About the Author

Continuing with the main character, Dean Nash, which Steve Bosworth conceived over twenty years ago as an image in his thoughts. Now after three years of writing following positive feedback from readers of *The Betrayal*, the second instalment is ready for publishing.

The Revenge

Steven Bosworth

The Revenge

Olympia Publishers
London

www.olympiapublishers.com
OLYMPIA PAPERBACK EDITION

Copyright © Steven Bosworth 2024

The right of Steven Bosworth to be identified as author of
this work has been asserted in accordance with sections 77 and 78 of the
Copyright, Designs and Patents Act 1988.

All Rights Reserved

No reproduction, copy or transmission of this publication
may be made without written permission.
No paragraph of this publication may be reproduced,
copied or transmitted save with the written permission of the publisher, or in
accordance with the provisions
of the Copyright Act 1956 (as amended).

Any person who commits any unauthorised act in relation to
this publication may be liable to criminal
prosecution and civil claims for damage.

A CIP catalogue record for this title is
available from the British Library.

ISBN: 978-1-80439-766-4

This is a work of fiction.
Names, characters, places and incidents originate from the writer's
imagination. Any resemblance to actual persons, living or dead, is purely
coincidental.

First Published in 2024

Olympia Publishers
Tallis House
2 Tallis Street
London
EC4Y 0AB

Printed in Great Britain

Dedication

Time is free, but it's priceless. You can't own it, but you can use it. You can't keep it, but you can spend it. Once you've lost it, you can never get it back. 'Harvey Mackay'

Temet nosce – Know Thyself. The two most powerful warriors are patience and time.

Brendan.

Please enjoy part two of the trilogy.

S.

Acknowledgements

I would like to thank all the readers of *The Betrayal* for their positive feedback which has driven me to complete part two of the trilogy. I would like to thank Sally and Richard for their detailed proof reading and support along with friends, family and other readers who have been patiently waiting.

ONE

Driving rain falling from dark skies continues to batter against the windows, signalling its sympathy for this sad day. I sit waiting in a little roadside cafe for contact from McGough. My clothes are soaked and stick to my skin from the earlier swim in the River Thames, following my escape from the warehouse explosion. I can feel the coldness from the wet clothes, as I sit on a red plastic seat staring out through the café windows which are partly covered with condensation. A people carrier vehicle stops on the road outside, and a frail old man exits from the rear passenger door. He gradually makes his way to the entrance of the café, and is wearing a long dark blue trench coat and matching flat cap. Opening the door, he removes the cap, unbuttons the coat and slowly makes his way into the café. Then with a big smile across his deeply wrinkled face, he greets another old man with a firm handshake. As they both sit opposite each other at a nearby table, I realise it isn't McGough, and take a deep sigh. I continue to look through the cafe window into what feels like nothingness outside with my reflection showing the emptiness inside myself.

Glancing around the café, I notice it is rectangular in shape with mixed-coloured tables and chairs placed onto the dark tile-effect laminate floor. The wooden window frames are painted white, but with the excessive moisture over many years, the paint is beginning to flake away from the woodwork. The lower section of the walls are covered in light grey wood panelling, and as with the window frames, some of the paint is showing signs of blistering and flaking away. Above the panelling, the walls are painted off white, and as my eyes continue towards the kitchen at the rear of the room, ever darkening stains can be seen on the walls caused from all the cooking. This place needs a good decorating, I think, as I look across to the pictures of old London landmarks which hang from the off-white walls. I try to imagine London in those days with the busy dockyards, and cobbled streets of these vintage scenes. It is certainly a different view today.

Visually scanning the room for any danger, I gradually take more notice of the people sitting in the café. I had already given them the once over when I arrived, but it is a good time to recheck. Looking around the room, closest to the door, a man and woman sit opposite each other holding hands, and gazing into each other's love-struck eyes. The two old men are sitting on the next table talking, and beyond them are an older couple. The man sits reading a newspaper and the woman is engrossed in her knitting. There are two other separate couples sitting near the centre of the room casually talking, and nobody here appears to be a threat.

The café is approximately half full on a wet Sunday afternoon, and my nostrils are now filled with the smell of cooking bacon. My senses connect to the noise from the small television set which is attached to the far wall. The football highlights from yesterday's matches are being shown, but my eyes are drawn to how precariously the cables hang from below the television as my view is obstructed by a young waitress walking towards my table. She is wearing a black tee shirt, dark trousers and black trainers.

"What can I get for you?" she asks in a strong cockney accent.

"Just a large tea, please," I reply with a smile, looking back at her. I instantly notice her bright red dyed hair and facial piercings. She is about twenty years old, and has a pretty smile, which is hidden by the dark lipstick she is wearing.

"Do you want any food?" she asks abruptly.

"No, just a tea, thanks." She turns and walks away quickly. My mobile suddenly begins to ring then vibrates on the table top and looking at the screen, I recognise the number.

Pressing the accept call button, I place the handset close to my ear. "Mr Nash, finally, after all this time you decided to make contact. We all thought you were dead?" he queries in a frail voice.

A police car races past outside with sirens blasting, as I reply, "Well, my sabbatical has finished, so I thought it was time to resume working." I watch another old man enter through the doorway and sit at another table.

"What makes you think we want you back, Nash?" He coughs.

"You made the first contact with me; I didn't contact you!"

"Very true, it was excellent news to hear of your existence. Now are you fit to carry on with active duty, or as is common in our politically correct society today, do you need some time to re-adjust?"

"John Wagstaff spoke your name just before he died," I reply, with my thoughts returning to Wagstaff's final few minutes alive. The waitress brings the mug of tea, and places it on the table before walking away quickly.

"Yes, it was sad to hear of his death, but life goes on. Ideally, you need to come in for debrief. However, there are more pressing issues to concentrate on."

Quickly remembering how uncompassionate McGough was in the past, I am not surprised by his replies, and the conversation continues. "What is the pressing issue?" I ask.

"Your pal Mr Neal, old boy, he needs to be retired from active service, and I thought seeing as he tried to kill you, maybe, a little payback could be the order of the day?"

"I suppose that this is a test of loyalty again, is it, sir?" I reply, beginning to feel slightly uncomfortable, but not surprised by this request.

"Well, time has moved on, Nash, and yes, I need to know if you are a rogue agent or someone who can be trusted once again. Now let's leave the debrief for another time. I understand from Mr Neal that you have kept yourself fit, and your performance during the warehouse robbery still means you can shoot straight, so back to work, old boy." He coughs then continues again, "Now, one of Neal's old passports has been activated at Heathrow airport today."

"His destination?" I ask.

"The other side of the world, old boy, to the great land of Oz and the city of Sydney." I suddenly remember a conversation, where Shaun mentioned he would move to Sydney, and live there, if anything happened.

McGough continues, "Now, I assume you will need some new attire after that river swim along with a new ID, passport and an agency credit card, so I have arranged for the necessary items to be placed in locker number three hundred and forty-five at Heathrow, terminal three. It requires the usual pin code for access that I'm sure you will remember."

How does McGough know about my swim in the River Thames? I muse to myself, as he pauses for a few seconds, coughs to clear his throat and begins again, "Nash, you are booked on the next flight to Sydney in four hours with Qantas. The bag inside the locker contains all the usual details and some essential items."

McGough then starts to laugh. "By the way, in case you have forgotten, you're still one of England's most-wanted criminals, so maybe, a little discretion is the order of the day, old boy." The conversation stops, and he quickly cuts the call without even saying goodbye and my thoughts remember the last time I held a discussion with McGough and the events which followed, and the hairs rise slightly on my neck as a shudder runs down my spine.

Feeling through all the pockets of the trousers and stolen jacket I am wearing, I take out all the cash and place it on the table in a little pile. Beginning to separate the coins away from the £20 note, the change is counted out. Looking at the menu, I check the price for the mug of tea, and put this money to one side. The remaining coins are ranked in order of value and, quickly, I calculate that there is less than

£30 left sitting on the table. Sighing to myself and reflecting that I've stayed in expensive hotels in the past where a single alcoholic drink cost more. Only £30 to my name, that's not a good start to a new life, especially with most of it coming from a stolen jacket. Standing, I pay for the drink then place the remaining loose change along with the £20 note into my trouser pocket as I walk from the café, and begin to head towards the nearest tube station.

The journey towards terminal three, Heathrow, reminds me of old times, and knowing deep down that agents will be observing my every move makes the whole trip more exciting, and nerve wracking at the same time. The thought of still being on the most-wanted list of criminals only adds to the flavour of my current travel plans. Reaching the east Putney tube station, I notice a baseball cap on the ground, and bend down to pick it up. Starting to walk towards the tube entrance, I slowly pull the wet cap onto my head. The coldness from the rain-soaked hat is instantly felt through my hair and as a water droplet hits the back of my neck, sending a shivering sensation down my spine. I hope that the hat will partially shield my face from the surveillance cameras as I reach the staircase and lower my head slightly and begin to descend the steps of the station.

Quickly checking the route, I buy a ticket with the last of the wet change from my pocket and gradually make my way through the crowded station. Even on a Sunday afternoon, the station is packed, and clearly there is still a large police presence. The usual background noise echoes in my ears from all the people walking and talking along with the tannoy system announcing carriages arriving. My mind quickly jumps back to when I had the daily commute to Harper and Harper before the events which are now reshaping my new life.

Standing on the platform, thoughts return of an old mission in Budapest, and the escape I had to make. These thoughts are broken by the tube rumbling to a stop and in front of me the doors slide open, exposing a packed carriage. Stepping into the carriage, I stand near to the access door and grab onto one of the vertical handrails for support. The tube doors close, and as it pulls away everyone lunges forward slightly from the motion. Once the carriage is moving, I gradually look around, and see a familiar person sitting to one side.

It is the old gentleman I used to see all those weeks ago who is reading a copy of the *Telegraph* newspaper from the sports pages backwards and drinking a cup of tea. My mind briefly remembers the helicopter explosion, and the tragic carnage afterwards as the carriages begin to bump and sway as we move through the tunnel at speed. A wave of sadness suddenly washes over me, which I try to block out by concentrating on the station stops. Seeing the signs for Acton Town platform approaching, I scan over the platform for any threats, and check the exit point before the tube lunges to a stop. The doors slide open, and I quickly make my way out of the carriage, and up the staircase, checking for CCTV cameras. The noise heard outside the station is deafening even at the weekend with sirens everywhere, as the fire brigade are still trying to extinguish the warehouse explosion, so quickly walking forward and keeping my head down, I reach the waiting line of black taxi cabs that are parked outside.

Selecting the first cab, I open the rear passenger door and climb inside.

"Where to, sir?" the cabby asks.

"Terminal three, Heathrow," I reply.

"No problem, sir, this weather isn't fit for ducks hey, and it looks like you have been swimming too."

Staring back at him, I reply, "Something like that, it's rain that soaks you through." We both laugh.

"Very true, gov'ner. Did you hear about the big explosion earlier near the Thames?"

Trying to hide my guilt, "Yeah, I heard a bang, but wasn't sure what it was."

"I thought it was another helicopter crash after the last one.

Everyone is still on edge even though it was a few weeks ago."

"I was out of the country at the time, but it must have been terrible."

"I had just dropped a young couple near there before it happened. They say it was all linked to the Pearson robbery with the car chase."

Trying to hide my guilt even more, I ask, "Have they caught anyone yet?"

"Not heard anything, gov'ner, but if they have, the old bill won't say anything yet."

"You could have some truth there." I heave a deep sigh.

"I heard from another cabby that the gang escaped the country. One thing is sure; they do not have to drive a black cab around London like me to earn an honest living."

"Yes, very true, but you never know, the perpetrators might have been some disgruntled cabbies wanting a little extra cash." We both laugh as the signs for terminal three appear.

"OK, boss, that's £18.80."

Reaching in my pocket, I have the soggy £20 note left, and handing it through the screen, quickly checking his ID badge. "Keep the change and thanks." He unlocks the door, and I climb out.

"Cheers, gov'ner, and hope you have a great day too." He opens his door window, shouting across the street after me.

I nod, smiling, and turn to head for terminal three departures entrance. I quickly choose a point by a side wall directly underneath the arc of movement of a surveillance camera which allows me time to check out the other security systems that lead to the locker area. This way, I can find a safe route when there are gaps in the surveillance curtain, and the position according to where the camera lenses are pointing. I wait a few minutes, scanning for any people that could be undercover police or agents, not knowing for sure if McGough hasn't tried to set me up now that all authorities will be notified about Wagstaff's death. Experience has taught me that sometimes it is better to be more open than sneaking around since anyone after you will find it difficult to get close with crowds of people around. Once the camera timings have been calculated to give me a big enough window to reach the locker area, I take one final look around then commit myself to walking across the entrance.

Moving away from the wall towards the locker area, I am constantly checking the camera timing as I go. I try to remain calm so people in the outside world believe I have no fear or doubt, although, my heart rate says otherwise. When I am nearly halfway along the front entrance lobby, my eyes suddenly pick up two agents on the far side of the open space, heading towards my direction. The small curly cable earpiece gives them away.

Keeping calm and remaining focused is something that was drilled into the students during the training programme, and my past experiences help control any fears. Therefore, slowly dropping and resting on one knee, pretending to tie my shoelace, allowing me to disappear from their line of sight and regain the upper hand once again. Still counting the timing of the camera, I know that ten seconds is a short time, but long enough to still make it to the locker area. So, watching the agents through the forest of legs the seconds tick away… two, three, four, I see them move away towards the front entrance doors. Five, six, seven, I slowly rise to my feet as the final seconds count in my head eight nine then picking up the pace I continue to walk the remaining distance finally reaching the locker area breathing a small sigh of relief. After checking all is clear, I walk inside and quickly begin searching for the locker number three hundred and forty-five whilst trying to avoid being noticed, I count the rows of locker doors, as I move along three hundred and thirty-one, three hundred and thirty-nine and finally three hundred and forty-five is located.

Almost in my sub conscious my fingers press the numbers seven one one two, and the electronic lock whirs into life as the mechanism de-latches. It is strange how certain numbers stick in your mind, especially when your life depends on them.

The sound of the airport tannoy system in the departures entrance was almost completely drowned out by the noise generated from people's shoes on the hard floor tiles, merged with the sound of voices, but it now fills the room with an eerie echo. Pulling the small plastic handle, the locker door is opened to reveal a medium sized green rucksack. Quickly lifting it out, I place it onto my shoulder and begin to walk towards the toilet block area at the back of the locker space, where I can safely check the contents.

Entering the block, and searching for an empty cubicle, I locate one and walk inside closing the door behind me. Taking the bag from my shoulder the top flap is unzipped, and I place my hand inside feeling various items. I lift out a new passport and credit card, a mobile phone, a hotel address in Sydney, and a boarding pass for the Qantas flight at twenty-one zero-five p.m. Finally, in the bottom of the rucksack I feel the softness of some fresh dry clothes and a pair of trainers. Quickly removing my jacket and my wet clothes, I drop them onto the floor, and climb into the fresh tee shirt and blue trousers. Removing my wet socks, I stand on the cold wet clothes, as I pull on the new pair of socks. My feet now feel comfortable, as I slide them into a new pair of black trainers. Checking the remaining pockets of the rucksack for any useful equipment, I return the passport, mobile, cards, and boarding pass into the small front pocket, and then throwing it over my shoulder, bend down to gather the wet clothes together from the floor.

Walking out of the cubicle, the wet clothes, and outer coat are dropped into a waste bin, and as I replace the baseball cap, my mind is now filled with the next challenge of the security check, and finally onwards to the departure gate for the flight. Taking out the boarding pass I look at the details, and compare it to the name in the passport ensuring they match. Continuing to the security area there are police everywhere standing around. Reaching the control, I scan across the rows of passengers trying to find the fastest moving line so my time in this area is minimal.

Looking around, I try to assess which police are the most observant, or those which are just standing as a threat. I notice the security check on the far right seems to be moving fastest with plenty of security personal not really taking much notice, but as I walk over in the direction of this line, two police officers appear from behind a large advertising board. They stop, and stand with a menacing stance. However, I sense they are not really taking much notice, as I join the back of the security check queue. My heart begins to beat faster as earlier in the entrance lobby, but I need to remain composed to make it through this area. 'What happens if I am noticed?' flashes through my mind, but feeling an inner confidence knowing that my documents have different names should give me a fighting chance.

Getting ever closer to the front of the queue, I remove the rucksack then take out the mobile from the front pocket. Now at the start of the inspection line, I reach down, taking out a grey plastic tray, and place it onto the stainless-steel flat surface. Lowering the bag into the tray along with the mobile, and finally the baseball cap, my disguise is now gone and feeling completely exposed I continue towards the body scanner.

Walking into the scanner a security guard asks "Have you removed your belt?"

Quickly lifting my t-shirt slightly, I reply with, "I'm not wearing one."

"OK." He waves me through, and I pass without any buzzing sounds.

Continuing to walk to the collection zone at the end of the moving belt, a police officer looks across and gradually walks towards my direction. Noticing him approaching, I avoid any eye contact but my mind is racing, 'What shall I do?' Just take it easy and relax, I tell myself.

Waiting for the plastic tray to exit the x-ray machine feels like an eternity. Finally, the tray holding my bag passes along the belt, I reach forward, lift out the baseball cap placing it onto my head first, then taking the bag push the mobile into the front pocket, and swing the rucksack across my shoulder. Lifting the plastic tray from the conveyor belt, I walk and drop it into the stack at the end next to where the police officer is now standing cradling his MP5 sub machine gun.

He stares at me intensely, as if trying to figure something out. I begin to walk away still avoiding any form of eye contact, but checking the emergency exit areas just in case I need a quick exit. Once I am twenty metres away, I hear him click the radio and know for sure I am made.

Suddenly, a second officer walks over to my direction, and asks, "What is your destination today sir?"

"Sydney, Australia officer." Looking at the large brown moustache across his top lip.

"Very nice. Can I see your boarding pass and passport?"

"Certainly officer." I reply, as I remove them from the rucksack and hand the documents over.

The first police officer has now made his way to stand behind me whilst the other passengers walking around this human obstacle casually glancing to see who is causing the obstruction. The second officer flicks through the pages of the passport stopping at the photograph page, and then stares at me.

"Is there a problem officer?" I ask.

"You seem to be travelling light for such a long journey, and your boarding pass doesn't have a cargo luggage receipt?"

"Well, believe it or not, my luggage got stolen, and I was intending on doing some clothes shopping in duty free along with replacing a small case."

The officer digests my answer in an attempt to scare me, but I'm not intimidated in any way, "Hmmm OK sir, thank you for your time, I hope you have a safe journey." He hands back my documents, as I smile and continue on my way, leaving the two officers together talking intently.

"What's wrong Jeff?"

"Chris something doesn't quite feel right, why would a guy travelling to Australia not have any luggage?"

"Like he says maybe, it was stolen?"

"Hmmm, what did you think was suspicious about him Chris?" Jeff asks.

"I thought he looked similar to one of the photo-fit images from Interpol, but you examined his passport, did it look fake?"

"No, it's one of the latest generation biometric passports and appeared genuine." Chris replies and continues, "I think it's best to call it in just in case, they can always stop him at the departure gate."

"If he gets there Chris!" Jeff replies.

"I will report it to command, and we can casually walk through duty free to see where he is going." The two policemen begin to follow in my direction.

"Covering your tracks and blending into any situation is how all agents are successful." One of my mentors once said. His words, "Never stand out from the crowd!" still burn a hole in my thoughts, as I quickly begin to shop for a few clothes, and personal items for the long journey. Some type of bag is critical, so locating a black holdall, I pay for it using the credit card after remembering the pin number, and then continue towards the clothes shops. I need practical yet comfortable clothing along with some sunglasses and toiletries. Keeping note of the time, and the fact that, I am still one of England's most wanted, I gradually begin to pick out certain simple clothes avoiding anything with large prints, or emblems to ensure it's more difficult to be recognised by security cameras, and other agents against any other of the general public.

Once I have collected enough items, I walk to the nearest toilets, and entering a free cubical remove all the items from the packaging, and place the articles into the holdall. Checking my watch, I only have fifteen minutes before the flight boarding will commence so gathering all the packaging together, I leave the cubicle, and place it into a rubbish bin. As I begin to walk towards the departure gate my emotions are calm and collected.

Reaching the queue of passengers waiting at the gate there are people standing everywhere. Some people have huge suitcases just for hand luggage, and others like myself have a simple bag or rucksack. I notice the sign above the gate shows the flight number, and the flashing image below stating *'Flight Fully Booked.'* The boarding staff at the gate request first, and business class passengers along with any parents and children to enter the aircraft. My thoughts remember the last flight to Brazil when Burns, and myself killed the brothers which feels like a dim and distant memory already. Passing through the turnstile after scanning the flight barcode, I continue to walk down the aircraft bridge trying to blend in. Entering the large jumbo jet, the air stewardesses from Qantas are welcoming everyone on-board.

Finding my seat, I get settled in for the journey as drinks are passed around, and placing my head against the seat back, I close my eyes and try to relax for the journey ahead. At that moment, I hear a couple of familiar voices as the two police officers from earlier enter the aircraft, and stand near the cockpit. Opening one eye casually, I watch an air stewardess join the two officers. One of the officers requests the passenger list and begins to scroll through the names turning over pages of the document. Watching his reactions, his eyes stop at a certain point, and then raising his finger, points at a name on the list and begins to speak with the flight attendant. Now opening both eyes, I try to slide myself gradually down the large comfortable seat underneath the direct eyesight of the officers, who are now staring directly down the aircraft. The pilot opens the cockpit door, and joins the increasing crowd now standing at the front galley of the aircraft.

A muffled discussion can be heard, and then the two officers slowly begin to walk along the main isle of the aircraft. Stopping at my row of seats, the officer with the large brown moustache turns and looks in my direction.

"Mr Deddington, I am so glad you made your flight. I hope all is fine?" he asks.

"Yes, Officer, thank you, and I managed to collect a few clothes for my trip."

"Well, that is good news. Could I see your passport again, sir?"

"It is in the rucksack." I point at the overhead locker, as I begin to move from the seat.

Now standing and manoeuvring into the aircraft aisle, I reach for the rucksack, then open the front flap, and take out the passport handing it over to the officer. He takes the document, and begins to examine the condition of the photograph and the quality of the passport.

"Hmmm it all seems OK." I hear him say as he hands it back to me.

"How long are you staying in Australia for Mr Deddington?" He continues.

"It will be about six days all together, I have the return flight details if you need to see them?" I try to remain calm and collected.

"Yes, please Mr Deddington." I take the return flight documents from the rucksack, and hand them over to the officer.

"I see you have an open return ticket?" I watch his eyes scanning through the documents in an attempt to find any discrepancies.

"I have several meetings to attend in Sydney, and then in Melbourne, and hope to be travelling back quite soon." I stare at the officer maintaining eye contact whilst trying to enforce my innocence.

The captain then walks behind the officer, and starts to speak, "I realise you have a job to do, but you are now holding up a commercial flight. If you want to remove this passenger for questioning then please do so, but I request you make this decision now otherwise, I will have to report this incident to air traffic control." The captain then turns and walks back in the direction of the cockpit.

"That will be all Mr Deddington, have a safe journey." The officer lifts his right hand and returns my documents, then he turns and begins to walk towards the front of the aircraft with the second officer following.

As he reaches the front galley area of the aircraft, he casually turns his head and takes one final glance at me, as I'm replacing the rucksack into the overhead locker. I can sense he is clearly not happy with what he has seen, but the return flight, and passport have all been arranged by the agency so it is way past his pay-scale for decision making.

I am only glad that the captain placed him on the spot to make a choice, and thankfully this was in my favour. As I take my seat again, one of the air stewardesses arrives with a tray of drinks.

"Mr Deddington, I am so sorry about the officer, please accept our apologies, what drink would you like sir?" She asks.

"It's OK, and not your fault, the officer was only doing his job. It's a typical hazard with the business I am in." I look at her trying to laugh.

I pause for a few seconds, as she looks at me, "I will have a large gin, and tonic after that interrogation." She hands over a large gin in a glass tumbler together with an Indian tonic water.

Settling back into the seat, I lean my head against the backrest, and close my eyes for the long journey ahead. My thoughts begin to replay the events of the last few weeks with the robbery, the death of Thomas, Josef, Ramone and Carlos along with the kidnapping, and unfortunate death of Wagstaff and his grandson. I remember the look on Burns face after Shaun took the shots, and the betrayal he must have felt. I could feel his eyes cutting through my body, and burning my insides. My thoughts then turn to Lloyd, and how I felt when he died in my arms. I had only known him for a few days, but he had an aura around him that flowed with support and confidence.

I felt guilty that he out of all the people, got killed in the robbery, but equally if he lived, I may already be dead hunted by Burns, and Lloyd himself. It's a cruel thought to wish for the death of one person, but if it saves your own life, its survival of the fittest and on this occasion, I was the lucky one. I continue to think about Shaun, and the feelings he must have running through his mind over the death of Chloe and their unborn child. My thoughts search for the reasons for my disappearance, and I start to remember the debriefing for operation Ottoman and the key suspects that had been targeted for elimination along with a woman spy for extraction. I can still see her face in my thoughts, and the darkness of her eyes at that critical moment. The hairs begin to stand up on the back of my neck, as I remember the events following the operation.

My thoughts return to Sophie, and how she could play with my emotions, and pull at my heart strings in an attempt to manipulate the situation both before the robbery and afterwards. I thought how strange it was that she arrived in Brazil, and the venom in Burns voice when she tried to disobey him. I still sense her lips close to mine, and the feeling of being loved, but I also remember her betrayal with Nick. His face now fills my mind, as I try to picture my past life with him and the current situation following Wagstaff's death.

I think back to how life was simpler as a finance accountant, but a huge part of me has been missing this excitement which flows through my body now. The reality of my situation starts to sink into my soul and the badness from my past starts to overwhelm the pleasure, I feel today. I have done so many wrong things in my past after orders, and decisions that were not my own. Maybe, I should have been more selective with the orders, I was given, but the training that I was subjected to, removed my ability to think, and make decisions. If I had disobeyed a direct order, and affected the outcome of an operation, this would have led to my certain death.

Much of my life has been shaped by intensive training, and following orders so to have the opportunity to think for myself, and make my own decisions as a finance accountant made me feel free from this life, but the constraints of being caged in an office generated frustration. How can I have the best of both worlds with a simple life and freedom? Clearly with my past I'll always have enemies, and will always be looking over my shoulder.

I need an escape plan which will help cover my tracks, and allow me to disappear, but I know it cannot be done alone, so I will need the help from a few friends to support me along the way. I start to think about which people I can trust, and one name now fills my thoughts.

TWO

Meanwhile, on the Monday morning, whilst Nash is travelling to Australia, a solitary black S Class Mercedes Benz car is driven along a quiet country road just outside the suburbs of Hitchin. The vehicle begins to slow down and the driver, who is wearing a dark grey suit stares through the rear-view mirror then he begins to operate the indicator. The vehicle begins to turn right between two highly ornate yellow sandstone gateposts that have elegant black wrought iron gates hanging from each side. The car continues past a section of cobbled stones, and along a tree lined driveway which then changes to gravel towards the main entrance of a large red brick detached house.

There are several other prestige vehicles already parked at the front of the property with drivers standing in various locations keeping watch on the building and the main driveway. The men are dressed in long black coats and all have an ex-military stance and swagger about them. The Mercedes Benz stops close to the front of the building and the house butler quickly opens both the entrance doors. The driver climbs out of the car and looks across towards the other men acknowledging them with a casual head nod. He walks around to the rear of the car opening the boot and takes out a dark grey trench coat and quickly pulls the coat over his suit jacket to protect himself from the driving rain.

The rain continues to lash against the long white framed Georgian style sash windows of the house as a person climbs out of the front passenger side of the car. This passenger then quickly opens an umbrella, and walks to the rear door placing his free hand on the handle. The driver reaches into the boot, and takes out a wheelchair quickly locking the frame into an open position. He then pushes the chair around to the rear passenger side of the car where a frail man opens the door, and slides into the chair supported by the two large men. The reaction from all the other drivers standing outside confirms that the master has arrived as they stand to attention. The frail man is pushed in the wheelchair along the gravel by the driver in the direction of the entrance with the second person carrying the umbrella protecting all three of them from the driving rain.

Standing by the door, the butler greets the guest "Mr McGough sir how wonderful to see you again." The driver and passenger turn, and walk away from the house as the butler pushes McGough along the large extravagant hallway. The two men from the car, walk towards the direction of the other men standing outside, and shake hands with their colleagues, as McGough disappears inside the house.

The butler continues to push McGough along the hallway which has very high light green painted ceilings. The walls have a dark brown dado rail running along the complete length, with white walls above the rail, and dark brown wooden oak panelling below. The hallway has light oak parquet wooden flooring set in a herring bone design which leads to a grand staircase which is set across three levels of the house, and is panelled with the same design of dark brown panelling and dado rail with white painted walls. There are various portraits hanging from the staircase walls, and a light green stair runner carpet covering the centre of the steps. The butler then stops next to a large dark oak door on the left-hand side of the hallway, and pushes it open. McGough is manoeuvred through the doorway, and then turned into a large dining room which already has several men waiting which include Victor Grant an established businessman, Roger Hopkins, a well-known political committee member and Graham Eaves, a press secretary for the Commons.

The butler turns and leaves the room quickly, closing the door behind, and returns to the entrance doors to welcome the next person arriving in a black Bentley limousine, which has just stopped outside. Another man can be seen climbing out from the passenger seat and walks towards the house entrance, welcomed by the butler again.

"Mr Rupert, I hope all is well." Rupert Vaughan gives a smile, and does not reply.

The butler closes the doors as inside the dining room, McGough is greeted with a firm handshake from the other men who have already assembled as a waitress passes around the room with a tray of drinks offering either glasses of wine or tumblers of whisky. The butler re-enters and helps with the drinks and preparations around the table.

The Right Honourable Rupert then enters the room dressed in a dark blue heavy pin-stripe suit and announces, "Is everyone here?" All the men nod in agreement.

"Shall we all take our seats at the table gentlemen; we have a lot to discuss."

He gestures to a long mahogany dining table which is laid out with a large ornate candlestick holder neatly placed in the centre. The table has twelve setting arranged with a dark red leather table mat, paper pad, pencil, pen and two silver table coasters placed neatly. The men all take a seat apart from McGough who is pushed by the butler again to an empty position next to the host. As the men mumble, and get comfortable, the waitress and the butler leave the room closing the large dark oak door. There is only one empty table place setting.

"Rupert what is all the urgency about?" McGough asks.

"Dean Nash has resurfaced." Rupert replies then coughs.

The room goes deadly silent as McGough continues, "We all had our suspicions that this day would come, and it has."

Rupert stares at McGough and says, "An informant told me that this information was available on Thursday, why were we not told Edward, it is now Monday?" McGough stares across back to Rupert.

Rupert continues, "My contact within Interpol overheard a call on Thursday morning that Nash was part of the warehouse robbery, and he had been arrested by Intelligence Director John Wagstaff who had taken him in for questioning."

"It was as expected, and was not an issue until the events of Sunday changed the state of play." McGough replies.

"Following the explosion of the warehouse by the Thames?" Rupert asks.

"Correct, and we also believe Nash was involved with the death of Wagstaff."

"Do we know if Nash had any legal representation?" Victor Grant asks.

"Yes, Victor he did, and I also have good information that he never mentioned anything about the robbery or the involvement of Burns."

"What is the issue?" Roger Hopkins asks.

"The problem is Roger, Wagstaff had already been starting to sniff around, and had also sent out agents to investigate Nash's past." McGough answers coughing.

"His files are clean and untraceable; nothing leads to us in any way." Rupert announces.

"There is some other information which is more concerning." McGough looks across to all the men.

"The issue we have gentlemen is that Nash's personality has changed, and he couldn't remember me in any way, but he had a level of aggression far worse than before."

The rooms goes silent again.

"The main question is, what is the next course of action for Nash, Burns and Director Wagstaff's team?" Rupert stands looking at the men.

"We must protect our integrity and the code."

"Wagstaff's team won't be a problem." McGough smiles.

"Why do you say that Edward?" Rupert asks.

"I removed the agent that Wagstaff had sent." The men gasp.

"That will open up a major enquiry for sure." Roger replies with nervousness in his voice.

"I can cover that; I have a man on the inside." McGough responds.

"What about Burns? We know how much of a loose cannon he is; how can we control him?" another man asks.

The men all start talking amongst themselves concerned over their reputations, families, and future business contracts. McGough takes a sip of his whisky and looks across at all the men who seem to have fear in their eyes.

He smiles to himself, and leans back in his wheelchair, "I have a suggestion gentleman!" McGough coughs then continues, "I have already made contact with Nash, and I think we can use him to tidy up Burns, but we all need to keep our nerve and remain calm."

"That's easy for you to say, where is Nash now?" Rupert asks.

"I've sent Nash on a little journey." McGough coughs.

"A journey? What for?" Rupert replies.

"To meet his old friend Neal."

"By Neal you mean Shaun Neal that waste of space you saved last time." Rupert speaks with aggression in his voice.

McGough, looking like a little school boy after being disciplined replies, "Neal can act as a diversion for Nash."

"A diversion what for Edward! The pair of them need to be eradicated." Roger stands, and starts to walk around the room continuing to speak.

"What gives you the right to not only to contact Nash, but to then send him away on a little holiday without *in pectore* approval?"

"I was appointed as the head cardinal spokesperson and with my position also given all tactical command to protect the '*in-pectore.*' In fact, I believe you were the main person wanting to distance from final decision making." McGough stares at Roger.

Roger returning to his seat replies with, "Yes, well, it's not your own private government agency, we should have at least been made aware."

"Gentlemen bickering between ourselves will not solve anything. The main focus now is protecting the cardinals." Rupert announces as McGough stares across at Roger with disgust in his eyes having his control undermined.

"What about Burns, how will he be silenced?" Graham Eaves asks.

"Graham, I have sent a team to intercept him making sure our front doorstep is swept clean."

"One team of how many men?" Rupert asks then sits down.

"I've handpicked a few good assets for the operation so leave that to me." McGough replies.

"We left it to you last time! And look what happened!" Graham snaps then continues.

"There is not only Nash and Neal loose, but that damn nemesis of Burns running around laughing at us."

"Look Neal and Nash have unfinished business, and once that is over, I can get Nash after Burns if the assets have failed." McGough replies.

"How do you know Burns will surface again, and god only knows what he is planning next?" Rupert speaks then takes a sip of water.

"Burns loves action and money. He will be planning another operation, and my team will be very close to his every move."

"There seem to be many uncertainties; it doesn't feel clean and simple and has too many moving parts for my liking, Edward." Graham replies.

"I will have a personal meeting with Nash offering him what he wants."

"What is that Edward?" Roger asks.

"The chance to take Burns out. I'm sure Burns will surface soon enough, and that will be all the bait Nash needs."

"Edward, I think that you are right about a personal meeting, but

I am very nervous we don't have any concrete plans." Rupert looks across to McGough.

"Nash, what will we do with Nash?" Roger snaps.

"When Nash swallows the bait, I'm sure he will fight with Burns, and that should take the pair of them out." McGough replies.

"If it doesn't?" Roger asks.

"We can deal with that situation if it occurs, but I have several more chances to handle any fallout. Nash and Burns must be eliminated."

"So is it agreed that Burns and Nash are both priority targets!" Rupert looks across the other cardinals.

"Unless we look at a new opportunity?"

"What opportunity?" Rupert asks.

"Get Nash back on-board, and reinstate the cardinal programme."

All the men look around to each other.

"I think, I can speak for everyone Edward; Nash must be eliminated in order to protect the future plans."

"We may not have a future, if the current agent intake doesn't meet the grade." McGough smiles at the men.

"It is too risky; Nash must be removed. Is that agreed by everyone?" Rupert asks the group of men.

They all nod in agreement, and the order is now cast with McGough to plan a meeting with Nash, and then remove both Burns and Nash permanently. There is still an undertone to the meeting that many of the cardinals are not in agreement with McGough's actions. The meeting quickly begins to draw to an end, as the men stand saying their goodbyes. McGough sitting in his wheelchair keeps twitching around feeling very uncomfortable with the whole meeting. The noise of the doors opening and closing followed by car engines starting, and vehicles driving across gravel echoes in the distance as Rupert says goodbye to Roger and Graham, and they leave the room closing the door behind.

"I wasn't very impressed with some of the questions from the other members, it's undermines my authority." McGough stares across at Rupert.

"Edward what do you expect, you make decisions without informing the rest of us. You keep information hidden for days. We shouldn't be involved with Nash or Burns, it's not our problem any more."

"We need to protect the faith of the society, and I for one believe that we have a duty and responsibility to complete all our business foreign or domestic."

"Edward your duty and responsibility is your own feeling of self-importance, and your actions recently are affecting everyone." Rupert takes the last sip of his whisky.

"What are you trying to say Rupert?"

"I'm saying that the elders have held a ballot over your recent actions, and a decision has been made which is final. The decision is that you are relieved of all duties when this sorry mess is tidied up."

"So, the elders have voted against me, and I wasn't even given the opportunity to speak?"

"Edward the world has changed and our previous enemies are now our new trading partners. What was left of the old iron curtain cold war is long gone, and our closest enemies appear to be our old friends and employees."

"For you people sitting here around this table maybe, but none of you are knee deep in the mess I awake to every morning."

"Edward those days are gone, and we as a society need to adapt and change in order to survive." Rupert reaches into his tweed jacket inner pocket and pulls out a light brown envelope, then hands it over to McGough.

"What's this, my P45?" McGough asks.

"Something like that Edward, open it please."

McGough snatches the envelope, and tears open the end flap, then he pulls out a white letter unfolding it. "I'm sure the settlement figure will be to your liking. We have already transferred to funds to a Swiss bank account with the account details on the reverse of the letter."

McGough not even turning the letter over grasps it between his hands and tears it in half throwing it to the ground.

"Do you really think it's about money? Is this what our society has now become? Well it was never about the money. It was for king and country, and no amount of money will ever buy that level of loyalty."

McGough turns his wheelchair around and, quickly begins to head for the door. Reaching for the handle, Rupert now holding the empty tumbler of whisky replies, "The cardinals have spoken and their word is final. Tidy up the loose ends and enjoy your retirement Edward."

McGough mumbles to himself, "I will tidy up the loose ends all right, and you will be first on my list."

"To say, I'm disappointed Rupert is an understatement, your betrayal of this code breaks all conduct and challenges the complete disciplines of our society."

"The elders recognise your efforts and sacrifices over the years, and offer you the opportunity to retire gracefully Edward."

"Retire, hmmm we will see about that!" McGough coughs then reverses his Wheel-Chair away from the table, turns and wheels himself towards the door. He reaches forward and snatches the door open.

Pushing himself through the doorway, McGough slams the door behind and continues along the hallway, where the butler stands holding the entrance doors open and gestures to the two men outside. He must be able to sense the anger that is welling inside McGough from the expression on his face, and smiles saying, "Nice to see you again sir, and wish you a good day."

McGough stops for a second then replies "Thank you James, and

I wish you all the best for you and your family. Please take care."

"When will we be seeing you again sir."

He smiles, and replies, "Maybe sooner than you think James, maybe sooner."

McGough is greeted by one of the bodyguards where he is pushed towards the waiting car. He then begins to climb onto the rear seat as the driver holds the passenger rear door.

"I would like a moment alone gentleman." McGough instructs the bodyguards.

Once McGough is safe inside the car, the door is closed and the wheel chair is disassembled, and then returned to the boot. Now sitting on the back seat, McGough reaches inside his jacket taking out his mobile. He unlocks the screen and scrolls down the contact list stopping at a particular name. He presses the call button and the mobile begins to ring. He lifts the mobile to his ear.

"Yes, sir, what is the plan?" A posh English voice asks.

"Operation Last Supper is GO repeat Last Supper is GO," McGough answers.

"Yes, sir, understood. Operation Last Supper is a GO," the voice replies.

McGough presses the cancel call button, and replaces the phone back to his inside pocket as the two bodyguards re-enter the car. The large black Mercedes car then drives away from the detached house as the rain begins to ease.

McGough's instruction signifies the start of operation Last Supper and in the basement of a luxurious house in the Kensington district of London, the handler sends out the orders via text message which simply reads *'Last Supper is a GO.'* This command now begins a chain reaction of events that will change the lives of people forever.

*

At the Bridge End bistro, near to Tower Bridge, the restaurant is filled with lunchtime customers. The brick walls, fixtures, and fitting of the restaurant have an industrial theme running throughout the building with large bi-fold doors that overlook London's landmarks of Tower Bridge and the River Thames which flows quickly below. There is modern easy listening music quietly being played in the background with groups of customers all laughing, and talking at the tables.

One table has a group of eight smartly dressed men all casually enjoying an early lunch meal, and bleeps can be heard from them receiving text messages on their mobile phones. The men instantly stop eating and talking, then look around the table to check out the messages being received on the phones. Staring across to each other, they all stand and place their serviettes across the plates which have their unfinished food on them. The eight men then take out cash and throw down the money, forming a pile in the centre of the table to cover the cost of the meals. A waitress rushes across to the table, asking what is wrong, but the eight men simply ignore her, and walk out of the busy restaurant past all the tables of on-looking customers who are completely surprised by their actions.

Outside the building, the men split into two groups and climb into two matt black Audi Q7 SUV vehicles, which are parked near to the restaurant in roadside layby spaces. The vehicles have the side and rear windows blacked out with tint material, and both cars sit on large black alloy wheels that fill the wheel-arches. Once all the men are inside the two cars, the lead vehicle begins to move with the second car in close proximity driving at high speeds in the direction of Lambeth Road. After just a few minutes, they finally turn along Barkham Terrace in Kensington district of the city. Slowing down outside the building labelled number five, the two cars stop and park on the small side street.

The car doors open, and all the men having similar build and appearance climb out, and continue towards the large gloss black front door of the white property. The clean-shaven team aged around mid-thirties in age having short cropped hair make no conversation between themselves on the few steps to the front door. The men in quick succession enter the house and gather in the main hallway. The lead man clearly knows the direction and begins to walks along the narrow dark hallway which is separated in half by a staircase on the right-hand side. There is a small passageway heading towards the rear of the property. The air is filled with a musty smell which probably comes from the old dark red threadbare carpet hanging on the steps that leads to the upstairs of the house.

The men continue along the left-hand side of the hallway, and stop at a dark brown door which is underneath the staircase. The first man places his left hand onto the old round brass handle, and the door is pulled open hinging from the left exposing a steep wooden staircase, which is illuminated by single light bulb hanging from a loose cable that runs along one side of the wall. Holding the door open, the remaining seven men pass through the doorway, and continue down the wooden steps with several of the men holding onto the wooden handrail which flexes and moves with each footstep.

The first man at the top of the staircase closes the wooden door with a firm thud, and follows as the last man down to the basement. Entering the dimly lit lower basement of the building, a solitary figure can be seen sitting at a small wooden dark oak desk, which has a green leather inlaid writing pad set into the top surface. There are four brown A4 envelopes resting on the top of the desks with the words 'Team A, Team B, Team C and Team D' clearly written on the them in large black letters.

The eight men then stand before the man like school children in-front of the head-teacher as the orders are given out, "OK, men, I will not repeat myself so listen up. Each of you need to split into pairs, and take an envelope for each team. I don't care which envelope you take or which pairs you divide into, but you have twelve hours to complete the mission. Inside the envelopes are all the information required on the selected targets. If anyone gets caught or identified, your removal will also be arranged by your colleagues. Now, gentlemen, you are on a strict timetable and the clock is now ticking. Any questions?"

"No, Colonel." The men's reply is synchronised.

The colonel continues, "There are untraceable weapons for all of you in the steel cabinet behind, so good hunting, and see you at the agreed rendezvous point tomorrow."

"Yes, sir."

"Good afternoon, gentlemen." He then stands, lifts a dark brown briefcase, and then climbs the steps out of the cellar. The basement door can be heard opening and closing followed by a firm thud as the front door is closed. The men quickly divide into pairs and then taking an envelope, look through the targets, their addresses and usual movements.

It quickly becomes apparent that some of the targets have common interests, and meeting points and the eight men quickly filter these patterns. The remaining targets are then arranged for eradication via their placement on a map, or distance to travel in the allocated hours. Once the plans are agreed and the workload shared, the men turn around and begin emptying the steel cabinet of all its contents of weapons which includes handguns, rifles, knives along with several packs of plastic explosive.

Concealing the weapons in their clothes, the men return back up the steep staircase, and then continue out of the house stopping by the two parked vehicles. The four teams of hit men then separate with two pairs continuing on foot, and two pairs each taking one of the vehicles they arrived in. One pair of assassins quickly flag down a taxi, and the other pair continue on foot to a tube station entrance of Lambeth North. The two vehicles drive in different directions, following addresses that have been programmed into the sat nav systems of the cars. Twenty minutes later, an elderly man walks out of a house in

Phillimore Gardens Kensington, and stands in the street waiting for his chauffeur. A large black BMW 7 Series arrives, and stops by the kerb. The driver who wears a smart black suit, and drivers cap quickly climbs out leaving the rear passenger door open. Not realising much difference, the old man leans forward slightly, and reaches for the rear door handle.

The driver quickly walks behind the old man and holding a silenced handgun next to the back of his head, quickly fires off a shot that sends blood and brain matter onto the window and roof of the black car. The assassin throws the hat into the car, then closes the rear door and begins to walk away with not a care in the world. The hunt for the cardinals is now on.

The message and instructions from McGough begins the chain reaction of events to systematically eradicate the cardinals. The Colonel from the house in Barkham Terrace, can be seen walking to another property in Blackfriars Road. Opening the light grey front door, he walks inside the freshly modernised property, and continues to the rear of the building into a large open plan dining and kitchen area.

The house is painted with white and light grey walls along with light oak laminate flooring running throughout. There is a modern look to all the furniture, but the walls are absent of any pictures or personal items. Lifting a dark brown briefcase, he places it onto the glass topped dining table. Sliding his right hand into the leather bag, he removes some architectural drawings. Gently unfolding the large building drawings and site plans, he runs his finger along various outer perimeter walls, then taking out a plastic scale ruler, pencil and notepad from the briefcase begins to measure wall lengths and thicknesses writing down the scaled lengths onto the notepad.

A knock is heard at the door so he stops, and sliding his hand once again into the leather briefcase, he removes a pistol, and slowly walks towards the front door. Standing twenty away metres from the door, he can see the image of a person standing outside through the frosted glass. The person can then be seen walking away outside, and the Colonel continues cautiously as he reaches the door. Standing to one side he reaches for the handle, and slowly starts to open the door. On the front step of the house, he is greeted with a brown envelope which has been left. Reaching down, his mobile begins to ring. Tucking the pistol behind his trouser belt, he reaching for the mobile, and presses the call accept button hearing a familiar voice as he bends down to lift the envelope.

"The first cardinal is dead. Well done old boy."

"What about Nash, where is Nash?" The Colonel asks.

"It's in the information inside the envelope, now take this inside or do you want to continue the conversation on the doorstep?"

The Colonel turns and closes the door asking, "What happened earlier?"

"Well it wasn't pretty he was clearly given his marching orders."

"It's expected he couldn't continue with his own little war without upsetting them." replies the Colonel.

"Very true old boy, and what about you. How are you?" The contact asks.

"Me, well, it was a close call really, just had a bullet wound, but only in the flesh. That arsehole Neal blew it up big style. Why did he send Neal?" The Colonel walks back to the rear of the property, and sits back at the table placing the envelope, and handgun onto the building drawing plans.

"He didn't completely, Neal was acting on his own. You guys killed his girlfriend after the warehouse robbery and McGough fed information to Neal. He knew Neal would take the bait and gave away your position."

"Hmm, thought, McGough might do that."

"Killing Wagstaff and his grandson, was well out of order, you know that." The posh voice replies.

"I didn't, it was that prick Neal who hit them both. I just wanted to hurt Wagstaff as I was instructed."

"Instructed by whom, that command didn't come from McGough?"

"It did, the message came from McGough's mobile." Colonel snaps

"It wasn't sent by McGough that's for sure." The voice replies.

"So, someone else in the agency is playing their own little game hey, hmmm, very interesting."

"What happens next old boy?" The old posh voice then coughs.

"Patience, patience, lets tidy up the cardinals then wait for the next opportunity."

"What shall I say if he makes contact?"

"Tell him nothing." The Colonel replies.

"You haven't seen me or spoken with me OK, and McGough will probably try to kill you now?" The old voice has hesitation in the reply.

"Let's hope I get him first hey!" The Colonel laughs.

"Do you want any more information old boy."

"No, I should have enough for now." The Colonel begins to look through the information from inside the envelope.

"Keep your head down Colonel and good luck with the hunt."

"Yes, and many thanks for all the help and support." The mobile phone conversation ends.

The mobile suddenly vibrates as a text message is delivered. 'Number four is out. Five, six, and seven within the hour. 'The mobile vibrates again and looking at the message it reads 'The doctor's surgery is fully booked.' Smiling to himself, the Colonel opens the envelope and starts to look through the information, and sees that Nash is travelling to Australia. He closes the plans and returns them to the brown briefcase along with the notes he has written.

Sliding the handgun and envelope into the case, he closes the flap and clicks the studs shut. The Colonel then walks out of the house closing the large grey front door placing a small cigarette, but end into the gap between the door and frame, then continues along the street whilst observing his environment. He reaches a car park and walks to a blue Ford Mondeo, opening the door he slides onto the driver's seat. Placing the briefcase on the passenger seat he closes the door then starts the engine and drives away.

Sitting in an upmarket Chelsea London restaurant, Rupert Vaughan and Graham Eaves enjoy a late lunchtime meal. The men are talking over the events that have shocked London recently, and discussing what should be the focus for their next monetary fund portfolio, and the future business plans to maximise on their capital already invested. The waiter brings over a bottle of chateau-neuf-du-pape red wine and places it on the table. One man's mobile begins to ring, and he removes it from his jacket.

He looks at the screen then looks across to his business partner, pressing the call receive button, he tries to hear the conversation over the noise from the busy restaurant.

"We are under attack Rupert!" The frail old voice shouts out.

"What? What do you mean Roger?" Rupert asks as a single bullet shot is heard.

Rupert shouts "Hello Roger, Roger can you hear me?" The conversation goes quiet.

Rupert looks across to his partner and says, "Graham, there is a problem? Roger said that we are under attack and then the sound of a single gunshot."

"You are not serious Rupert." Graham asks.

A few people look across as Rupert, now standing at the table with a look of shock on his face stares across to Graham still holding the mobile to his ear.

The waiter looks across and with a single movement of his hand reaches inside his trouser pocket. With a casual movement of his fingers, he operates a small detonator device held in the palm of his hand. A small 'BANG' echoes through the restaurant, just slightly louder than a firecracker, as the bottle of red wine explodes sending shards of glass and red wine liquid in the direction of Rupert, and Graham killing them instantly. It is clear that the explosion is controlled device and the tally now stands at nine cardinals with only three more to go.

THREE

A black Jaguar can be seen stopping by the main entrance of Whitehall as the prime minister climbs out from the rear of the car, and quickly steps inside the building. The sad news of the death of John Wagstaff and his grandson washes through every office, as people stand whispering like church mice. Reaching the office of Home Secretary Allen, the prime minister pauses for a few seconds, then takes a deep sigh and pushes the door open. The room has an eerie silence which hangs heavy in the air due to the loss of Wagstaff and it feels that the security of the entire country is now at risk. People stand around almost in a state of shock suffocated of any conversation wondering what will happen next, as PM requests the intelligence contingency plan is to be implemented immediately, as the agencies try to piece together the jigsaw puzzle that ultimately lead to the death of Wagstaff. The list of likely replacement candidates is withdrawn from the Home Secretaries office safe and the PM quickly runs his finger down the names of people who could never fill the impossible footsteps of the vacant role.

The two men then walk towards the main office, where a group of high-ranking security personnel from Police, Military, and all the Intelligence agencies all anxiously wait outside. As all the people enter the brightly lit room, the smell of fresh furniture polish engulfs the air. The PM and Home Secretary take their places at the head of the table, as all the other remaining people quickly withdraw their individual chairs, then the occupants take their seats around the table.

"How can anyone follow in his footsteps?" is asked around the round table.

"How safe can we be now, when John was taken in such an open kidnap?' The discussions continue with some being quite heated.

"Ladies / Gentlemen can we get back to the agenda for the meeting, the choice of candidate to fill the role. We all miss John, and know he will never be replaced, but a successor is required." The PM speaks with confidence.

Many of the replacement candidates are quickly eliminated, and after much deliberation three names finally begin to surface at the top of the list, Atkins, Blake and Rushton. A sealed box voting system is used, and the selection committee write their candidate on the paper, and put them into the box with the PM casting the final vote. The box containing the slips of paper is then taken to the side of the room, and two independent people begin to count out the votes with three piles of paper gradually beginning to form.

Its eyes to right with Atkins seen as the clear winner with six votes against the next highest of only three. An immediate meeting with Atkins is requested along with the Home Secretary in order to establish a clear level of stability and send a message to the murderers that it's business as usual. The Home Secretary nods to his assistant who quickly makes a telephone call, and then walks out of the office. On this cold, wet and miserable Monday, the newly appointed Director of Intelligence walks out of another small Whitehall office, after having been waiting with the other candidates for the decision, into the main passageway.

The Home Secretaries assistant quickly reaches Atkins, and the pair of them begin to walk along the corridors of power. Atkins wearing a dark grey suit along with carrying his raincoat draped over his left arm reflects on the journey both in the actual steps he is taking and the selection of him for this vacant position. Atkins wonders, how he will try to fill the empty role of his old mentor Wagstaff, but also knows deep down that this will be an impossible task. As he continues towards the office, his heart beats faster, and the feeling of sickness rushes through his body with the apprehension of a personal meeting between the prime minister and the home secretary. The security of the entire country and all the commonwealth nations now begins to rest squarely onto his narrow shoulders. The Home Secretaries assistant tries to hurry Atkins along, but he continues to walk at the same pace knowing that this moment is special and from here, the burden he needs to carry will require all his experience and knowledge to complete the role.

Finally, they reach the office door which has a deep dark oak colour. The assistant places their hand onto the handle, and then knocks on the frosted glass panel. Waiting for the words 'Enter', he pushes it open and Atkins takes a long sigh before entering. The PM and Home Secretary are seated in a small office still discussing the events of the last few days, as Allen begins to takes a call just at that moment when Atkins enters the room. Quickly trying to finish the call, the home secretary looks across to Atkins and from the expression on his face, it is quite clear he is not in agreement with the selected successor.

"Well, it wasn't pleasant, but it needed to be done. He is just too old fashioned for our new business opportunities so cleaning up Burns will close that door for good." He finishes his call.

The PM stands and with a strong handshake welcomes Atkins to the team, "Robert, I am very pleased that an apprentice of the master will be taking the role. I feel it is a fitting memory to John."

"Yes sir, I am sure, John is looking down on us right now swearing and cursing." Atkins replies smiling.

Home Secretary Allen looks over his half round glasses, and with a fake smile welcomes Atkins, "So finally the big job at last hey, Robert are you ready?"

"As ready as Mr Wagstaff has mentored me to be sir." They complete a handshake.

The PM smiles, and continues, "Robert, you have a very big task at hand, where do you feel you need to start."

"Sir, the warehouse robbery, the helicopter explosion and the death of John, I suspect are all linked, it is too much of a coincidence to all happen that quickly."

"Hmmm, well, as you know all the resources within this building are at your fingertips and disposal."

"Thank you sir, and I'm sure that, I will need them."

"What makes you feel that these recent crimes are all related?" Allen asks.

"Home Secretary, Interpol has informed me today that, they are still working on a case which occurred several years ago in Hungary. This case appears to have similarities with the use of explosive charges and destruction following a robbery of a national bank. Clearly there appears to be a team that keeps completing a theft to raise funds for a cause."

"Yes, well, I wouldn't read too much into Interpol's intelligence, Wagstaff never rated the information which was shared." Atkins stares at Allen with a look of surprise.

"Very true, sir, but I do feel that this could link certain evidence, so I would like to send a couple of agents to see what is similar."

"Excellent idea, a little bit of cross fertilisation always helps." Atkins smiles at the PM nodding in agreement as Allen looks away with doubt on his face.

"Robert, we need to close down these awful events and move on, the country needs it, and frankly everyone in this building needs it too. If you require any gears to be greased and any walls to be knocked down, please don't hesitate to contact ourselves directly right?" The PM stares at Allen.

"Yes, PM, if you need help with anything Robert, you have my direct mobile so call me anytime."

Atkins smiles, and replies, "Gentlemen, I can't thank you enough for the help and support. Your confidence in me gives me a lot of encouragement, I won't leave any stones unturned, and I am sure that this can be tidied up thoroughly and quickly. I will, of course, need a headed letter of approval from yourselves to take authority of this complete investigation."

"Well, of course, Robert, no problem at all. Do you have the letter already drafted Allen?" The PM asks.

"*Err! Yes,* of course, Prime Minister, but is it not better to wait a couple of days?" Allen seems suspicious and nervous of the request from Atkins.

"Patrick, this man needs to complete the investigation, and we have just said that we need to support him in any way, so get the letter out, and we can all sign it now." The PM snaps.

Allen reaches into his desk, and takes out the headed letter. Removing a pen from his jacket, he hands writes the name of Robert Atkins into the blank space of the paragraph giving him full authority. He is clearly not in agreement with the PM's instruction. Sliding over the letter and pen, both the PM and Atkins also sign the letter and Atkins then starts to lift the document.

"I just need a copy for the files." Allen asks and places the letter onto a desk top scanner and whirring can be heard as the letter is digitised.

Handing the original to Atkins, Allen stares in contempt at his new intelligence director, as Atkins gently folds the document and pushes it into the inner breast pocket of his jacket. All three men nod in agreement, and the new Director of intelligence then shakes hands with two employers, and starts to walk out of the office with the weight of the commonwealth on his shoulders.

Opening the office door, he turns slightly and smiles back at the PM and Home Secretary, "I will be in touch soon gentlemen, once I have more information, it will not take me long. I will head over to the metro command centre and have a discussion with Mr Kingsbridge."

"Please keep the both of us involved and report any issues

immediately to Robert." Allen replies with a fake smile.

"Yes, of course, sir, just one thing, if you do think sending a couple of agents to Hungary is not good idea, I will, of course, leave it."

"I never said it was not a good idea, but that case was years ago and any evidence could be corrupted or lost by now. Hungary had a lot of close ties to the Soviet Union Atkins, and we all know what they were like. I have a contact in Hungary so will make a couple of discreet calls."

"Yes, sir." Atkins replies, and walks out of the office closing the door behind. Home Secretary Allen was clearly shaken by the question.

"I don't think the Hungarian connection is anything PM." Allen tries to shrug off the idea.

"Patrick, in these times, it is worth just checking. There may be some similarities as Robert mentioned. Give him some support at this time."

"Yes, Prime Minister." Allen replies, but is clearly not happy.

Director Atkins walks out of the building, and noticing the bad weather outside pulls his outer jacket on. He is deep in thought after his discussions with the prime minister and home secretary, as he slowly walks back to his car. An agent opens the passenger rear door and Atkins climbs inside. The agent then quickly walks around to the driver's side, slides onto the seat then closes the door. The engine is already running, so the agent engages drive on the automatic gearbox.

"Where to, sir?"

"Metropolitan Police Command Centre please Shaw."

The car drives away and his first journey in charge commences. The car speeds across London city and reaches the entrance gate for the main command centre where two police officers dressed in fully body armour stop the car.

Lowering the driver's window Shaw announces, "Director Atkins to see Commander Kingsbridge.

The police let them pass and the vehicle continues to the front of the building and stops. Atkins jumps out, and quickly starts walking towards the direction of the entrance doors, where he is instantly met by a man in his mid-fifties standing outside the building who is wearing a full police uniform, has light grey hair, and a slightly overweight figure. As Robert approaches, the man outstretches his hand to welcome Atkins him with a firm handshake.

"Director Atkins what a pleasure to see you, what an honour with your visit to see us on your first day in charge?" The man asks with a level of sarcasm in his voice, and coughs to hide a laugh.

"Commander Kingsbridge, well firstly, it might be a good idea to introduce me to the team in the main command centre." Atkins replies assertively.

"Well, of course, sir." Atkins can sense from Kingsbridge's actions, he does not approve of the appointment.

Two large police officers stand guard each side of the entrance door, and one man reaches forward to open it as Atkins and Kingsbridge enter. Walking into the building they continue along a brightly lit corridor, and then turn into a room. As the door is opened, the noise from all the people talking and clicking away on computer keyboards buzzes around the room. Atkins turns and sees a large wall covered in individual screens which show the present surveillance from hundreds of cameras placed all around the capital.

Helicopter video footage is being played along with dashboard camera car chases, and the four bottom screens on the right-hand side of the wall show cameras following suspects. Standing in front of the screens, Kingsbridge and Atkins look towards the operating staff. Atkins coughs with nervousness not being a regular speaker.

"OK everyone, a few seconds of your valuable time, please." Kingsbridge announces loudly.

All the people look forward towards Kingsbridge and Atkins and the room goes silent, "Ladies and Gentlemen, I would like to introduce Intelligence Director Atkins who will be in charge of the investigation going forward following the sad news of John Wagstaff's death."

Atkins walks slightly forward and stares across all the faces that look back at him for inspiration, "Thank you, Commander, I will only say a few words. Although, I worked very closely with Director Wagstaff, he will never be replaced, and I will not attempt to be like him, but what I do know is that if Director Wagstaff was here today, all he would ask from each and every one of you is to try your best. All the knowledge and experience in this room along with the latest technology is at our fingertips, so we will quickly need catch his killers."

Atkins looks across all the faces and says, "Thank you, and please continue." People simply lower their heads as the humming noise returns with keyboards and telephones starting to be operated. Commander Kingsbridge beckons a man over who has been standing on the far-left side of the room. A short man with a close shaven head and dark eyebrows approaches.

As he reaches the two men, Kingsbridge announces, "Director, this is Chief Inspector Mulberry who is responsible for everything you see in front of you."

Atkins shaking hands asks, "Hello Inspector Mulberry, can you get me up to speed quickly."

"Sir, of course." He turns slightly and gestures to a woman sitting on the front row.

"Officer Kelly, pull up the video footage from the Sunday afternoon at the Bermondsey trading estate near to Bermondsey beach warehouse district." Mulberry orders.

"Yes, sir, I will run it onto the main screen." She replies.

The images and footage begin to roll, and Mulberry starts to commentate, "OK, sir, this is what we have currently, a call was made by a member of the public who reported hearing gunshots, as they were walking along the river bank side and Mulberry indicates on the screen with a laser pointer. The call came through to the Met Command centre, and two police armed response vehicles were dispatched, and you can see them driving at speed." He points to the two vehicles approaching the area.

"Where is the helicopter at this time?" Kingsbridge asks.

"Sir following the previous attack, the police helicopters now film from a safe distance of thousand metres both with colour and thermal imaging. The crew were already airborne on city surveillance when the call came in."

"The police cars pass this white Audi car that was seen leaving the warehouse area at speed, and the two vehicles are directed to the building by the member of the public who waited near to the scene." Mulberry points to the white car and the two attending police cars.

"The witness has been checked out sir and the statement which was taken at the scene confirms all facts are correct." Kingsbridge speaks to Atkins with Mulberry nodding in agreement.

"Correct, sir." Mulberry replies taking a sip of water from a plastic cup.

"The white Audi car?" Atkins asks.

"Good question, sir, it has been found near to Heathrow airport terminal four car park. There were blood stains, and finger prints lifted that are now under forensic examination as we speak." Mulberry continues.

"OK, sir, this is when it gets interesting. The helicopter has already confirmed that the four officers entered near this door at the front of the building. It then picks up two individual heat sources leaving from the rear. There is a difference in timing of around three minutes between when the first and second suspects leave the building. The first suspect runs parallel to the river in an opposite direction away from the building, and the second suspect can be seen running directly towards the river." Mulberry pauses for a second.

The TV screens are suddenly filled with the explosion of the warehouse, and the main control room falls silent again. Mulberry continues, "This second suspect can then be seen to reach the low bank area and then jumps into the Thames. The river diving team were deployed within ten minutes, in the area, and currently have not found a body or any traces. The thermal imagining heat source was lost, and we are sure this suspect knew this would happen."

"So, the second suspect must have known about body heat dispersion. OK, what about the first suspect?" Kingsbridge asks trying to be interested.

"Sir, all CCTV in that area was not active at the time of the incident, and we believe they could have been affected by a signal blocker. The surveillance helicopter also suffered with intermittent live video footage. The forensic teams onsite are still completing a collection of evidence from the warehouse, but the main focus is currently with a white van inside the building. It's clear sir that, both men knew how to avoid the helicopter thermal imaging cameras, and we feel are highly trained probably ex-military personnel."

"Wait, wait, a van which van?" Atkins speaks with an annoyed voice.

"Sir from the warehouse, it was badly burnt out but we have a couple of prints."

"Excellent, who is it?"

"Sir the forensics team has confirmed it was Wagstaff's I'm afraid."

"Damn. Look both the van and this white Audi car must be on some road traffic cameras somewhere, Christ they drove almost half the way around London city." Atkins turns and stares at the wall of TV screens.

"Are they the same team from the robbery is the biggest question?" Kingsbridge asks as Atkins ponders.

"To have two teams of ex-military trained personnel in almost the same area of London within a few days of each other it seems highly unlikely, sir." Mulberry announces and coughs slightly.

"Commander, Director Wagstaff did confirm to myself that he believed the robbers were ex-military trained with the use of explosive shaped charges and efficient gun handling skills." Kingsbridge looks at Atkins.

"Correct Director." Kingsbridge replies, as the men walk away from the front of the room and retire to a smaller office as a secretary brings in fresh drinks.

"Have you been able to establish who Wagstaff had been contacting?" Kingsbridge asks inquisitively.

"We were hoping you could tell us sir; we have a dead end at the minute." Mulberry looks towards Atkins.

"How about his close agents Preston and Wilson? Have they been spoken to yet?" Atkins requests keeping his theory silent.

"Sir, they both mentioned a person of interest called I believe Nick Burns?" Chief Inspector Mulberry replies.

"Fuck that's not good news." Kingsbridge snaps.

"Why is that Commander? What do you know?" Atkins replies keeping Wagstaff's intelligence information secret.

"He is trained assassin, from a now disbanded government kill squad."

"*Ahh*, yes, Kingsbridge, you were military intelligence before this Police secondment." Atkins replies.

"I can't say more than I have already done so." Kingsbridge replies submissively.

"Well, are we tracking this Burns suspect now?" Atkins requests.

"Sir, Men like Burns know how not to be tracked, and are trained to disappear." Inspector Mulberry replies.

"They can also make mistakes like everyone else, so I want a full track on him and any of his known acquaintances over the last ten years. Is that clear." Atkins instructs then takes a large sip of tea.

The tension in the room is broken by a knock on the door and a Sergeant enters, "Inspector, sir, the forensics have just been delivered from the white Audi car."

"Excellent who is it?" Atkins asks excited.

"The blood and finger prints have been confirmed as a person called Shaun Neal."

"Christ are you sure?" Kingsbridge asks.

"Yes, sir confirmed," the sergeant replies.

"OK, thank you, Sergeant Reynolds." Kingsbridge takes a big sigh as the Sergeant leaves.

"Another man from the past and the same government assassin team?" Atkins asks. Kingsbridge simply nods his head in agreement.

Atkins stands and begins to walk towards the door, "Let's get moving gentlemen we need some information on these guys before the scent gets too cold."

All three men stand and walk back towards the main control room with Kingsbridge the last in line looking very downtrodden. Re-entering the room, Atkins speaks confidently, "Inspector Mulberry do you mind, if I address the team again?"

"Please go-ahead, sir." Mulberry stands back slightly.

"OK, everyone listen up, we have several new leads, and we need everyone focused. The white Audi left at Heathrow had finger prints and blood stains from a person called Shaun Neal. Do we have a picture of this suspect?"

An officer uploads an older picture onto the big wall screen, and Kingsbridge looks away very embarrassed as the six feet tall image is seen. Atkins continues, "I want this driver's face matched to the car then we can trace it backwards, hopefully to an area near the warehouse. There must be some surveillance along that route."

Commander Kingsbridge now tries to stop Atkins, "Sir, this is not the time for chasing Neal!" Atkins is now on a roll.

Staring at Kingsbridge Atkins continues, "Right, I want this team splitting into three, team A on the left, concentrate on the white Audi car that was left at Heathrow. I want to know where it came from and if Shaun Neal owned it. Then confirm who left it and where they went too?" Atkins passes for a second.

"OK, this section is team B as he gestures with his arms splitting the centre of the room. I want you to trace the warehouse van, do we have any definite details colour, partial registration?" Atkins gestures to the screen.

"Sir, we have a few details. We know from some evidence on the licence plate holder that it was a hire van." An officer replies from near the back.

"OK, I want to know where it was hired from, when and by whom. We also know now that John Wagstaff's fingerprints were evident so it must have been the vehicle that transported both him and his grandson after being kidnapped. We must be able to trace it back to Nuthurst."

"Sir, two police officers reported seeing a white Hertz rental van leaving the village of Nuthurst the same morning, as Wagstaff was kidnapped." A Female officer speaks out.

"They didn't think to stop it? The director of government intelligence disappears, and they didn't think to stop a white hire van?" Atkins with a level of disgust in his voice continues.

"So, trying again to match the drivers, and I'm sure that a second or even a third person was required for the kidnap of Wagstaff and his grandson so look for two passengers. Atkins looks to third team.

"Team C (Pointing to the right), I want you to concentrate on facial recognition and try to trace the two people that were seen leaving the warehouse, we must be able to locate their movements."

Commander Kingsbridge takes out his cell and starts to type a message.

"What are you doing Commander?" Atkins leans over and

whispers in his ear.

"Err just a message to my wife saying that I will be late home."

"Hmmm, I doubt that very much since you got divorced last year and I'm sure if I request all your phone records for the last twelve months, I will find a certain pattern of numbers will keep appearing." Atkins turns and walks away.

Kingsbridge shocked replies with, "I don't know what you mean sir."

"Oh, yes, you do. You are now excused from this investigation on direct orders from the PM and Home Secretary Allen."

"You do not have the authority." Kingsbridge snaps.

"Really." Atkins takes out a headed letter signed by the PM and Home Secretary Allen. Commander Kingsbridge snatches it, and as he begins to reads it all the colour and emotion disappears from his face in shock.

Kingsbridge hands the letter back Atkins who replies with, "Don't leave town Commander, I will want a formal chat old boy. You are now suspended pending an internal affairs investigation." Kingsbridge storms away with a few of the officers lifting their eyes watching him leave.

Atkins turns and watches the multiple TV screens as video footage is being played back second by second. The facial recognition software scans through every face trying to make any match as the officer's stare at their computer screens.

Suddenly, an officer shouts, "Sir, I have something."

"Play it through the main screen." Atkins instructs.

On the screen the white Audi car can be seen following a white Hertz van and at a set of traffic cameras, the faces can clearly be seen as Neal in the Audi and Burns as a passenger in the van. The driver of the van is completely covered and unrecognizable.

"We know that at least Burns was in the van, but who was the driver?" Atkins mumbles to himself.

"Everyone be aware to that they are either working together or we need to check, if Neal is simply following. Both vehicles head towards the warehouse area and the route is lost."

"Sir, some clear facial recognition on the white Audi driver from Heathrow."

"Excellent, who is it?"

"Suspect Neal, sir."

"Right, so we know he went to Heathrow, and possibly he may have taken a flight out from the UK. Trace from where the car was dropped, the clothes he was wearing and place a block on his passport. Trace any credit cards bank or government issued." Atkins instructs the complete room.

"Sir, confirmation that Neal's credit card paid for a one-way ticket with Qantas to Sydney Australia, and his passport was cleared through to departure."

"OK, inform the Australian authorities to hold Neal at port of arrival. Do not deport." Atkins replies.

"Sir, what about Burns and the second suspect?" Mulberry asks.

"All in good time Inspector. If Burns did the robbery, he will not be leaving town quickly without the money, so we need to try and find the money."

Atkins stares at the large wall of TV screens with his arms cradled looking for inspiration. His mind is running over who the heat sources in the river was and the significance of kidnapping, and killing Wagstaff in the whole line of events. Maybe, Wagstaff had worked things out and was trying to piece the final parts of the puzzle together.

"I'm returning to Whitehall, keep me informed of all changes. Find both Burns and hopefully the river swimmer. Chief Inspector Mulberry please take this card." Atkins hands him a card with his mobile number.

"Yes, of course, sir." Atkins leaves the control room and the

Inspector stands staring into nothing wondering what has just happened.

He has a new boss with a different set of instructions. The chief's mobile begins to ring, and as he takes it out a familiar number appears on the screen.

He lifts the mobile to his ear pressing the answer button at the same time, "Yes, sir how can I help you." He walks to a quieter corner of the room.

"Sir, Shaun Neal has been recognised, and it has been confirmed he boarded a flight to Sydney Australia yesterday." Mulberry continues to listen.

"Sir, Director Atkins has requested that Neal be detained at the port of entry."

The voice on the mobile gives a specific instruction and the Mulberry acknowledges the command. Then the Chief Inspector walks over to one of the desk Sergeants who is operating the control screens and leans over to whisper in his ear, "Remove the detain order to Australian boarder authorities for Neal." The Sergeant gives a casual nod and enters a special restricted screen with another person's log in details changing the request.

The surveillance teams continue to track through film footage from car parks, shop and airport security systems along with road traffic cameras in the desperate attempt to link Burns, Neal and the Thames swimmer all to one place. Another team track the owner of the burnt-out warehouse, as a third team continues to investigate the money warehouse robbery. In the meantime, German Interpol share intelligence that two known ex-military personnel have been found in the remains of a farmer's barn with a cross check of their passports confirming they were in the UK at the time of the robbery.

A lone officer suddenly watches some evidence film footage from a road traffic surveillance camera noticing the van, and white Audi travelling along the same road with a distance of three hundred metres between them approaching a busy crossroads.

"Sir, I have the two vehicles but only the driver's face of the Audi." The facial recognition software confirms the Neal.

Chief Inspector Mulberry quickly walks across to a large illuminated map of the city, and says, "OK, what is the time and location?"

"Location is along Purley Way near the A232 Beddington junction. The time is eight twenty-eight a.m." The inspector indicates the vehicles on the map with a big black spot.

Another officer shouts, "Sir, I have the same two vehicles with a location along the A23 near the Ritzy Cinema at a time of eight fifty-nine a.m."

The inspector shouts, "OK, Guys listen up we have a direct route here back towards Nuthurst."

A third officer then speaks, "Inspector, I have suspect vehicle Audi on a surveillance camera on the M25 travelling at high speed at seven forty-six a.m."

"OK, so looking at the times we know both vehicles were close to Nuthurst so one must have been either following or joining at the warehouse."

"Sir, we haven't been able to confirm the driver of the suspect van, what shall we do?"

Another officer shouts, "Sir, I have Burns identified near to Cherry Gardens and then entering Bermondsey tube station at zero nine fourteen a.m."

"Track that tube and see where he leaves it."

"Sir, he only stays on the tube for one station, then leaves at London Bridge, and he isn't seen again."

"What he disappears? that is not possible at London Bridge unless he changes all his clothes, and complete appearance! Check again." the officer lowers her head and tries to find him.

The Inspector takes out his mobile and calls the number for

Atkins. The phone starts to ring, "Atkins here."

"Director we have confirmation that Nick Burns was at the warehouse along with Shaun Neal. We also have confirmation that Burns was seen leaving the warehouse, and entering the Bermondsey tube station at zero nine fourteen a.m."

"That's good progress do we know where Burns went afterwards?" Atkins asks.

"We are still tracking that Director, but we appear to have lost him at the next stop London Bridge."

"Lost him?" Atkins acts concerned.

"Yes sir, we cannot find him leaving the tube carriage at London Bridge."

"Maybe, he never actually got onto the tube at Bermondsey. It might be worth send a couple to police down to investigate."

"OK, sir." Mulberry replies.

"Any news of the swimmer yet?" Atkins requests.

"No sir, we are drawing a blank." The officer replies.

"OK, well, keep me informed. What about Neal in Sydney?"

The Inspector looks across to his Sergeant and asks, "We have no news on that information at this time sir."

Atkins replies with, "Well, contact both Sydney airport and Qantas airlines to inform them of a possible suspect that requires holding in custody."

"Sir, I will make contact with the authorities." Mulberry stares across to the Sergeant.

Chief Inspector Mulberry's mobile then begins to ring, and seeing the number on the screen he walks to a quiet corner of the room to take the call and Atkins casually looks across.

"Mulberry, there are many patients in the doctor's surgery, what is the status at HQ?"

Mulberry replies, "Atkins has relived Commander Kingsbridge of his authority. Nick Burns has been recognised as the passenger in the

Hertz hire van and escaped to Bermondsey tube station. Atkins has requested that police officers are sent to Bermondsey tube station to search for Burns."

"That is unfortunate about Kingsbridge, but expected with his actions. Send the police to the tube station and investigate."

"Sir what of Atkins?" Mulberry asks.

"Leave Atkins to me Mulberry. Carry on." The phone call ends.

Mulberry walks back to the area close to the Sergeant, and looks across at him giving a fake smile. Meanwhile, Commander Kingsbridge begins his journey back home. As he begins to turn onto the driveway of his house, a man is seen walking a dog past the gateposts as the electric gates open. Kingsbridge waits a few seconds, and the person moves to the right allowing the commander to pull into the driveway. Suddenly, the man turns and with a silenced pistol fires several bullet rounds at the door window of the commander's car.

The glass shatters, and a several bullets hit Kingsbridge. One bullet hits the right temple of his head, and the second through his right eye socket killing him instantly. As he slumps over the steering wheel of his car, it continues to move forward, and drives into the large garage door. The assassin bends down to pick up the spent bullet cases whilst watching the electric gates closing then walks away as though nothing has happened. He takes out his mobile and sends a message to number ten.

FOUR

Arriving in Australia on the Tuesday morning, I join the long queues for passport and immigration control. The fear of my documents being highlighted as a suspect do not even register in my thoughts, as I continue down the line. Finally, reaching the front of the queue, I hand my documents over, and the immigration officer simply flicks through the pages and stamps the passport. Easily passing through the security checks, I walk past the security dogs which are sniffing all the bags just before the exit of the airport and continue towards the overhead signs for the hire car area. As I exit the airport, I pause for a few seconds, then take a few breaths and enjoy the release after such a long flight overwhelm my emotions. I continue to walk outside heading towards the car hire collection area. Taking out the documents from my bag, and check which company the hire car is booked with. Finding the AVIS stand, I walk into the Portacabin, and am meet by a very pretty woman in her late thirties with long blonde hair, and large round rimmed glasses sitting behind a desk.

"G'day sir, and how can I help you?" She asks.

"Hello, I have a reservation under the name of Deddington." I hand over all my documents.

"Ah, yes sir, here we have it, for three nights, right."

"Correct." Her name badge reads Karen.

"Only three nights? It's a long way to travel for three nights. Are you here for business?" Karen asks.

"Only for a business meeting, no pleasure on this trip, my boss likes to keep me on a short string Karen."

"You can say that again, Mr Deddington. You must be very

important."

"Important hardly, expendable probably fits the phrase better."

We both laugh, as she starts to fill out my information on the computer system.

"OK, Mr Deddington, I just need you to sign this hire agreement in these three places, she indicates them with a small cross next to each box."

"I need to take a refundable deposit for the hire car of $1000 dollars is that OK sir." She requests.

"Yes, no problems at all. Does the car have sat nav?"

"It's an automatic Holden Commodore, which has built-in sat nav, I hope that's OK."

"Well, at least the steering wheel is on the same side of the car."

"You certainly have come at the best time of the year with this weather, I bet it's not this nice in the UK?" Karen smiles.

"Very true, this looks fabulous outside."

"Where are you stopping in Sydney?"

"The Park Hyatt hotel in the Rocks area."

"Oh, very posh, OK Mr Deddington, we are done. Here are you go sir; these are your car keys. The vehicle is parked on the central parking lot in bay number one hundred and seventy-six. Please try to return it with a full tank of gas at the drop zone B4." She holds out her hand with the keys.

I notice she wears a very large diamond engagement ring set in a lion claw mount.

"Certainly, many thanks for your help." I reply.

"No worries and hope you have a great stay."

I leave the office and continue along the pavement towards the parking lot. Seeing the AVIS section, I walk along the lines of parked cars, and reach bay one hundred and seventy-six. Unlocking the hire car, I place my bag into the trunk, and then walk around to the driver's side. Opening the door, I slide onto the leather seat and start the engine. I switch on the air conditioning and then programme the sat nav for the Park Hyatt. The journey to the Sydney quayside takes around twenty minutes, and as I reach the rocks district, my first vision is of the magnificent harbour bridge along with the arches of the Sydney Opera House in the back ground. I have only ever seen these monumental buildings on television or in advertisements before so to see them in the flesh is awe inspiring. Finally, arriving at the hotel, I drive the car into the underground parking area, and find a suitable parking space. I remove the bag from the trunk and then after locking the doors, follow the signs leading towards the reception and main check in.

My mind drifts back to Brazil, and the last hotel check in when Burns and I were hunting the brothers. Reaching the main reception, I hand over my passport, and the man behind the counter checks through all the reservation details. Handing me a piece of paper, I read the top which says check in form. I complete all the basic information taken from the fake passport, and tourist visa, and hand over the agency credit card. The man on reception hardly says any words, but gradually completes all the document checks and tasks in a methodical manner. He takes the credit card, and transfers the payment then hand back the card wrapped inside the printed slip.

After what feels like ages, he hands over the magnetic room key which is placed inside a folded cardboard holder. He points towards the direction of the hotel lifts and explains that my room is on floor fifteen. Walking towards the lifts, I reach the control panel and press the up-arrow button. The lift door opens, and then I enter inside, after waving the access key over the magnetic reader, and then press the button for the fifteenth floor.

The doors close and images begin to rush in my mind back to different operations, when I have been exposed to dangerous situations. After several seconds, the lift stops with a judder and the doors slide open breaking my thought process. Walking on autopilot,

I continue towards the room in a pre-programmed manner counting the room numbers along the corridor. Reaching the door, I stop and wave the access key over the lock system and the mechanism whirrs into action. Pushing the dark heavy door open, I enter the room and push the key into the slot near the door. My eyes are instantly drawn to a small black suitcase which has been placed near the foot of the bed on top of the sheets. The large sixty-inch television shows the name of 'Mr Deddington' across the screen, and a welcome notification. Lowering the bag onto the floor, I find the TV remote and quickly switch off the screen and walk towards the large panel windows. I stare through the open curtains of the hotel room at the Harbour Bridge and can see in the faint distance, a group of people dressed in grey overalls climbing up to the top of the arch.

A darkness now engulfs my thoughts when the task at hand of tracking my old friend Shaun begins to take hold. Inside the hotel room, I turn and walk back towards the bed. Reaching the case, the zip is opened, and the top flap is lifted to reveal some shirts neatly folded. Lifting out the shirts and placing them on the bed next to the case, my eyes are now focused on the weapons which were hidden underneath.

Within the rows of weapons is a map which shows the last known location of Shaun Neal and a note from McGough which reads 'Happy Hunting.' Another strange feeling now begins to flow through my body as the reality of hunting your once best friend to his death now sends a shiver along my spine. His death will be all over my hands, but in a way, it feels as though, I will be saving his life from being hunted any more. All our previous conversations begin to race through my mind, as I try to remember any information that could lead me to him. It feels very strange that my only focus now is finding out, where he is hiding with all my past feelings and adventures along with the great times we have shared falling into insignificance. Studying the map, I suddenly remember the area of a district and the name of a small apartment Shaun mentioned once.

Quickly calculating the distance from the map, I can see that Kent Street is twenty minutes' walk from the Park Hyatt hotel. Gathering a pistol from the case along with two clips of ammunition, I place one magazine into my trouser rear pocket, and the other is pushed into the handle of the Beretta handgun. The top slide is pulled back and a round is loaded into the chamber. The gun is made safe by applying the safety catch, and then tucked behind the belt at the back of my trousers. Replacing the clothes and zipping the case back together, I place the bag on my shoulder and then lift the case from the bed.

Reaching the door, I remove the room key from the slot and place it inside the cardboard wallet. Entering the corridor, the door is closed, and I continue towards the lifts and then down towards the garage parking. Placing the case and bag into the trunk of the car, I leave the key on the top of the passenger front wheel, and then return back to the entrance lobby. Finally, reaching the outside world my ears are instantly filled with the sound of noise from cars horns, helicopter rotor blades and blasts from ships horns in the harbour, as I start to walk in the direction of Kent Street. The clean streets are filled with people talking and going about their daily business, as I continue to walk along the pavement. The glasses I am wearing protect my eyes from the sun's rays, but the warmth from the sunshine sends a burning sensation through my skin.

Finally, after twenty minutes of walking, I turn into Kent street and instantly notice the designer style buildings. Remembering the name 'Whitechapel', I reach the building entrance. The building has commercial offices on the first two floors then private residential apartments. Waiting outside a woman exits from the side door, and I gain access to the stairwell.

The information I have already confirms that Shaun is in apartment 4a and climbing up the staircase to the desired level I open the door and walk towards apartment 4a. With my senses on full alert, as I reach the front door, I take a deep sigh, and standing slightly to one side, try the door handle. The white door opens easily which leads directly into the kitchen with white high gloss cupboards, and light grey flooring. Slowly moving into the apartment, I turn to see Shaun sitting behind the dining table with a revolver pistol resting on the top surface not even trying to hide.

"Come in Dean, I've been expecting you." Shaun announces.

Continuing to walk into the room my emotions are now overpowered by the thought of having to killing him.

"Come and sit at the table." I slowly walked over.

"So, I guess McGough has sent his little boy to tidy up the mess eh? Well you tell him from me I gave everything for his precious little private wars over the years." Shaun lifts the pistol and points it at me. Noticing the half empty bottle of whisky on the table and the way he is slurring his words confirming, I know he is drunk and the pain of losing Chloe clearly claws away at his insides. I slowly reach for the pistol tucked into my belt and gradually begin to remove it.

"All I want to know is why Dean? Why out of all those people to die on that day did Chloe have to die?" Shaun has tears in his eyes then lowers the gun.

I stare across at him then decide to leave the pistol tucked in the belt, as I lean against the kitchen unit worktop opposite him.

"Shaun all I can say is, I'm sorry that Chloe died that day, it wasn't my intention to kill her you must know that."

Shaun takes a big gulp of whisky, then asks another question, "How did you do it, how did you manage to escape all those years ago? I wish I could escape now?"

Not giving a reply to Shaun he continues in his drunken state confused, "McGough wanted to try and hide that failure and blamed all of us, but when you escaped, well, that did just stir up the hornets' nest and what finally broke the cardinal programme ultimately."

Shaun empties the whisky from the glass then pours more liquid from the bottle, "What now Dean, between us, what happens now?"

My handgun presses hard into my back almost urging me to use it, as I reply, "He wants you dead Shaun."

"How I feel at the minute Dean, I don't really give a shit. McGough sent you to kill me, a test to check your loyalty to him?" Shaun coughs.

Shaun looks terrible, with a greyish look in his face from a broken heart and the gunshot wound.

"If we don't end it today, he will send a team here to eliminate you, there's nowhere to hide. I found you easy enough." I reply

"I know, but I did leave you a few clues to follow."

"Clues which clues?" I ask.

"The bag in the locker, the boarding pass, the passport, the hotel details, the information at the hotel! Do you really think McGough planned all that? He couldn't plan to tie his own shoelaces without us, he is pathetic." Shaun has an aggressive tone in his voice as he takes a big swig of whisky and lifts the gun again.

Another tear rolls down his cheek, "I did blame you for killing her, but I know it wasn't your fault." Shaun forgives me as he lowers the gun.

"I never could have known she was in the crowd Shaun." I reply, as I begin to walk closer to him.

"I know that now Dean and sorry for Sunday, but what happens next?" He asks again knowing that I have been sent to kill him.

"Were you really my friend or just someone sent to monitor me by McGough?" I ask.

"At first, Dean, it was just a job. I owed McGough and watching you gave me some level of freedom, but I'd like to think that we became friends in the end."

I notice more blood slowly oozing from the gunshot to his leg, "How's your leg?"

"You didn't have to shoot me Dean. Christ!" He begins to smile.

"It was the only way to save your life; Burns would have killed you in an instant. You did kill John Wagstaff though."

"Did I? oh fuck, well, it saved you a job eh." Shaun tries to laugh.

"You could say that. I'm sorry Chloe is dead." Replying with sympathy in my voice.

Nodding his head, he asks "When did McGough make contact?"

"It was Friday last week, when I was travelling back from Brazil."

"Brazil! What the hell were you doing there?"

"Helping Burns tidy up a few loose ends. I remember everything now Shaun, and I know what happened with you."

"Well, best not talk about that geezer?"

Changing subject quickly, "McGough sold me out after the Turkish operation went wrong and left me to die." I reply.

"Turkish op, which op?"

"Operation Otterman? The female agent who wanted to defect."

"That must have been a special op because it wasn't any that I was aware of. Let's face it Dean he sold us both out to do his dirty work, and we both fell for it."

Just then the front door barges open and a guy around thirty years old dressed in a red tee shirt and jeans enters holding a handgun. His hand is shaking with adrenaline, as the gun is pointed towards the direction of Shaun who quickly picks up his revolver and points back at the man even in his drunken state.

"What the fuck do you want bastard!" Shaun asks as the man just stands there.

Suddenly, behind Shaun the glass breaks, and he slump forward onto the table as the familiar sound of a silenced bullet, and thud from a sniper's rifle registers in my brain. Quickly removing the gun from my trouser belt, I grab a fresh loaf that lies on the worktop and placing it endways to the gun barrel, shoot a bullet into the man by the door close to his heart killing him stone dead with the loaf acting like a sound suppressor to muffle the sound.

Dropping to the floor, I crawl across to Shaun and placing my arm around his waist he whispers "Goodbye Dean my friend, at least I will be with Chloe and my child soon. You kill McGough and save yourself from this life." My thoughts suddenly rush back to Lloyd and Wagstaff.

More glass breaks and a fragment hits my arm as another bullet strikes Shaun in the back of his head. He slumps instantly on the table top and takes his last breath, and as I drop to the floor for protection. With the piece of glass still in my arm, I quickly crawl out of the kitchen towards the front door past the man who I shot. Searching through his pockets for any information, a red dot laser sight begins to scan around the room, which confirms it was a sniper. Not finding any evidence, I need to find this assassin quickly, and crawling my way into the corridor reach the doorway.

Standing and leaning against the apartment doorframe, I pull out the piece of glass and then tear off a piece of the tee shirt. Pulling the strip of cloth around my arm acting like a tourniquet. I continue down the corridor and the stairwell. Reaching the street level, I stare across to the high-rise buildings opposite trying to pinpoint any open windows and see at the top of the tenth storey office block one small window ajar. Moving quickly towards the entrance a man dressed in dark clothes, and carrying a long holdall bag can be seen opening the staircase door. We both stop and stare across at each other wondering what will happen next. After a few seconds, he turns and heads back down the staircase with me now in hot pursuit. As I reach the basement, the assassin can be seen climbing into a blue BMW car.

The engine starts, and with the tyres squealing he speeds out of the basement towards the exit ramp, as I run behind. Removing a small magnetic tracking device from my pocket, I manage to throw the device that attaches to the rear of the car near to the number plate position. A tiny red flashing light can be seen from the device, as he disappears from view.

Quickly heading back to the Park Hyatt Hotel, I walk down into the basement around to the rear passenger side of the car and lifting the key from the top of wheel where it was placed earlier, and the car is unlocked. Removing the bag from the trunk, I sit on the driver's seat placing the bag onto the front passenger front. Removing the handheld tracker monitor, I can see that the assassin has already begun to make his way onto the expressway heading towards the A4.

Starting the car engine, I begin the journey in pursuit to see where he is going, and who he is going to meet as the tracker bleeps against a basic digital map. I quickly check the cars sat nav screen to see where the A4 expressway road routes from Sydney lead too and notice that this road joins with the M1 and then possibly onto the A1 which could ultimately lead to Brisbane or any other cities on the east coast. I check the tracker and see that he is heading north, but not knowing where he is planning to go, I can only try and follow his GPS location using the tracker which has a location range of fifty kilometres. Thinking what big cities could be north on the east coast Brisbane seems a logical assumption due to the airport which has quick links out of Australia. Quickly calculating the distance and average speeds along with any possible detours, a journey time of at least ten and a half hours could be ahead, and I hardly have any provisions of food or water.

This is not the best start to a journey across Australia which goes against any possible survival training planning, I have done in the past. Settling into the journey, I begin to follow the assassin's route which now begins to head towards the Terrigal central coast area. My mind begins to play back the events earlier, when I visited Shaun and remember entering the apartment and walking into the kitchen area, where he could be seen sitting against the dining table. The emotions racing through my body didn't know whether to run over and hug him or take out the pistol and shoot him. A sadness then fills my thoughts, as I remember seeing the half empty bottle of Glenfiddich whisky, and his glass on the table top as he tries to drown his pain.

The torment that he must have been experiencing along with

knowing that, I caused the death of Chloe and his child must have been eating away at his insides like rats stuck in a trap. The sound of breaking glass followed by the thud from the bullet punching into his body still echo in my ears, and a strange side of me feels as though he was finally released from his pain and suffering. I can picture the look on his face, as the colour from his life drained away onto the table top with the bullet shot to his head, but it also feels that his death has still has not fully sunk into my soul.

Driving out of Sydney and along the M1 expressway, the scenery starts to change from high rise buildings, and large private houses to open scrub land, trees and farmland. The road side is littered with signs everywhere for camping areas, as I continue along the tarmac road entering into the national park. After a few more kilometres, I pass the sign for Terrigal, and instantly notice driving along the high street that the road junctions are completely devoid of any traffic lights.

So, having to slow down at every crossroads, I cautiously pass through the criss-cross roads following the bleep on the tracker. The distance from Sydney is already ninety minutes, and from the bleeps on the monitor, the assassin appears to be following the A49 along the causeway that heads towards Newcastle. A quick distance check confirms that Newcastle is around one hour from Terrigal.

I check the fuel gauge, and check the outside temperature deciding that this may be a good time to refuel, and pick up some water and food. Seeing signs for a road side service station, I indicate and pull onto the forecourt. Stopping next to the fuel pump, I climb out after opening the automatic filler flap, and am instantly hit by the warmth from the daytime sunshine. I unscrew the cap, select the correct fuel and insert the nozzle beginning to fill the tank.

After the tank is filled, I replace the cap, and close the filler flap, lock the car and continue into the shop to pay for the fuel and collect a few supplies. Reaching the door, it opens automatically, and I am instantly hit with a blast of cold air from the conditioning system and continue towards the line of refrigerators. Sliding the door open and collecting two bottles of water, I walk towards the prepared food selecting two packets of sandwiches and bags of nibbles that can be eaten on the journey. Reaching the till, the food, water and fuel is paid for, and I return back to the car. Checking the tracker which has been left on the front passenger seat, I can see the assassin still on the A43. Settling behind the wheel, I pull away from the forecourt and continue along the A43 passing towns with names such as, Swansea and Belmont heading towards Newcastle.

 The tracker suddenly makes a continuous bleeping sound, and as I look over, I can see that the target has stopped in a roadside diner car park. I continue to follow the direction seen on the tracker map, and twenty-five minutes later, notice the signs for Greg's roadside diner. Gradually slowing down, I see the targets car which is parked near to the entrance door of the restaurant.

 I wait close to the kerbside around hundred metres away from the diner waiting for him to exit the building. This way, I can keep just enough distance between us so hopefully he will not see me following. I begin to open one of the sandwich packets, and bottle of water and quickly reflect on the adventures in my first few hours in Australia. Suddenly, a familiar image emerges from the restaurant, as the target walks towards the BMW car. Never even looking across towards my direction, he opens the driver's door and climbs inside. The engine starts, and he quickly reverses away from the parking space then joins the main road and continues on his journey. I gradually lower myself down into the seat as he quickly passes by me. With the engine on my car already running, I engage drive and continue to follow him with the tracker still emitting a signal.

 With him around five hundred metres in-front, we continue on the A43 and then join the A1 just past the twelve mile creek boarder signpost. The signs for Myall lakes are quickly seen, as we seem to be on a route towards Port Stephen. The traffic on the roads is sporadic with lorries seen passing on the opposite side. Between the assassin, and myself are several campervans which helps to conceal me following him on the coast road.

Continuing past the town signs for Possum Brush and John's river we head towards the main signage for Port Macquarie. As I enter Port Macquarie, the first thing that is noticed are the large painted roadside rocks showing various cartoon characters, and I notice looking at the clock that Port Macquarie is nearly two hours from Port Stephen.

Looking across towards the sea, the swell of the waves deepens and lengthens, and the signs for Crescent Head become evident. Lots of surfers can be seen bobbing on the waves waiting for their point break in the late afternoon sunshine. Camper vans can be seen parked everywhere, as surfers are seen crossing the roads dressed in wet suits holding their boards. Beginning to think about how simple a life it would be just to park up a camper, and go surfing every day, my thoughts then turn to the matter at hand and avenging Shaun's death. A sense of guilt now falls across my emotions, as I feel a sadness for killing Chloe, his unborn child and ultimately Shaun. My throat suddenly goes very dry as the significance of the situation starts to burn deep.

Passing the road signs for Kempsey and Valla Beach, a road sign for Coffs Harbour is seen. Glancing across to the check the car distance and clock, I have been driving now for nearly five hours, and a slight cramp in my left leg starts to increase. The tracker still shows that the target is continuing to drive, but I need a break and driving along notice a roadside diner called the `Happy Frog`. Stopping on the roadside, I stop the engine and climb out, with a stiffness in my back and my legs feeling a little rubbery, I walk towards the café and opening the door walk inside.

The décor is quite basic, but the café is filled with people talking and enjoying food and drinks. Sitting down a waitress arrives, and an order is placed for a large coffee. I need something to keep me awake on this road trip. I visit the bathroom and return to the table as a large mug of coffee is delivered. I sit in the café thinking over the challenges ahead, and try to remain completely focused over thinking how to kill McGough inflicting just enough pain to revenge Shaun's death.

Looking around the café, I can see couples of all different ages, and families enjoying their time together. After a large coffee, I walk back to the car and continue along the main road, and then pass *'The Big Banana Coffs Harbour'* and see that the sign is written along a huge banana which is placed parallel to the road. Heading away from Coffs Harbour along the A1 in the direction of Byron Bay, I head past towns such as South Grafton and Clarence river which is quite a built-up area. Maclean is the next town which is also built alongside the Clarence river. I notice it is a smaller town large building called the Bottom pub. I pass through Woodburn Flicker river town next which has brightly painted buildings along the main street along with a food and liquor store called Lennox Head.

I continue driving on the M1 and clearly the Gold coast is a surfer's paradise, as I pass Tweed Heads South the Robina district. There are surf shacks and camper vans parked everywhere. Once I have driven past Pacific Pines, the tracker signals a slight change in direction, and I begin to drive away from the coast, and head inland into more built-up areas and suburbs. Passing a large Ikea superstore, I finally reach the outskirts of Brisbane as the daylight draws to a close with the darkness of the night illuminated by building lights. Continuing to follow the tracker signal, we cross the Story Bridge and drive past Chinatown into the Fortitude Valley area travelling along Brunswick Street. The assassin stops, and I drive past noticing his car is parked by the Mantra Terrace Hotel. I continue past and a little further down the road see a blue neon sign for vacancies hanging by the City Palms Motel, and pulling onto the driveway, I continue underneath the bright yellow archway sign, and stop the car in a parking space at the back of the motel.

Climbing out of the car, it is locked, and I walk towards the reception along a path past a row of large palm trees. To the side of the motel, a bright blue wooden staircase is attached to the outer wall of the building. Reaching the blue reception door, I open it and continue into the lobby area with my nose overwhelmed by the smell of pine air fresheners. Walking towards a light coloured tall wooden desk at the side of the room, a thin frail middle-aged man with a receding hairline, and round rimmed glasses who is dressed in a black tee shirt and beige trousers suddenly walks out from a side room.

"Well, G'day, sir, and how can I help you today?" He asks.

Quickly looking at him, I reply by saying "I would like a room for one night is that OK?" The hairs on the back of my neck lift show, as I take an instant dislike to him.

"Yes sir, no worries sport, if you would just like to complete this registration document, I will find you a room." He hands over the sheet of paper and pen.

"How will you be paying sir?" He asks in his deep Australian accent.

"Cash." I reply quickly filling in the form with a false name and address, then handing it back to him with a fake smile.

"OK great sir, now I have placed you into room twelve that is back out through the main entrance door and up the first staircase to the left. If you need anything there is a person here until 8.00 pm and afterwards an emergency number in the room OK?"

"OK, thank you." I reply nodding.

Walking out of the lobby, I return to the car removing my bag and suitcase from the trunk, and then continue back up the blue staircase to the motel room. Reaching the room, the key is inserted and the door opened.

As I enter the room, my eyes quickly scan around the open plan space from the right to the left. I notice that the room is simple, but is equipped with a small kitchen, and a few basic electrical appliances.

Continuing to look around the room, there is a dining table and four chairs placed close to a wall that is covered in dark green floral wallpaper. As my eyes pass the door for the bathroom, a double bed can be seen to the far-left corner of the room with a floral settee placed in-front of an old-style TV. My nostrils pick up the faint smell of cigarette smoke which hangs in the air from a previous tenant. I walk over to the bed, and lowering my bag and the suitcase onto the top bed-sheet, I take out a change of clothes. After replacing the clothes, I remove some more equipment from my bag which includes another pistol magazine, a knife and another personal tracker device.

Walking out from the room, I continue back down the staircase and onto the pavement heading back towards Chinatown following the tracker signal being emitted from the car. Cautiously crossing the road, the signal bleeps quicker, as I reach the Mantra Terrace Hotel.

I notice his car has disappeared from the road side, and instantly think that the tracker has either been removed or fallen off. I recheck the screen and see that actual position has moved slightly and slowly make my way into the underground car parking area. The assassins BMW car is parked in a corner space, and I begin to walk over in the direction of the vehicle looking around the area for any evidence of him or any possible motion sensors or cameras, as I reach the car. Understanding some of the assassin's techniques, he will attempt to try and cover his tracks in and possibly even disappear quickly.

He may even plan to change his car if he senses that I am close by. Walking around to the back of the car, the small tracker LED flashes confirming it's still attached, but with it so close to the boot lid he may have already have seen it. Deciding to remove it just in case, I take out a second tracker, and place it well into the rear passenger wheel-arch hiding it from sight. Feeling inside my pocket, I remove a motion sensor and place it under the driver's side sill. This way if the car is being dumped, he will at least rock the car taking out any final possessions confirming its position. Finally, I walk back towards the

City Palm motel stopping at a take away for a burger and chips, then return back to the room. After eating the food, I retire to the bed, and take some well-earned rest.

Awaking in the morning, I check the condition of the motion sensors and see that the car has not moved. I make a coffee, have a quick, facial wash to wake myself up and then decide it is best to head towards his hotel, where I can try to monitor his actions. Reaching the Mantra Terrance hotel lobby, I enter past the security gate and into the main lobby area. There are fifteen people in the lobby with some just sitting and talking. More people can be seen just standing, and there are three people who are currently checking out. I continue towards the small coffee shop area to the front of the lobby, and remove a copy of the latest Sydney Herald newspaper from the display rack.

Finding a suitable area, I sit in one of casual armchairs at the rear section of café which allows me to see the street outside, and the movements of all the people inside the hotel lobby. The waitress comes over and an order is placed for a coffee and a bacon sandwich.

I remove the mobile tracker from my pocket, and place it onto the table top. The device looks very similar to a mobile phone and quickly checking the screen, I confirm that the trackers are still working. Opening the front page of the Herald, I settle down to wait for the target to surface. Trained assassins will usually make a base, and then walk the area to carry out any threat assessments before waiting for the next orders to be delivered. After several hours of waiting combined with a few coffees, my patience pays off as the assassin, who is now wearing a different set of clothes and baseball cap, walks through the lobby towards the street outside.

His change of clothes now allows me to size up his build and shape profile, and assess what his possible weaknesses could be, just by how he walks. With the coffees and sandwich already paid for, I wait a few seconds for him to exit the hotel, and continue to follow him keeping the copy of the newspaper.

Slowly placing a pair of sunglasses over my eyes, and a baseball cap on my head, I keep a distance of about seventy-five metres away from him. The sunshine casts great shadows across the street from all the high building, as I slowly begin to follow the target past shops, bars and restaurants. He is very nervous continuously looking around, as though he senses something is wrong, but I also need to check I'm not being set up so using reflections cast in vehicle door mirrors and shop glass frontages, I check to see if anyone is following me. After walking around the city for around one hour, he is seen taking a mobile from his pocket. The mobile is placed to his ear, and he starts to talk. Stopping next to an office building, he enters through the main door.

FIVE

Slowly strolling past the door, I casually glance through the glass, and check the different nameplates of the companies listed, and then continue towards a small shop. After buying a bottle of water, I select one of the public benches, and sit underneath the cover of a tree opposite a road which appears to run parallel to the back of the office building. This position allows me to observe both the front door and the rear exit of the building if the target tries to escape. Lifting the newspaper, I turn to the rear page pretending to read the sports page, and slowly start to flick backwards through the paper thinking about the assassin and who he could be meeting inside.

I return to my thoughts about Shaun, Wagstaff and what level of revenge I can start to inflict on this assassin. I try to remain focused, but my emotions want to lash out at someone, and an inner pain rips at my insides indirectly blaming this assassin for their deaths. Another fire starts to burn deep inside over the thoughts of Burns, and the fact that he was using me before he would probably have killed me. All of these thoughts combined with the conversation between McGough, and myself starts to flow through my body, as I remember how I was left for dead in the past. I am filled with anger, and pain beginning to shake as the adrenaline rushes around my nervous system.

'What is happening to me?' crosses my mind, as I continue to try remaining focused, but clearly there is a lot of unfinished business which needs to be wiped clear before I can move forward. Away from my vision, the assassin is standing talking to a younger man in a small meeting room. The assassin gives his account of Neal's death and also the fact that other man was seen at the apartment. The young man smiles, and hands over an A4 envelope which contains information for his next target along with a few recent pictures.

Meanwhile, I stare into the unknown waiting for the target to surface and gradually glancing at my wrist watch notice that he has been inside the building for nearly twenty minutes. Then as if by magic, he is seen walking towards the glass front door. He pulls it open, and passes through the doorway before returning to the street heading back towards the direction of his hotel at a fast pace. Folding the newspaper and placing it under my arm, I quickly jump to my feet and begin to follow with anger in my eyes, as I replay what could have happening inside the building. It's clear he has met with a contact or handler, and has probably gathered information on his next contract.

Following him back to the Mantra Terrace hotel, I watch him walk past the main lobby reception. Removing the handheld tracker from my pocket, the devices are rechecked that they are still working, and I casually begin to walk back to the City Palms Motel. Reaching my room, I quickly place all the contents back into the two bags, then walk over towards the bed and lower myself onto the top-sheet. I close my eyes and continue to think about where the assassin could be moving to next. As I rest, the assassin can be seen taking out a laptop from his rucksack, and starts to investigate his next contract killing.

He gathers information about an address and known accomplices then begins to plot a route. He then begins to check, and clean all his weapons ensuring they are all precise. After a few hours of rest, the mobile tracker begins to vibrate confirming that the motion sensor has been activated. Quickly gathering the bags, I walk out towards my hire car. Placing the bags into the trunk, I climb in and drive towards the Mantra Terrace hotel. The movement tracker now begins to signal that the car is changing position, and as I reach the end of Brunswick Street, he can be seen driving the car in the opposite direction away from the city. Knowing he doesn't recognise my car; I pull into the road side and wait, until he passes.

Quickly turning in a small side street and leaving some distance, I begin to tail him back onto the coast road, and then continue towards the M1 motorway. Over the road lanes a sign for Cairns is seen. Slowing down, I give more distance between the assassin, and myself as we continue along the M1. I pass the signs for Palm view and continue through this small town which has shops on one side of the main road and car parking spaces on the other. The next town is Yandina which has signposts stating that this was an aboriginal district for over forty-thousand years. I continue past the signs for a ginger factory, as I head along the A1 Bruce Highway. The next town is Glanmire which borders the Mary River and the journey is already two hours long.

Entering another small town called Biggenden, I see a public bar which is painted light blue, and a convenience store that has across the front and sides of the building a huge sign consisting of a yellow band with four large painted red X's indicating Castle main beer logo. In the main street, I notice the wide central reservation which is planted with roses in full bloom along with low hanging telephone cables spanning the wide roadway. Continuing along the Bruce Highway, I see a sign at the side of the road which has the painted image of a woman backpacker in high heels and short skirt and the name of Colosseum Creek road house. After nearly five hours of driving, I need a break so pulling into the parking lot, I stop the engine and reach over for the tracker. Checking that the target is still driving, I climb out of the car, stretch my back and then walk towards the signpost indicating the direction of the restaurant. I reach the doors that open automatically and enter the small shop area. There is a lady in her late fifties standing behind the counter all dressed in black. I walk along the yellow coloured floor tiles, and ask if it is possible to have a coffee.

She smiles, and says, "Take a seat honey, I will bring one right over."

Walking into the restaurant the yellow tiles change to a dark brown flooring and my eyes notice the white table clothes which hang neatly over the evenly spaced tables. Pulling out one of the wooden chairs from a vacant table, I look around the room which has a few people sitting around, and over the bar is a large green Victoria Bitter sign hanging. After the lady brings over the coffee then take a few moments to try, and think about my next plans and what to do next. The people sitting in this room don't even realise who I am, or what I have done. Casually, I glance over to the tracker to see if the assassin is still moving, then remember, why I am here.

Leaving the table, I pay for the drink, then use the restroom on the way out of the building then walk towards the parked hire car to continue my journey, and climbing back into the driver's seat, I start the engine, then continue along the A1. Settling back into the vehicle the time seems to disappear, and after another hour, the tracker device starts to vibrate indicating that the target vehicle has stopped, and checking the map see it is near a city called Rock-Hampton. He is at least three minutes in front of me, and I only hope that he is not changing his vehicle. As I enter the outskirts of Rock Hampton, there is a large statue of a Bull at the side of the road with the words *'Welcome to Rock Hampton'* carved into the stonework below. I continue past a large sign for the Fitzroy River, and the tracker vibrates and bleeps again to confirm that the motion sensor has been activated. Briefly stopping in some road side parking, I recheck the map and just then the assassin can be seen driving his car back towards the direction the of the A1. After giving him plenty of distance, I continue to follow him once again with my thoughts constantly thinking about what I will do to him once we finally meet.

The day is now beginning to turn into the darkness of the night, as I look at the speedometer, and realise that I have driven over eight hundred kilometres today. The car headlights illuminate a roadside sign of a town called Marlborough. Watching his brake lights illuminate, I see the indicator signal begin to flicker with his intention, as his turns right pulling the car into a parking lot in-front of the Marlborough Hotel. Slowing down, I take this opportunity to approach him a little closer, and as I pull onto the gravel surfaced car-park, he quickly glances across in my direction, then enters into the building walking along the short-covered veranda.

Stopping the car engine, I watch him disappear into the building hoping this is not the place for a gunfight, and take out a small bladed knife then slip it into my trouser pocket. Climbing out of the car my back is stiff from all the sitting, but as I follow him the stiffness eases. I now sense that he must be, aware of my presence after seeing me in Brisbane and now driving onto the parking lot. Pushing the main door open, I take a deep sigh then enter the bar area. I quickly scan around the room looking for him, but only notice two gambling machines which have lights flashing away. The small bar has a couple of high stools near to the counter. Noticing he isn't in the main bar area; I continue to scan around the remainder of the room seeing a pool table with a red cover cloth at the far-right side. The wall behind the pool table has a large map of Australian with pictures of famous landmarks, which I quickly glance at before seeing an area with simple wooden table and chairs. Seeing that he is not in these areas too, the only place left is the restrooms, so I continue towards the direction of the signs pointing to the rear of the bar area.

The headcount in the restaurant bar area confirms only two possible threats. One threat is from two big truck drivers who are enjoying large steak dinners, and the other threat could be from four diners who appear to be travellers probably driving along the coast road in the old VW camper seen in the parking lot. Slowly taking out the small knife from my pocket, I cup it into my hand, then gradually begin to push the light green toilet door open.

The fluorescent tube lighting in the restroom area flickers slightly as the starter motor buzzes, which keeps making the area almost plunge into complete darkness, apart from a small light bulb near the mirror that is placed above the bathroom sinks. The next noise to fill my ears apart from the distant music being played in the bar area, is the whirring sound being emitted from the large ceiling fan, as it oscillates about its axis in an attempt to circulate the pungent smell of raw sewage waste which keeps filling my nostrils.

Entering the room fully, I stand close to the exit door, as it closes behind me slowly, suddenly one of the toilet cubicle doors swings open and the assassin walks out staring at me.

"I knew it was you that had been following me since Sydney." He says casually with a strong Australian accent as he begins to walk towards the wash hand basins.

"What did you expect after killing my friend." I reply.

"We don't have any friends in this business, only enemies foreign and domestic." He throws some water on his face.

"The training and orders teach you those answers in life on the other hand you need friends." I reply, slowly lowering the knife in my hand and noticing his concealed gun.

"McGough spoke so highly of you Nash and I suppose you could say it's a pleasure to meet, but killing you, I will do that for free." He slowly starts to move his right arm.

"Do you think I haven't seen that concealed gun tucked in your belt?"

He stops suddenly then turns to stare at me, as we both look each other up, and down trying to weigh up any weaknesses in our opponents, he is similar build to me with tanned complexion and a small tattoo on his right arm. His shoulder length black hair glimmers from the splashes of water which glistens in the flickering lights.

His dark brown lifeless eyes stare at me with death written deep into them, as I notice his weakness.

"I've heard a lot of stories about the great Dean Nash, I was expecting more to be honest, but it seems that killing you will be easy."

"Well that is my disguise, and by the way you can, of course, certainly try." I prepare for combat as he tries to stare me out.

I walk three more steps closer towards him, then begin to pick out more of his facial details, as well as, the large scar to his left neck. My experience remembers that this weakness indicates thinner skin in this area and an opportunity to overpower him.

"I've always wanted to go head to head with you Nash so let's go."

"I'm not going anywhere." Lunging forward, I take a swipe with the blade cutting his neck close to the jugular vein near to the thinner old scar tissue.

"Christ, I never saw that fuckin blade, you're fast for an old man Nash." He lifts his hand and feels the warm blood already dripping quickly.

"There is plenty more for you yet." I smile across at him.

The assassin jumps forward and grabs me around the waist pushing me into a wall. As I hit the wall a tile breaks, and cuts my arm, as he starts to lift his knee into my groin, and punches my mid-section with a feeble attempt, but already I have the advantage. Clasping both my hands together, I strike him straight in the centre of his spine causing him to loosen his grip, and he drops to the ground in pain. I jump to the right, and stand waiting for his next move, as he slowly starts to stand dripping blood onto the floor from the knife wound. He lifts his hand to his neck, and sees how much blood is pumping from the wound, and begins to move in my direction trying to wrestle me to the ground again. I sense he is already weakening from a simple knife cut, and kick him across the face breaking his nose. He rolls around on the floor and then moves his arm for the concealed gun.

"Enough of this shit." As he pulls out the silenced handgun.

"I bet you can't dodge a fuckin bullet Nash." He snarls with his hand shaking slightly, and pointing the handgun at me.

I quickly throw the knife hitting him in the shoulder that locks the joint, and severs the main bicep tendon as he tries to take a shot.

As he drops the gun to the floor, I quickly run forward, and spinning him around grab him across the neck, and now standing behind him take out the knife from his shoulder, and with two quick actions cut the extensor tendons on his arms near the elbow joint which renders his arms useless. Finally, I push the knife into his neck as he tries to fight against me kicking at my shins, but he is no match and sensing he is weakening more with every movement, I lower him to the ground as he starts to cough from the blood filling his airway. Reaching for the silenced handgun which he dropped onto the floor near the washbasins, I stand away from him slightly and begin to question him.

"So, who sent you to kill Neal? Was it orders from McGough?"

"Fuck you Nash!" He snarls.

Lifting the pistol, I shoot him in each kneecap, and I ask him again, "Who sent you?" I stand on one of his knees as he shouts in pain.

"Fuck you Nash, I won't talk!" He shouts.

"Then you're no use to me." I raise the gun and fire two bullets into his head at close range knowing that I'm wasting valuable escape time.

Quickly dragging his body into one of the empty cubicles, the door is closed, and I begin to check his pockets for any information. Taking out his car keys and wallet, I exit out of the cubic re-closing the door behind, and walk over to the wash hand basins. Switching on the taps, I remove his excess blood from my hands and then casually look into the mirror and notice the cut to my arm. I remove some paper hand towels from the dispenser, and run some water on them then layer it around the cut. Returning back into the restaurant, I sit at the bar and order a coffee as though nothing has just happened and slowly check the time on my watch to see it is eighteen forty-five p.m. Luckily, the black clothes I am wearing help conceal the fresh blood. Taking out his wallet, I begin to thumb through the different layers removing credit cards which have his name printed on them which reads Michael Hughes. There is some cash and a couple of old pictures with the rest of the contents just being receipts and a few scraps of paper.

Slowly looking around the room, one of the truckers has already left, and the other guy is not far behind him which just leaves the four travellers, and the young man behind the counter. All of whom don't seem very interested or very threatening. After drinking the mug of coffee, I stand from the table and then walk out of the hotel bar and towards the parking lot. I continue over towards Michael's car, and unlock the door then slide onto the driver's seat. Beginning to check through the car, I am, after any information or evidence of his last and next contracts. There are a few papers left in the front passenger side door bin. Reaching over the papers are removed, and I look at them under the interior courtesy light, one document is for a flight request for Cairns, there are the hire car papers and a room booking at Palm Cove with no name just a reservation code. Opening the glove box, nothing is seen inside, so grabbing the room and flight booking information I leave the remaining hire car documents and climb out of the car.

Walking to the rear, I open the passenger door, and lean inside and the rear seat of the car is checked and a dark brown thin leather jacket is removed. I walk around to the back of the car which has a green holdall bag sitting in the trunk. Quickly unzipping the bag, and trying to use the pathetic interior light from the trunk, it is evident that there are some blank passports, a few big bundles of cash and some weapons.

Lifting the bag from the trunk, I close the lid then lock all the doors, and throw the keys and empty wallet into a rubbish bin near to where his car is parked. Returning to my hire car, the bag is placed on the back seat and after climbing into the driver's side, but realise that my body needs to rest, and I can already feel where he has punched me in the stomach aching slightly. My best option is to continue to the next big city and find some accommodation for the night. Taking out my mobile, I begin to look for the next city towards Cairns and Mackay which is around two and a half hours drive away, and it seems the best option. I begin to look for a motel for the night, and find the International Lodge motel. Checking they have a room for tonight, the booking is completed and the directions typed into the sat nav system of the car.

Once again, I continue driving along the Bruce Highway, now in complete darkness with the occasional signpost for Mackay hanging from the side of the road, as I follow the directions. My thoughts hardly register over the death of the assassin and during my past, it was always the survival of the fittest so better him than me replays through my mind. During this journey the feelings of loneliness and failure begin to wash over my emotions, as the demons of the darkness start to take hold, and tighten their grip around my throat.

Knowing that my fate could also be as swift as that of Michael Hughes, the positive energy which normally overflows begins to drain from my soul like sand running between the fingers of a clenched fist. Trying to battle with these feeling of self-doubt and failure, I know, I need to stop somewhere, and recalibrate my thoughts and the signs for Mackay suddenly, become welcoming as a wave of comfort washes these dark emotions away. Now summoning my usual confidence, the main objective is to look for the motel and get some rest.

Passing by the marina area the dark sky is filled by a brightness from the succession of ships cabin lights moored at the quayside, and in the distance the yellow neon lights for the International Lodge motel send a warmth into my soul.

There is smaller sign hanging underneath the motel name which reads no vacancies, so I hope that I managed to book the last room. The motel is on a small side street close to the Blue-water Lagoon area of the city, and as I approach the street, lights illuminate the off yellow building, as I draw onto the car parking area. Finding a space, I climb out of the car which now begins to feel like a part of my body, and walk towards the reception that still has a person on the desk. I notice the time tick over to twenty-one p.m. on the large digital clock on the wall. There is a young man sitting behind the front counter, as I enter through the doorway.

"*G'day!* Can I help you, sir?" He asks.

"I have a room reservation for tonight." I reply.

"Ah, yes, you booked it about three hours ago correct?"

"That's correct, the name is Deddington." I reply.

"I was just going to leave for the night, you were lucky."

"Luck sometimes is my middle name." We both smile.

"OK, I need you to complete this registration document, and I have placed you in room eighteen which is across the parking lot and at the far end of the building second floor. It was our last room."

"No worries sport." I reply.

"What part of the UK are you from?" He asks.

"In the north not far from Manchester."

"Oh, right, not been that far north, but made it to London though."

"Lucky you." I answer not really interested.

"You have complimentary breakfast cereals included in the room rate along with tea and coffees. There is milk in the fridge."

"OK, Mr Deddington, that will be $75.00 for the room, can I charge it to the card you used for the reservation?"

"OK, that card should be fine." I reply.

Handing over the room key, I smile back at him, then walk outside towards the hire car. After removing the bags and locking the doors, I climb the staircase heading towards room eighteen. Opening the door for the room, I walk inside and lower the bags to the floor. Switching on the light for the room, the LED bulbs illuminate the four corners of the apartment just enough to make out a double bed, a table and two chairs along with a white sink unit. Lifting the bags up again, the room looks a little basic, but for my needs tonight it will be fine, then walk towards the bed.

As I collapse onto the soft bed, I quickly fall to sleep with exhaustion following the long journey, and the killing of the assassin. As the morning breaks, I awake from my sleep still fully clothed. Moving off the bed, I walk towards the bathroom to remove the blood-stained clothes from yesterday's fight placing them into a plastic bag, then take a shower to freshen up for the day ahead. Now feeling more awake, I eat some breakfast cereals, and gather my things together before heading out of the room. Leaving the room, I continue along the walkway, then down the staircase to the towards the parking lot with the sound of birds singing in the nearby trees filling the air. I stop at a waste bin, and dump the blood covered clothes in the trash then reach the car. Pressing the remote, the doors unlock and the bags are placed inside.

Continuing to the driver's side, the door is opened, and I slide onto the seat once again. The engine is started, and as I re-join the Bruce Highway, the image of the motel fills the rear-view mirror of the car, and my thoughts briefly remember the assassin, and his final evidence of ever knowing him dumped in a waste bin. As I continue this endless journey to Cairns, the sound which now fills my cars is of waves crashing against the rocky coastline. The left side of the road is boarded by a sheer rock face and to the right, the white spray from the sea can be seen rising from the impact caused by hitting the rocks. My mind returns back to the black thoughts which caused anxiety and nervousness last night, and what might have triggered those feelings.

These emotions are probably punishment for all the bad things I have done in the past, but taking hold, and battling against these dark emotions will always be an inner battle in my life with only the strong surviving.

Even the most trained killers still have a soul and my old handler used to say 'Blank out these thoughts or they will eat you up inside.' I have seen in the past how agents could not blank out these feelings which claw at your insides like a wild animal trying to escape. Many people attempt to simply close off these thoughts, but they always haunt you. Several previous colleagues both male and female couldn't control these thoughts and the aftermath only has two ends. One solution to their pain is to try, and kill enough people to bury it or the worst cases are that agents take their own lives to end the voices they constantly hear in their heads. Most agents try to remain focused and controlled, but eventually they will crack under the emotional turmoil, and from the false image they try to portray to everyone they meet.

My mind changes to the journey to Palm Cove and checking the car sat nav, see I have over eight hours' drive ahead. Wishing, I had planned a flight enters my thoughts as the suburbs disappear and open land begins to fill my vision. Driving past the signs from Mount Ossa National Park, I also feel that I understand why so many people visit Australia to travel around and explore the countryside. I pass signs for the Bloomsbury BP overnight parking area, and continue along the A1 towards Gregory River camp site and onwards and Bowen. I notice signs for Mundubbera Caravan Park, which has a huge Mandarin shaped house on the advertising boards. After passing through Alligator Creek, the next big city is signed posted called Townsville, which I enter and stop next to the Exchange Hotel for a break and some food. There is a large canopy across the front of the hotel which has dark green painted steel legs which span across the pavement, and as I walk underneath the overhanging structure, I see the main entrance door. Opening the large glass front door, I enter the room and walk over towards the large bar which has shelves full of spirits and alcoholic drinks.

Ordering a coca cola and burger I take a seat at one of the tables and watch the large television screens showing the latest sports news. The room is quite empty with only a few men standing or sitting enjoying a drink and some food. I don't sense any fears in this area, but also know deep down that there could be trouble ahead. I need to start planning what to do with my future and how to live in the shadows again. A big part of me wishes that I had never met Nick Burns, however, I could not continue working in that office as a finance manager, and it was so dull.

The experiences in the last few weeks have been both traumatic, and exciting showing me that something was missing, and so my thoughts then turn to the next chapter of my life, and which route I should take. My mind is filled with all the past operations, the training with the agency, and it feels like my soul has been imprinted with a route, and discipline that was not my own, but this training also gives a certain comfort deep down.

My deep thoughts are broken by the waitress bringing my drink and burger. She places the two items in front of me without a word spoken, and just smiles, as she walks away. Taking a sip of the drink, I lift the burger from the plate, and take a mouthful of the food. You sometimes forget how enjoyable a simple burger tastes as my thoughts drift back to previous operation, when I hadn't eaten for several days. Finishing the food and the drink, I walk towards the bar and pay for them then slowly walk towards the restrooms. After using the toilet, I then continue back outside in the direction of the car, but sense something doesn't feel quite right. For a split second it felt as though I was being watched, so slowly, I look at the people in the street and glance across to the cars parked nearby.

On first impressions nothing appears to be wrong, but on closer inspection, I can see two men sitting in a dark grey Holden car which is parked around hundred metres behind mine. The two men are talking to each other, and casually look across in my direction. Slowly walking towards my car, I unlock the doors and slide onto the driver's seat.

Sitting inside the car I adjust the rear-view mirror slightly, and am able to see one of the men lift a mobile phone to his right ear and begin talking. Whether this is just a coincidence or something more, I start the car engine, and slowly drive towards the main road with intention to head towards the Bruce Highway to see if they follow. After a few seconds, I also see their car start to move and follow in my direction. Quickly looking at the cars sat nav map, I see a route, and I can take with several turns so continue down Flinders street then at the roundabout turn along Wickham Street following the one-way signs. At the end of Wickham Street, I turn right and turn along The Strand, and checking the rear view mirror the grey Holden is following. I turn off the Strand along King Street then back along Flinders Street passing the roundabout and then past the front of the Exchange hotel, and they continue to follow.

Pulling next to the side of the pavement, I stop a little further up the street from the hotel and watch the grey Holden stop. Clearly, they are following me so the first thought is to try and escape from them, or maybe, I could try another solution and approach them. Stopping the engine of the car I climb out, and then walk along the pavement at speed in their direction hoping that they will not try and shoot me in a busy public street. Almost reaching the car, they suddenly speed away, and try to turn their heads avoiding any facial contact and continue along Flinders street. This may be my only opportunity to escape and quickly returning to the car, I drive away at speed joining route sixteen and the road back towards the Bruce Highway. I wonder who the two men could be, and if they have placed a tracker on the car.

Managing to stop on a shop parking lot, I quickly look around the underside of the car and around the wheel arches, but don't find any tracking devices. I need to move quickly and get to Palm Cove and leaving this country far behind. Continuing once again on the A1 highway, I drive through Ingham before passing Cardwell, and just after Mission Beach see the first road signs for Palm Cove, as I continue through Wooroonooran National Park. My mind is filled with thoughts of who the two men were in the car, and why they were following me. Maybe, I was already under surveillance from the Australian authorities, and they had tracked my hire car or maybe, it is something else.

SIX

Earlier in the day, in a small forensic laboratory, a man and woman wearing long white coats quietly complete their work using various pieces of medical equipment. The room has a clinical smell which hangs heavy in the air from all the cleaning products, and the chemicals that are being used to prepare samples. The matt white painted walls and ceilings have blades of sunshine reflecting onto them after penetrating in between the light grey vertical blinds that hang against the windows. The air conditioning system works almost silently apart from an occasional creaking sound from the rotating louvers, as waves of refreshing cool air flow into the stuffy laboratory. Below the unit and down the left side of the laboratory there are six waist high side windows that overlook the main car park. Underneath the windows and running along the full length of the left wall is a long light grey worktop with storage cupboards built beneath.

Through the windows a row of eucalyptus trees can be seen casually swaying in the light breeze, and in the distance a whirring noise can heard as a gardener sits on a tractor lawnmower cutting the grass at the far side of the parking lot. The right-hand wall opposite to the windows has posters detailing various working procedures for the medical equipment in the laboratory.

The far wall of the long thin laboratory has a white board with hand written notes plastered across it and a computer desk is placed underneath with a few papers scattered on the top. The entrance door is set into the opposite wall which has a small desk placed at a right angle to the door opening. On the top of the desk is a telephone and small desk calendar which shows pictures of Australian wildlife and famous landmarks. In between the two long walls are the pieces of forensic equipment such as microscopes, fume hoods, chromatographs, spectrometers and centrifuges used for sample investigations. Near to the rear of the laboratory are three different industrial freezers / refrigerators.

Doctor Isabella can be seen looking at particle fragments through a microscope lens, while her assistant Chris is at the end of the room, typing on the computer keyboard entering evidence onto the government database system. Isabella lifts her head, rubs her sore eyes, and then slowly glances across the room with her light brown eyes, she is around thirty years old with shoulder length hair dark hair and athletic body. Being quite pretty, she doesn't wear much makeup and her height is close to five feet seven inches. The desk phone begins to ring, so standing, she gracefully walks over to the desk with her part open white laboratory jacket flowing around her. She lifts the receiver and answers.

"Oh, hi yes, Sarge." She listens to the request.

"OK, right now?"

"Course, I know where that place is, we will be on our way." She lowers the receiver and shouts across to Chris.

"We have a job to do Chris, so gather the tools and equipment, we have to go now."

"What about this report Issy?"

"That will have to wait, this is a big case Chris."

Chris who is in his late twenties has a masculine figure with blonde hair and blue eyes, he stands and walks towards the windows. He bends down and starts to open the doors of the under-counter cupboards, then begins to remove various boxes of equipment. Once the two of them have quickly gathered all the relevant boxes of equipment together, Isabella sits on the swivel chair closest to the entrance door, and changes her black high heel shoes for a pair of flat walking boots. Standing she removes the white lab jacket, and places it across the back of the swivel chair. Chris can be seen removing his jacket placing it across another desk, and they both then continue out towards the car park carrying the boxes of equipment with them. After loading all the equipment, and boxes into their white forensics van, they climb inside the vehicle and drive away.

Meanwhile, at a small hotel, three police cars are parked next to a blue three series BMW. Two police officers can be seen standing outside on the wooden porch of the motel stopping people from entering. Inside the hotel bar, two officers are sitting at separate tables taking statements from the people that are inside the restaurant. Outside the restroom, one officer can be seen guarding the entrance door, while inside another officer stares at the body of a person inside one of the toilet cubicles. The deceased is slumped against the right-hand side wall of the cubicle with their head leaning downwards. A white van arrives at the parking lot with the blue lights flashing which has the words 'Police forensics' written across the sides.

It parks parallel to the vehicle which has 'Private Ambulance' signage along the sides in small white writing against the black vehicle. Dr Issy and Chris climb out of the white van and continue towards the rear of the vehicle, opening the hatch. They begin to take out white paper overalls from clear plastic bags, and climb into them. Finally, they take out various boxes from the back of the van close the doors, and begin to walk towards the front veranda of the building. It is now late morning, but the sunshine is already beating down as the sound of a kookaburra shouts in a nearby tree.

As they reach the motel steps one of the officers speaks, "G'day Chris how you keeping sport? My it's no place for a Sheila in there?"

The woman replies, "Officer Stanley, that doesn't sound like an equal opportunities statement." They both smile at each other.

"G'day Issy, well, it's a mess in there, I was only thinking of you, the Sarge is inside waiting for you guys."

"Many thanks, but I'm old enough to look after myself." she

replies.

The two forensic officers walk inside the restaurant to see the four people sitting together talking to one officer, while the second officer talks to the barman making notes on some documents. Seeing Chris and Isabella, they point towards the restroom signage hanging near to the bar. Isabella lowers the boxes to the ground, and reaches into one of them removing two pairs of light blue slip over shoe covers and white paper overalls.

Handing a pair to Chris, they both pull these onto their shoes then climb into the white paper overalls. The two officers continue in the direction of the restrooms with Issy at the front. As they reach the toilet area, the officer standing outside the toilet door, pushes it open. The two enter to see the Sergeant standing talking on his radio.

"Roger control the forensic team have just arrived on site. Can you confirm, if the hotel owner has been contacted yet?"

The radio crackles, "No word on the hotel owner yet Sarge."

"Isabella, Chris, well, what a wonderful sight for you two guys this morning hey, just after brunch."

"No worries Sarge, what do you have for us?" Issy asks.

"Well, there's a dead body in the dunny with what looks like two bullet holes in his head."

"OK Sarge can you confirm if any of the people from the bar have been in the restroom." Chris asks.

"Christ Chris, it's hardly Grand central station. The barman found the body when he was locking up and noticed the blue BMW outside as well."

"I take it there are no witnesses?" Chris asks.

"You will be right there." The Sarge replies.

"What about the four other people in the bar." Issy asks.

"They are travelling down to Sydney, and were stopping last night." Sergeant Haynes replies.

"What time is the Doc is coming?" She asks.

"Christ love, he is still on golf course until at least midday, but I think we can all deduce the guy is dead, I haven't tried any first aid but you can have a go if you would like too."

"Do you think the blue BMW is his car Sarge?" Chris asks, looking at the body.

"It's highly likely; the doors are locked, so I have requested a locksmith to open it."

"OK Sarge thanks, can you give us the room." Isabella requests.

"Sure thing, hun, it's all yours." The Sarge walks out closing the door behind.

Isabella and Chris both take out cameras from the bags, and begin to walk the crime scene starting from the entrance door, and Isabella starts to use a dictation machine, "Today's date is twenty eighth September 2010. Onsite is the Forensic team from Mackay Police Station and the two officers are Chris Taylor and Isabella Arnold. We have been requested to complete a forensic examination of the evidence, in connection with the body of a male that has been found at the Marlborough hotel with the address of thirteen Railway Street Marlborough Queensland Australia."

She continues, "On entering the male toilet restroom, to my direct right are four toilet cubicles, and the body has been found in the cubical number three. Number one is the first cubicle which is closest to the entrance door. The body was found by the barman of the hotel."

"Continuing into the room the left side has three white wash hand basins which all have a mirror attached to the wall above them. The floor is covered with a mixture of buff cream quarry tiles near to the main wash hand basins, which then pattern into the remaining white tiled flooring covering the rest of the room. The lighting in the restroom is basic florescent tube strips, and two lights have flickering starters affecting the illumination. The ceiling is a yellowish colour showing signs of plaster having fallen or broken away and the vertical walls are covered in white tiles floor to ceiling. There are no windows in this room and the only ventilation is from a large ceiling fan." She stops.

"Chris, takes a picture of all the wash hand basins and the mirrors along with each of the toilet cubicles. We will also need to check them for fingerprints and any possible DNA sampling. Can you ask one of the officers to fetch a halogen spotlight from the van."

She continues, "To my right behind the entrance door, several of the white wall tiles are smashed with broken fragment particles lying on the buff flooring." She takes a picture of the broken tiles and fragments on the floor.

"There are no hand dryers only paper towels that are available through a hand operated dispenser. Chris takes more pictures of the dispenser, and we will also need any fingerprints from the operating lever front and sides. The contents from inside the trash bin require bagging and tagging." She instructs.

"Next to the broken fragments on the floor, is a pool of congealed blood that needs to be collected. Smear marks can be seen from, where it appears that the body has been dragged into toilet cubicle number three. In the centre of the blood pool, it appears to be two circular holes that are from first investigation matching the two bullet holes seen in the deceased head. The bullet holes measure approximately eight millimetre in diameter and have a pitch of twenty mm apart." She lowers a thin clear plastic ruler over the holes and takes several pictures with the camera flash illuminating the room.

"Chris we will need to remove these tiles, it is possible that the bullets that are buried in the flooring below."

"OK Ma'am, I will ask the officer to bring the tools from the van."

Just then one of the officers brings a halogen spotlight and hands it through the doorway to Chris. He clicks the button sending a beam of light into the darkness.

"Would you mind fetching the hammer and chisels too?"

"Sure, I have nothing else to do sport!" He replies.

Isabella stares across at the officer then continues "Walking towards the cubicle number three, blood streak marks are seen as the body was dragged along the tiles and then placed into the cubicle."

"We need any fingerprints from all the door locks and latches." She requests.

Isabella now stands opposite the dead person, "The deceased is slumped in the cubical fully dressed with what appears to be two bullet holes to the head that appear to match the diameter and distance from the floor markings." She holds the same thin plastic ruler against the bullet holes.

"The deceased is casually dressed in blue jeans and a black tee shirt. His training shoes are clean and all his clothes appear to be in a new condition." She takes more pictures.

"I am now entering into the cubicle and taking pictures of the head wound. There appears to be scorched bone indicating that the bullets were fired at a close range. The deceased also has a knife wound to his left neck and a cut to both of his arms in several positions. The shoulder joint also has a large cut from a small narrow blade."

Chris continues to take pictures as Isabella continues to talk, "Bruising has already begun to develop around the dead male's neck confirming that some type of physical stress took place prior to death. There could be fibres and skin traces under his fingernails, so we will need to bag the hands."

"OK Boss." Chris replies.

"The male appears to be around thirty years old. I cannot determine time of death until the doctor on duty arrives."

She switches off the Dictaphone, "OK Sarge, we can have the coroner in now to move the body and place him on the stretcher to wait for the doctor." she shouts out.

"OK Issy, by the way the locksmith is here and is getting ready to open the car doors." The Sergeant replies.

"Great we will be out shortly. Make sure he is wearing gloves."

Izzy instructs.

"OK Chris, I think we have covered the pictures, you stay in here and start taking finger prints from all the areas we discussed, and I will look outside at the car."

Isabella walks outside as the locksmith finally clicks the doors open,. "Have you touched the door handles at all?" She asks, annoyed that he is not wearing any gloves.

"No Ma'am." He replies.

She looks at the Sarge, and he shrugs his shoulders, "OK, don't touch anything, please allow me to open the door." She walks over and clicks the driver's handle.

The locksmith stands to one side as she pops the door open and then prepares to climbs onto the driver's seat for starting the search of the car, "Yes, your work is done here!" She stares at the locksmith.

The Sergeant walks over, "OK Trev, thanks very much, I will give you a call later."

"What's going on here Sarge." He asks.

"There has been some trouble inside the hotel Trev, I will call you later OK, send your invoice to the office." The Sergeant pats him on the back and gives him a fake smile.

Isabella starts the Dictaphone again, "Opening the driver's side car door of the Blue three series BMW, documents can be seen on the passenger front seat, one document appears to be a rental agreement. Opening the rear driver's side door, the back seat has nothing evident." She continues to take pictures then walks around to the rear.

Opening the trunk, she continues, "Again the trunk of the vehicle has no bags or any personal possessions evident."

"I continue around to the front passenger side and opening the door, there is a small empty plastic water bottle which is stuck between the seat side and lower sill, that will be bagged and tagged for evidence. Now leaning inside, it is clear that the glove box lid has been left open." She takes pictures and then closes the door and walks over to the closest rubbish bin.

"Reaching the nearest trash bin which is twenty metres from the suspect's vehicle, it appears to have a male's wallet inside along with." She stops and reaches into the bin.

"Sarge, I've found the car keys." She waves and jingles them at them at him smiling. He gives a fake smile back and then scowls at an officer that had been trying to find the keys.

"Sheila Holmes will have this case solved by lunchtime." The Sarge looks across, as Isabella returns to the car and places the keys in the ignition confirming they are correct for the vehicle.

Walking back into the building she heads towards the restroom, where she begins to assist Chris with collecting the remaining evidence. Isabella starts by dusting for fingerprints from all the door catches from each of the toilet cubicles. Chris starts to chip away at the grout, so that he can remove the floor tiles easier. Outside the hotel, a black Holden Commodore car arrives into the gravel parking lot, and screeches to a stop sending dust into the air. The engine stops and the driver's door flings open quickly. A man aged around forty-thousand years old with light brown hair, and dressed in a dark grey suit begins to climb out throwing a cigarette to the ground. The passenger door opens and another man about fifty-five years old dressed in a dark blue suit with a scruffy black and grey beard can be seen. He rubs his right hand over the short cropped dark black hair which shows signs of grey, and then takes a partly smoked cigarette from his mouth.

He throws it into the gravel, then stamps on it aggressively. His dark sunken eyes which have large bags underneath them, slowly stare around the area looking for something, then he turns and gestures to the door. The other man stares across to the police officers who are trying to understand what these people are doing. The two men both start to walk towards the main entrance doors. Sergeant Haynes is alerted by one of the officers who is standing guard by the top step on the veranda. The Sergeant walks outside and joins his officers.

"Sorry gents, the hotel is closed Police business."

The older man speaks, "Yes, we know, and you must be Sergeant Haynes?"

"I could be." The Sarge replies as the guys reach the bottom of the wooden steps.

"Ah great, my name is agent Clifton from the federal bank robberies task force. The man to my right is agent Wilkins." The men take reach into their inner jacket pockets taking out their identification badges flashing them quickly as the three officers stand tensely.

"What's your business here?" Sergeant Haynes asks.

"Did you not get the message from head office?" Clifton replies.

"No, Agent Clifton, I did not." Haynes speaks slowly and clearly.

"Right sorry about that, but we have tactical command of this crime scene."

"Is that so agent Clifton?" Haynes seems confused.

"Yes, Sergeant Haynes, we need to observe what is happening and then take the evidence back to Sydney."

"Who is your boss and where are the federal documents giving you tactical command?" Haynes asks.

"I don't have the paperwork with me, it was sent to your main offices in Mackay this morning."

"No one has notified me, so you aren't entering without official confirmation." Haynes instructs.

"Please Sergeant Haynes, I don't want to make a fuss in front of your men. If you just call your office, I am sure this problem can be cleared up very quickly."

Sergeant Haynes lifts his personal radio and presses the call button beginning to speak, "Control, Haynes here, I, have two agents from the federal bank robberies task force who are informing me that they have tactical command of the crime scene. Can you confirm if the official documents are at the office?"

"Hi Sarge, Denise here I will check with the front desk and report back."

"It's a lovely morning, Sergeant isn't it, just a shame we have a deal with this mess hey?" Agent Clifton tries a fake smile as the other agent looks around uninterested.

"Sarge? Are you there Sarge?"

"Yes, Denise receiving. We can't find any documents but the chief wants a chat." The radio crackles and Sergeant Haynes returns back inside the hotel restaurant as the other officers stand guard protecting the door.

"Haynes, Brooks here. Now I was woken by a phone call this morning from some government tosser in Sydney about a robbery and two agents who are heading our way. They believe that the dead man inside is an accomplice to a recent robbery and murder." Brooks coughs.

"Ok chief so why has nothing been in the news."

"Do I look like a fackin Clark Kent Haynes? How the fuck do I know? Now, you are to give over tactical command and assist where required in this enquiry. Now don't be an arsehole about this Haynes. The assistant governor still wants your balls in a jar after that last time."

"Well, last time two men just arrived from nowhere without any documents." Haynes smiles.

"Last time there were under fackin cover agents, and you blew a fackin two-year drugs case."

"This isn't drugs boss, it's a dead body."

"Look just get it tidied up OK." Brooks snaps.

"OK boss." Haynes is obviously unhappy with the decision, as he clicks off the radio and begins to walk back outside to speak with the agents.

Opening the door agent Clifton sees, the expression across the Sergeant's face clearly knowing he is not very happy to hand over command.

"OK agent Clifton, the site is yours, we will assist with your investigation."

"Thank you, Sergeant Haynes." Clifton smiles, and quickly walks past the three officers into the diner.

The agents walk towards the direction of the restrooms, as if they already know what has happened inside. One of the police officers outside who is standing next to his boss asks, "What's the problem Sarge?"

"These fackin agents don't look to be the real deal Simms."

"How do you mean Sarge?" Simms seems confused.

"Well would you fly or drive from Sydney on an urgent case?"

"What are you saying?"

"I think these agents were already in the area to be here this quickly, and I think they are either looking for the deceased or his killer." Haynes ponders.

"Do you reckon they were involved?" The officer asks.

"Yes, and have been waiting for us to tidy up their mess." The Sarge walks back inside.

The agents reach the restroom and pushing the door open see the forensic team collecting evidence and one man speaks out,. "Morning all, we are agents from the federal bank robberies task force and now have tactical command of this investigation. Please bag all evidence and arrange for it to be transferred to our vehicle, and we will take it back to Sydney."

"Excuse me agent, but I work for Sergeant Haynes, so I only take instruction and orders from him." Isabella replies.

The Sergeant reaches the restroom door, and hears the raised voices in the discussion beginning to develop between Isabella and agent Clifton. Taking a deep sigh, he pushes the door open and enters giving instructions, "It's OK Isabella, the chief has cleared the agents request." He takes another big sigh and continues.

"Bag and tag everything as the agents have requested. Our hands are tied on this investigation."

"But Sarge!" Isabella answers back.

"No buts Isabella, just do it."

"Sarge, can we speak outside?" she asks.

Haynes smiles, and walks back outside. Clifton nods towards the other agent to follow and try to catch any news what they are talking about. Isabella follows Sergeant Haynes outside onto the wooden steps with agent Wilkins close by. The Sarge reaches the door turns, and opens it for Isabella, then after she passes, slams it shut in the face of agent Wilkins.

"Your job is inside!" Haynes snaps at the agent, as the Sergeant holds his foot by the base of the door smiling, until he can be heard walking away inside.

"Sarge who are these guys?"

"I don't know Isabella, but something isn't right." A car drives past the front of the hotel, slowing to see what is happening.

"Look, this has all the details of a professional hit." Isabella replies.

"What makes you say that?" Haynes asks.

"Well, the tattooing and burning around the entry wounds confirms that the deceased was shot at point blank range, and we can't find any finger prints?"

She continues, "The knife wounds on the body are clean, sharp and precise."

"So, the killer cleaned up after the murder, and may still be close by then?" The Sarge replies as his mind starts to tick over.

"Exactly, Sarge. I have never heard of this task force before either." Izzy appears concerned.

"Well, Chief Brooks seemed pretty scared, so the instruction must have come from a high office somewhere."

"Do you want me to lose a few things Sarge?"

"It's too risky Isabella, and we don't have the resources to complete a full investigation anyway."

"I have an old colleague in Sydney who might know this task force, and I can complete the investigation in my own spare time?"

Haynes pauses for few seconds then continues, "OK ask around, but be discreet and don't keep a record of the evidence you have taken."

The door opens and Clifton appears, "We will take the car with us too."

"I can arrange a low loader to transfer it to protect the evidence that's normal protocol." Haynes replies.

"That won't be necessary all the main evidence is inside anyway, and HQ have asked for the vehicle urgently, so we will drive it back." The forensic team continue to collect as much evidence as possible, under the watchful eyes of agent Clifton and Wilkins. Clearly the local police team are not in agreement with the decision which the chief has been instructed to follow. As requested by Sergeant Haynes, Isabella manages to gather a few pieces of evidence even under their close supervision. The two agents spend more time talking and messaging on their cells, but there is a clear underlining fact that they don't really seemed to be bothered over any investigation of the samples. Some words are exchanged between the agents that Isabella and Chris don't fully understand with a tension in the restroom only broken when the doctor finally arriving.

"OK, where is the body?" Asks the doctor as he bursts into the room.

The body is now lying on a black covered stretcher in a black body bag on the toilet floor. The doctor in his mid-sixties with a full head of white hair along with a slim build and walks to the body carrying his old medicine bag. He is dressed in dark trousers and a golfing polo shirt.

"Excuse me, who are you?" Agent Clifton asks.

"I'm the *Doctor,* young man! Now move out of my way unless, of course, you are allowed in court to determine if this body is deceased?" Clifton stands back slightly as the doctor unzips the body bag.

"Well, if he wasn't dead, he certainly is now!"

"Doctor, how are you?" The Sergeant asks.

"Was doing fine till this call came, I was on the tenth with a par round. Now who are these jumped up little shits."

"Doctor McGee, this is agent Clifton and Wilkins, they have tactical Command, and we are here to support. The body has been requested back in Sydney."

"Support my fackin arse, this is on my turf, and I am the only assigned doctor on call today, so I decide where the body goes and where the autopsy will take place."

"I'm sorry doctor but the body has to be taken back to Sydney for the autopsy. We have a court warrant to confirm."

"Really, well, you had better show me this court warrant or I will be ringing the deputy forensic minister." The doctor snaps.

"The documents have been sent to the Sergeant's office this morning."

"Oh, how convenient, what by snail post? It's now twelve thirty p.m. and looking at this body it's been dead for nearly sixteen hours and any toxins or poisons that could be inside are probably beginning to break down."

"Excuse me, doctor, no one has mentioned poisons. It looks like gunshot wounds to the head." Agent Clifton announces.

"Well, you boys from Sydney seem to have all the answers, but you wouldn't be here unless you are trying to cover your own arses. Well, it's not going to happen on my watch so you go and get your warrant and then we can move the body anywhere you like? But for now, it goes to the local mortuary."

"Doctor, there is no discussion on this point." Clifton snaps.

"You are exactly right, and my word is final so wind your neck in and don't try to intimidate me I'm too old in the tooth. Charlie get in here!"

"Doctor, with the cause of death being gunshot it's surely a simple matter of the death certificate."

"Oh, and now you're a fackin coroner too hey? I suppose you have your own pathology lab in your pocket too!" Clifton walks off with a flea in his ear taking his mobile out of his pocket as the doctor zips up the black bag, "Now then Charlie, this body is to go to the local morgue and prep for a full autopsy to begin ASAP."

"OK Doc." The two men lift the trolley and wheel it outside to the waiting private ambulance.

Sergeant Haynes whispers, "What are your first thoughts on the death?"

"Well, for sure the gunshot wounds to the head are what finished him, but a quick look at his face shows traces of possible toxins that seem to be leaching out around his lips and there is some bruising around his neck. He could have been dying anyway and not known about it."

"OK, Doc, thank you."

"Is there any news on the killer, Haynes?" The doctor asks.

"No why?"

"Well, if there is poison or toxins, the killer may have been subjected to them too."

"Do you think we are at risk?" Haynes asks concerned.

"It's a bit fackin late to ask that now Sarge, but no, after sixteen hours we should be fine." The doctor smiles.

"Now, I have got to finish my golf game. I will touch base with the morgue later today to see the progress."

"Thanks Doc, and have a good day, and speak soon." The doctor smiles, and walks out of the restroom.

The two agents are now close to each other whispering clearly concerned about the body going to the local mortuary, and Clifton walks outside following the doctor. As the two men reach outside, Clifton approaches doctor McGee.

"Doctor, thank you for the support inside, but I am still concerned over the body being transferred to the local morgue. I am worried about contamination of the evidence, and it would be better in Sydney."

"Look I have told you once, I am the signing doctor, and it will be my name on the death certificate. That can't happen in Sydney, and besides after three days in an ambulance the body will just be dingo food unless that is what you want?"

"Doctor, please you have it all wrong we have better equipment in Sydney, and our team of experts can help."

"There are standard procedures, and equipment required in every federal mortuary so no stones are left unturned."

"What about if we fly the body to Sydney would that be better?"

"Why not fly your experts here? Even in this little backwater I'm sure we can achieve the same results, and your experts could help train our team? Now please excuse me."

As the doctor climbs into his car, Clifton takes a small black tablet looking shape from his pocket and drops it onto the car floor mat. The dropped tablet is almost invisible on the car mat and as the doctor closes the door, he starts the engine and drives away staring at Clifton with a look of disgust across his face.

The second agent walks outside and stands next to Clifton who then says, "Ring team B, and intercept the ambulance crew."

Agent Wilkins quickly takes out his mobile and begins a conversation confirming the route to the local mortuary.

"What about the doctor?" Wilkins asks.

"Golf can be a dangerous competitive game." Clifton smiles, and walks over to their car as Chris begins to carry out the first box of evidence.

Now finally alone with the evidence, Isabella quickly searches through her collected box of samples, and finds a spent bullet round from the floor along with a smudged finger print from the deceased neck. Beginning to walk outside, she quickly removes the two forensic bags that she left on the top, and places them into her pocket as she walks to the car. She slides the clear plastic box containing the evidence bags into the agent's trunk next to the one box Chris has already placed. Agent Wilkins walks over to the abandoned car, and opens the door.

"We haven't finished wiping down for any evidence yet!" Isabella shouts across.

The agent takes out a pair of latex gloves and pulling them onto his hands, slides into the driver's seat.

"We can dust it for prints, and collect any evidence in Sydney. We have wasted enough time here." Clifton replies slamming the trunk lid.

He walks around to the driver's door, opens it, and climbs inside quickly starting the engine, and engaging reverse gear. Wilkins in the deceased car, completes the same actions, and both men drive away without thanking anyone or saying goodbye.

"Good riddance." Sergeant Haynes whispers under his breath.

"Did you get any evidence Isabella?"

"Yes Sarge." She replies.

"Great get back to the lab and run the tests under John Doe papers, and be careful."

Haynes, still staring at the two cars disappearing into the distance says, "Officer Ellis."

"Yes Sarge."

"Get on the radio to that private ambulance company and see if there's any trackers on the vehicle, these boys may want to hijack the body or dispose of it."

The officer makes some calls on his radio as Haynes begins to move towards the hotel and asks, "Any news on the owner Trigg?"

"No Sarge." Just then Officer Ellis runs over to Haynes.

"Sarge, the ambulance company have confirmed they have a tracker on the vehicle, but it stopped about ten minutes ago, and hasn't moved since. The guys inside are not answering the radio."

"OK Ellis, take Trigg with you, and go to investigate. Be careful, and no hero shit. I will try to get in touch with the chief and get some state back up." The Sarge walks back inside the hotel, and continues towards the young bar man.

"Close the hotel today, go home, and if anything looks suspicious please call me anytime day or night." The Sarge hands him a card, and then gestures at the two other officers.

"Guys, it looks like we may have some trouble brewing. The ambulance and crew have gone missing. Tidy up here, and make sure the barman goes home safe, and check his place over just to be sure. Remember he is our only witness who may have seen the killer. Somebody is trying to cover this up, so meet back in the station in a few hours, and keep your eyes open."

"Where are you going Sarge?"

"I need to speak with the chief over a few things."

"Just then the radio crackles."

"Sarge, control here can you respond."

"Yeah control, tell me." Haynes replies.

"Sarge, we have a report that doctor McGee has just collapsed, and died whilst playing golf."

"He was fine when he left here." Haynes replies then continues "OK control, I will travel there now to check it out. Has Trigg or Ellis radioed in yet?"

"No Sarge no word."

"OK, keep trying them over."

"Will do Sarge." The controller clicks off the radio.

SEVEN

Sergeant Haynes with a concerned look on his face reaches the car, opens the door, and climbs inside. He quickly drives away from the hotel with the blue lights flashing and heads in the direction of the golf club. Meanwhile, Clifton and Wilkins drive out into some scrubland, and stop both cars.

Clifton climbs out first and says, "OK, take the boxes from the trunk, and place them into the black Holden."

"Yes boss." Wilkins starts to move the boxes as Clifton takes out a pair of latex gloves. He pulls them onto his hands as he walks over to the BMW hire car. Opening the doors, he starts to check through the car for any evidence. "Wilkins, have you taken anything from the car?"

"No boss why?"

"Some documents are missing, and I bet I know who has them!" Clifton snarls.

"OK, both boxes are in the trunk." Wilkins replies.

Passing his lighter over, Clifton answers with, "Light it up, and let's get out of here."

"OK boss, where to next?"

"Palm Cove, Nash must be heading to Palm Cove, and we must stop him or we are next on the hit list. Come on let's go."

Clifton rushes over to the car as flames begin to engulf the blue BMW. As they drive away at high speed the fuel tank ignites sending a huge black mushroom cloud into the sky, and an explosion blows through the stillness of the bush. All of the collected evidence is burnt in the process.

Trigg sees the black cloud rising about one mile upfront as they drive along the main road, and shouts, "Christ fella what the fuck is that."

Continuing to drive along the highway towards the direction of the rising black smoke, Ellis suddenly stops the car, and looks across to the left, and he can see a fresh set of tyre tracks in the mud of a lane which goes into the shrub-land. He turns onto the lane, and after about one hundred metres looks closer, and notices a black van shaped vehicle in-front of them through the trees.

"Control over, Trigg tries to request support." The radio simply crackles.

"Try another channel, Trigg?" Ellis replies.

Switching through the radio channels, Trigg tries all the different stations, but no signal. He takes out his mobile, and checks the signal strength, as Ellis continues to drive slowly towards the front of the black private ambulance stopping short by eighty metres.

"No signals anywhere, very strange, never experienced this before!" Trigg has concern in his voice.

"I don't like this shite Trigg lets drop back." Ellis replies.

"Nah, pull forward, let's check it out."

"With no backup? Nah mate I'm happy to be a hero, but this just an't right."

Gradually, the rear doors of the ambulance slowly begin to open, as two men start to climb out of the van holding fully loaded machine guns. The clean-up team have just killed the two-man ambulance crew, and are in the process of pouring sulphuric acid over their bodies along with the hitman Michael Hughes in the back of the vehicle, stopped when they heard the police car approaching. Both cleaners are fully ready for action, and the police officers are sitting ducks as they debate whether to stay or go.

"Why is there no fackin signal, this is strange." Trigg scratches his head.

"Is it a black spot around here?"

"Could be." Trigg replies looking confused.

One cleaner can be seen keeping low as he starts to walk into the nearby shrub-land attempting to sweep around behind the two officers blocking off their escape. The second cleaner waits behind the ambulance, with his gun fully prepared as the police officers are more engrossed in trying to understand why there is no signal. The two officers have not even seen the bullet holes riddled along the side of the ambulance just as the radio crackles.

"Trigg, is that you Trigg?"

"Yes, control where have you been early lunch?"

The signal breaks up again, "Trigg crackle check crackle report crackle."

"Come in control repeat again. Ellis back the motor up, to see if we can get out of this damn black spot."

"Too fackin right mate." Ellis slams the gear lever into reverse, and backs the 4x4 truck backwards away from the ambulance as both cleaner's watch.

"Trigg repeat, Trigg come in." Control repeats.

The signal clears, "Yeah, yeah don't have a heart attack what's all the fuss?"

"Sarge Haynes, has asked to check with you guys. Doctor McGee has been reported as dead."

"No way control, he ate nothing from the hotel restaurant?"

"It appears to be a heart attack." Control replies.

"Christ control, what is it today."

"What is your situation? The Sarge is concerned."

"Well, if we can do our damn jobs, we can then report that there was a big explosion, and black smoke rising near to Arkwright's farm, we were just going to investigate, but now we have found the private ambulance abandoned." The radio goes silent.

Suddenly the sound of gunshots is heard as the first hitman fires bullet rounds into the police car punching holes in the body, and breaking the rear windscreen. The second hitman runs up the road firing into the front of the vehicle killing Ellis and Trigg outright, as blood can be seen spraying the inside of the vehicle, and across the bullet ridden front windscreen.

Flying particles of plastic are thrown into the air as bullets punch though the radio and dashboard as the radio controller loses all communication and the two officers can be seen collapsed in their seats from the amount of ammunition which has hit them. The bullets then stop hitting the car as an eerie quietness floats through the woodland, and the two hitmen look at the damage they have caused to the police car. One of the hitmen walks across to the driver's side of the vehicle then opens the rear, and front doors.

The inside of the car is covered with broken glass, fragments of plastic, and the two officers are seen covered in blood, slumped in the bullet punched seats. The hitman leans inside the car, and drags Ellis out of the driver's seat then pushes him across the rear seat onto the ground as the second hitman walks back to the ambulance. Now sitting in the blood drenched driver's seat, the hitman starts the engine of the vehicle, and the car is then driven into the bush, and is stopped close to a deep ravine approximately two hundred and fifty metres from the road. The second man can be seen climbing into the front of the ambulance, and follows the same route into the shrub-land, and stops behind the police car.

A canister of sulphuric acid is poured over the two police officers, and then one of the cleaners leans into the vehicle engaging a forward gear, and the car is then driven off the ravine edge. As the police car drives off the edge, it begins to roll forward, and after a few seconds crashes upside down into the bottom of the ravine sending out a huge explosion followed by flames, and more black smoke into the sky. The ambulance van is also placed into gear, and races off the edge crashing close to the police car again sending smoke, and flames into the sky.

The two cleaners collect all their equipment, and return to their green car that was parked just off the highway slightly covered in a few branches. One man takes out his mobile, and send a text message through to a named contact which reads 'Clifton, housekeeping has changed the bedding over.'

The only evidence left on the track are a few spent bullet cases, and as the cleaners drive away, they make sure to flatten as many cases as possible in an attempt to cover their assassination of the police officers and the ambulance crew. The cleaner who is driving stops the car briefly, and watches the flames reduce in height, but thick black smoke can still be seen rising high into the sky from the burning tyres. The driver looks across to his accomplice with a large smile across his face, and then drives away at high speed heading for the A1 in the direction of Cairns.

"Sarge come in Sarge?" Cheryl in control activates the radio.

"Sergeant Haynes, receiving control."

"Sarge, we have a strange broken message from Trigg confirming that they had located the private ambulance. Both Trigg, and Ellis also reported that they had seen an explosion, and black smoke rising. Their location was close to Arkwright's farm. Then the communication was lost."

"Lost what do you mean lost?" Sergeant Haynes replies with concern in his voice.

"Well, the signal was very poor, and kept breaking up, but there was a strange noise which sounded almost like gunshots." Cheryl has nervousness in her voice.

Haynes, just indicating into the golf club car park takes a deep breath knowing that his worst fears have just been realised, and responds back to Cheryl, "I have just arrived at the Woodpark golf course. Send Mike and Tommy to the golf course. I will then head over towards Arkwright's farm to investigate. Could you also speak to the state department, and give them the Code one for help?"

"Sarge, do you mean Trigg and Ellis are at risk?"

"Cheryl, I am planning for the worst, but hoping for the best, and if I'm wrong then the worst I will get is another suspension, but if I'm right well, let's not go there yet. Are my instructions clear?"

"Yes Sarge." Cheryl replies with sadness in her voice.

Sergeant Haynes sits in his car for a few seconds, to compose himself, wondering why all these things have happened in his district. Several people can be seen walking towards his vehicle, and as he looks back at them, he takes a deep sigh, and prepares for what could happen next. As instructed by Cheryl, Mike and Tommy begin to drive towards the Woodpark golf club, completely unaware as to what has happened to their fellow offices in the line of duty. Sergeant Haynes on the other hand can sense deep within his body, and is fully aware of what has probably happened to his colleagues, and is just trying to prepare himself for the worst, and losing some of his officers, but also some of his good friends that he selected, trained, and has seen grow into impressive law enforcement officers.

Isabella and Chris, now finished at the crime scene, tidy away all the final equipment from the hotel, then after loading it all into the van, drive back to the forensic laboratory. The young man locks the hotel doors, and begins his short walk home after a very long night.

Mike and Tommy now travelling to the golf course were supposed to ensure he is safe, but for now the man is on his own. The young man reaches his apartment door, and inserting the key into the lock opens the door. As he enters the room he continues into the centre of the apartment, and suddenly, there is a blast of light and a muffled sound echo through the room as a bullet penetrates his head and as he slumps to the floor. The gunman fires two more bullets into his head, and two further rounds at his chest. Making sure the target is dead the gunman silently leaves the apartment, and climbs into a waiting car that is parked close by. Meanwhile, Isabella still has the two small bags of evidence in her jacket as they reach the car park of the forensic lab. Isabella collects the evidence and places it into two fresh bags, then after entering the laboratory locks it into the safe. The desk phone begins to ring, and Chris takes the call,

"What are you serious?" He has a look of shock in his face as Isabella stares across.

"We will be on our way now Sarge." The call cuts off.

"The Sarge wants us both at Billy's Ravine." Chris looks across again to Isabella.

After making sure the safe is locked with the precious evidence, she grabs the keys for the forensic van, and then the pair of them make their way out of the laboratory onto the car park. Unlocking the vehicle, she senses being watched, and looks around at the few parked cars, but sees nothing out of place. Climbing into the car, she starts the engine as Chris quickly opens the passenger door causing her to jump slightly as he enters the vehicle. They drive away from the parking lot, and begin the drive to Billy's Ravine. In the distance of the parking lot, a green car is parked at the side of the main high street, and slowly begins drive away following the forensics van. Isabella and Chris pass some small talk about today as they continue to drive towards the ravine.

"What is it today Chris? We have spent years with nothing to do, and suddenly all of this?"

"Yes Issy, this is really strange."

"Did you manage to speak with your friends over the Sydney task force?" Chris asks.

"Not yet, I was going to call them later today."

"Something certainly doesn't feel right?" Chris looks at Issy.

"Very true Chris, I feel a little concerned that this has happened here in our quiet town." The two of them arrive near to Arkwright's farm.

Sergeant Haynes can be seen standing next to his car with a look of shock on his face, and tears rolling down his cheeks. Isabella stops the car, and quickly climbs out.

"What is it Boss? Are you OK?" She asks.

Trying to remain focused he replies, "Trigg and Ellis's patrol car is in the ravine along with the private ambulance from the hotel earlier. On the road are spent bullet cases. I think this was professional hit."

"Isabella, I want you to go back to the laboratory, and start work on the samples. I'm sure this will lead to some information we are looking for, however at least two of my men, and I suspect Doctor McGee have been killed."

"Well Sarge, I can help Chris first then travel back together."

"No, I think it is best if Chris collects any evidence from here, and I will bring him back later." Sirens can be heard in the distance as the firemen can be seen driving along the road. Stopping by Haynes vehicle, they jump out, and start to look at how they can attempt to put out the fires.

Haynes repeats, "I would prefer if you can start on the samples, and I can then speak with the chief over the evidence."

"OK, will do." Isabella walks back to the van with Chris staring at her wondering what is happening.

She speaks with Chris, and then the pair of them can be seen taking the boxes from the van, "Chris, the Sarge want you to stay here and collect any evidence." Isabella instructs.

"OK, no worries boss." Chris replies.

"I will go back to the lab, and get started with the paperwork from this morning's evidence from the hotel. You know what the chief medical examiner is like."

"Yeah he can be a real pain in the ass." The Sarge will give you a lift back to the laboratory later, just make sure everything is bagged and tagged, if there is anything left after the fire. Make sure you collect as many of the spent cases so we can match them to any of the bullet rounds."

"No worries." Chris replies.

After instructing Chris to go and support Sergeant Haynes, she walks back to the van, and then begins the drive back to the laboratory. Reaching the parking lot, she parks the van near to the entrance doors, and slowly walks to the laboratory with her head slightly bowed still in shock over the last few hours.

Opening the air tight seal lock, she continues into the room to begin working on the John Doe evidence.

Walking to her desk, she instantly notices that the computer screen is still on standby which was not how it had been left earlier in the day. Unlocking the computer, and booting up the system, everything seems to work OK, so maybe, the cleaner had touched the button by mistake after passing her in the outside corridor. Returning back to the safe, she takes the two evidence bags out, and places them onto the work counter next to the digital microscope. Walking back to the computer she begins to type away on the keyboard completing the records sheet for John Doe. She then tries to collect forensic evidence taken from the spent bullet round and fingerprint. She switches on the microscope, and takes a strip of film tape. Holding the fingerprint image onto the film tape, it is slid between two glass slides. Placing the slides onto the glass inspection table of the microscope, the lower light illuminates through the fingerprint image, and as she adjusts the lens to generate a clearer image, a picture is taken. The image is then scanned, and transferred onto the international criminal records computer system.

The computer screen shows a copy of the print as the database begins to read the information of the print details quickly searching for a possible match. Red lines can be seen illuminating different shape details of the friction ridges from the print as the search begins. In a parallel activity, she removes the finger print slide, and places it onto the work surface. Lifting a pair of tweezers, she takes the spent bullet round out of the evidence bag, and gently lowers the bullet onto the glass slide of the electronic microscope. The table height is locked in position, and as she stares through the eyepiece, the lens is re-adjusted.

Instantly, the bullet's rifling can be seen on the screen, and this detail of the twist and diameter is then scanned to confirm the type of gun that was used. Again, this data is loaded into the criminal database and the result comes back very quickly with a one hundred per cent match of a Glock handgun showing a right-hand twist of one in 15.74 and nine millimetres parabellum round. The bullet is removed from the microscope table, and then a section of the material is cut, and taken to the refractometer so that material composition can be checked to find out which company manufactured the bullet head. Isabella also noticed a shiny surface coating on the bullet head, so lifting the bullet head, she takes a small scraper and removes some of the material onto another glass slide. Placing some of the material deposits into a spectrum analyser, it begins to spin, and quickly confirms the coating is made of Teflon. She then places some of the main bullet head body material into a refractometer and after several minutes, the bullet material is confirmed as a lead content specification used by Winchester. Isabella's attention is then suddenly drawn to the computer screen that has been scanning the fingerprint image. The screen has frozen, and is flashing with big red writing that reads 'Image Blocked Level Eight Access Required.'

Just then the silence is broken by the telephone ringing, turning slightly she stands, and walks over to answer the call. Lifting the receiver, she answers with "Hello Mackay Forensic laboratory."

"Isabella, its Chris you need to get to the Billy's Ravine urgently, it's a right mess, I need some help." Chris has lots of distress in his voice.

"OK Chris, I can be there shortly, is the Sarge close by?"

"Sarge, Isabella wants a chat." Chris shouts, and Haynes who walks over.

"Haynes here."

"Boss, I have started to run the tests on the two samples."

"It's not a good time now Isabella, I need your help here."

"Yes, I know Sarge, but the fingerprint image through the database has thrown up a message."

The Sarge curious asks, "What does it say?"

"It reads 'Image Blocked Level Eight Access Required' and there is more, the handgun used from the rifling is a Glock. The bullet material is from the Winchester ammunition factory, and the bullet had a Teflon coating. What do you think Sarge?"

"It definitely sounds like a professional hit; Teflon is used to puncture bullet proof vests. Use Code number 864375 for the access code for level eight. Lock the evidence in the safe, and make your way down here. By the way, be very careful."

"OK Sarge, will be on my way now." Haynes clicks off the mobile.

She clicks onto the screen, and then inputs the access code. The nerve endings on the back of her neck send a signal to her brain instantly causing the hairs to stand slightly as a breeze touches her skin. Suddenly, a few loose pieces of paper gracefully drift towards the floor. She quickly glancing around the laboratory, but senses nothing is different as the computer carrying out the fingerprint scan bleeps. Turning back towards the screen she reads the big red bold writing which states 'MATCH.' Clicking on the keyboard, the details of the finger print owner are seen on the screen along with a picture of their face with a confirmed identity. The screen of the computer suddenly goes blank, and the air conditioning system stops working. Isabella looks around the room, and notices the ceiling lights have stopped working and the lack of humming noise from the freezers, and refrigerators confirm they have stopped working too.

Nervously, she stands from the chair and begins to walk in the direction of the only door in the room as an eerie silence completely overtakes the laboratory. Reaching the door, she tries the handle to open it, but the catch is locked shut. A gradual panic now begins rush through her body as a familiar voice breaks the silence, "You were instructed not to take any evidence from the crime scene, but you still had to break the rules. That was a mistake!"

"Agent Clifton, what a surprise, how did you manage to get into a secure police facility?"

"That's my business, Dr Isabella, now hand over the evidence."

Isabella turns, and see's agent Clifton standing with a gun pointing at her and he says, "Give me the spent bullet case, and finger print image evidence."

"I have already run the print through the national criminal database and know the name of the victim."

"Well, that is certainly unfortunate, what about the bullet?"

"It is from a Glock handgun, and the bullet is made from Winchester lead ingredients with a special Teflon coating."

Agent Clifton coughs, and walks over to the computer. She continues, "Now the evidence which has been sent is impossible to be removed from the secure server."

"Nothing is impossible, difficult maybe."

"You are not from Sydney or any special agency task force, are you?" She asks trying to switch on her mobile phone in her white laboratory jacket pocket.

"Where I am from is none of your business, but what will happen to you well, that's another story."

Isabella now starting to shake slightly with both fear, and adrenalin rushing through her body quickly thinks about what she can use to defend herself. Seeing a scalpel underneath a red notebook on a nearby table top she slowly begins to move towards it.

Clifton starts to lift the gun more in her direction, and continues, "Now we need to make this look like a robbery, and attack that went wrong so, I want you to start taking off them clothes."

"I'm not taking my clothes off for you!"

Clifton lurches forward, and smacks her across the face with the butt of his handgun breaking her nose. She drops to the floor, but doesn't show any weakness in front of him. She stands with blood now dripping from her nose and mouth, and pretends to smile as she starts to take off the white laboratory jacket. Placing it next to the red handbook she covers the scalpel. She then begins to slowly unbutton her white blouse beginning to expose her lacey black bra as Clifton begins to smile with excitement.

"I'm going to fuck you hard bitch." Clifton stares at her.

She turns slightly, and in one quick action she takes the blade, and slashes across his face at the top of his cheek, and through the bridge of his nose. In an equally fast action, she drops to the floor and swipes Clifton's legs causing him to fall hitting the hard-ceramic floor tiles, and in that instant Clifton drops the gun and Isabella reaches for the weapon.

"Arghh you fackin bitch." he shouts out as Clifton holding his face turns to see her standing with the handgun pointing at his head.

He stares at her as she quickly moves the gun towards his leg and fires a bullet round into his left kneecap, then lifting the gun fires another round into his right shoulder. Clifton stares at her as he still tries to undress her with his eyes smiling.

"You're far too beautiful for this type of work, and it's going to be a shame."

Clifton looks past her as she replies, "You didn't think a Sheila could not only disarm you, but use your own gun, so which agency do you work for?"

"I will tell you nothing bitch. I would rather die first!" He spits a mouthful of blood into the floor then smiles at her with blood now covering his teeth.

"That's your choice, you fuckin bastard." She begins to lift the gun towards the direction of his head as he moves around slowly on the floor from his injuries.

Clifton coughs and begins to shake violently as white foam begins to ooze from his mouth and in an instant, he is dead after eating a cyanide capsule.

Isabella quickly runs for the emergency panic button, and with both hands presses it, but as she lowers her hands a single gunshot echoes through the laboratory. Blood and brain matter are scattered across the white wall. Isabella begins to drop to the floor as agent Wilkins stands over her body. Wilkins dressed in a police uniform, quickly turns to the desk where the microscope is and grabs the bullet round, then with the pistol handle smashes both of the computer hard drives. The main entrance door to the laboratory unlocks automatically, and the assassin quickly walks towards the direction of the exit standing next to the wall, waiting for the emergency team to arrive.

The main door suddenly flings opens inwards, and two police officers carrying handguns rush inside. Both officers are shot in the head with a silenced pistol, and drop to the floor next to the door. The assassin then simply slips away slowly walking out of the laboratory, down the corridor and out of the police station where he then continues outside towards the parking lot. Wilkins opens the door of a Green Holden, and can be seen driving away from the car park just as four more officer's rush along the corridor towards the forensic laboratory.

The officers are wearing full body armour holding sub machine guns, and burst into the room standing in complete shock. The only noise that can be heard is the sound of Isabella's mobile starting to ring inside her laboratory jacket pocket. One of the officers hears the mobile phone ringing, and reaches for Isabella's white jacket. Lifting the mobile from the pocket, he sees the name across the screen then takes a big sigh. He then presses the answer button which reads across the screen 'Sarge (Dad).'

As Wilkins continues to drive down the main street of Mackay, he takes out his mobile, and after typing away on the keypad of the mobile, sends a message. 'Cleaning operation compromised. The mice have the cheese. The trap needs to be emptied. The cat is missing.'

After a few minutes, a reply is received 'Traps will be emptied tomorrow. The cat is returning home next flight back from Cairns. Continue to pursue.'

'OK understood, Pied piper out.' Wilkins continues to drive towards Cairns.

Word quickly starts to spreads in the news following the death of police officers and the national newspapers, and television channel reporters start to arrive en masse at the local police station looking for gossip, and the latest news. The small town of Mackay has never had such a large influx of people in a couple of hours, and news vehicles are parked everywhere blocking roads. A press conference is called and inside the station one of the conference rooms is laid out with rows of seats, and a small stage at the front with three table. The two outer tables have large pictures of the four police officers, and Dr Arnold. At the centre table there are several microphones laid out, and sitting behind table is Sergeant Haynes, a lady around fifty years old, and another man of similar age. Television news film crews stand at the sides of the room with news reporters weaving their way along the rows of chairs to sit down. Haynes is almost in tears following the death of his daughter, and fellow colleagues but he is trying to remain composed. Questions are being asked, and the Chief Inspector tries to deflect the press from asking any direct questions to Sergeant Haynes.

"It has been a very sad today with the death of four serving police officers in the line of duty along with our doctor of forensics."

"Chief Inspector, can you confirm that there were two male suspects inside the police station?" A male reporter asks.

"I can confirm that two suspects were inside the police station, and one of the suspects was shot, and killed by Dr Isabella Arnold who died in the line of duty, and is in fact the daughter of Sergeant Haynes."

"Chief Inspector, do you have any leads?" One reporter asks.

"We have some very strong leads, and will be working with the government agencies to catch the remaining suspect as soon as possible."

"Is the death of doctor McGee also linked to this case?"

"We understand that doctor McGee passed away playing golf, but the autopsy needs to be completed to confirm the final cause of death."

"Chief Inspector, can you confirm or deny the reports of a dead body that was found at the Marlborough Hotel are linked to the death of the officers." A lady reporter asks.

"We are still gathering evidence at this time, and currently have not found a direct link to join all these events." The Chief replies.

"Sergeant Haynes, do have any words to say?" Another lady reporter asks.

Pausing for a few seconds, the Sergeant looks across to the chief, and begins to talk, "It has been the saddest day of my life not only losing my daughter, but also fellow colleagues with these tragic events. I can assure everybody that I will not rest until the people who have done this terrible act are caught, and prosecuted."

The room goes silent, and then the chief inspector continues, "Now we are only a small town so I ask that all roads are kept clear, and there will be no further questions at this time."

EIGHT

Wednesday morning, at Broadhurst Industries seems just like any other day for the young security guard who looks very casual resting in the large office swivel chair of the security building as a white Mercedes Sprinter van approaches the gatehouse. Broadhurst Industries is a tier one sub-contractor that manufactures precision components for military projects, and employs over thousand people between the shop floor and office areas. The factory is located near to Bury St Edmunds on a small business park, and from the outside is fronted as a logistics company. Lord Broadhurst, the Chairman is a frail old man at nearly eighty-five years old. His second born son Richard is already running strategic parts of the business portfolio with Richard's eldest son William, already showing an active interest after completing his degree as he starts to learn the ropes of the business. This manufacturing site is a small hidden part of the Broadhurst Empire that covers property ownership worldwide including silent partners in well-known hotel chains and sub contract businesses specialising in land acquisition. The company also has strong ties with a small shipping, and logistics business used as an umbrella corporation to deliver military components worldwide to customers.

Lord Broadhurst keeps out of the public eye, and uses his government acquaintances to win military contracts worldwide. The company has developed many of the weapons, and equipment used in modern warfare globally. The vans brakes squeal slightly, as it stops just level with the front window of the main gatehouse building. The driver switches off the engine, and the whole vehicle shudders slightly, and as moves in his seat; he pushes the driver's door open and a large well-built guy starts to climbs out from behind the steering wheel. This man has a military look about him with short cropped hair, and square chin as he walks over towards the security cabin. A large digital clock inside the security cabin flicks onto twelve forty-five p.m., and the young security guard is lethargic from his early lunch. He is messing around with his cell phone looking at the status of his friends on social media, and paying no attention to the driver or the van.

The driver reaches the window, and leans through the glass opening slightly, and in a deep Queens English accent says, "I say old boy, I have a jolly urgent delivery for your Dr Newton on the second floor, and can you let me through?"

The security guy is that engrossed with his friend's status logs, he never even looks at the guy or his papers which are part of the company security procedures. He simply asks,

"Dr Newton you say, he's that research boffin, isn't he?"

The driver replies, "Well, you tell me old boy; I've just been told to deliver a parcel at the main reception marked for his attention to pick up personally."

"OK boss, no problems, I will just let you through." The security guard pushes the button for the gate release as the main access gate motors begins to whirr into action.

The driver walks back to the van, opens the doors, and slides back behind the steering wheel. In doing, so he looks into side mirrors of the van, and stares back towards the rear of the vehicle nodding his head. The right van rear door slowly begins to open, and daylight begins to flood inside, but quickly disappears as the door closes again without making any noise apart from a faint clink from the door catch. The driver starts the van engine, and begins to drives towards the large security gate that has begun to lift open. As the driver starts to pass by the large steel gate posts under the lifting gate he keeps looking into his rear mirrors as though he is looking for something as he now enters the secure facility. The young security guard returns back to the large black swivel chair, and leans back down in his seat. He takes his mobile in his left hand, and starts to flick through social media updates using his right hand fore-finger. Suddenly, there is the sound of a faint *'THWACK.'* Blood spatters suddenly appear on the mobile screen and as the guard looks up, he sees a faint smoke cloud disappearing, a person in a black mask and overalls with a silenced pistol is looking at him through the open window of the security cabin.

He looks down at himself and can see that he has been shot in the chest. Blood begins to blot onto his light blue shirt as he begins to panic with fear of dying. He takes a deep breath, and starts to try and move in the chair, but the pain has just started to hit his nervous system like a sledgehammer smashing against his chest. He can already begin to taste fresh blood in his mouth as he starts to wet himself with shock. The gunman fires another shot *'THWACK'* and once again a small cloud of smoke erupts from the barrel as a spent bullet case hits the ground. As the smoke begins to clear, the young security guard has been shot in the centre of his forehead, and is twitching in the chair, still holding the mobile which is logged into a social media page.

The assassin quickly runs around to the back of the gatehouse, and shoots a bullet through the locked door mechanism with a 'THWACK' as the barrel lock snaps. They place their hands which are protected by white latex gloves onto the handle, turn the handle, and walk into the gatehouse. The assassin walks over to the young man who is now completely dead, and collapsed in the chair, and begin to drag him out by placing his hands under the armpits of the body. The man is thrown under the large security control counter like a rag doll, and is shown no sign of respect.

Taking the dead security man's dark blue jacket that was hanging on the back of the swivel chair, the gunman throws it across his face, and the light blue shirt in an attempt to cover the blood drenched body. The guard's mobile phone in all the disturbance has fallen onto the floor with the screen still showing a picture of a guy smiling at the top of a mountain. Picking up the cell from the floor, the assassin switches it off, and throws it into the waste bin under the control desk, thus ending the complete life of the young man in less than a minute. The assassin begins to remove the black overalls, and underneath he can be seen wearing the same type of clothing worn as the security guard. The assassin takes up position by the control desk.

The new security guard turns around, and sees the blood pool that had started to form by the base of the swivel chair which is running out of the dead guard. He kicks the blue jacket down slightly in an attempt to soak up the mess, but also notices where the bullet has punctured a hole into the back of the chair.

He kicks the base around one hundred and eighty degrees in an attempt to try and hide the problem. The new guard now looking like any other security guard stands watching the large bank of video screens which are inset into the counter which shows all the cameras that cover the office areas, shop floor, warehouse and surrounding gardens. The assassin is about twenty-five years old with blonde short hair and blue eyes. His slim athletic build is supported by his arms as he leans on the counter watching the white van travelling towards the main reception. He lifts his head, and continues to look from the gatehouse window noticing the brake lights illuminating as the van stops near to an area with tall dark trees at the edge of the main building. The rear doors open, and ten people all dressed in black overalls, and carrying large green holdall bags climb from the inside of the van. The people can be seen waiting near to the trees.

The van doors close, and the Mercedes sprinter slowly continues to drive away heading for the reception, and the ten people start walking towards the back of the building using the van as cover. The advertisement signage on the side of the van reads Aces High Courier Services, and as it reaches the main entrance of the factory, the front desk security control man looks through the large glass doors watching it stopping. The driver keeps the engine running, and grabs a medium sized cardboard box from the front passenger seat, and opens his door to get out. Pushing the door open fully, he jumps out, and then slams it behind himself as his feet touch the pavement. The driver continues to walk towards the main office doors then pushes the right door open walking into the reception heading straight towards the front desk.

"Excuse me sir; you should have left that parcel at the rear gatehouse, why have you driven through the site to here?" asks the security man on the main reception.

"Well, the young guy at the rear gate sent me through when I said this parcel was urgent for Dr Newton on the second floor." replies the driver, reaching the counter.

The driver dressed in dark blue jeans, and white polo shirt with Aces High Courier Services seems a little nervous, and is sweating across his forehead as he reaches the desk. His right arm is slightly behind his back as he places the parcel on the counter. The parcel is around three hundred mm square with 'Dr Newton, Broadhurst Industries' written across the top of the box in black pen permanent marker. The mature security man around sixty years of age takes the parcel from the counter, and checks the weight, then tries to look for more information.

The security man looks at the parcel, and says, "I will just give Dr Newton a call to come and collect. What is the company name, and address on the delivery note?"

The security guard looks at the driver, and smiles, as he starts to reach for the desk phone to contact Dr Newton. The driver leans back slightly, and takes a silenced pistol from behind his back that was tucked in his trouser top underneath the polo shirt, and points the gun straight at the guard's head pulling the trigger quickly. The colour from the security guards face begins to drain to a light grey as his expression starts to change from friendly to shock. The driver's finger clicks the hammer, and a single round emits from the barrel with muffled *'THWACK.'* The bullet enters the forehead area of the guard's head passing quickly through forming a blood mist cloud from the back section of his skull.

The blood spray cloud can be seen starting to drift across in the still air of the reception as the guard begins to collapse to the ground still holding the box. The spent bullet round still manages to reach the large grey marble wall which is around fifteen metres behind the security guard. A small dust cloud can be seen clearing, and a white chip mark can be seen in the highly polished surface.

The driver looks at the guard falling to ground, and laughs saying, "It's from Fuck You Enterprises.com and the address is going to hell old boy."

The assassin turns, and looks back towards the van then waves his left hand. The side door slides open, and three more people dressed in black overalls climb out of the van carrying large green holdalls, and start to make their way into the reception area. Two more people climb out of the van with one person dressed in black, and the other person dressed in the same security uniform of the Broadhurst Company. The person in black clothes closes the side door, then transfers onto the driver's front seat, and starts to turn the van around driving back towards the rear gatehouse direction. The man dressed in the security uniform pushes the left large glass door open, and continues towards the reception desk. The driver then walks around to the back of the reception, and kicks the body of the dead security man under the counter. As he moves the body the blood has begun to seep out from the bullet wound to his head which is beginning to cover the light grey speckled marble flooring. The armoured gunmen are now near the main reception desk when the driver speaks out with tension in his voice.

Firstly, he points at the main desk, and says to the man dressed like a security guard, "Marcus, take charge of the reception, and block all calls."

"Yes Colonel." Replies Marcus.

The Colonel looks across at the main doors, and points at the green holdall bag snapping an order, "Lock the front doors with the chain and padlock and place the Claymore mines across the complete inside front of the building setting the detonator switches around the door locks and hinges."

The Colonel then stares across at two other men saying, "Hobbs and Reynolds help with the Claymore mines, and then follow me, and Britton through to the main restaurant area locking doors, and placing claymores as you go."

"Sir, Yes sir." Replies Hobbs & Reynolds.

Hobbs and Reynolds are both very similar with a height of six feet tall, and have athletic well-built bodies, they carefully lift the large holdall full of Claymore mines, and detonators then start to walk towards the main reception doors. With aggressive attitude, and body movements they don't even speak to each other as they start work on the doors.

The Colonel watches as the men reach the main doors, and then stares at then as they commence work, he then looks down at the green holdall near his feet, and zips open the green holdall bag taking out an MP5 machine gun along with a bullet magazine. The reflection of the gun can be seen in the highly polished marble as he pushes the magazine into the gun, and clicks the top slide engaging the hammer, and a round into the chamber. He places the gun on top of the reception desk, then reaches back inside the bag removing a pair of black overalls, and a black mask.

The Colonel starts to pull on the black overalls and instructs, "OK Britton, tool up, let's get started, remember though don't kill too many."

Britton starts unrolling the black masks which he is wearing on his head, and slowly covers the pink complexion of his face. He then unzips the last green holdall, and takes out packs of loaded magazines, and pushes them into the body armour webbing that is strapped across his chest. He takes out an UZI sub-machine gun, and clicks a full mag into the handle, and cocks the top slide making the firing pin, and gun ready. The Colonel and Britton then take out some smoke grenades and clip them onto their belts. Britton then bends down, and removes two radios from his holdall and passes one to the Colonel, the pair of them click the talk button to make sure they are working, and Britton slides his behind the webbing across his chest.

"Evans what is your status?" Asks the Colonel in a deep calm voice.

"Sir, we are at the rear doors of the building awaiting your orders sir." Evans replies.

"Evans, split into the three teams as discussed, you and three men make your way to the back of the restaurant. The other six split into two teams of three, headed by Stubbs, and Heaton taking the left and right sides of the shop floor sweeping through the factory pushing everyone towards the restaurant. Make sure all the doors are mined, and locked. We need minimal fatalities, but if any resistance is found or felt, killing a few people won't hurt the cause, but don't go trigger happy men."

"Sir, Yes sir, what about the van sir?" Requests Evans.

"Carla, will drive the van directly underneath the restaurant, and wait with Dale until Stubbs and Heaton arrive. Prep the C4 and timers then help guide the shop floor parasites up the stairs." Smiles the Colonel.

"Sir, yes sir understood." Replies Evans waving at the white van to stop.

"Over and out sir." Carla confirms.

The Colonel starts to roll on his black face mask, and in doing so darkness begins to fall onto Broadhurst Industries. As the men push their way through the office doors, people are having lunch sitting at their desks reading newspapers, looking at things on the internet, and siting in small groups talking as the men explode into the office area.

Absolute panic immediately begins to reign as huge bangs ring out around the open plan office areas as smoke grenades are thrown into different zones. People are suddenly stunned by the sound of machine guns, being fired into the office ceilings which send clouds of plaster dust floating into the air. The fireball of terror had started rolling, and the Colonel, and his team know that there is no going back.

"*OK, EVERYONE MOVE TOWARDS THE FUCKING RESTURANT.*" The men keep shouting.

People begin to stand from their seats in complete shock, and time appears to have stopped with all the confusion that is starting to flow through the office area. Armed men can be seen beginning to drag, and push people from their chairs towards the direction of the restaurant at the far back section of the office.

Panic starts to unfold in waves of terror as people start to run down the main walkways away from the men with their eyes burning from the smoke grenade clouds. Four Broadhurst employees are sitting in a group talking about the football match from last night about twenty-five metres away from the gunmen when the commotion starts. They all stand, and begin to walk over towards the armed men in an attempt to try, and reason with them. *'BURR' 'BURR' 'BURR'*, is all that that can be heard from the deafening sound of the machine guns as they are chopped down on the spot by three of the armed men.

"*NOW THE REST OF YOU FUCKIN MOVE.*" The men keep shouting.

The staff are looking at each other in shock, and disbelief as the smell of gunpowder, and smoke grenades begin to float through the air of the office. People are crying, and coughing from the fear, and shock of gasses emitted from the spent smoke grenades. Two women try to run towards the side exit staircase on the far-left side of the office, and are fired upon by one of the armed men. *'BURR' 'BURR' 'BURR.'* The bullets track a line along the wall punching holes into the plaster, and hitting the women with large *'THWACKS.'* The nine millimetres bullet rounds from the machine gun fired at such a close range, blood is sprayed across the white wall as the women start to fall towards the floor. The two women hit the wall, and try to hold themselves up, but their fingers drag the wet blood down the wall causing long thin red marks.

"*ARGHHHHHH.*" Is heard as the shouts of pain start to ring out through the office. The two women die near the staircase doorway unable to escape. People are already sitting having lunch when the machine gun rounds are fired at the far end of the office. People begin to look at each other, start to stand from the seats as the whole room echoes, and vibrates as the smoke grenades detonate. Three armed gunmen suddenly appear in the room, firing off machine gun rounds into the ceilings. All the people are completely trapped, and have nowhere to go. Several people have mobile phones on the tables and try to grab them.

One of the gunmen see's what they are trying to do and screams out, "*NO CELL PHONES* put them down." In a south African accent.

One man ignores his request and continues to lift his cell from the table.

'*BURR*' '*BURR*' '*BURR*' is heard as the man collapses and falls back into the table and chairs, behind where he was sitting with blood running onto the marble floor. The gunmen start to work their way into the centre of the room, throwing tables, and chairs against the walls beginning to clear a large central holding area.

"*WOMEN LEFT, MEN RIGHT, SIT ON THE FLOOR NOW,*" Commands the man with the South African accent.

One masked man starts to walk towards the kitchen area with his machine gun held horizontal, and kicks the kitchen door wide open. There are ten kitchen staff four men and six women dressed in white food stained clothes standing next to a large stainless-steel sink in complete shock. The gunman can see ovens switched on, and pots boiling on the top of large gas hobs. The air in the kitchen is full with the smell of meats being cooked with chicken and pork along with a big pot of curry bubbling away on the stove. Vegetables are all drained, and in large stainless serving trays waiting to be taken out front for serving. One cook who had just started to cut a large joint of meat can be seen turning around slowly, and is holding a carving knife. The chef stares at the gunman, and then suddenly, a microwave 'PINGS' indicating the food is cooked.

The gunman who shows no hesitation, fires several bullet rounds into the chef, and as he slides onto the floor, the remaining kitchen staff jolt in fear from the noise as the gunman lifts his gun across to their direction. Walking forward, the gunman pushes a trolley full of dirty plates and cutlery out of his way which then rolls, and hits the door on the dishwasher.

Indicating to the kitchen door with his gun he shouts, *"OUTSIDE NOW JOIN THE OTHERS."*

The men and women from the kitchen start to run into the middle of the room standing in shock, and disbelief that one of their colleagues has just been killed in front of them. They begin to divide almost in a trance forming small groups in the centre of the restaurant huddling together for comfort. More people are now starting to run into the restaurant dazed, and confused with eyes streaming with tears and coughing from the smoke grenade fumes with no one knowing what to do. A few people slide over on the shiny polished marble floor, and knock over some of the standing men and women.

"WOMEN LEFT, MEN RIGHT, SIT ON THE FLOOR NOW, NO MOBILE PHONES." The same gunman repeats his instruction.

The machine gun firing, and smoke grenades echo through the whole building causing the windows to vibrate as small pieces of plaster continue to fall from the ceilings where the gunmen have fired bullets. Dust and smoke start to circulate around the room like a net catching fish. Men and women are crying, and sobbing covered in dust and some in blood traces as the groups become ever larger as more work staff join them. Meanwhile, the other teams have started to make their way as ordered by the Colonel through the shop floor areas of the factory.

The left-hand team enters the factory from the north entrance, and locks the outer doors placing a claymore mine across the locks. They start to sweep through the factory silently but strongly with almost no sound. Inside the factory the machines are buzzing and whizzing with operators at lunch either in the main restaurant or in little areas on the shop floor. The right-hand team carry out the same exercise from the south entrance, and come across a group of men sitting having lunch dressed in blue overalls. Some of the shop floor workers are reading newspapers or books, and others are checking cell phones or talking with each other.

"ALL RIGHT EVERYONE UP AND HEAD TOWARDS THE RESTURANT NOW." Commands one of the armed men.

A well-built guy stands up, and says, "What is this, A Fucking Joke?"

'BURR' 'BURR' 'BURR' as a machine gun is fired, and blood spatters all over his colleagues, and across the table, and floor.

"DOES IT LOOK LIKE A FACKIN JOKE? NOW MOVE YOU FACKIN ASSES RIGHT NOW OR YOU WILL ALL BE FACKIN NEXT."

The remaining men stand in complete shock, and are pushed, and man handled towards the direction of the restaurant leaving blood spattered newspapers, sandwiches, and tea cups on the table where the man landed. A stream of blood now begins to flow over the table top, and starts to drip onto the floor near a metal hatch in the floor. The two teams of armed men continue pushing as many people as possible towards the restaurant firing machine gun blasts into the air. Shop floor guys keep appearing near equipment like Meerkats on scouting patrols standing and watching what is happening. All the men are well built, and have a menacing demeanour with almost full radio silence between them as they continue to sweep the floor areas. It is evident by their actions that they are all hardened professionals, and have carried out similar sweep, and clear tasks in the past.

The armed security man who is leaning on the counter in the rear gatehouse, can see everything which is happening both in the office, and shop floor areas of the building, and stares at the banks of screens. He has watched all the carnage unrolling in front of him, and has a look of both shock, and delight plastered across his face. He watches as the first of the shop floor staff push their way through a set of double doors, and reach the area at the base of the staircase to the left side of the building. They are met by two more heavily armoured gunmen standing in front of a white van pointing at the stairs which lead to the restaurant area.

"UP THE STAIRS NOW," Shouts one of the men in a strong London accent.

The men, in complete shock, continue up the stairs not knowing what is happening in front of them with the sound of gunshots, and bangs echoing through the building. The gunmen behind them continue to work around the shop floor, and suddenly, more screaming voices and more gunshots are heard. Panic is everywhere as the shop floor men reach the restaurant and are met by a final group of armed gunmen who start to push, and man handle them into the centre of the room. The last of the office staff are now entering the restaurant with the four gunmen close behind. The men and women are now separated into two shaking blubbering groups on the floor.

"JOIN THE OTHER MEN," Shouts the South African accent.

The shop floor men continue to enter the restaurant as the Colonel walks into the centre of the restaurant. He stares across the faces of the men and women deciding what to do next. There are people from all sides of the business, from directors to office cleaners. As the last of the shop floor people make their way into the restaurant and are followed by the two gunmen from downstairs. The Colonel lowers the machine gun so it is resting on its shoulder strap, and lifts his hands up to his face as he starts to roll up the black head mask revealing his face.

"Excellent work men." The Colonel nods his head in appreciation.

"Ladies and gentlemen, let me introduce myself, my name is Colonel Nick Burns, and I would like to thank you for your co-operation, and apologise that some of your colleagues have died during today's events, but unfortunately an amount of force was necessary."

Burns continues, "Now for the remaining people that are still alive, and I assume you would like to remain that way, if you all co-operate, and do exactly what I instruct you to do, no one else will be harmed, and this chapter in your lives will be over very soon." Burns looks across the people with a fake smile on his face, and speaking in a calm clear voice.

Coughing to clear his voice, "Are there any people in the room with medical conditions or maybe, any ladies that are pregnant, we are human after all?" Burns asks a general question looking around.

Several men and a couple of women start to raise their hands into the air, and Burns points at one of the gunmen, then at an area on the far left of the room.

"Collect a few chairs, and form a small hospital zone in that clearing, but please ensure men and women are still kept separate."

"Now everyone with a mobile phone would you kindly take them out of your pockets or bags, very slowly, and throw them into the centre of the room, where one of my team will collect them." Requests Burns.

One masked assailant starts to collect a few chairs from the side of the room, and places them into two small circles as people start to move very slowly reaching into pockets and bags for their phones, throwing them into the centre of the room. Another masked man starts to unwrap a thick black bin-bag, and walks towards the centre of the room grabbing handfuls of mobiles dropping them into the bag. The pile of phones continues to either 'ring' or 'ping' from text or emails being sent. Now that all the firing has stopped, and quiet is restored, phones outside in the main office area can also be heard ringing. The people with medical conditions begin to stand shaking, and shivering waiting for the next set of orders trying to hold back the fear racing through their bodies.

"The hospital ward people can move, making sure you leave your cell phones in the main pile." Burns indicates with his right hand sweeping towards the two circles of chairs being arranged.

Burns lifts the two-way radio from his jacket webbing, and raises it to his mouth pressing the talk button at the same time saying,

"Divert all calls to the answering system until further notice. Just leave one phone with access for incoming calls in the closest office to the restaurant." Burns lowers the radio, and pushes it back into the webbing.

"Now which person here is responsible for Human Resources?" Burns looks around for any motion.

A shaking hand, and arm can be seen being lifted from within the crowd of men and a faint Welsh voice says, "I am."

"Please stand, and introduce yourself, since you have probably never done this before!" Laughs Burns.

Burns watches this thin old man around sixty years old with thick rimmed glasses, and white hair dressed in blue suit stand and says in a nervous voice, *"My name is Ian Watts, and I am the HR Director."*

"OK Mr Watts, I would like you to select one of your team to go around this room and count the number of people here. I also need to know how many people are not on site today through absence or business trips. I need to know how many contractors and visitors are on site today, and I need this information in thirty minutes." Burns stares at Watts with a smile.

Watts standing looking across at the group of women, and with his left hand makes a gesture to stand requesting, "Gail Andrews, could you help me with this."

Mrs Andrews sits in the crowd of women shaking her head, and crying, "Why me?" In a very low voice.

"Mrs Andrews, please stand, and start." Burns asks in a calm voice.

Mrs Andrews is still sitting on the floor in shock not knowing what to do shaking her head in disbelief. She is around fifty years old, and is unaware that there are women gunned down trying to escape from the staircase in the office earlier.

"Now Mrs Andrews, I won't ask you again, either stand now, or start what I have asked, or I will kill Mr Watts, is that clear." Burns voice has a more serious pitch.

"OK, OK" Gail Andrews begins to stand, and is crying and shaking.

"Excellent, now one of my colleagues will escort you to the records computer. I want you to print off a full list of all staff that should be on site today. I then want these names cross referenced, and double checked against the people who are in this room."

"Now, of course, making any contact to the outside world it not an option."

Burns stares at Mrs Andrews with another fake smile and continues, "Any people that are not in the restaurant may be unfortunate casualties or absent, let's see how good your staff attendance systems are Mr Watt. Now will you please also go with Mrs Andrews since she may need some of your access codes."

Burns points to a fairly short stocky gunman on his right, and beckons him over, "Scotty, you go with them and watch, any issues, kill them both, we have all the access information anyway, but why have a dog, and bark yourself." Whispers Burns.

Scotty nods in agreement, and follows Mr Watts and Mrs Andrews into the main office towards the human resources department. Scotty reaches the outer area of the restaurant as all the phones that are ringing suddenly stop. The main office area is open plan sub divided into departmental area zones. The outer walls have glass offices, and conference rooms where directors and senior management teams sit. Closest to the restaurant is the sales & marketing zones followed by purchasing, IT then HR. The engineering and development zones are at the front sections of the office area. Scotty was part of the restaurant team assault entering from the rear of the building, and didn't see this section of the office other than on blue prints during the pre-briefings. Watts and Andrews reach the main central personnel computer, and start to print off the staff lists for that day. Watts is trying to open the security system to see how many contractors and visitors are on site that day, but the system keeps locking out.

"There is something wrong with the computers, maybe, the smoke, and bullets have affected the hardware." Mr Watts speaks in shaky nervous voice.

Scotty lifts the two-way radio from his jacket and presses the call button, "Security, can you unlock the visitor and contractor files from the main server for PC terminal, hold on a minute." Scotty leans forward to find the correct IP address.

"1190-1789-1975."

A voice on the radio replies, "Unlocked, and completed."

Mr Watts looks at Scotty, and says, "You have fully locked our systems?"

"Just get on with your task, so I don't have to kill you man." Replies Scotty.

Ian Watts clicks a few buttons on the keyboard, and the lists being to appear. Mrs Andrews is sending the information to the main office printer, and starts to move, "Wait here Ma'am; we will all walk over when he has finished his lists too." Scotty requests.

"What's the printer you have used Gail?" Asks Ian.

"The HP desk jet main server." Replies Gail.

"Ah yes, found it thanks, don't worry everything will be fine." Ian tries to reassure Gail.

"Let's hope so." Says Gail.

"I didn't notice Michelle in the restaurant." Gail whispers to Ian.

"Enough talk you." Scotty speaks as they begin to walk towards the printer.

The printer is already whirring, and buzzing as the pages begin to be fall onto the support tray as the three reach it. There is a very faint noise of "Ah" heard on the right side of the office, near to the stairs exit sign that is being partly masked by the noise from the printer working.

Neither Watts nor Andrews have heard the noise, but Scotty has, and starts to look over in the gradual direction, and see's what appears to be a body lying against a wall. Through the maze of computer monitors, chairs and desk partitions he sees a pair of legs moving slightly. The legs, now clearly seen to be a woman's, move even more, and as the printer finishes running off the list of staff names sheet by sheet, the noise of the woman seems to get louder in the silent office. Scotty looks back at Gail, and pointing with his left-hand requests.

"Mrs Andrews, collect all the sheets, and bring them over to me."

As Gail starts to collect the sheets from the in-tray of the printer, she stops, and turns looking towards the stairway exit and asks, "What's that noise?"

"Bring the sheets here now, then head back towards the restaurant. The Colonel expects you both to start the head count." Scotty snaps out.

"No wait Ian, that's a person over there, and I'm not prepared to leave them alone if they are injured!" Gail replies straining to look over towards the direction of the noise.

"You will go back to the restaurant NOW!" Growls Scotty.

Watts and Andrews are still standing close to the printer, trying to decide what to do. Either ignore the gunman's request or be submissive to him. Scotty then starts to lift the two-way radio from his jacket pocket. Gail is holding the paper sheets, and then starts to roll them into a tube type shape that is easier to hold, and grasps the tube in her right hand.

"Colonel, sir we have a situation out in the main office area, one of the staff injured earlier appears to be alive. Can you send someone to investigate, Out?" Scotty asks.

The Colonel hears the request, and replies, "Scotty you go, and investigate with Mr Watts & Mrs Andrews, whoever it is, silence them, there is nothing we can do!"

Scotty looks at Ian & Gail, and gestures over towards the direction of the body with his Uzi sub machine gun. Scotty is a gunman around thirty years old, and is thinner in build than the other guys with a short-cropped beard that can now be seen since he has removed the black facemask. Meanwhile, in the restaurant, the Colonel still holds his two-way radio, and lifts the receiver in the direction of his mouth, pushing the talk button, "Heaton & Stubbs, report in."

"Sir Heaton here, team two has completed a second sweep of the right-hand side of the factory floor, and confirmed no more staff." Heaton growls in a gruff Yorkshire accent.

"Sir Stubbs, team three confirming the same for the left side." Stubbs answers in a strong Northern Ireland accent.

"Men can you confirm the body count for any resistance found." Requests the Colonel.

"Sir total of four male fatalities on the right side." Heaton confirms.

"Sir another six men killed on the left side." Replies Stubbs.

"Heaton & Stubbs, meet at the lower restaurant staircase, collect the C4, and timers from Carla and Dale then sub split your teams into three groups of two starting roving patrols across the entire shop floor area. Use a figure of eight sweeping pattern keeping radio communication to a minimum, but anything suspect must be reported immediately. Check all doors, windows, and make sure all are locked, and mined. Place the motion sensors in Z sequence across the factory floor, and place the C4 charges next to mains electrical, gas, water and air systems. Once the motion sensors are set, set the frequency so we can track the signals here upstairs." The instructions are said with harshness in his voice.

"Over and out sir." Both men reply and start to make their way through the maze of machines and gangways en-route to the restaurant.

"I will take Taylor." Says Heaton to Stubbs.

"OK, let's send Lewis and Brough together, and I will take Swifty." Replies Stubbs.

Both men nod in agreement as they continue to walk. Meanwhile Scotty, Gail and Ian are almost within five metres of the groaning noise, which now is quite clear. Gail starts to walk quickly towards the noise thinking that it may be her daughter who she didn't notice in the restaurant. Scotty is walking fast to try, and be there first to avoid any possible conflict. As the three people reach the two women bodies, the faces of Gail and Ian change. Gail's face looks revealed as she notices that neither of the women are her daughter, but then realises that both of the women are very familiar, and looks across at Ian only to see the colour draining from his face in complete shock.

One of the women is his daughter, and the other is his ex-wife, both gunned down in cold blood for being in the wrong place at the wrong time. Scotty looks down to see the two bodies lying in a large pool of partly congealing blood, the bullet exit wounds clearly visible through the blood drenched clothes of the women. The ex-wife is clearly dead since she was closer to the arc of fire of bullet holes seen on the wall, and clearly has more exit wounds near her back, and side of her abdomen. The daughter is still breathing, but very faint, and fast almost panting. Blood is still trickling from her body with air bubbles clearing showing that she is hit in the lungs, but the blood also has blackness to it confirming that the heart is hit, and the body is dying as vital organs begin to close down. Scotty turns around only to hear Ian screaming out in absolute pain, and terror.

"Arghhhhh, my Grace, my beautiful Grace." Watts collapses into a pile on the floor, and then starts crawl on his knees through the pool of blood towards his daughter.

As he reaches his daughter, he pushes his left arm under her limp body and turns her over, holding her in his arms. Watts is now covered in blood, and is weeping continuously as he starts to wipe her long blood drenched blonde hair away from her beautiful face revealing her light blue eyes. The partly congealed blood has caused her hair to stick against her the greyness of her dying face.

Scotty turns, and looks at Watts saying with no emotion in his voice, "There is nothing that can be done for her Watts, time to go."

Watts looks up at both Gail then Scotty, and as the expression on his face turns from fear to aggression starts to scream out,

"YOU! YOU FUCKING BASTARDS! IF IT WASN'T FOR YOU! MY BEAUTIFUL DAUGHTER WOULD STILL BE ALIVE AND NOT DYING IN HER OWN BLOOD!"

"Mr Watts, time to move." Scotty insists again.

"YOU! And all the others Go Fuck yourselves, I am stopping here with my beautiful daughter." Ian shouts out.

Gail starts to move towards Ian to give him some comfort in his loss. In doing so Scotty takes his left hand, and places it on Gail's right shoulder,

"I wouldn't, if I were you." He whispers in her ear.

Gail suddenly stops and turns her head slightly to look at Scotty saying, "I am going to help Ian, if you don't like it then I'm sorry, but he needs some help."

The situation is beginning to get tense, and Burns has heard the screaming of Watts even in the restaurant. The men and women in the restaurant have also heard Watts screaming, and shouting, and begin to look towards the direction of the main office area through the large glass open doors. Burns raises his right hand, and beckons Reynolds over from the right-hand side of the room with a single arm gesture. Reynolds who is standing with his MP5 pointing towards the ground sees the movement and reacts instantly, walking quickly over to Burns.

"Reynolds, go, and see what the fuck is keeping Scotty, I have given him a simple job, and it sounds like a fucking amusement park ride out there." Burns instructs Reynolds with calm yet pissed off voice.

Reynolds quickly starts to walk in the direction of the open large glass doors at the front of the restaurant, and as he reaches them Burns shouts out,

"Reynolds, shut the doors would you on the way through." He looks back at Burns, and nods his head submissively, pulling the large doors closed. As Reynolds makes his way down the main walkway of the office between the rows of desks, the screaming, and shouting from Watts can still be heard.

"THIS IS NO WAY FOR ANYONE TO DIE, LET ALONE MY BEAUTIFUL DAUGHTER!" Sobbing uncontrollably.

He can see Scotty trying to speak with Mrs Andrews trying to take her away from Watts with Gail saying, "Leave me alone, I must help Ian, go and find someone else to harass."

Reynolds can see that the situation is now well out of control, and as he reaches the two of them, he lifts the MP5 and clicks back the hammer with his right hand. Mrs Andrews stops and Scotty turns slowly to see Reynolds now standing with the machine gun pointing at them.

'BURR, BURR, BURR, BURR.' Shots ring out as Reynolds guns down Gail and Scotty without even a moment's hesitation. As the empty bullet cases start to hit the light grey carpet, a cloud of smoke emits from the barrel of the gun and another two bodies lie dead on the carpet. Reynolds then turns slightly, and looks at Watts holding his dying daughter supported with his arms, and fires another small blast of bullets rounds into both the daughter and Watts. 'BURR, BURR, BURR, BURR' is muffled slightly as the noise reaches the restaurant doors, but men and women jump with fright as the shots echo around the office.

Burns still standing in the middle of the restaurant talks to himself in a calm voice, "Oh dear another two hundred grands less, but made a small amount of profit."

Everyone in the restaurant is now shaking with fear after hearing that two more of their colleagues have been executed in cold blood. Some of the other gunmen in the restaurant casually look towards each other almost in shock themselves, not fully realising that Reynolds has gunned down Scotty as well.

Reynolds walks over to Mrs Andrews's body, bends down slightly, and grabs the roll of white papers with blood staining from her right hand, and quickly turns walking back towards the restaurant. Burns mind starts to work overtime as he plans the next stages of the situation as Reynolds pushes the large glass door open. Reynolds walks calmly over to Burns, and hands him the tube of papers. Without a single sign of emotion, Burns turns to the staff sitting on the ground, and says.

"OK, I need another volunteer to continue with the head count, do I have any takers?" Burns looks around at the men and women with no one trying to make any form of eye contact.

"Has Scotty decided to leave us, as well?" Burns asks Reynolds and he replies by nodding his head in agreement.

The staff of Broadhurst Industries are now in absolute fear for their lives, knowing that Burns promised no more deaths and already killed two more colleagues. Men and women are sobbing, and crying, holding on to each other shaking like young children. Burns and his team have them exactly in the position where they want them, being completely subservient. Burns knows that hostages can react in different ways during hijack situations, and being strong from the beginning enforces he will maintain control, and overpower any rebels with a quick death. If he is willing to kill three people just for fetching sheets of paper what could he do next? This also shows that he will not bow down to anyone, and trying to negotiate with a person like this for the police will be impossible.

Burns continues to look around the men and women, and asks again, "Ladies and gentlemen, if I need to ask for second time, there may be many more people joining Mrs Andrews and Mr Watts."

A young man starts to raise his arm, and says, "I'll do it to stop any more deaths."

Burns looks at the man, and beckons him to stand speaking, "Please introduce yourself hero."

The man speaks naturally in a nervous voice, "My name is Phil Bentley, and I work in the IT department."

The man is around twenty-five years old and is dressed part casually in a white shirt with no tie and light grey trousers. He has short red hair and bright blue eyes. His face is covered with designer stubble of a week or so, and he has a weak build. Burns beckons him over and Bentley begins to pick his way through all the men sitting around on the floor. People look up at him almost in shock that someone has volunteered to finalise a death list. After what appears to be an hour, Phil finally reaches the heavy built Burns who is nearly six feet tall. Bentley is a little shorter in height, and looks up slightly towards Burns as the paper having the list of names is rolled up, and handed over. Phil takes the tube of paper in his left hand and Burns starts to reach in his lower jacket pocket for a pencil.

"Now Mr Bentley, I want you to go around everyone sitting in here now, and with this pencil, place a tick by their name. Once you have completed this task, please speak out, and say sir, head count complete." Burns instructs with has calm collected voice.

Bentley stands at arm's length away from Burns and begins to move.

"Excuse me, Bentley, have I asked you to move?"

"*Error,* No, sir, you haven't." Bentley replies with a look of shock on his face.

"I instructed all of you to do exactly what I said otherwise there would be consequences!" Burns snaps at Bentley.

"*Errrrrr,* yes sir, you did." Bentley replies with even more nervousness in his voice.

Burns starts to move his right hand in the direction of the pistol holstered on the left side of his waist-belt. Bentley sees the action, and begins to close his eyes thinking that he will be killed next. In the same instance he starts to wet himself with absolute fear. Burns un-holsters the pistol, and points it at a large fat man who is sitting in the group of men at the edge. He is around fifty years old with a brown overgrown beard and long greasy unwashed dark hair. The man is wearing black trousers, and a sweat stained white shirt. Sensing a nervousness, he starts to look in the opposite direction of Burns attempting to avoid eye contact. Burns 'clicks' back the hammer of the revolver, and looks across to Bentley who is screwing up his face expecting to feel the bullet when a single bullet round *'BANG'* echo's through the restaurant. The bullet hits the fat man in the back of his skull sending blood and brain matter exploding all over everyone sitting in a six feet radius of the exit wound covering them with blood, hair, bone, and brain tissue.

Everyone in the room suddenly stops crying, shaking, and sobbing as the big man starts to collapse to the floor in a direction away from the other men. His head and body hit the floor with a solid *'THUD'* as blood from the wound begins to spill out onto the grey marble flooring. A few women instantly start screaming with fear, and disbelief that another colleague has been killed in cold blood.

"Now what does our hero have to say?" Barks Burns.

Bentley begins to open his eyes, and stands there in complete shock still thinking that he is next as Burns re holsters his pistol, and stares into Bentleys fear filled eyes. Bentley's trouser leg is darkened wet with piss, and has formed into a small pool on the floor by his feet. Bentley's eyes are full with tears of both fear and joy, since he hasn't been executed yet. He doesn't know whether to smile or cry, but takes a great sigh of relief.

"Now hero move your fuckin ass, you have less than nineteen minutes and forty-eight seconds, to finish the headcount, or the next person to depart from here will be you." Burns barks out the instruction.

Bentley runs over towards the hospital area to start the head count as Burns looks across towards Reynolds and Hobbs, and instructs the men, "Gents move the dead bodies from inside this room, and line them up just outside in the main office. Then carry out a recount of the bodies in the main office area."

"Sir, Yes sir." Both men reply.

He looks across to the opposite side of the room and speaks, "Carla, Get the equipment from the van and get me some communications fast. I need to make my broadcast, and inform

"Sir, Yes sir." Carla replies in a strong confident feminine voice.

Evans nods in agreement, and the two of them head off down the stairs in the direction of the white van. Burns then looks around the gunmen, and carries out a quick headcount talking to himself quietly, "Hobbs, Reynolds on body patrol, Carla and Evans on communications."

"Stubbs and Heaton, working on shop floor, Marcus on Front desk." He mumbles on, "Scotty one less, Dale, Britton and Swifty on crowd control. Perfect."

Carla and Evans reach the van, she opens the side door saying, "Be careful Evans, there's enough C4 in here to flatten the site let alone empty the restaurant."

Evans replies, "My, Burns is pissed off today, what's wrong with him?"

"Better not ask, but if this plan doesn't work, he'll be going out with all guns blazing." Carla answers.

Carla carefully climbs into the side of the van, and lifts out two large green holdall bags that were near the front passenger seat base, and then turns, passing them to Evans who is standing at the open side door. She then briefly looks across the white bricks of C4 layered in piles around the rear wheel arches of the van, and checks the remaining blocks.

"How much C4 did Burns find in the end Carla?" Evans asks.

"Two hundred and fifty kilos." Replies Carla from inside the van.

"Two hundred and fifty fucking kilos, is he fuckin real?" A shocked Evans asks.

"Very much so Evans. He has asked for radio transmitters too." Carla answers as she reaches the side door, and begins to climb out.

The two of them make their way back up the stairs towards the restaurant, and decide to stop talking in case anyone hears them. They reach the restaurant, and see Burns patrolling around the hostages deep in thought as the other gunmen, stand around the hostages in a deadly silence.

Burns points at the large glass doors and instructs, "Clear the first desk, and tap into the main hard-line closest that first glass office. We will use this office as a command area."

"Now ladies and gentlemen, my other assailants will continue to take care of your well-being while I prepare for my broadcast." Burns smiles.

"Mr Bentley, how many people have you accounted for?" Burns asks calmly.

"About fifty per cent of the list so far sir." Bentley continues to walk through the crowds of people on the floor asking their names.

"Britton, when Mr Bentley has finished, could you bring him through, and I will confirm the head count for the broadcast." Burns gestures to Britton as he starts to walk out of the restaurant through the large glass door being held by Evans. Burns continues towards the direction of the first glass office which has the words 'Sales Director' written in large black lettering. The hostages can see him taking the machine gun sling from around his left shoulder, and some watch him lower the gun onto the desk in the office.

He then sits down in the large director's office chair, and lifts his feet placing them onto the desk. The doors finally close as Hobbs and Reynolds return from the body counting exercise and stand in the glass office doorway.

Reynolds knocks on the glass door, and asks, "Permission to enter sir?"

"Ah Reynolds, Hobbs what's the head count look like?" Burns asks leaning back in the chair looking at the ceiling of the office with his black boots scrunching up the papers that have been left on the desk.

"Sir, not including Watts, Andrews, the fat man and Scotty, there are four men and two women." Replies Reynolds.

"Sir, was it necessary to kill Scotty?" Asks Hobbs.

"Scotty, and a few more of these guys are fairly new to this Hobbs, and I don't quite have the same level of trust in them, so sometimes an example has to be made." Burns replies in a calm voice, still staring at the ceiling.

"Make radio contact with the roving patrols, and ask for an update." Burns requests.

"Nineteen people dead that's £3.8 Million less, but with no Scotty, we will still be ready to retire." Burns leans forward, and looks across to Reynolds and Hobbs.

"Gents you have my complete trust, I had planned to kill Scotty from the very beginning and planned his loss against the hostages that have been killed." Burns looks towards the left of the office, and starts to read the sales calendar of events planned for the year with various military events, and exhibitions.

"There are some people on this team, however, that I do not trust and Scotty will not be the last. I will need your help once the shit starts to hit the fan." Burns takes a short sigh.

"Now go, and check on the roving patrols and watch for any disruptions in the restaurant, people will need the toilets and arrange some drinks." Burns shows some level of compassion.

"After all we can't afford to lose many more hostages or we may be bankrupt." Burns smiles, as Reynolds and Hobbs give an informal salute, and start to reach for the radios.

The Burns leans back again in the chair and closes his eyes thinking about the speech he has rehearsed so many times, and replays it over and over again in his head. Carla and Evans have cleared a desk outside the sale director's office, and taken out two laptops from the holdall bags. Both have connected the electrical and network supplies.

Evans is breaking into the main server system of Broadhurst Industries with stolen passwords, and client address information, and Carla is arranging the communication systems with the outside world. Marcus on the main reception, has blocked all external phone lines, and network communications and Jones is in the rear gatehouse protecting the rear. He has also installed a playback recording informing any people contacting the company that the secure server network system has failed, and will be operational in a few hours. Phil Bentley is still going around the people sitting on the floor, and keeps asking for their names. He has covered the hospital area, and the group of women and is finally working his way around the men

One man says to Bentley, "Why does he want this information, are we hostages, and being held for ransom?"

"I don't know." Bentley replies as he reaches the young man dressed in a dark grey suit.

Bentley completes the list, and then stands in the restaurant holding the sheets of paper aloft. Britton walks across and takes the papers, and then instructs Bentley to sit back down with the group of men. Britton walks out towards the Colonel and slides over the pieces of paper.

"Excellent, and before time." As Burns checks his watch.

He quickly counts through the numbers of names on the lists and confirms the final amount. Carla and Evans have fully completed the computer links, and connected a portable camera system. Burns tries the camera, and sees his face on the screen of the laptop.

"OK, dial in the number."

Carla starts to call the number and the Skype system begins to ring. The call is taken, and Burns begins to speak, "Could I speak with the Director of British Intelligence."

"I am sorry sir, but who is this?" A lady replies.

"Tell them, it is Colonel Nick Burns."

The call goes quiet, and then a male voice can be heard. "Colonel Nick Burns, well that's a voice I haven't heard in a long time, what can I do for you?"

"Is that Atkins? Well, what happened to John Wagstaff?"

"You know full well, what happened to John, you killed him on Sunday." Atkins replies.

"It wasn't me that killed him, from my recollection of the day I believe your undercover agent Shaun Neal took care of that."

"Enough of the past Burns, what do you want now?" Atkin asks.

"I have a very important announcement and would like this message to be broadcast internally, of course, to begin with, it might be worth you gathering the rest of your little team including the Home Secretary Allen."

Atkins speaks with his secretary off line, and requests the relevant people to attend. After several minutes, people begin to enter Atkin's office, and the call is transferred onto a large wall projector screen.

Burns face can be seen plastered across the screen smiling as people take their seats.

"What does this idiot want now?" One man asks.

"Is he working another undercover operation for the British government?" Another voice is heard mumbling.

"Quiet everyone." Atkins speaks.

"OK Burns, we are all here now, what little gem of wisdom do you have for us?"

Burns cough's, clears his throat then adjusts himself on the chair, he leans forward, and starts to speak, "To the Government of the United Kingdom, I Colonel Nick Burns confirm that my team, and I have taken over the Broadhurst weapons development facility, and now hold a total of five hundred and four staff hostage. We hereby request the ransom of £200,000 for each employee at Broadhurst's."

Burns now stands in front of the portable held camera demanding his money, then turns the camera, and scans around to reveal the staff sitting in groups on the marble flooring shaking and sobbing. He scans across the large wall sign of Broadhurst's to confirm the place.

He then moves the camera towards a TV screen showing the time and date, ensuring proof of life. People around the office sigh in disbelief and there is a pause for a few seconds and Burns continues, "The monies demanded will be split between evenly between my colleagues, and the families of my fallen British Armed Forces comrades that have been killed in conflict by the weapons produced and sold by Broadhurst Industries over the last thirty years to our enemies. These include The Falklands, both Gulf Wars, Bosnia, and finally Afghanistan." Burns then turns the camera, and walks into the main office area and the sales director's office at Broadhurst's.

"I have detailed reports, and files showing where these weapons were sold along with all the official government documents from the Cabinet confirming that these transactions of arms sales were for training exercises only." Burns then starts to move the camera over piles of Home Office and Ministry of Defence documents and folders.

"The last remaining documents are, of course, in the old archive files of Broadhurst Industries, and I have already started to extract this information." Burns then turns the camera to a large digital clock on the wall.

"The time as you can see is two nineteen p.m. on Wednesday fifteenth September 2010. You have until six p.m. Friday seventeenth September 2010 to arrange for the monies to be transferred to a Swiss Bank account, that I will give the information in the next twenty-four hours." Burns continues.

"Of course, any form of rescue attempt will result in the death of all the hostages at Broadhurst Industries, and I will go public with this information delivering it to all the major news networks." Burns warns.

"I do, of course, fully understand that Her Majesties forces would like to set up camp on the front lawn, and they are more than welcome providing no one enters inside the fenced surrounding land of the factory." He smiles to the camera.

"It is also worth noting that any rescue attempt could force me to detonate the Two hundred and fifty kilos of C4 explosive that I have distributed, and armed around this site including the two large ammunition silos. Please keep your distance!" Burns warns again, and the signal stops.

NINE

My nose is overwhelmed with the scent of salty air, and as the skin on my face tingles from the warmth of morning sunshine magnifying through the windows, pain suddenly takes a vicious grip on my body with not even the softness of the bed giving any comfort, as I begin to awake. The sound of waves crashing against rocks then lapping against the shoreline in the faint distance can be heard as my thoughts try to blank out yesterday's events that continue to resurface. Trying to eliminate these black thoughts, I open my eyes that begin to sting immediately from the bright sunlight revealing a blurred vision of the room. Continuing to lie in bed, my senses are alive with listening to the calming noise of the sea, and the singing of birds as they jump around in the trees causing the leaves to rustle. The noise of a car engine starting outside, and the *'Burr'* from the tyres, as it splashes through some standing water on the road below fill my ears. I stare at the white ceiling of the room, and turn my head looking towards the direction of the open balcony doors to see the early morning sunshine shining like a lighthouse through the gap, casting shadows around the furniture onto the light oak flooring. The white painted room is complemented by the light grey curtains gracefully flowing with the sea breeze passing through the window with the occasional aroma of eucalyptus entering the room. Suddenly, a kookaburra shouts out its distinctive call, and now the truth of where I am fills my thoughts, Palm Cove Australia.

The thoughts in my mind drift towards the recent weeks and today lying in bed, I hope that this is the dawn of a new chapter in my life. Throwing back the white duvet cover, I begin to peel myself from the bed sheets and pillows; finally sitting upright I swing my legs over the side of the bed. As my feet touch the cool wooden flooring, I gradually rise from the large king-size bed and walk towards the open balcony doors, passing by the two holdall bags I placed there last night. Turning around, I walk past the chair near the TV in the corner of the room as my feet begin to feel the heat being emitted from the sun warming the laminate floor. Grasping with my right hand for a pair of sports shorts, I step into them covering my naked body. The white flecked grey curtains float, and twist even more violently with an increased breeze entering the room and reaching the balcony doors, I push them fully open exposing my body to the warmth of the morning sunshine.

    Walking out of the room onto the balcony I see three large yachts moored out at sea bobbing in the waves that are not strong enough for surfers, but several people out in kayaks are seen trying to exercise. Looking across the road, and leaning on the safety fence of the balcony, I see the main beach of Palm Cove protected with rows of coconut and eucalyptus trees. People are jogging along the shoreline, and dogs can be seen taking their owners for a walk along the pavement in the shade of the trees. Glancing towards the right there is a storekeeper cleaning fallen leaves from the pavement with a hosepipe, and the excess water runs onto the street. A red Audi convertible drives through the water with a splashing sound. To the left, there are different types of cars pulled into parking spaces near the edge of the large trees, and finally a large blue motorhome parked near the overnight rest stop, and for-most people it looks like any other ordinary morning in Palm Cove.

    Across towards the far right, more cars are parked with people moving around. Finally, I stare at the car that even at this distance has small traces of blood along the passenger's side of the rear door from yesterday's events. I make a mental note that the car must be cleaned before it's disposed of so all traces are removed. The Omega watch strapped to my left wrist shows a time of nearly seven a.m., and it has been over twelve hours since my last meal, but last night's actions fill my memory, when I climbed out of the car, and walked towards the boutique hotel reception carrying the two holdall bags. I remember showing the night service manager the booking confirmation, and thought how strange it was that without any discussion or identification he gave me the keys and pointed out the direction to the room. The staircase was tough after that late drive, and after opening the door, I continued through the doorway into the room. The warm refreshing shower after the several hours of driving along black isolated roads, and the comforting sight of the shimmering glow being emitted from the city lights of Cairns all race through my mind.

With the smell of fresh bacon floating in the air, most of the breakfast bars are starting to serve food, and where better place. Turning around walking back into the room, closing the balcony doors, I continue in the direction of the bathroom part sliding the door shut, and then standing near the sink, I reach for the toothpaste with my left hand and squeeze some paste onto the toothbrush.

I start to brush my teeth, and also stare at myself in the mirror with a chin covered in two days of facial stubble, and the short hair on my head standing up everywhere. After placing the toothpaste tube on the glass shelf, I switch on the cold-water tap, and fill the glass beaker from the shelf, and spit the toothpaste into the sink. After washing the toothbrush under cold water, it is placed carefully back on the shelf, and finally lifting the beaker to my mouth, I rinse out my mouth spitting the final residue in the direction of the plughole.

Replacing the beaker, I cup my hands to collect some water throwing some onto my face and hair. Using my wet hands to brush my hair flat, I take the soap bar from besides the sink, and rinse the it under the cold running water to make a lather for washing my face. The stubble prickles against the palms of my hands as they move over the skin, and then finally with cold water, I wash off the soap from my hands and face and turn off the tap. There is a white hand towel hanging near the sink so with a grasping action, the towel is lifted to my face and the water is absorbed.

Staring at myself in the mirror, thoughts drift back to two days ago when I drove many hours along the A1 Bruce Highway. The long wall mirror in the bathroom begins to reflect the cut on my left shoulder, and the bruising around the wound. Bluish bruising has started to appear on the upper left bicep and ribcage area from the fight yesterday. The dark grey tiled floor in the bathroom, and the white shower cubical are covered in drops of blood from the cut, as I remember sewing the wound together again last night after it split in the fight.

There is a small cut to my left eyebrow, and a split in the top lip that now stings from the toothpaste. My stomach and ribcage now begin to ache from the punishment that has been inflicted to them, but all can be covered with clothes. Walking out of the bathroom a black polo shirt is hanging on the back of the chair near the TV, so with a single motion I take the shirt and throw it over my head engaging my arms through the armholes.

Taking my sand coloured combat shorts folded on the chair seat, I step into them and button up the fly. Twisting to the left and bending down to take the flip flops from the bag the injury to my rib's stabs with a deep throbbing pain down the length of my abdomen, until I stand back upright with the flip flops on my feet. Placing the cell in my left shorts pocket along with the apartment keys and cash I had taken from the asset's wallet, the Rayban sunglasses are lifted from the sideboard and placed over my eyes, as I walk towards the apartment door. Noticing that the handle on the door, and the cream tiles on the floor have blood stains and drips covering them, I walk towards the bathroom, and grab some toilet paper from the roll with my left hand, switch on the cold tap and begin to wet the paper. After soaking the paper, it is squeezed to remove any excessive water leaving a fibrous pulp.

Switching the water off, I look down and quickly remember that. I need a bag for the blood drenched clothes and walking back towards the open door, I bend down to clean the blood from the floor, and from the door handle of the apartment.

Opening the apartment door blood drips can also been seen on the steps so closing the door, I continue towards the staircase, and bending down begin to rub at the evidence. The congealed blood isn't too difficult to remove from the smooth cream tiles, and as I make my way down the staircase towards the side gate, the blood stains disappear. Turning right and walking parallel to the beach past the shops, bars, and restaurants sitting along Palm Cove beach, I drop the wet bloody toilet paper into a rubbish bin that sits along the main road.

After the last nights late drive, I didn't manage to have any food and my stomach is aching for a big breakfast, coffee, and orange juice. Feeling inside my right shorts pocket, there is some Australian dollar notes that include one $50 and three $20 bills. My mind thinks about the things that have been done over the past few months, and linger like the numbness from a toothache, but another side is beginning to show. The side that now finally starts to want my life back seeking forgiveness for all the in human acts that have been carried out against others, and maybe, return back home. The fresh sea air is calming and relaxing, as it fills my lungs, and I begin to think about what it would feel like to walk hand in hand with someone special right here today. My nose is filled with the smell of bacon being cooked at The Rising Sun Restaurant and stopping at the menu board, I look at the breakfast menu hanging in a glass fronted wooden frame. Bacon, Eggs, Hash Browns, Toast, Beans, Coffee and fresh Orange Juice all for $25, sounds like a real bargain.

Stepping inside and taking a seat at a square table with four chairs which is placed near to the road, I watch the world go by and wonder what a new life could offer to a man like me. People are still jogging along the beach dressed in casual sports clothes, and there is an elderly couple looking me as they walk past the front of the restaurant.

"G'day sir, what can I get for you today?" asks a female waitress.

Turning and looking towards the direction of the voice, and I reply, "G'day Ma'am I'll take your big breakfast with a large coffee and orange juice."

The waitress is about thirty-five years old with dyed blonde hair and slightly sunburnt skin. She is quite slender, but the short dress she is wearing with white trainers doesn't suit any fashion style. I smile back at her, as she writes down the order.

"Are you just passing through, honey or just here for a few days?" she asks.

Cautiously replying back, "Just passing through from Brisbane on the East Coast; I'm planning a dive on the outer reef tomoz. Do you know any good tour guides?"

"Hey, Yeah, Silver streak are always good and professional, if you call into one of the local tour shops just down the road here, they can plan a trip for you." she replies.

"OK, that's great thanks." Not quite the answer I was looking for, but and it tells me that she is not from around here otherwise she would have closer contacts.

"Are you from around these parts?" I ask.

"Nah from Adelaide, and only work here in the summer months to catch some surfing and sun rays." She smiles back at me.

With a return smile I ask, "Do you have any of today's papers at all by any chance?"

She turns, and starts to walk towards the kitchen area, and points to the left side of the restaurant at a newspaper rack, and replies, "Help yourself honey."

I stand and walk towards the paper rack, scanning the headlines to find any news from the events in Sydney then Brisbane and my journey to Cairns. Looking through the different paper titles, Sydney

Morning Herald, The Australian, Brisbane Courier Mail and The Canberra Times all the stories talk about the killing of police officers in a town called Mackay. Taking the latest copies of the Sydney Morning Herald, and Brisbane Courier from the rack, I return back to my seat with the newspapers still in my right hand, and slide onto the cane wooden chair, and placing the papers on the table. Starting to look down the front cover page of the Herald, the smell of fresh coffee floats in the air, and sensing the waitress making her way towards the table bringing the drinks. I look up slightly, and see she is holding the two drinks on a small square red plastic tray. The coffee is in a large white coffee cup and the orange juice in a large glass with condensation all around the outside.

She reaches the table, and leans slightly towards me placing the drinks on the next to the newspaper saying, "There you go Babe, found any interesting news or gossip yet?"

Looking back at her, and I reply, "Just flicking through, but you never know. Ask me again in thirty minutes!"

She smiles, and then turns away walking towards a young couple that have just sat near to me enjoying the morning sunshine for breakfast. Hearing her talking to them, I continue to look through the paper scanning for any possible news checking the front page, and read that a woman Forensic doctor was killed in a police station followed by the death of two police officers. Two further officers were killed, and burnt at a piece of scrubland in their police car, but there is no mention of me. Closing the Herald, I repeat the same with the Brisbane Courier and again read a similar story, but nothing is mentioned over the man I killed, Michael Hughes. Reading between the lines it sounds as though a government clean-up team was sent to remove Michaels body and got caught up with the local police.

Rechecking the date of the papers, I hear a vehicle in the distance drive through a puddle of water on the road, and pull up stopping around fifty metres away from the restaurant facing the beachside parking. The sound of two doors opening and closing can be heard then the positive sound of a sliding side door as you would imagine from a van or minibus. Peeling my eyes away from the newspaper columns, and looking towards the noise from the doors, and I see a Black MPV with blacked out windows. There are two thick set men dressed in dark grey suits having short cropped hair and dark Rayban sunglasses with clean shaven faces standing next to the side door of the MPV. It is clear by the build that they are ex-military in those suits. Their tell-tale stance of neatly crossed hands resting near their stomachs tries to hide the pistols in shoulder holsters. My attention starts to be drawn to the faint 'whirr' of an electric motor, and then a voice that causes the hairs on the back of my neck to lift.

"Mr Nash, it's been a long-time old boy! How are you keeping?" asks the frail old voice that instantly recalls an image in my thoughts.

I look towards the direction of the voice, and see McGough approaching in an electric wheel chair travelling along the road towards the restaurant frontage. Looking back at the man, my mind tries to remember his face, as I see him reaching ever closer to the wheelchair access ramp for the restaurant. Rising from my seat, and gradually pushing the cane chair backwards making a slight scraping sound, I stare at him being jolted around in the wheelchair as he makes his way along the bumpy road. Reaching the bottom of ramp, the electric motor whine increases, as it gradually starts to climb the obstacle creaking, and knocking as the ramp flexes with the load.

"Well, Dean, are you going to clear a seat for me at your table, and order me a large pot of Earl Grey Tea? That is, of course, if you want me to join you for breakfast?" McGough continues to smile as though I am one of his old long-lost friends.

Standing, I push a chair away to my left-hand side closest to the ramp beckoning the waitress over at the same time.

"It wasn't this difficult the last time we met hey?" He smiles across at me.

"No, that is true, but you certainly look better for it!" Replying assertively.

"Relax, I'm not your enemy Dean." McGough moves in his wheelchair trying to make himself comfortable.

The waitress comes over to the table with my breakfast, and says, "There you go honey, you never mentioned you'd be having company? G'day sir, what can I get you?"

"Thank you dear, an earl grey tea please, and some light toast, I don't have the appetite like this man here for that large breakfast." Replying in his old broken English accent and gesturing to me.

"I didn't know company was expected otherwise I would have waited!" I snap back towards him.

As the waitress walks away quickly, I look towards the guys standing by the black MPV. "Do your monkeys want anything?" I ask sharply gesturing with a head movement.

"Dean, please we are not your enemy. Have you forgotten about us, and everything that has happened in the past?" McGough speaks calm and quietly.

"Hmm, well, my mind now remembers a lot Edward, and I remember what happened to me." I reply.

Quickly trying to change the subject he looks across, and sees what I am reading then asks, "I did not take you for a newspaper man Dean? I hope your recent actions have left no tracks."

"Look, I didn't invite you or your men here, what are you doing checking up to see if I'm still alive?" I respond back sharply with a nasty streak.

"I have never doubted your skills to survive." McGough stares at me.

"So why did you have Shaun killed by the other hitman?" I ask.

"You seemed to be taking too long, and I needed to close off the loose ends."

"Loose ends! I had only been in the country less than one hour, and was at his apartment!" I snap back aggressively.

"Dean, you were sent to complete a contract that you didn't follow, so a backup was sent to ensure the job was done. Neal was a big mistake, he let me down and worse he let you down."

"Well, your little assassin was resting in a little backwater hotel toilet near Mackay, but it looks as though your cleaning team have managed to fuck up that job too!" I reply lifting my knife, and fork to start my breakfast.

"That's unfortunate, but expected, that little problem is already going to disappear soon enough. Here is the flight information by the way, from the car." McGough smiles as he replies, and slides over a brown envelope.

"Dean, we have another problem, and I need your help?" He asks.

Chewing a large fork full of eggs and bacon, I take a big swallow, and respond with, "WE have a problem? It's not my problem, it's yours!"

"One of your previous employers has been compromised, and is being threatened by a group of terrorists. The terrorists are holding the large majority of the workforce ransom." McGough explains.

"What has this got to do with me?" I reply.

"Well Mr Nash, you will be given a formal briefing back in the UK, but you are the only man that knows the facility, its layouts, security, and possible entry points." He continues.

"We were planning to send in a group from a Special Forces team for extraction, but several of the hired help are ex Government employees, and the PM doesn't want to embarrass the country, and indeed the cabinet with another scandal, so your name popped up on the top of the list."

"I'm sure you made that list Edward, so let's get this straight, what are you asking from me is to go against ex Special Forces trained mercenaries, and take them out?" I reply.

"Well, that's pretty much the game old boy, but there will be one main difference in this operation." McGough takes a sip of his coffee, and makes a deep cough.

"You'll be on your own, we all know how much you enjoy working solo, and this will be perfect for you." He smiles back at me.

"There is also an added bonus with this contract, your old mentor Nick Burns is running the show, so maybe, some well-deserved payback is in order hey Nash?"

"How do you know Burns is running the hostage situation?" I ask.

"Let's just say the video he shared with the government sealed that piece of information."

"When has this hostage situation taken place." I reply.

"Yesterday in the UK." McGough answers.

"Yesterday, and it takes twenty-four hours on a plane to get to Oz? Hmmm, something doesn't quite add up Edward." I reply.

"I was already in the country for some other business and this came up, so I thought, I would drop by, and say hello." He thinks quickly trying to cover his response.

"I know what I think, you knew that Burns was going to plan this hostage take over, and you knew I was still in Australia, so you jumped on a plane to be out of the way, but your assassin Michael upset the balance. You were expecting to meet him here today and not me."

I continue, "Am I right, and I'm sure Burns is acting for you, and probably gone native to fund the next Cardinal programme?"

McGough twitches around in his chair, as if my questions have made him uncomfortable, and he pauses for a few seconds, before giving the answer, "I wouldn't say Burns has gone native as such, but for sure, we do not know who is sending him orders now. In answer to your other question I knew you had already killed Michael and with your training, suspected that you would use the room booking so thought it was a good place to meet. As for the cardinal programme that was closed many years ago. You should know this because you caused its closure."

A little surprised by his replies I try to break them down, "Burns has gone rogue, and the agency want me to tidy up the mess right."

"Well, you are an expendable asset Nash." McGough replies.

"Thank you so much, and this makes me feel better?" I snap back at him.

The waitress then brings over the toast with butter, jam, and marmalade. I sit back slightly in my chair and lower my knife to the table with my right hand, and lift the glass of orange juice to my lips. I take a large gulp of cool orange juice, and take a look around the restaurant. I look down towards the left and lower the glass back to the table.

"Dean, operation Ottoman was a nightmare for the agency, and it exposed highly influential people in the government so the cardinal programme had to be closed. Measures were put in place to stop it ever operating again." McGough leans forward.

"We don't know who Burns is working for any more, but we need you to find out and then kill him. He is a rogue agent and must be stopped."

"So, how many agency men do you have watching us as we sit here talking just having breakfast?" I lower my head towards the table, and lift the knife starting to cut the Hash Browns and continue.

"I've counted ten so far with the young couple, three men, and two women jogging by the beach not to mention the road sweeper who keeps checking his mobile, and, of course, the two rent a mob idiots over by the MPV."

"Dean, you never fail to impress me with your observational skills and talent, that's why we employ you." Replies McGough.

"Don't try bull-shitting here old man. What's in this deal for me, what's the payment for carrying out this small request for you?" I ask.

"Well old boy, the Home Secretary has offered you pretty much anything you want due to the significance of Lord Broadhurst, and the top-secret information stored in his business. What payment would you want from your country for this small ask." McGough smiles back, leaning in his chair, and staring at me.

"Anything hey, hmmm." I lean back in my chair slightly and with a smile on my face ask, "Well, how about my life back?"

McGough suddenly leans forward, coughing with a look of shock on his face, he takes a deep breath, and growls, "Well that's not quite the answer I was expecting! What, are you becoming soft in your old age?"

I finish my breakfast, and slide the plate to the left side of the table, "I wouldn't say soft, but maybe, more educated."

McGough leans on the table staring at me over his thin rimmed glasses, and responds, , "Well Nash, actually that's a very big ask, and how would we know that you wouldn't just sign up with another interested party?"

"Edward, it is becoming clear over the last few weeks that there is a long queue of interested parties who want me either dead or want my employment, and you sitting here today puts my life in danger one way or another. My past work is something that I now need to leave behind." I stare back at him.

"It's as woman Dean, have you found true love?" Laughs McGough.

"Well, let's just say that, I do have a new love in my life, and it's to enjoy the rest of my life, and stay alive." Replying with a big smile.

"How is someone like you going to survive in Civvie Street? There is nothing finer to start the week than blowing up a few baddies on a Monday morning, with the smell of fresh gunpowder and C4." McGough leans back again slightly in his chair and continues.

"Remember though, that no matter what you try to forget, you will always carry around all that pain and guilt. It haunts some men for the rest of their lives, and no retirement will ever cure that illness."

I lean forward slightly, and begin to feel anger welling deep inside as I reply, "Well, what do you recommend Edward, just to carry on until finally I get a bullet in the back of my head, but, of course, that is what the agency would like, easy, clean, and simple with no comebacks hey!"

I lean back with a slight smile on my face and continue the conversation, "What have you achieved for your country, all that pain and guilt from your orders must sit deep inside chewing away at your strong values." I ask McGough.

"Well Nash, this question is not about me, it's about you, and what have you achieved. From my side, I can say hand on heart that I have served my country with honour, pride, and dignity and my life, although, evil to some people has ensured that everyone in the British Empire feels protected and safe."

McGough continues, "Even with all the kill orders that I have given or sanctioned over the last thirty years, I can still sleep well at night knowing that everything was done for the greater good, Can you Nash? Or does all that guilt and suffering feel like you are being suffocated?"

I stare at him knowing that he is right, and that my past will haunt me for the rest of my life, I try to gain some higher ground in the conversation.

"Well, from my side your conscience is far from clean, and whatever guilt I feel is nothing compared to what you must be carrying around inside yourself, no matter how much you try to hide it. I was only the hired help; the orders were always yours."

McGough seems a little shaken with my words but continues, "Orders, yes Dean, its survival of the fittest so the weak and frail need culling to maintain the natural balance. Your responses are now beginning to question loyalty so retirement may be the best option for you after all."

I lean forward with a level of anger welling inside as McGough speaks, "If you neutralise Burns and find out who he is working for and ensure minimal hostages are killed and, of course, you make it out alive! I will grant your life back, but the chances of you even getting inside the building very remote."

I stare across the table at him, and can tell from his few chosen words that he has already given the order for my execution. I have now become a disposable asset and the future now seems to be set so asking a further request, "I will, of course, need this in writing, just for old time sake old boy?" Smiling across to McGough.

"I will arrange the paper work in the next few hours, and have it emailed across." He growls back with a look of disgust across his face.

I'm sure he is wearing a wire and know that everything is being recorded. I think of one last thing to say that might just save me, and trying to flush him out, I ask, "Well, I'm surprised that you have given up so easily without even so much as a fight, but I still need to give you the final information over the whereabouts of the cash from the sorting house robbery."

McGough's eyes open and light up like floodlights on a football pitch. He takes a few moments to give his answer, "Robbery what robbery, I'm not sure what you are talking about."

"The money sorting house robbery carried out on the August bank holiday weekend. The robbery which I helped carry out with Burns, who I understand was following your direct instructions."

McGough cough's then moves his hand across his shirt clearly switching off a microphone device. He looks at me then replies, "Burns, didn't complete the robbery for me, he is working for someone else." McGough has nervousness in his voice, and the look of fear running through his eyes. He turns, and starts to move away from the table.

"So, if the orders were not from you, which organisation sent them?" I ask confused.

"Perhaps, Burns has been playing a game with you Nash, like he has with us all, as I say you need to find out who he now works for. Goodbye Mr Nash, and I look forward to seeing you back in the UK soon. Watch the flight mind you only have a few hours." He quickly reverses the wheelchair, and moves away from the restaurant. He is clearly shaken by the final discussion.

I watch McGough continue towards the MPV, and see the two agency men assist him back inside the vehicle. One of the men stares across and as they close the doors, and I observe them driving away along with all the other undercover agents who suddenly start to disappear from the areas where they have been waiting. My cover has been compromised in this country, so I need to depart quickly.

After McGough leaves, I walk back to the hotel room knowing that he might give my address, and information to the local police just for fun, but also confirming I have four hours before my flight home. Entering into the room, I lift the bag onto the bed, and begin to check through it, quickly stacking up the cash, passports, and weapons into three neat piles. I know the weapons are no use to me now, as I'm travelling back to the UK, but the cash and passports could be.

Counting the money, there is almost $50,000 Australian dollars, and I know this will be confiscated at customs unless I can arrange a bank transfer. Taking out my mobile, I check on the internet for money converters who can transfer this money forward. As with much of my life, hidden bank accounts are a way of life, so finding a company registered in online transactions is the only option for now. I note down the address and office hours and place the money back into the bag. There are six passports registered in different countries, and all are traceable through the agency, so are not worth keeping for any escape plans, but could be used to throw them off my scent and worth keeping for now. The two handguns, snipers' rifle, Ingram machine gun, and smoke grenades require to be disassembled then wiped down for any prints. Finally, these items will be wrapped in newspapers ready for disposing in general rubbish bins later, but for now they are replaced into the holdall.

I take the blood drenched clothes from last night, and place them into a plastic bag taken from the bin in the room. These will need to be incinerated to hide any of my traces so a small BBQ or fire pit will tidy up these loose ends. Placing the two bags by the main door of the apartment, I take a hand towel from the bathroom, and quickly begin to wipe down the room gradually working towards the door leaving no evidence and just smudged fingerprints. After closing the hotel door with the hand towel to avoid and skin contact, I walk down the stairs, and place the keys into the security drop-box. Waiting for a few seconds, I return back to the Holden ready for the next leg of my journey and unlocking the car the bags are placed into the trunk. I am not fully sure, if McGough men have either fitted a tracker or tampered with the car, so a quick inspection is carried out. Nothing is found out of order and opening the door, I start the engine. Typing in the address of the money transfer office one hundred and fifteen Abbott Street into the sat nav, the system begins to search for the most suitable route. My mind is filled with making sure my connecting flight to Melbourne, and finally towards home are all correct and on time. I pull away from the kerbside parking which is at the opposite side of the road to the apartment building and driving slowly, watch to see if I am being followed.

Continuing away from the coast, and the rows of large private houses, I head inland along Highway forty-four which takes me into the centre of Cairns. The cars sat nav announces I have reached the offices, and stopping fifty metres down the road, I wait for a few minutes in the car, to check any possible threats and any escape routes before climbing out. Locking the doors, and walking to the entrance of the Money Gems offices, there is a small sign in the window that reads 'International money transfers' seen hanging behind the glass in big black writing. Pushing the glass door open, I walk inside the offices, and my eyes are immediately filled with the sight of old, and well used, damaged furniture, and a large ceiling fan slowly rotating and creaking. The office area is dimly lit with a smell of stale cigarettes and mould with light grey venetian blinds hanging by the windows. In the centre of the room is are two large wooden desks with a middle-aged woman sitting behind one, and a fat older man sitting behind the other. To my left is a large well-built man sitting on an old blood red leather sofa who can be seen reading a newspaper, and I guess for sure is the bodyguard. I walk towards the woman who sits painting her broken and damaged fingernails with bright red varnish. She wears a tight leopard print dress, and her dyed blondie hair shows the dark brown roots. The skin on her face is all creased, and shrivelled by the amount of sunbathing abuse she has carried out in the past.

"G'day sport can I help you?" She asks without even lifting her head.

"I would like to send some money via bank transfer to an offshore account." I reply.

"Basic commission is thirty-five per cent plus handling charges and exchange rates." She lifts her head and smiles.

Knowing it's not my money anyway, and I will lose it at customs otherwise, at least I will get something from the deal I reply with, "Yeah, that is fine no issues."

She stops painting her nails, and with a look of shock and points at the fat man, "He will help you." Then gives a fake smile showing her blackened teeth and red lipstick.

Walking over to the man, I take out the cash and place it on his desk. He stares at the cash, and then looks at me saying, "I take it no questions asked." Nodding in agreement, I sit on the chair opposite.

The old man with the last few hairs left for a comb over, scowls at me through his octagonal framed glasses with the arms pressing against the sides of his head. The bottom of the rims rest on his fat cheeks, and he leans over to take the cash. He quickly begins to count it, and after a few minutes replies, "OK, there's $52,000 dollars. I take it you want Stirling so after our commission, and exchange rates you are looking at £20,000 pounds into your bank."

I nod in agreement, as he starts to complete his paperwork by tapping hard on the keyboard entering information.

"Have you got the transaction account details." He asks.

Taking out a small piece of paper from my pocket, I hand over the account number, sort code, account holders name and the international bank codes. The man continues to type in the details as the noise of a chair behind me scraps on the floor, and the woman stands up. Her high heels echo on the laminate flooring as she walks over in our direction.

"Fancy a brew Sidney? How about you Sonny?" She asks.

Sidney nods his head, as I reply *"No thanks I'm fine."*

"Suit yourself Sonny." She walks in the back room in a sensual way trying to show off the remains of her once nice figure. She reaches the kitchen area, and the sound of water starting to fill a kettle can be followed by the noise of cups, and spoon being moved.

"OK sir, the transaction paperwork is completed, I just need you to sign these couple of documents, and we are done." His printer begins to whirr as papers get regurgitated onto his desk. His shaking hand passes the documents over along with a pen as the secretary returns with a big mug of coffee. She lowers it on his desk and spills a few drops on the paperwork.

"There you go Sidders, I'm glad at least someone values my services."

Sidney smiles back at her saying, "Thank you Dorothy."

She then walks over to the bodyguard placing another mug of coffee on the table in front of him giving a big smile clearly trying to impress him with her short dress, trying to show her chest, and legs off as she wiggles her hips walking back to her desk. I notice the guard's reflection in another glass door as he simply lowers his paper, and lifts the drink taking a quick sip.

The look on his face clearly shows he is not impressed, and as he lowers the drink, he rubs his finger through the long handlebar moustache that covers his top lip across his old, and well-defined chiselled face. He gradually looks across in my direction, and I notice he has a false eye in his left socket, which I imagine was probably lost in one of his many battles. After signing the papers with an unreadable scribble, I hand the documents back to Sidney, who with a shaking hand takes them back and places it onto a pile of other transactions that is about eight centimetres thick with signed documents.

I stand, and hold out my hand towards Sidney who a little shocked as he returns the action. Grasping his shaking, sweaty, and clammy hand I say, "Thank you Sidney." The hand is released, and I turn walking out of the office back towards the car.

Reaching the car, I open the door and climb into the driver's side looking back at the office, and I notice the image of somebody standing staring at me through the glass door with a ponytail evident its clear the bodyguard is checking me out. Starting the engine, I reverse out of the parking space and head towards the nearest car wash for cleaning off the blood before I return it, and still needing to dispose of the weapons and blood drenched clothes before I arrive at the airport, I notice a small parking lot with large green waste bins and a BBQ area. Pulling up and stopping, I climb out, and take a good look around to see how many people are around only seeing two families enjoying the morning sunshine. Taking the holdall from the trunk, I walk towards the row of wheeled bins, and throw packages of wrapped gun parts into each bin along with the holdall bag.

Next, I walk over towards one of the BBQ areas with the small bag of clothes, and a few sheets of newspaper, and quickly start a fire placing a few pieces of wood collected from around the ground to give the fire more heat. Once the fire is hot enough, I place the bag of clothes onto the flames that quickly ignite but send some smoke upwards. After a few seconds the smoke reduces, and the only thing left are the burning embers. I sit staring into the crackling dying fire thinking about my next course of action and what to do next. Once the fire is completely out, I brush the now cold ashes to the ground then climb back into the car closing another chapter in my life, as I drive for Cairns airport, and the long journey back to the UK. Arriving at the airport, I leave the hire car at the returns area then continue towards the departure hall entrance doors. Checking the status of my flight, I proceed to the check in counter and as usual try to blend into the crowd. After receiving my boarding pass, I wait in the que for the security with different emotions running through my body.

I sense no guilt whatsoever over killing Shaun's assassin, but begin to feel a release from this life following my meeting with McGough. Once security is cleared, I continue towards the business class lounge, where I try to remain concealed until my flight is called. I start to reflect back over the times that I had shared with Shaun, and understand how he must have felt a level of revenge over me killing Chloe. I also remember back the first time I met Shaun all those years ago in agency training. Shaun's agency class was several years after mine, and I found it strange that even with our drunken nights he never made any mistake to talk about our common agency background. McGough's programme operations management kept a lot of information hidden from the agents, and would challenge agents against each other to complete assignments.

My thoughts are broken by my flight back to the UK being called so leaving the lounge, I continue to the departure gate with my mind now focusing on the next assignment, but deep in the back of mind is how to plan my escape from the grips of McGough. Boarding the flight, I am shown to my seat, and relaxing for the return flight home my mind is filled with, who could I trust, and my thoughts return to an old friend and work colleague, and start to remember the last time we had met during a secret mission called operation Cosma in Hungary back in 1998.

TEN

Operation Cosma Budapest May 1998.

My mind replays the events, and I recall when I had arrived at Budapest airport. Departing from the plane, I continued past the basic rows of shops, and the small cafe then walked down a double staircase to the luggage hall. The airport was fairly quiet for a Tuesday afternoon, with only minimal security seen, and after collecting my luggage, I walked past the passport control counters, and continue through the lower area of the airport to the hire car offices. Reaching the Hertz car rental counter, the paperwork was completed for the pre booked car, and the assistant handed over the keys. Leaving the airport building, I walked underneath the canopy, and continued down the long ramp towards the car parking zone past the lines of waiting taxis.

    Reaching the Volkswagen Golf parked in space C21, I checked the condition of the vehicle then unlocked the doors. The boot was opened, and the bag placed inside. Once the lid was closed remember glancing around before I returned to the driver's side then onto the seat. Switching on the ignition and starting the engine, I have vivid memories of the Garmin Street Pilot GPS sat nav. It was the first digital sat nav I had ever used, but I still took out the road maps just in case. The address for the hotel was typed in, and as the route was calculated, I made the final adjustments to the seat and mirrors, then pulled away from the airport car-park for the two-hour drive. The roads were eerily quiet, as I continued along E341 towards Szekszard with only an occasional passing car and Sat nav instructions for any company.

Reaching the town of Szekszard my instructions were to check into the Zodiac hotel, then wait for the next set of orders that would be delivered. Finding the hotel, I parked the car on the small courtyard area, then climbed out to stretch my back. I removed a pair of walking boots and long black coat from the bag which remained in the trunk, then removed the bag, closed the boot lid, and continued towards the reception for check in. Once all the room card documents were finished, the receptionist handed over the door card, and I walked to the room. Checking the essentials of the room were all OK, I left my bag on the bed, and returned to the outside to assess the situation around the town, and in the late afternoon, tried to find my bearings and locate escape routes, surveillance cameras, and vantage points for observing the target of the operation.

I recollect walking along the cobbled streets, and passing an area with a large white church which was now illuminated with halogen lights to my left, and a bus station on the opposite side of the main road to the right. Behind the bus station were shelters, and a series of small shops interlinked with darkened passageways. Heading towards the first arched passage, I noticed a small car park but unfortunately with access gates padlocking them closed. I continued towards a second arched passageway which lead to a narrow side road, as I reached an area of derelict ground, there were a few cars parked and a small track which lead across some fields. Casually scanning around no camera's or buildings directly overlooked the ground, so this could be a possible escape route. I walked back towards the hotel, and I recall the Nokia 5110 mobile phone which was began to vibrate which confirmed a message has been delivered. As I checked the message it read 'Target still in Budapest No further instructions today.' With the time now close to eight p.m. it was time for some food, and stopping near to a small restaurant, I quickly checked over the basic menu outside and walked inside.

I was greeted by a young man, and I asked in German, "Are you still serving food?"

He replies, "Yes, but we will finish serving by nine p.m." He then shows me to a table, and handed me a copy of the menu.

Sitting at the table, I casually looked around the restaurant which had dark wood doors and flooring, and off-white walls. The ceilings were a light green colour and around the windows were large wooden shutters. There were only a few people in the restaurant eating food that include three men dressed in work clothes, a man, and woman enjoying a dinner, and two more women drinking some wine. The room had very basic décor with simple pictures, and lighting with the faint sound of Hungarian music being played through the speakers hung from the walls. The tables were covered in pure white clothes with red leather placemats, and cutlery neatly placed. As I opened the menu, the waiter returned, and I ordered a glass of local red wine and a jug of water, then decided to order pork fillets in mushroom sauce. The waiter brought the wine and water to the table along with a side plate of some crusty warm bread and butter.

I enjoyed some of the warm bread along with a drink of wine, and remember how hungry I was, as I waited for the food to be prepared and reflected back on the operation, and the target that had been selected.

My mind then drifted back to the briefing for the operation, and I remembered being summoned to one of the interrogation rooms. Waiting in the silent dimly lit corridor outside room three my heart beat remains constant until the voice was heard from the other side of the door, "Enter Nash" The handler instructed.

His words still echo in my ears, and even now nearly three days later, the hairs rose on the back of my neck. I opened the door and entered the room. The handler was sitting close to a small dark wooden table smoking a large cigar, and enjoying a drink of whisky. Lying on top of the table was a brown A4 envelope which was clearly visible from the single table lamp placed in the centre of the table. There was no other light in the room but this illumination, that was enough to see his chiselled facial features.

"Nash, I hear you are ready for the operation?" He asked.

"Yes sir I am all prepared, as I have been trained." I replied submissively standing up straight with my hands at my side like a child in front of a headmaster.

"Hmm, well, we will have to see about that, what happened in Dusseldorf?" He asked taking a large inhalation of his cigar, and blowing out the smoke which caused his face to almost disappear.

"I got the job done sir."

"You certainly did that Nash!" He snapped.

"I do not regret my actions sir; the target was cleaned as requested." I replied.

"Half of the fuckin German secret service too I recall." He raised his voice slightly.

"That was unfortunate but I had planned for worst case."

He lifted his hand, and threw forward the envelope, "Well, better plan for this target Nash he is a diplomat and will have a few bodyguards who could get in the way." I leaned forward, and took the package.

"I was going to send your old friend, but I thought this little task might suit you better. I will not arrange for your extraction this time once you are on your own." The handlers grin could be seen even in the dimly lit room.

"Now, I want the job done for the end of the week, and don't come back if you make the same mess as last time." He snarled.

"Thank you, sir for your words of encouragement." I replied confidently.

"Encouragement!" He stared at me over the top of his reading glasses.

"*Encouragement!*" He repeated.

"Look the only reason I am sending you is for a lesson in doing what you are instructed to do. The only reason I am sending you is to follow my fucking orders and my orders alone. You are not paid to think you are paid to kill and the only *encouragement* you need is that if you don't follow my orders, I will have you fucking killed. Is that encouragement enough!" The handler snapped.

"Yes sir, that is fine, all the encouragement I need. May thanks for the support." I replied back smiling.

"Now get out of my sight." He turned away slightly.

Turning I walked out of the room, and closed the door behind, then a second voice was heard, "He is right sir, he did complete the mission."

"I know he did, but it was nearly a political incident, and that is what I am annoyed about. I can only blame the Russians a few times you know."

"He is the best you know that sir."

"I know, and that is what worries me sometimes he is too good, and I sense he is starting to kill for pleasure." The hander replied.

"Is that a bad thing sir?" The second voice asked..

The reflections of the operation briefing were broken by the young waiter bringing the food, and after not eating for several hours I quickly started to cut up the pork fillets. The food tasted great with lots of flavour, and I devoured the meal along with the wine. After I had paid for the food, I begun the walk back towards the hotel, and as I reached the front car park area, I'm surprised to see my room light illuminated. Knowing full well, that all the lights had been switched off before I had left, thoughts raced through my mind that there was someone inside.

Maybe, room service has prepared the bed for the night, but looking around at the poor quality of the hotel decor that wasn't the answer I was searching for to my question so either someone has been in the room or they are still there. Realising that I hadn't taken ownership of any weapons yet now fills me with a level of both fear and excitement, as I reached the door. I checked the handle, and it was quite clear the door was unlocked, so as I took a big sigh, I begun to open the door slowly with my hand shaking slightly from the adrenalin that rushed through my body.

Gradually, as I entered the room, my heartbeat raced with every footstep and continuing into the small hallway which had a door to the bathroom straight ahead. A second door on the left lead to the bedroom. I recall pausing for a second then tried to listen for any sounds which came from the room, but nothing was heard. I pushed the bedroom door open and looked around the room. I am instantly drawn to the contents from my bag which had been thrown onto the top-sheet of the bed. Suddenly, a noise from the bathroom was heard as the toilet flushed, and quickly lifting a drinking glass from the bedside table, I turned on the spot and positioned myself ready to pounce onto whoever was in there, and I could force the glass into their face. As the bathroom door begun to open a familiar person appeared.

"What the fuck are you doing here, and why have you been searching through all my stuff." I asked with a raised angry voice.

"Now relax Dean, it's not how it looks." He replied holding his hands in the air submissively.

"Christ Chris, you like to live dangerously." I lower the glass.

"What were you going to do with that glass offer me a drink?" He asked.

"I was going to smash it into your face before breaking your neck." I replied.

"If that was your intention then please carry on." He smiled back then both shake hands.

Now immediately relaxed I asked again, "Why have you caused all this mess with my stuff."

"Dean, it wasn't me, I got here about five minutes ago, and found it like this."

"Well, what are you doing here?" I asked.

"McGough, has sent me with your supplies and looking at this mess it's a good job the weapons were not here." We both walked into the bedroom and I pulled together the few clothes.

"I thought no-one else would be here?" I asked.

"I'm just passing through heading towards Austria, to tidy up that KGB mess, and boy what a mess heads will roll for sure."

"Yes, I heard a rumour it all went wrong." I replied.

"So, who do you think has caused this mess?" Chris asked.

"I have a feeling that I had been followed from Munich, where I had a connecting flight so it's probably a rogue agent looking for kicks, but I will catch them."

"Are you all set for the op?"

"Why what's happening here?" Still not fully convinced it wasn't him who had trashed the clothes.

"I thought you were here for operation Cosma?"

This code name is only known to the closest team members of the cardinals, so knowing that Chris was a friend and not foe I replied, "Not happening today but a couple of days so just doing a recki at the moment."

"Still not giving much away hey Dean?"

"That's what we had been taught." I replied.

"True, so shall we get the bag of tricks from the car." Chris asked.

"Yeah, but let me go first in case anyone is watching so I can get a mark on them."

"Are you still going to stay here tonight after someone doing this?" He asked.

"Where else can I go at this time, and besides in a few minutes, I will have some weapons for self-defence."

"OK, let's move." I lifted the empty bag from the bed then opened the door.

Slowly, we walked outside, and I scanned around for any possible movements from curtains flickering in windows or lights being switched off in rooms. I stared across to the windows and doors that overlooked the front of the hotel, and made sure none were being opened or closed suddenly. Finally, I looked for any people who could be standing around outside, maybe, having a last smoke or drink before bedtime. The quietness of the outside had an eerie feeling as we both begun the walk to Chris's car with no-one stirring that was both welcoming, and worrying since the rouge agent could be anywhere. As we continued towards the car parked just at the side of the road, the silence of the night was broken by the occasional passing car, but everything else was quiet with an absence of any people that was strange for a busy city. My senses were on high alert waiting for any threats as Chris unlocked the car then begun to open the trunk. I handed the empty bag across to him as the increasing noise of a car approaching could be heard. Chris clicked open the case full of weapons, and suddenly, a police car is seen making its way towards us.

"Chris, we have company, but don't turn around quickly or they might get suspicious." Alerting him to the forthcoming danger.

"Who is it?" Chris asks

"The police but we are standing next to a car parked by a hotel getting a bag out."

"Not one full of weapons though Dean?"

"Continue filling the bag Chris don't worry."

The headlights of the police car shine in my face, as I casually watch their approach, "They are slowing down Chris, how are you doing with the guns."

"Nearly done just some ammo left. I had it all prepared. The rifle is zeroed to one hundred and fifty metres as per policy so I'm sure you will be able to sort it if a bit more range is needed. OK Dean, done."

Chris leaned back and lifted out the bag slowly, and handed it over to me then closed the trunk. Taking the bag, I instantly notice the increased weight then shake his hand, and said, "OK Chris, thanks for the package now take care and keep safe."

"You too Dean." He replied.

Turning, I headed back towards the hotel with the weapons slightly clinking together caused by every footstep. Noticing that the police car has now continued past where Chris is standing, it then turned around in the street, and at an increased speed drove in the reverse direction with its red and blue lights flashing. Hearing Chris open the driver's door, I turned around and gave him a wave in the barely lit hotel entrance. Chris's face is partly illuminated by the interior light of the car, and as he returns, he waves, and gives me a small smile of friendship wishing me all the best. He climbed inside then closed the door, and as the car engine starts, the noise of Chris driving away could be heard. As I reach the hotel room door, it was opened, and I walked inside placing the heavy bag onto the bed.

Sitting next to the bag, I begun to take out the cold metal weapons, and ammunition placing them onto the bed sheet. A pair of Beretta handguns, and fifty rounds of nine millimetres ammo including four spare clips. An Ingram nine millimetres sub machine gun with three fully loaded magazine clips, and a Mauser 7x62mm snipers rifle separated into the stock, and shortened fluted barrel which was screw cut for a sound moderator. Attached to the action is a tactical day / night vision scope, and with the rifle was the over barrel sound moderator, and forty rounds of ballistic tip ammunition along with a pair of ten round magazines. There was a selection of hand tools and cleaning kits for the guns, and finally six smoke grenades, and four anti-personnel mines with fifty metres of fuse wire. I begin to check through each weapon to ensure all magazines fit correctly and all top slides operate to eject spent bullets and finally I start to assemble the snipers rifle. I realised the time is fast approaching one a.m., so ensuring all weapons were unloaded apart from one of the handguns, I place the guns, and ammo back into the bag then slide one handgun underneath my pillow. After using the bathroom, I double check the door was locked, then leaving the key turned sideways in the mechanism return to the bed for some rest.

Meanwhile, at another area of the city at the Mercops hotel, two police officers leaned against the reception desk talking to the night manager. Both officers were around forty years old with one man quite athletic, and the other a little overweight asking questions, and exchanging small talk conversation to the old man sitting behind the reception.

The larger of the officers asked, "If I decided to bring my wife here for a meal could you arrange a good table, and discount?"

"I'm sure we could offer an excellent meal package Officer." The manager replied trying not to intimate the officer.

The second officer then asked, "So how many customers do you have in the hotel tonight?"

"We have ninety per cent occupancy today, and for the next three nights."

The first officer replied, "Do you have a full list of the clients who have checked in over the last four days?"

The manager replied with a little nervousness in his voice, "Yes, the hotel has to carry that information for administration reasons, but."

"But what?" The officer replied.

"I am not allowed to divulge that information."

The overweight officer leaned forward, and whispered, "You are when a government diplomat is staying here tomorrow so we need a full list of the clients along with their passport information, and which company had made the bookings, and I need it now!"

"I will have to speak with my senior manager to gain permission."

The athletic officer leaned over and lifted the receiver handing it to the old man in an intimidating manner, "Better call him then hey?" The manager took the phone with his slightly shaking hand, and begun to press the buttons, and lifted the receiver to his ear, "Good evening sir, sorry for the late call, but I have two officers from the Diplomatic Protection Service requesting our client lists before the visit of the VIP tomorrow. Can this list along with all passport information be released due to client confidentiality?"

A mumbled voice could be heard, and the manager removes the receiver from his ear then said, "He wants to speak to one of you."

The older officer took the phone and raised it saying, "This is Sergeant Olger Pertrovnic from the DPS."

The officer continued to speak,. "Yes, that is correct we need to check for any possible suspects in readiness for the diplomatic visit."

After a few seconds, the officer smiled, and handed the receiver back to the manager, "He wants to speak to with you again."

Taking the phone, the manager replied with, "Yes, OK sir, I will, as instructed, and sorry for bothering you at this late hour."

The manager replaced the receiver, and begins to tap away on the keyboard, in a few seconds the printer can be heard whirring, as sheets of paper are seen emerging from the machine. The old man turned and reached for the papers handing them to the outstretched hand of the athletic diplomatic officer. The police then turned and walked out of the hotel to a waiting car outside.

My morning begun with the sound of a helicopter flying slow and low over the hotel, I leaned over to reach for the mobile to check for any new messages, and one was delivered twenty minutes ago, which said 'Target had left Budapest will be at the Mercops for one night.' Realising that my window of opportunity is only limited, I needed to check the rifle for accuracy, and finalise the killing zones along with the any safe escape routes. The hotel itself would be very heavily guarded along with the entry and exit roads, but if I could get inside then this could be an option. Trying to hit the target in the car would be difficult being a single person unless the car is damaged. Another message is delivered, 'Four-man team plus driver with two cars on diplomatic plates.' Reading the message, I got up and prepared for the long day ahead which started with a simple breakfast. Leaving the room, I walked across the small forecourt, and entered the small basic restaurant. Looking around there were trays of orange juice by the glass, and a coffee machine where you selected your drink. To the far right was a counter with a basic selection of salami meats, cheeses and bread rolls. Taking a plate, I removed some of the cheese, and meats then walked to an empty table. Returning to the machine, I made a coffee and collected an orange juice.

After eating the breakfast, I returned back to the room, and changed into some more suitable clothing. Taking the bag, I left the room, and headed for the car unlocking it with the key fob and lowered the bag into the trunk. Closing the lid, I opened the driver's door, and slid onto the seat as a helicopter passed over again clearly completing any overhead surveillance. Starting the engine, I drove away from the hotel and the city heading for an area, where I can test the rifle accuracy.

Looking at the distances, that I may need to fire the rifle at, it needed to be zeroed for about four hundred metres that would give enough range out to six hundred metres. I continued along the M5, until I noticed a small side road that lead to a large forest. Pulling into the gateway, I noticed an old rusty gate barely hanging from the posts with a sign in Hungarian, I climbed out and walked around to the rear of the car, and listened for a few minutes, with the only sounds being that of the slight wind rustling branches and a few sheep bleating in a distant field. Opening the boot lid, I took out the longish black jacket, and passed my arms into the sleeves then reached for the pair of lightweight walking boots and changed my footwear still listening and waiting.

Confident that the area is clear, the rifle was removed from the bag, and slipped underneath the long black jacket. An old beer can and glass bottle had been thrown into the gateway so bending down to pick them up, I continued into the forest looking for an area, where I can set up the targets with a sufficient backstop. After walking around for ten minutes, a suitable area was seen inside the forest where the targets can be set onto a small mound of earth with a good backstop. The box of bullets was taken from my pocket, and I walked away from the targets counting the strides in the straightest line possible. Once four hundred is reached, I turned and looked back at the two small targets against the brown leaf backdrop. The rifle was removed from under the coat, and leant against a nearby tree, while I loaded the bullets into the magazine. The rifle was lifted, and I looked down the telescopic sight taking aim at the beer can lowering the cross hairs onto the centre of the can. Confident in the position, I pushed the magazine into the rifle, and retracted the bolt allowing a bullet to be loaded into the chamber. Composing my breathing, the safety catch was clicked forward and the trigger pulled.

 I recall watching through the scope as a puff of brown dust erupted as the bullet struck the ground just below the can. The muffled metallic sound echoed from the shot, and a small amount of white smoke rose into the air from the end of suppressor. I noticed the horizontal plane looked good, so I adjusted the elevation by a number of clicks. The empty bullet case was placed into my pocket and another round was loaded, as I constantly listened for any people. This time taking aim I re-fired, and the beer tin jumped into the air with a ping as the bullet round strikes home. Knowing that the bullet hit the target, I reloaded another round, and aimed for the neck of the glass bottle.

 The shot was taken again, and the glass fractured with a breaking sound as the top of the bottle disappeared leaving enough of the main body for a second bullet to be fired, and sure enough the zeroing looked fine. I unload the magazine, and then walked over to the targets carrying the rifle, but made sure all the cases were counted. I scrapped a small hole into the earth with the heel of the boot, and pushed the broken glass and beer tin into the ground, and recovered the soil hiding any evidence. Knowing that the rifle was accurate gives a higher level of confidence, and as I placed it back under the coat, I continued back through the forest and returned towards the direction of the parked car. I remember waiting a few minutes, and watching a pair of red fox cubs playing running around, and chasing each other before I moved closer to the car in case anyone was close by. Hearing that all was clear, I unlocked the car, and then returned the rifle to the bag. After changing the shoes and removing the coat, I started the car engine, and begun the journey back to my hotel. I need to check out the Mercops hotel so returning back to the city, I parked near my hotel, and took a casual stroll along the pavement that passes by the Mercops hotel to view the threat level.

As I approached the road, two police cars could be seen clearly guarding the main entrance road near the main doors of the lobby, and as I continued past them, a dark blue Audi A8 was parked very close to the pavement which had light blue diplomatic number plates. A man dressed in a smart suit leaned on the side of the car having a cigarette, and flicked the ash across the roof. He was about thirty-five years old with an amount of designer stubble. I noticed he was wearing a shoulder holster for a pistol. I as looked into the hotel lobby, two more guards could be seen sitting in the reception area again about thirty-five years old, and well-built, but there were two guards missing, they must be the close protection team. Finally, I noticed a third police car parked on a parallel side street which covered the rear entrance. It was evident that the information on the five guards appeared to be correct, but there were at least four more police officers protecting the target so hitting him here will not be easy.

I crossed the road, and walked towards a small antique shop that was almost opposite the hotel. I looked into the window of the shop, but not at the items for sale, instead I was using the reflection from the glass to look at building behind checking out the windows, and as I looked upwards, confirmed that the buildings close by all have similar flat roof designs. A message was delivered to my mobile which read

'Photographic evidence is required of the kill.' I read the message, and took a deep sigh, this now completely changed using a sniper's rifle and in order to get evidence I needed to be close, and this would mean only one thing direct contact.

A ground floor level assessment of the buildings, and its layout would take several hours, and was needed for any closer access to the target, but with the police and protection teams in close proximity it would be difficult for this late change of plan. I needed to get close enough, but the protection team will already have a list of the staff members employed. I continued to look into the reflection of the window as an opportunity presented itself. A man could be seen exiting the rear of the hotel, and from his clothing I could see he was a janitor. He must be finishing his morning shift, as he begun to walk along the street. Following at a distance, I noticed that he is a similar build, and age to me, and I continued for around fifteen minutes, and then stopped next to a three-storey building. He opened the front door and continued inside, as I casually walked past the building. I noticed the mailbox on the front wall having three flat numbers and names.

I turned and walked towards the direction of my hotel via the Mercops. When I was one hundred, and fifty metres away from the main entrance of the Mercops, the target and all the bodyguards were seen protecting him as he climbed into the back of the blue Audi car. My heart sunk to think that he is already leaving, but I have not seen any luggage being loaded into the car. The car drove away with one police car at the front and one to the rear. A third police car stayed at the car park, so I hoped that the target would be returning soon. I now had a full image of the target and what he looks like in the flesh.

Knowing I cannot do anything more for a few hours, and hunger was beginning to call, I see the signs for a restaurant called the Bella Napoli with an Italian flag hanging outside, and an illuminated red neon sign hung in the window which said they were *'OPEN.'* I walked through the open doorway, and as I entered the restaurant my eyes were immediately greeted by a long brick lined arched room, and it instantly reminded me of an underground bunker.

The sombreness of the dimly lit space the atmosphere was broken by the sound of Italian music playing. The waiter showed me to a table, and asked what you would like to drink, as I sat down before beginning to read the menu. A diet coke was ordered, and my mind quickly drifted to the contract that needed to be completed tomorrow. As with many other times the thought of this possibly being my last meal pales into insignificance the feeling of just another day at the office for anyone else. Selecting my starter and main course, the waiter returned with my ordered drink and my food choice was written down. The escape routes are replayed in my head along with the image of the old man seen in the street. His main facial features confirmed that, it concurred with the information and picture from the Cosma folder of the target.

Next were the defining features of the close protection body guards. There was a woman about thirt-five years who seemed to be very close to the target. The second guard was a man with designer stubble about two metres tall with a well-built body about thirty-eight years old. This guard looked as though he could probably be able to handle himself in a fight. There were two more bodyguards both about thirty-five which again both looked very tough, and I had already seen the final guy who was the driver, and I'm sure would have access to any additional weapons in blue diplomatic plated Audi A8.

A plan is being formulated in my head which would give me the maximum chance of success, and the only open point was what was noticed today, all the body guards seemed to be very relaxed, and this could well be there downfall but everything now depended on the janitor. After finishing my food, I returned to my hotel room and then laid on the bed. I ran through different scenarios of the plan in my thoughts, but some of the plan needed to remain flexible and adapt to the situation that could unfold in-front of my eyes. Some of my old training techniques started to filter through the ideas, but the main instruction was to *'blank out any emotions for the victims'* along with the final set of orders *'Failure is not an option.'* burnt deep into my soul. The reason for the target being selected for elimination was never discussed, but equally, it is probably better not to know. Thoughts returned to the target folder which showed pictures of his wife, the family, and any close friends. I remember trying to plot possible interception ideas which I could have used to gain leverage, but the opportunity to kill the target cleanly was always the easier option. The body guards would always be present so taking them when there are only local police to support would be simpler than if the hit would have been closer to his home or working office.

Arising from the bed, a handgun and silencer were removed from the bag along with a pair of thin black gloves and a lock picking kit. The room was exited, and I continued onto the street and headed in the direction of the janitors flat. I needed certain items from the janitor, and as I reached the building, I looked up to confirm that the lights inside the flat were switched on and I took the pair of thin gloves from my pocket, and pulled them onto my hands. Stopping at the main entrance door, a lock picking case was removed, and various tools inserted into the mechanism. After a few seconds, the door lock opened and I continued towards his flat not knowing what could be waiting inside. As I walked up the stairs, the silencer is attached to the barrel of the handgun and returned to my jacket pocket. As I reached the flat entrance door, I paused for a few seconds, and listened outside the apartment with the only sound heard that of a television playing inside.

This should hopefully mask any noise that might be made as the lock picking tools were inserted into the door mechanism and a faint clink was felt as the door was now free to be opened. The handgun was removed from my jacket, and the lock picking tools were placed back into my pocket, as I gradually begun to push the front door open.

I remember the music from the television was being played quite loudly, as I continued into the flat. My heartbeat was elevated, but my concentration was completely focused on any possible threats from inside the apartment. Directly in-front of me was a very small hallway with wooden flooring which lead down into what appeared to be the living room at the far left. To my direct left was an off-white coloured door which had a small picture of a cartoon seagull attached to it. The hallway was light blue colouring to the walls and ceilings, and I recall a noise could be heard opposite to the living room doorway which sounded like a saucepan, and I assumed this must be the kitchen. Gradually moving forward, I reached the kitchen doorway and heard water beginning to run from a tap and slowly moved around the doorway and there was the janitor with his back to me as he stood by the sink.

He was dressed in casual jeans and a white tee shirt and was completely unaware of my presence. Knowing that I only required his ID badge and uniform, I fired a bullet round into the back of his head, and he dropped quickly to the ground with blood spattered against the wall above the sink. I continued through into the living room which then lead into the bedroom of the apartment to check for any other people, but I could see from the clothes hanging in the wardrobe, and items in the apartment that he lived alone. I took his uniform and ID badge which were in the bedroom, and returned to the living room, and reduced the sound on the TV to ensure no neighbours complained.

I walked back into the kitchen, and switched off the oven avoiding the blood pool that was already seeping out from the gunshot to his head, and recall suddenly, hearing what appeared to be a woman walking in high heels in the direction of the apartment. My heart stopped, as the keys were heard being pushed into the door lock mechanism. I only had a few seconds, and quietly walked into the bathroom then stood behind the main door. The entrance door to the apartment was opened, and then the footsteps entered the hallway. The clicking of high heels was heard as the person passes the bathroom and continued down the hallway. I slowly lifted the handgun, and gradually begun to open the door. The person could be seen entering the living room, and I quickly shot her in the back of the head.

She dropped sideways, and hit several of the pictures that were hanging on the hallway wall, and my heart missed a beat, as she then dropped to floor as the picture frames clinked against the wooden flooring. I recognised that the woman was in several of the pictures which now lay around her, and must either be his girlfriend or a family member. I cannot afford to be seen leaving any living witnesses, so I knew that there was no choice other than to kill her. Checking that she was dead, I exit from the apartment close, the entrance door and continued back down the staircase towards the direction of the building entrance door. Leaving the apartment block, I headed back to my hotel, and felt no remorse or regret for the two assassinations which have just been performed. We were trained that nothing can affect any operation from becoming a success, so the death of civilians was unfortunate but part of the job. Compassion was not allowed and was always classed as a weakness during training, and recalled that during training several candidates were removed from the programme due to this weakness and died in the line of duty.

My hotel room was reached, and I start to get mentally prepared for the assassination tomorrow morning along with any problems that could arise from trying to flee the country. I ran through the plan over and over in my head, as I fell to sleep. Awaking the next morning, at four thirty a.m., I quickly gathered all my belongings together. The room needed to be wiped down, and the car had to be moved to the safe place so it was easier to escape. I had decided to park the car on the waste ground near the back of the town, and this would allow me enough time to slip away easily once the target was cleaned. Getting dressed into the janitor's uniform, the silenced handgun was removed from the weapons bag and a magazine was loaded in to the handle, and the safety catch was applied.

I placed the gun into a small rucksack which was taken from the janitors flat, and then a small fixed blade knife was also removed from the weapons bag, I checked the sharpness of the cutting edge then return it to the holster, and it was pushed behind my trouser belt. Finally, three small grenades were removed from the weapons bag, and placed inside the rucksack. The janitor's rucksack had a small metal thermos flask which was taken out and checked, it contained some homemade goulash which was still warm. The flask was then returned to the bag, and the final part of the disguise was to change the picture on the janitor's ID badge to myself. Sticking a passport picture onto the ID badge, I hung the lanyard around my neck, and looked into the mirror and checked all the main elements of the disguise. The weapons bag was taken out to the car along with the small rucksack and my clothes bag.

All were placed onto the rear seat, and I remember the freshness of the air in the morning, and wished I had a coat. Checking through my clothes bag, I found a thin jumper, and pulled it over my head. The car engine was started, and the heaters were turned on. The vehicle was driven away from the hotel car park, and I headed towards the waste land at the edge of the town which was only a couple of minutes away, but would give me an advantage if the town is suddenly became locked down.

Pulling the car onto the waste ground, I recall the gravel surfaces made a rustling sound, and I stopped the car to look around for any signs of people that could have been watching. No window lights or people were seen, so I climbed out of the car and took the rucksack from the rear seat, and then locked the car. As I walked back into the town, I casually kept glancing around for any signs of other people moving around in the darkness of the morning. I reached the rear entrance of the Mercops hotel and noticed that there was one police car parked just down the road, and two diplomatic plated cars were parked close by to the hotel entrance. The police car had two men which were sitting inside, and each of the diplomatic cars had a driver waiting. The targets seven series BMW was parked inside the compound of the hotel, and as I walked in the direction of the rear entrance of the hotel, a diplomatic bodyguard suddenly appeared from the shadows smoking a cigarette.

"Can I help you?" He asked in Hungarian.

"I am the janitor starting my shift." I replied holding out the ID badge.

He took out a pocket torch and shone it into my face then looked at the badge. Next, he lifted a radio and made a call. I noticed, he was about mid-forties and his face had a very bad complexion of heavy pitted indentions from acne in a younger life.

"Confirm Petre Polvanic as Janitor?" I heard him ask.

"Confirmed he is on the clearance list." He stared at me again trying to intimidate me as he allowed me to pass, then he took another large inhalation of his cigarette.

I nodded my head submissively then started to walk away.

"What is in the bag?" He asked.

"My lunch." I replied quickly, and continued towards the rear doors of the hotel.

I sensed he was walking behind, but didn't stop, until I had reached the doorway. I stopped, and turned around and removed the flask from the rucksack.

"Do you want to try some of my homemade Goulash?" I asked.

He snatched the flask from my hands, and unscrewed the lid to sniff at the contents, "Ah just like what my grandma made in the past." He smiled, gave me the flask back then turned, and walked away.

I returned the flask to the rucksack and walked into the hotel past an emergency floor plan map of the building. I quickly took important details from the map which were the same as the information already supplied from the operation briefing. I continued towards the main workers locker area just down the corridor from the main kitchens. I walked past the kitchens, and through to the staff locker area to check the list of any jobs that the janitor may need to complete. Checking through the VIP clients, I see the target is in room two hundred and fourteen, and there is work required in room two hundred and nine which was along the same corridor. Collecting the trolley, I placed the tool bag onto the trolley along with the room access keys and my rucksack, then began my way towards the service lifts. Opening the door into the main hotel lobby, I noticed there was a diplomatic bodyguard leant over the main reception counter talking to the pretty young girl by the desk. I recall when he looked across but he didn't seem very interested.

This was the second weakness that I have seen with this team. Reaching the service lift, I pressed the button for the second floor, and entered through the doorway. The doors slid shut, and I removed the handgun from the bag and pushed the pistol behind my trouser belt as the lift was moving. The doors '*pinged*' and then slowly opened.

I began to walk out of the service lift and looked quickly at the room signs attached to the wall opposite the lift entrance, the direction arrow pointed left towards two hundred and fifteen, so I turned slowly, and could I see two more bodyguards sitting on chairs outside room two hundred and fifteen, which was at the end of the short corridor. Both men instantly stared at me, as I begun to walk in their direction. I recall reaching room two hundred and nine and knocked on the door to make sure there were no occupants inside, then I took the access card, and swiped it across the door lock section activating the mechanism with a whirring sound. Entering into the room, the door was left open, and I remember from the job board that a ceiling bulb required changing. Switching on the lights, I found the bulb which was broken, and I placed a chair underneath so that I could climb onto the seat to complete the exchange. Just then a voice is heard.

"Excuse me." I look at the doorway, and see one of the bodyguards standing in the doorway,

"Yes, can I help you?" I replied looking at her dark brown short hair and blue eyes. She was wearing a shoulder holster for the handgun underneath her dark grey suit jacket.

"The guest in room two hundred and fifteen has an issue with the television controls I wondered if you could help?"

"I could certainly have a look, I'm sure it may be something simple. I'll finish this job then be right over."

She smiles, turns then leaves. I can't believe my luck to be asked to enter the room where the target was, this was their third mistake. Quickly completing the bulb change, I then replace the chair, and close the door to room two hundred and nine, and start to walk down the corridor.

The bodyguards are now standing each side of the door waiting for me to arrive. I walked down the corridor and slowly removed the pistol from behind my back and casually placed it onto the trolley underneath a white rag. I had already clicked off the safety catch in readiness to use it.

The male bodyguard lifted his hand, and said, "Could I check your ID badge?"

"Certainly, I replied, your friend outside checked it before I entered the hotel at the start of my shift." I held the ID badge for him to look at.

Then he knocked on the door, "Sir the janitor is here to check the television?"

"It's about time." I hear from the other side of the door in a rough old Hungarian voice.

The chain was removed from the door, and it began to open. I started to push the trolley into the doorway, and then the male bodyguard said, "You will not need your trolley to tune the TV?" and placed his foot by one of the wheels.

"What happens if it is an electrical fault?"

"Then you come back to the door, and we will hand you the tools you require. We have an important client inside, and we can't just allow you to walk inside."

"OK fine." I replied.

"Signa, complete a body check of him." He asked.

"Lift your hands." She said then she started to check my arms, legs, and around my body, she didn't even feel the small knife under my belt.

"Take your mobile out, and leave it on your trolley?" The male bodyguard instructed.

"Yes sir." I replied.

I entered the room and can remember seeing clothes all over the floor along with bottles of beer and some drinking glasses. The bed was a complete mess, and I recall there was the smell of women's perfume still hanging in the air. An elderly man walked out of the bathroom with a white towel wrapped around his waist, and pointed at the television set then returned to the bathroom. I instantly recognised that this was the target. I walked over to the TV, and turned slightly to see that the main door had been left open, and the body guards stood staring at me. I lifted the TV remote controller which was on the top of the bed-sheets and switched on the appliance. The screen was all fussy with no clear picture, so I pressed the source button and could see that the target had selected the wrong input signal. I noticed there was a small handgun on the bedside cabinet closest to the bathroom along with a pair of women's black tights that looked similar to the ones worn by the women bodyguard. He had clearly kept himself entertained last night.

I bent down, and looked for the TV cable, and started to track it along the carpet edge towards the bedside cabinet. I noticed his clothes are already laid out on a chair to wear today which included a red tie, blue shirt and dark grey suit. Quickly lifting the small handgun, I checked it had a full magazine, and loaded a bullet into the chamber. The gun was then pushed behind my trouser belt, and I walked back towards the television. I pressed the remote controller button again, and restored the picture.

The target walked out of the bathroom again combing the last few hairs on his head, and said in a gruff voice, "It's about time, what was wrong with the dam thing?"

He stood in-front of me still wrapped in the white bath towel with his hands on his hips, and large pot belly which hung over the towel like an elephant's ear.

"Sir, the cable was loose by the wall, it is reconnected now."

He grunted at me then walked away. I began to walk towards the door as the male bodyguard turned his back to me that was the last mistake this team would make.

Close to the door was a small armchair with two thick cushions, I quickly grabbed one cushion, and held it behind my back. Removing the gun with my other hand, I made sure the safety catch was released then reached the door, and placed the gun inside the cushion acting as a sound suppressor. The male bodyguard was shot in the back of the head with blood and brain matter hitting the wall opposite, and he fell forwards. Quickly reaching for my handgun from the trolley, I shot the female bodyguard in the chest then fired another bullet round into her head. I fired a second round into the male bodyguard, and then turned around and took my mobile phone from the trolley. I walked back into the suite room and closed the door behind me and continued towards the bathroom. Suddenly, he walked out and sees me holding a handgun at his head.

"Please, please don't kill me, there is $100,000 cash in that case over there which has untraceable serial numbers, take all of it and please leave me alone." He dropped to his knees, and tries to sob.

"I have a family and need to be here for them." He said.

"This is not about money, and I'm sure your wife knows about your infidelities, you have upset the balance of the cardinals, and in doing so have been placed on the list."

He looks up at me with a tear in his eyes just as a bullet round is fired into the centre of his forehead. He collapsed to the carpet, and I fire two more rounds into his head then two rounds were fired into his chest. Next, I make safe the handgun, and place it back behind my trouser belt, and removed the mobile phone from my pocket. Taking a pair of latex gloves from my pocket, his body was moved so that he was lying on his back. Several pictures of him were then taken, and I walked over to the bag of money. There were ten bundles of notes each with a bank seal which reads $10,000. Two bundles of cash were removed from the case, the I sea split and then the cash was thrown around the room, onto the bed and finally some on the dead body which hopefully would make it look like a robbery.

Having the remaining cash staring back at me, I removed eight bundles of bank notes from the case and placed it into my trouser pocket, and then made my way towards the door. Opening the door, I looked at the condition of the two body guards outside, then turned the trolley around and continued back down the corridor towards the service lift with my work complete. After returning the trolley in the locker room area, the small rucksack is removed and continued back outside into the daylight of the morning.

The first bodyguard which stopped me earlier had his back to me, as I approached him, so I removed the pistol and fired a single round into the back of his head. He dropped forward, and landed face down onto the ground, I took out the flask of goulash, and poured it over him then dropped the vessel near to his body.

I walked quickly back onto the side street then continued towards the direction of the area where my hire car was parked. Reaching the wasteland area, I opened the car door and climbed inside then started the engine and placed the rucksack onto the front passenger seat. Looking into the rear-view mirror, I see my exit is clear and began to drive away. Suddenly, as I started down the old track, the rear window of the hire car shatters with a hole evident from a bullet round which had hit the centre of the screen. Another bullet round hits the passenger headrest so pressing the accelerator downwards to gain distance I continued with my escape. The pinging sound of another bullet punching a hole into the rear car body was heard followed by the distant sound of police sirens. I continued along the lane, and recall looking to my left seeing several police cars being driven at high speed from the direction of the town centre heading towards my position. A bullet round strikes the car again and looking into my side mirror, a person can be seen standing on the roof of a six-floor office building. The distance between the sniper, and myself must be at nearly two kilometres range.

My main focus at this time was to head towards the direction of the motorway network in an attempt to reach Budapest airport, and my flight home before the country is on lockdown, but the car was damaged, and there was a bag full of guns on the back seat so my best option was to escape before the airports are closed. I already had an outbound flight booked for ten thirty a.m., so I should have had plenty of time to reach the airport. The hire car could be dropped off at the airport parking with nothing traceable to me.

As I started to reach the slip road for the E71 which joins the M7 motorway, police cars could already be seen waiting in the distance so quickly turning the wheel, I continued along route seven which was a parallel road but smaller with hopefully less police presence. As I drove along Route seven a red car could be seen in my rear-view mirror overtaking other vehicles in pursuit. There were no police lights flashing, but with a rear window shattered my vehicle was quite obvious and easy to track. Watching the approaching car, I could see that there was a man driving and with no other passengers evident.

I recall the chasing vehicle suddenly sped up, and crashed into the rear of my car which pushed my vehicle forward slightly. The chasing car increased speed once more, and then tried to push my car towards the edge of the highway, but I sensed his actions and depressed the accelerator ramming into the car in front of myself which quickly pulled to the side. It was now becoming clear that it will not be as easy, as I thought escaping out of Budapest. I checked the time for my flight and saw that I did not have much time for this vain attempt of pushing me from the road. I took a handgun, which was resting on the passenger seat then started to slow down, and the red car immediately began to try, and overtake me. As he tried to pass me, I used the handgun and fired several bullet rounds into his car. Blood splatters could be seen on the windows, and I knew that he was hit. I managed one final shot and hit him in the neck, and his car violently swerved and hit an approaching lorry on the opposite land with a head on collision which caused the car to explode on impact. Flames and debris, touched the side of my car, as I drove past.

My car began to fill with the smell of diesel fuel and burning rubber, and I knew, I needed to ditch the car and carry on with my journey, but the distance to the airport was still over forty kilometres. I checked the time again and quickly realised that I would not be able to make the flight. Suddenly, the front windscreen shattered, and a burning sensation was felt in my left shoulder and looked across to see that I had been shot. Seeing a small side road, I pulled off to the right, and then managed to stop the car near to a couple of trees that could help with cover. Another bullet hit the side of my car, and I reckoned that the sniper from earlier has found me again and needed to be stopped. I climbed out of the passenger side of the car, and used the car as protection, as I started to move towards the rear of the vehicle. I recollect the sniper shooting out the vehicle side window that sent glass particles flying everywhere, but the sniper had made one big mistake, I now knew their position and from the clothing it was the same person from the roof top earlier. Opening the rear passenger door, I managed to reach inside, and took out the holdall which held the rifle inside.

The sniper took a couple more shots, whilst I quickly assembled the rifle, but their time will soon be over. Loading a magazine into the rifle action, the operating handle was pulled back, and a bullet round was loaded into the chamber. Slowly the rifle was lifted so that the barrel protruded slightly through the smashed glass. I looked through the telescopic sight and could see the sniper approximately seven hundred and fifty metres away from me near the centre of a road bridge trying to hide amongst the metal framework. Already knowing that the rifle is zeroed, I checked the wind direction, and made the final adjustments with the magnification.

Another random shot was heard hitting the car, and as they start to reload a fresh bullet into the chamber their hand movements gave away the final details that were needed. The safety catch was unclicked and looking through the telescopic sight the cross hairs were aligned onto the main target, the sniper's head. I could now see more details of the person, and it was a man in his early thirties. He was wearing a black Bennie hat and dark clothing and looking at his face, I could see he had a strong shaped chiselled chin. With a final breath the trigger was squeezed and I watched the bullet round strike the sniper just above his top lip, and I watched the blood and brain matter erupt from the back of his head, and then watched his body gradually collapse.

The opportunity to catch the flight was now a becoming a distant thought, as I removed the clothes from the car along with the first aid kit. I placed them into the rucksack, and I took out another magazine clip for the pistol and removed a smoke grenade from the bag. The pin was pulled from the grenade, and I walked away slightly throwing the grenade through a broken window of the car. The vehicle caught fire quickly, and my plan was to burn most of the evidence including my blood stains from the driver's seat.

I needed to check the wound in my shoulder, and find somewhere that I could lay low, until I worked out the next options for an escape. The first option now would be to head into Budapest city by using public transport or a taxi to try and find a hotel to rest for a few hours. I started to walk back towards the main road in the hope of maybe, catching a bus or a taxi, and after several minutes, I managed to flag down a taxi.

"Where do you want to go?" The driver asked.

"Into Budapest city, I am looking for a hotel to stay tonight?" I replied.

"My brother manages Hotel Canada next to the main train station, I'm sure he may have a room?"

"Yes, no problem, it would suit near the train station," I answered.

I opened the rear passenger door, and climbed into the taxi, and leaned back into the rear seat and noticed a booklet of train time tables. The schedule was taken out, and I began to look through the timetables to see the easiest way out of Hungary. There were several options to look travelling to Vienna so placing my head against the seat headrest, I watched the world go by from the windows, and reflect on the morning events.

I could feel my shoulder already aching from the bullet wound, and needed to remove any cloth fragments, the bullet round and then try to stop the bleeding, before I can travel without being noticed. After almost an hour of driving, the taxi stopped outside Hotel Canada, the driver climbs out along with myself, and we both then walked inside to the main lobby.

"Hello, Hotel Canada, ah, Mr Petrov, how can I help you?" The man behind the counter asked.

The taxi drive replied, "Hello do you have a room for this client and is my brother David available?"

"One moment please, I will just check."
The man on the reception used the desk phone and called somebody, and a person entered from a back office. The taxi driver smiled, and

gave the man a big hug. I could hear them say brother and started to laugh at each other.

"Yes, of course, we have a room." The manager replied.

"What name shall I use on the reservation?" The manager asked.

"Joerg Schmidt please." I replied.

"Because it is before midday, you will need to pay for an additional night. It that a problem?" He asked.

"Yes, that is fine." I answered handing over my fake passport.

The manager started to write in a large leger, and works out the cost for the room then said, "The bill is 23,500 Forint." I hand him over Ft 25,000 in cash.

The taxi driver saw the money, and said, "Hey don't forget my taxi journey, it is 12,500 Forint. I removed another Ft 15,000 from my wallet and gave it to the taxi driver who quickly took the cash and walked away smiling.

The manager took my cash, and then walked in the rear office, leaving the man behind the counter who could speak little German. He wears round rimmed reading glasses and his hair had been shaven, I noticed a small tattoo on his hand as he handed over the room reservation document and asked, "You need to complete this visitors card registration."

I took the card and pen, then gradually looked around the lobby, and saw a black vinyl two-seater settee behind me. As I completed the paperwork for the room, a young woman exited from the lift began to walk in my direction. I casually watched her, and recall her bright orange skin tight skirt and black lace top. Her long wavy black hair was quite messy, and she looked as though she had just risen from a bed.

Finally, I noticed the high heeled black Sillitoe shoes with lacing around her ankle and lower calves, and at that moment, I realised she was a prostitute looking for new business. Her eyes stared through me as she walked to the settee and sat down. She continued to look at me in a provocative manner. but I am far being interested in her at this time. After I had received the room key which was attached on a piece of chain, I made my way to the lift still sensing that the woman was still watching me.

The doors opened, and I recollect being greeted by a bright red carpet that was covered in dried chewing gum and other black stains. As I walked inside, I pressed the button for the fourth floor, and turned to see the prostitute walking over towards the reception as the doors juddered shut. The lift kicked into life banged against the sides, as it travelled up the shaft. Reaching the fourth floor the doors slowly opened to reveal a dark musty smelling corridor, and as I stepped out there was more red carpet covered in black stains. The lights in the corridor were dirty with cobwebs and broken glass shades, as I continued along the floor looking for room four hundred and fourteen.

I pushed the key into the door lock, and the turned the mechanism, then pushing the door open, I remember my ears instantly being filled with the noise of flies which could be heard from inside the room. Switching on the lights the room overlooked the main train station, but this view was obstructed by a yellow tinted net curtain which hung from a broken rail. I walked across the threadbare carpet, and closed the heavy red velvet curtains before placing my rucksack onto the bed.

The white sheets were covered in small insects just waiting for me to venture inside, but I walked into the bathroom and taking one of the towels from the rail, walked back into the bedroom, and begun to swot the flies with the towel killing as many as possible.

After brushing the insects onto the carpet, I returned to the bathroom with the first aid kit from my rucksack and removed my clothes. I needed to attend to the wound on my shoulder, so switching on the shower, I removed a hand towel from the radiator and ripped it along its length to make two long strips, then after removing my clothes stood inside the cubicle to check the condition of the injury, I could feel that the bullet has actually missed the bones and hit the muscle underneath my shoulder blade. I felt around to my back and could sense that the bullet had passed through the body which meant there was less change of infection.

Gritting my teeth, I placed my index finger into the bullet hole to check if there was any debris inside or any broken bone but feeling nothing knew it was not a serious wound. Blood ran out of the wound and down my body, and as I looked down could remember seeing that the white shower cubicle tray had turned red. Fighting against the sensation of pain and feeling faint, I cupped some water in my right hand, and tried to tip it into the wound making sure it had been washed out. Stopping the shower, the injury was now throbbing, and I taking one of the ripped strips of towelling, I tighten it around my armpit and shoulder in an attempt to make a tourniquet before drying off my body.

Taking out two pieces of gauze and a self-adhesive dressing from the first aid kit, I covered the gauze with some of the antiseptic cream then stood facing the bathroom mirror. Removing the towel tourniquet, I could see that the bleeding had eased enough to quickly place the gauze, and dressing onto the entrance hole of the wound then turning slightly, repeated the same task for the exit injury. Finally, I used the second towel strip to complete the bandage for now. I will need to get the holes sewn at a later date, but wanted to ensure there is no infection, and that I could travel without being noticed. I walked back into the bedroom, and remembered opening the door to see cockroaches running around on the carpet attempting to flee from me.

After getting dressed, I lay onto the bed, and closed my eyes with the sound of the road traffic, trains and people's voices filling the room from the broken windows on the room. The trains passing by the hotel rumbled along the track causing the windows and doors to rattle, as I began to think about an exit plan, and the only real option now would be to catch a train direct to Vienna, where I could then plan a flight home. Hunger started to overtake my body, so I rung down to the reception and asked what could be available. The man replied that there is no food at the hotel but he could arrange for a meal to be delivered.

I ordered a simple Margaretta pizza and after about twenty minutes of waiting, there was a knock on the hotel door. Taking the handgun from the rucksack, I walked towards the door and lifted the small flap on the peep hole to see a delivery man standing with a large hot bag and the name of a pizza restaurant on his clothing. I slowly stood to one side of the door, and began to unlock the catch holding the pistol with my opposite hand.

I opened the door fully, and I could hear a woman's voice further down the corridor and as the delivery man handed over the pizza. The prostitute from earlier walked past my room smiling in a provocative manner. I stared at her with no emotion then paid the delivery man and simply closed the door. My time at the hotel was now limited, so I needed to eat and move quickly, overhearing her conversation I knew she was being asked for information over clients at the hotel. Whilst eating the pizza, I noticed the train timetable in the room, and checked the station opposite at Soroksari Ut, where I could catch a train to Vienna. Finishing the food, I packed the rucksack then quickly gathered all the clothes and towel which had my blood on them. I removed the plastic liner from the bin and placed everything inside. After wiping down any remaining blood from the bathroom, I left the room and headed towards the lifts. I had a new plan in my mind to catch the thirteen forty-five p.m. train from platform six and checking my wrist watch I had nearly thirty minutes to spare.

The lift doors opened, and I walked inside then pressed the button for the first floor, so that I could leave the lift and continue down the outer staircase of the hotel to prevent being seen in the hotel lobby. Reaching outside, I disposed the bag of bloody clothes in a street side rubbish bin which was en route to the railway station. The noise from the city was quite overpowering, as I slowly walked over towards the entrance of the train station.

I quickly noticed there were two police officers standing near the main entrance doors who appeared to be more interested in the women passing by, as I continued to move towards the main ticket hall. Reaching the pay-point window, I purchased a train ticket for the journey to Vienna which used train S25 from Soroksari Station then it changed at Salzburg, where I needed to catch train RJX 42 and finally would continue to the main railway station at Vienna. The final train RJX 567 was from the main station at Vienna to the airport terminal station.

Whilst I rechecked the platform number and time, I had a sensation that someone was watching me, as I reached the train platform. I recall the thoughts kept churning over in my mind, as I waited for the train to arrive, but I tried to blank out, and think about the four-hour journey in front of me. People began to gather on the platform, and I observed two men walking along the station platform trying to act casual, but looking at their demeanour I could sense that they were agents searching for someone. All I needed to do was to remain calm and composed and I would be home dry.

Suddenly, I felt a pistol being pushed into my back and a man's voice whispered, "Where are you heading off to in a hurry Nash?"

Recognising the voice immediately I replied with, "Well, Alistair what a surprise."

"McGough, gave my contract to you for the diplomat."

"That's news to me, that contract was mine from the start!"

"No Nash, this was my contract, and you had taken the scalp and the money."

As the train started to draw into the station, "I guess you were thinking that you would simply hop onto the train to Salzburg and disappear hey Nash." He snarled.

"Well, that's certainly the plan and my plan will not change." I replied.

"I'm looking forward to killing you Nash, I only wished I had completed it during the training." He smiled.

The two Hungarian agents had walked past and reached the opposite end of the platform, where they had started to smoke cigarettes talking to each other. I only had a small window of opportunity to escape. Alistair was another agent from the cardinal programme but was always near the bottom of the class. He was smart, but not always smart enough. I needed to get the timing just right so that I could simply slip away. The agents started to walk back along the platform, and I slowly started to remove a knife from my right pocket. Unlocking the blade, I knew that Alistair has not even seen the two Hungarian agents so, as they approached, I turned slightly, and smiled at Alistair, then in one quick action, slit the side of his neck deep with the knife in my right hand and using my left grabbed the gun, and used it upside down to shoot one of the agents in the stomach. The complete action made it to look as though Alistair had taken the shot, and as he stumbled forward from the deep knife wound the second agent drew his gun, and fired several rounds at Alistair.

In the panic, people started to run in all directions, and I quickly moved forward and climbed onboard the train finding my seat quickly, and watched as more police officers suddenly reached the injured agent on the platform, and then started to turn Alistair onto his belly and handcuff him, but he was already dead from the fatal gunshots from the agent. I knew that McGough might send out a second assassin, but was glad that I managed to use this person to hide my escape on the train along with leaving an agent behind for the Hungarian government to investigate.

ELEVEN

My old thoughts from Operation Cosma are broken by the sensation of the plane landing back at Heathrow. After clearing passport control and security checks, I collect a hire car and continue along the M25 heading towards Hatfield, where I will be joining the A1 heading towards Bury St Edmunds, the sky is partly covered by broken cloud as the redness from the setting sun changes to a purple pink colour. I look at the digital clock on the dashboard of the BMW and see its eight p.m., but my mind is full of what the outcome could be, as I start to remember the conversation and meeting with McGough less than twenty hours ago. Focusing back on the road, I know that McGough has sealed my fate and even if an escape is possible, snipers will kill me at the doorway or near the main exits. I'm too important and know too much about the agency for them just to allow me to walk away to freedom, that is not an option here, and I must have a plan B. A fast escape route that would give me at least a few hours to slip away would be a bonus at this time. Lifting my mobile phone from the front passenger seat with my left hand, I start to roll through a few numbers of former contacts then see a sign for 'parking' at ¼ mile then begin to slow down indicating to pull into the layby.

    Reaching the parking, I pull the car to a gradual halt and press the brake then turn the key to stop the engine. The interior light switches on and numbers from the past appear on the mobile phone screen, with many of the old contacts now deceased, but my fingers stop at a particular name and number. I look through the windscreen and see the old red payphone near the end of the layby. Since any mobile phones and numbers are tracked and monitored, for any known agents active or not, using the landline could be a preferred option. Taking the ignition keys from the dashboard slot and placing them into my jacket pocket, I move my right hand into the lower door bin feeling for some loose change that was thrown in there earlier after buying a sandwich. Removing the change, the door catch is pulled, and the driver's door is pushed open at the same time. Lifting myself from the car seat, my face senses the dampness from the approaching darkness as the dew from the air begins to float heavy. My nose is filled with smell of the last silage cut of grass from the farmland and a blackbird shouts an alarm call in the distance which can be easily heard with the road being so silent.

Closing the car door with a positive 'clunk', it echoes in the silence of the countryside, as I start to walk towards the phone-box. The tarmac is already damp from an earlier rain shower, and my shoes scrub against the small stones and broken glass on the road surface. The phone-box has most of the red paint damaged or blistered from the side panels with many of the small glass window panes missing or smashed. Using my right hand, I open the heavy door and my nostrils are instantly filled with the smell of stale piss and mould with my mind flashing back to a distant memory. I look and see the phone receiver which is still attached and take it from its hanger with my left hand, checking the condition and looking for any insects or dirt.

As it's raised towards the direction of my left ear, the faint buzzing of the ringtone getting ever louder can be heard. Now fully inside the phone-box, the door closes behind with a solid *'THUD.'* The numbers are worn and the stainless cover is hammered, and damaged from people trying to steal the loose change coins. There are labels and graffiti all over the inside of the phone-box, but I remember being in far worse places in my life. As I start to punch the buttons of the keypad, they make a large metallic 'click' as they make contact, the receiver begins to ring as the number connects. I begin to take the change from my jacket pocket and gradually start to add a few coins into the money slot which makes a 'clinking' noise as they fall inside.

"Yes, hello, sorry the car is sold?" as a voice from the past fills my ears.

"Sorry mate, not after a car, how's tricks Chris? It's Dean." I reply

The phone goes silent for a few seconds then a reply, "Dean, my god what a surprise, it's a long time no hear, what are you up too?" Chris asks.

"I'm well, thanks, but need a little help! Would it be possible to meet up?" Replying quickly.

In the distance there is a faint noise of another car engine approaching from my right.

"Well, it's a little difficult at the minute, but since it's you. When do you want to meet?" Replies Chris.

A blue Audi saloon car passes by without slowing down on the main road which I watch from inside the phone box as the headlights illuminate the damp road surface.

"What are your plans tomorrow Chris?"

"Tomorrow, that's a bit fuckin short notice, where are you?" Chris snaps.

"Parked on the A1 just outside Stevenage, Sorry about this, but I've only been in the country a few hours and need to talk." Replying submissively.

There is a pause for a few seconds then Chris replies, "That sounds serious Dean; you are not that far away from me but I can't make it until tomorrow lunchtime. We can meet up at the Black Bull pub at Great Barton near to near Bury St Edmonds. It is about one hour from where you are?"

"Yeah, a pub might be a good place, so looking forward to seeing you there." I reply as the phone starts to beep for more money.

Replacing the receiver back on the hanger, my mind drifts to old memories of what Chris and I had been through in the past, as I push open the heavy old door and start to leave the phone-box beginning to walk on the noisy tarmac surface. The phone box door *'BANGS'* shut behind as the distinctive sound of another car engine getting louder and louder in the semi darkness. With travelling on a fake passport not known by the agency, they will have every single airport and ferry crossing covered in an attempt to track and monitor me. The hire car was booked on stolen credit cards and driver's licence, but with swopping the plates at a local dealer, this would give me a few days. I need a room for tonight, and I have no option other than switching on my mobile and start looking for some accommodation. After checking through various B&B's, the best option may be a travel lodge which I notice is quite close to Bury St Edmonds. After passing through Bury St Edmunds the next stop will be the Travel lodge and a stay over after my long journey from Australia.

    I briefly think about the meeting with Chris tomorrow before the final drive to the headquarters of Broadhurst Industries, and my mind is filled with thoughts that these could probably be my last few days alive. Stopping on the car park of the hotel, I walk towards the neon signs for the travel lodge then continue inside. The reception is basic and after the automatic check in, I fetch the room key from the safety box. As I walk along the corridor my thoughts flash back to Shaun, and the noise from the breaking glass and the rifle bullets that hit him. An uneasy feeling starts to chew away at my emotions, as I try to remain composed in these difficult times. Reaching the room, I open the door and walk inside, it is clean and basic but it's only a bed a need for the night. After the long journey from Australia, I undress and lay on top of the bed quickly falling asleep.

    I awake the next morning feeling more relaxed and after freshening up, walk down the breakfast room for some food. Cereals and toast are consumed, and I return to the hire car in the parking lot, and prepare for the next journey to Great Barton. Following the sat nav instructions after our telephone call, I begin to drive towards the small village of Great Barton, where I have arranged to meet Chris.

My thoughts drift back to the last time we met, many years ago after saving his life, and it is quite ironic that maybe, he is the only person who can help me now. Reaching the Black Bull pub, I pull onto the gravel surfaced car park and stop in one of the spaces. Climbing out of the car I take a quick look around the other cars parked, and then walk towards the back of the pub checking the exit doors. I am sure Chris is loyal but telephone calls can be traced and my capture could be priceless for some enemies.

Now satisfied that the area is clear I continue towards the main double entrance doors that lead into the pub. The main bar area is dimly lit with white washed walls and exposed black oak beams inset both into the walls and ceilings. Walking onto the light oak laminate flooring, my nostrils are instantly filled with the smell of wood burning, and looking both left and right, I notice the open fires lit at each end of the pub which gently releases heat from the burning logs. The bar is central to the pub with groups of tables and chairs placed around the room. As I continue into the bar area, I casually scan around the tables searching for Chris. Reaching the bar, a clicking noise of shoes walking on the laminate flooring echoes from the rear area of the pub as a young barmaid wearing black high heeled shoes, and a tight-fitting black dress showing off her curvaceous body walks behind the bar. She has short dark brown hair with red highlights and green eyes, "Good afternoon sir, how may I help you?" She asks politely giving a cheeky smile.

"Hi, good afternoon." I reply.

Just then a familiar voice shouts my name, "Hey Dean over here."

I quickly turn to see Chris at a table in the far-right corner of the pub near to one of the front windows. The sun's rays shine across his face, and he already has a pint of beer sitting in front of him on the table.

Giving him a quick wave, I reply to the barmaid, "I will have an orange juice please."

"OK, sir, I will bring it over." She replies smiling and begins to prepare the drink.

Walking over towards Chris, I casually continue to scan around the pub ensuring that I have not been followed or set up, and reaching the table lean down slightly to shake Chris's hand. He has a smile beaming across his face from ear to ear as though it's his birthday as he takes a big sip of his drink and asks,

"Dean, it's great to see you, I was so happy when you called."

Sitting down opposite him I reply, "Hi Chris, yes its, great to see you too. How the devil have you been keeping?"

"Well, stuck in these wheels isn't much fun, but the agency has looked after me really well, but without you I wouldn't be here at all."

"You would have done the same for me I'm sure." The young barmaid brings over my drink.

"Will you gents be ordering any lunch?" She asks standing by the table.

"If you could bring the menus over that would be great." I reply.

"Certainly sir." She smiles, and walks away quickly returning with the menu cards.

"The specials are on the blackboard at the side of the bar."

"Thanks very much." Chris replies as she walks away.

"My Dean, seeing a beautiful woman like her, well, that makes me want jump up and start dancing, anyway how have you been and what have you been doing? I want to hear all about it? The last I heard you were missing?"

"Missing in a certain way Chris. I've not got all the answers yet, but after the Turkish operation something happened and I'm still piecing all the parts of the puzzle back together."

"That Turkish operation was suicide Dean why did you volunteer?"

"It's a long story and for another time, but after that op I disappeared off the grid for years or so I thought."

I continue, "The agency kept a track on me with different undercover operatives with the last one being Shaun Neal."

"Shaun Neal? That name doesn't sound familiar, but there are so many sub agency departments it's hard to follow all of them. So, what happened to him?"

"McGough, sent me to kill Shaun in Australia four days ago, but he also sent an asset who actually did the final kill."

"Edward McGough, well, that's a blast from the past. I would rather sleep in a bag of snakes than work for that slippery bastard." Chris smiles.

"What brings you here." Chris asks.

"McGough." I reply.

"Oh shit." Chris answers.

"What has he asked you to do?" Chris asks.

"Remember Nick Burns?"

"Nick Burns hmmm." Chris pauses.

"The San Paulo job." I say.

Chris pauses for a few more seconds, then replies "Colonel Nick Burns?"

"Yes." I reply.

"Fuck Dean, he's real hardcore what does McGough want you to do?"

"Burns dead! And I'm the man who has been selected to do it." I answer.

"No way Dean that's impossible and certainly no way back. Burns will rip out your beating heart, and serve it to you on a plate for breakfast. I hope he is offering you a good deal?" Chris asks.

"My life back."

Chris bursts out laughing then says, "You're joking right." He looks across smiling then his expression changes as he sees the seriousness in my face.

"You're not joking." I nod my head in agreement as Chris stares at me in shock.

"Shall we order some lunch? What would you like?" As I lift up the menu.

"I don't know Dean, to be honest I'm still shocked over what you said."

"Ah steak, and ale pie perfect." I decide quickly after looking down the menu.

"What about the specials Dean. Can you go and have a look please? In this thing it will be last orders before I get there." Chris smiles.

Nodding I stand, and walk over towards the bar looking down the specials list noting down all the options. The barmaid is seen at the back of pub talking to a man and woman who casually look over in my direction and at that point realise that Chris may have been used to set me up. Walking back to the table, I don't know if he can be trusted, but could use him to throw the agency off my scent.

Smiling at him I sit and read off the specials board aloud, "OK, there is fish and chips, salmon tagliatelle, beef stroganoff, shoulder of lamb, and a nice squash nut roast?"

"Hmmm gee, the salmon sounds like the best option."

The barmaid reappears with a worried look across her face, "OK gents, have you decided what you would like to order." She asks with some nervousness in her voice,

"Salmon tagliatelle for me and another pint of lager shandy please."

Looking at the guilt in her eyes I reply, "I will have the steak and ale pie plus another orange please."

"OK gents, thank you." She takes the menus and returns to the bar.

"I'm just nipping to the toilet Chris."

"Yeah go for it, have one for me too."

Standing I turn, and walk past the bar towards the toilet at the back of the pub as the barmaid continues to watch my every move. I quickly stare at the couple sitting in the back of the pub trying to avoid eye contact, but I sense they are clearly watching our discussion and movements. I can tell that they are agents by how they sit pretending to talk. Chris may be innocent, but why are the agents here, they have either followed him, me or a trace has been taken from the phone call. Prior to the washrooms are a set of glass double doors that oversee the car park, and quickly glancing through the glass panel, a man can be seen walking around outside towards the hire car looking at the number plates with a mobile placed against his right ear.

Reaching the washroom, I throw a little water onto my face and stare into the mirror deciding what to do next. I must be safe here at this time since McGough had cleared all my flights and travel so these agents must just be tracking who I'm talking with, and why I'm, off course.

Something must have triggered the agent's response with them already in the pub, the only answer must lie either with Chris, the phone call or me. Quickly thinking about my escape options, if there is a tracker it could be inside me so I need to know otherwise I will never be able to escape. Returning back to the table the barmaid has brought the additional drinks along with some bread and oil. Chris has begun to drink his second pint of beer and eat some of the bread. It may be a good time to push him slightly for information over the agents being here, as I sit down opposite him.

"Chris, tell me a little about yourself, and what have you been doing since your retirement from the agency."

"Not much to tell really. After the agency sorted me with a new bungalow and had all the disability changes completed, I spend most of my time now painting, and taking photographs of scenery, where I can access anyway. I certainly miss the buzz from the operations and have done some freelance work for a security company but no one prepares you for retirement. Losing my legs has taken a long time to get over with the lack of independence, but I have adapted to life and enjoy every day now." Chris replies.

"It's great to see how independent you are," I answer.

"To a fashion, but the disability only affects your body, my mind is still willing, and very active. I tried to go back to the agency for a few months, but working in an office in a none important role didn't help so they offered me a great pension to finish."

"Hmmm I never really thought about keeping your brain active."

I sense Chris is upset over his treatment by the agency, but still think he is working for them especially with his skill sets.

"Anyway, what can I do for you Dean? You seemed quite tense on the phone." Chris seems concerned.

Being cautious over my reply, I think about what to say without sounding as though I have wasted his time,. "I'm sure McGough will want to kill me if I manage to escape so was after some ideas of what I could do."

"My Dean that's a major question, what disappear off the grid for good?" I nod at him.

"That will need a new identity, money from none traceable bank accounts, and the hardest thing removing your profile from every single face and fingerprint recognition system across the world. Mate you can't buy that type of clearance it's on another level."

"That's the only way."

"Every person on the planet is on some form of database and to be in none, well, that's impossible. I take it you are here to ask for help?" I nod in agreement as the barmaid brings over the food.

"OK gents, the salmon tagliatelle and steak pie. Enjoy your meals." She places the plates of food on the table then walks away very quickly.

Chris continues, "Dean, I can help with the ID and bank accounts, but clearing the face recognition well, that is way out of my depth."

"If you manage to kill Burns how are you going to escape? The agency won't just let you walk away with your skill set and history, you're far too open to any form of enemy contact. It's easier for them to just kill you." We start to eat the food.

"Look at your situation Dean, it's impossible." Chris continues.

"Nothing is impossible, difficult yes. All I need is a diversion and some help with the facial mapping. I know it's difficult, but the level of facial imaging can surely be changed."

"After what you did for me Dean, I will see what I can do but, I can't promise anything. How are you going to escape though?"

"You leave that to me. I'm planning a little diversion what can you suggest?"

"Where are you escaping from and when?" I have nothing to hide from not telling Chris the truth fills my thoughts and besides McGough will be expecting me to escape anyway as I continue.

"There is a situation at Broadhurst industries, and I have got to get in there before Burns blows up the whole place and most of southern England."

"Broadhurst! Fuck Dean that's a major military secure facility, there is no escape from there I saw the plans years ago."

"What was built can come down so leave that to me." I reply.

"OK a diversion, how about an officer down radio call." Chris smiles.

"No there will be cops everywhere on high alert anyway."

"OK, how about breaking into the communication centre, and hacking the mobile network causing them to be blind for a few minutes, that could work."

"Yeah sounds more interesting, how long could you knock out the comms for?" I ask.

"I have to get in first over the network through the firewall, but maybe five to ten minutes." Chris replies.

"That might give me enough time, OK try it out, and see how far you can get." I reply.

"When do you need it laid on by?" Chris asks.

"Ready to go in twenty-four hours."

"Twenty-four hours! Are you fuckin serious they are secure police and military hard lines! To break the encryption codes could easily take weeks?" Chris is shocked.

"I don't have weeks Chris, I have hours."

"Dean, I would do anything, but I don't know about this. Its deep major deep."

"Look Chris, I know you cracked the code before that's why you got a position in the unit so cracking it again must be easier." I smile at him finishing my meal.

"The new security software did have a little backdoor, but without looking I can't guarantee it's still there."

"Well, can the personal profile information be done?" I ask.

"I think that's possible yes, but I could only corrupt the programme for a few days, it is self-learning so a terrorist can't change anything and removing a profile will highlight on the system." Chris replies.

"I don't want to remove the facial recognition; I want to bombard it from different locations causing panic, and overpowering its software causing a failure." I ask.

"Well, that's easy enough with cloning technology. Yes, that idea could be done easily with multiple target location areas." Chris finishes his food and drink.

"OK, so get sniffing around and see what you can find out."

"So how will I contact you Dean." Chris asks.

"Leave that to me, I will contact you in twelve hours." I reply.

"OK, it's risky as hell though."

"That's why we were the best. Now can I trust you or are you going to sell me out." I decide to challenge him over the couple in the back.

"Sell you out? what do you mean? I came here because you asked for help why do you think I'm setting you up?" Chris's face has a look of surprise.

"Are the two agents in the back of the pub following you or me?"

"Agents what agents?" As the man and woman from the back walk out towards the front door staring at the both of us.

I jump up, and quickly follow them outside watching them climb into the back of a waiting silver Mercedes E class. I memorise the number plate, as it speeds away from the car park. Turning around I walk back into the pub as Chris has begun to make his way to the door, "They have gone, but I have the license plate details."

"Let me assure you Dean, I haven't worked for the agency in a number of years so if the agents were here, they must of either tracked my mobile or yours?"

"One thing is certain they are now onto the both of us. Sorry if my actions have led to difficulties for you Chris." I have remorse in my voice.

"Difficulties no, more like a bit of fun. Look leave this with me, and rest assured you can trust me Dean." Chris replies.

"OK, Chris, thanks." I continue, "You get going, and I will settle the bill."

We shake hands and then I turn and continue towards the car park. The barmaid appears and Chris ask for the bill with the thoughts of the two agents and the waiting car flowing through both our minds. Before unlocking the car, I have a quick check around the vehicle, then after the doors unlock slide onto driver's seat. I start the engine, and begin to drive off the car park as Chris emerges from the pub entrance. I begin to drive away, and suddenly, my mind clicks the pieces together and realising what might have happened. I stop the car and begin to turn around at high speed just as a large *'BOOM'* is heard.

Flames burst into the sky which then sends a mushroom cloud of black smoke bellowing upwards as a car is engulfed in fire. Stopping the hire car short of the pub, I already know deep down that Chris would have been inside and an agent must have set a car bomb to neutralise any help. It's pointless going to see if he is alive. I can tell from the sound of the explosion that a C4 charge was used and the heat from the blast would clearly have incinerated him immediately. Continuing to drive past the pub, I try to keep a low profile in an attempt to avoid any contact. The barmaid can be seen staring at the car park as a few neighbours begin to appear from nearby houses. It seems that McGough has killed another good friend so for sure his fate is now sealed, and his deathbed apology will be the only way to feed my anger against him. Not knowing for certain if Chris was killed by the agency, my mind is filled with who else could have carried out the assassination in such a public way as a car bomb. I need to lay low overnight, that will allow me to regain my thoughts, and plan my escape which is now my prime motive.

Pulling the car over to a small gate opening at the side of the road, I take out the mobile and click onto a hotel website search engine looking for cheap quiet places to stay for one night. After a few selections, a suitable hotel suddenly loads onto my screen, The King William pub at Cambourne. Quickly clicking onto the contact number, the call button is pressed.

The mobile is lifted to my ear with the ringing being heard and after a few seconds, a lady's Cockney voice answers, "The King William."

"Yes, hello do you have room available for tonight?" I ask.

"I will check, just the one night is it sir?" She replies.

By her voice I can sense she is around fifty years old, as she continues to speak, "We have a cancellation, but it is only a single room is that OK?"

"A single room will be fine for one night."

"Certainly, sir what is the name of the booking?" She asks.

"Jones, its Martin Jones."

"Have you stayed with us before Mr Jones?"

"No I haven't, I also see that you serve food?" I answer.

"Yes, Mr Jones, our kitchens are open at six p.m. until nine p.m."

"OK, that is fine I will be with you in about one hour."

"Could I take a credit card number to confirm the booking please?" She asks.

"Well, I was hoping to pay cash!"

"Oh right, but a card number would secure the room otherwise I will let someone else have it."

"I see your point hold on." I quickly grab a credit card which I had taken from the asset in Australia, and begin to read out the number, "9785 3451 2685 3497, expiry is 03/2014 and the code is four hundred and fifty-one."

"OK Mr Jones, that's great, well, we will look forward to seeing you soon.

"OK, many thanks."

The phone rings off, and I begin to type the address into the car satellite navigation system. Engaging first gear, I pull away from the gate opening and continue along the A428 in the direction of Cambourne with the roads surprisingly quiet with hardly any cars passing by. The hotel is located about one hour away from Broadhurst's in a quiet rural location so there shouldn't be any distractions from McGough or any other agents who will still be after me. Knowing all my cards will be tracked it's good to have some loose cash keeping below the radar, and with using a simple pay as you go mobile that was purchased from the airport, my digital footprint will only be seen through surveillance equipment, and a few simple disguises will keep them guessing.

This modern world with the latest technology makes it easy to track anyone keeping the general public safe but now in my situation generates huge problems when you want to disappear, and not being evident on any surveillance systems makes the authorities more focused to find you so it feels almost like living on a double-edged sword. After fifty minutes of driving, the village signs for Cambourne appear and the satellite navigation system instructs me to turn left and follow Mangrove Road ahead. I drive along a small narrow country lane enclosed by tall trees and houses very close to the roadside which leaves no pavement access.

As the road rises slightly, I emerge from the trees and continue along a gravelled driveway that borders a large grassed village green encircled with several detached properties and finally I see a sign for The King William pub. Pulling into the car park, I reverse into one of the parking spaces then reaching across take the baseball cap from the passenger seat and place it onto my head. Climbing out of the car, the sound of birdsong fills the air, as I walk towards the back of the vehicle. A bag is taken from the trunk then the boot lid is closed. Reaching the entrance doors, I scan around to see if there are any surveillance cameras and notice some placed on the black wooden soffit corners of the building.

The white washed pebble dashed frontage has small black framed windows covered with diamond shaped leading that almost disappear in the large ivy draping over the front of the property. I open the entrance door and continue inside reaching the main hotel reception where a lady sits behind a desk.

"Good afternoon, you must be Mr Jones, we spoke on the phone earlier."

"Yes, that's correct, a single room just for one night." I reply.

"OK, the room is £42.00 which includes a continental breakfast served between seven a.m. and ten a.m."

"Seven a.m. is fine for the breakfast." I reply.

"OK, do you wish to pay now or in the morning?"

"Yes, I will pay now." As I reach for my wallet.

"We just need you to complete this registration card so if you could fill this in that will be great?" She asks.

Taking £45.00 from the wallet, I hand it over to the woman and taking the card start to fill it out with my fictitious name and address.

"Are you in the area for business or pleasure?" She asks.

"Business I'm afraid, but it looks a lovely part of the country."

"Isn't it terrible about that company where all those people are being held hostage?" She mentions.

"Yes, it's such a shame, what is the latest news?" Pretending not to know much.

"The authorities haven't said much at this time, but I certain they must be planning some form of a rescue attempt I would have thought."

"You would like to think so." I reply not taking much notice.

"OK Mr Jones, I will show you to your room, our building is a bit like a rabbit warren. I have put you into room number eight that is at the back of the hotel so a little quieter. Follow me!" She stands.

I notice her dyed blonde hair, false fingernails and eyelashes as she tries to look younger than she really is. She wears a tight white flowery dress and cream high heels. We walk up a set of creaky green carpeted stairs that have a small gold and red coat of arms patterned design that is the same motif, as seen on the pub sign then continue along a narrow corridor, which has off white walls and light green gloss woodwork.

The floorboards creak with every footstep and with the ceiling being quite low, I have to keep lowering my head to avoid the large oak beams, as we finally reach the room. The narrow passages do indeed resemble a rabbit warren with paper signs pointing back towards the reception. She unlocks the door, and hands me the key then pushes the door open.

Pointing into the room she says, "OK, the WIFI password can be found on the desk along with any information about the hotel, there are tea & coffee making facilities to the right."

"Thank you, did you say that the restaurant starts to serve food at six p.m." I ask.

"Yes, that's correct six until nine. I wish you nice stay."

Walking into the room, my nostrils are instantly filled with the smell air fresheners trying to mask the stale musty air, and as I continue inside. I reply with, "Many thanks." As she closes the door behind her.

Placing the bag onto the same green patterned carpet near the door, I walk over to the first window to the side of the bed that overlooks wheat stubble fields at the back of the hotel. The field has a long hedge down the left-hand side that leads to a small wood with most of the leaves on the trees now beginning to turn brown. Walking over to the second window next to the television stand in the corner of the room, I look through only to see the flat roof of the hotel towards the restaurant area. Both of these windows could be both entrance and exit points for any assets trying to target me.

Quickly pulling the curtains shut on both windows, I walk into the en-suite bathroom. As the door is pushed open, a sensor picks up the movement and switches on the ceiling light, and quickly scanning around the bathroom it has all the basic fittings of a white toilet, sink, and shower cubicle with pale green walls with small traces of mould seen in the corners. It's still certainly better than many places I have stayed in the past and my mind quickly thinks back to some of the flea infested rooms from different parts of the world as the hairs begin to stand up on the back of my neck.

One particular experience from a stay at a hotel in Hungary suddenly fills my thoughts. Hoping that this room isn't the same quality, a deep sigh is taken and the light cord is pulled, and thankfully no sound of scurrying feet is heard, but I quickly check around to make sure there is no evidence of any animal droppings and walking over to the bed I peel back the bed-sheets checking for dirt or mess. After a short rest, I leave the room and continue along the corridor towards the doorway at the base of the staircase that leads towards the bar. As

I walk down the creaky steps the voices of people talking and laughing can be heard and quickly checking my watch the time is showing six thirty-five p.m.

Walking into the bar the southern accents ring out discussing football results from last night's big game and general chit chat. Slowly scanning around the bar area for any threats I continue towards the main entrance door. The large black cottage style door has a large set of catches, and ironwork, and depressing the metal bar, I push the heavy door forward allowing me to pass back onto the car park.

At each side of the tiled roof entry porch, picnic table are sets with men and women drinking, and laughing enjoying the last of the autumn light. Dusk is starting to fall fast, as I begin to take a casual walk around the small village back along the road that was used to enter the pub car park. Continuing along the narrow country lane I notice the signs for a public footpath and turning right walk past the large grassed village green, and reaching a small stile in the corner of the hedge, climb over it. Looking around the darkening wheat stubble fields the ground is dry with not having rain for weeks, and the birds sing trying to keep the ever approaching darkness from arriving, but I fear their calls are in vain.

The footpath continues along the field edge and down towards a small housing estate. Slowly, beginning to walk along the well-trodden path, my mind quickly pictures a simple life as a brown hare suddenly rises from its crouched position and lifts its head to assess my threat, then jumping to its feet bounces away further into the field generating more safety space. Standing watching the hare my emotions sense what it must be like to be hunted and thinking about escaping from Broadhurst's fills my confused thoughts, but I must remain calm.

Knowing that McGough had Shaun killed along with suspecting that he was part of Chris's death with me being so close sends a shiver down my spine, but not from being afraid. Payback fills my thoughts, and I hope that McGough will be at the command centre which gives me an opportunity to assess the best way to try and establish a weakness.

Plans of killing him before the op could be an answer, but this won't give me the advantage of surprise so it's better to wait until after. I know he will send his best assets to finish me, and I also know what techniques they will use since much of their training is based on my experiences. Reaching the small tarmacked path at the outskirts of the housing estate, I continue to walk along the almost pitch-black path enjoying the freedom and beginning to feel at peace, until I return to The King William car park. Glancing across to the hire car, a small piece of paper has been placed underneath one of the wiper blades, scanning around casually and looking at the people sitting down outside to check for any threats, I slowly walk over to the car. Slowly lifting the wiper-blade the piece of white ruled paper is removed.

I open the note to read 'Dean I'm so sorry how things have changed between us and wish we were back in our former lives sharing our special times and love together. X'

Signed with a single letter 'S.'

Reading the note again, the handwriting suddenly takes me back to a past life and an image of a face fills my thoughts. Looking around again my mind now thinks how could anyone have followed me to this place and known my location along with the car I'm driving, but more importantly who left the note. Then my thoughts return back to when Chris was killed and the assassins must have reported in my car. The feeling of being watched now penetrates through my usually unbreakable skin and now feeling vulnerable again makes me anxious and nervous.

Just as I begin to plan my escape to try and win back my freedom this curve ball smacks me straight in the face knocking me for six. Reality now sets in, and as I walk towards the pub entrance, I'm sure that McGough arranged for a note to be written and copied in her handwriting then planned for Chris's assassins to place it here in an attempt to scare me, but a note won't alter my thoughts.

This does now lead to another problem to solve knowing that someone has got this close to me and not knowing what they look like is the worst fear of all. Opening the door of the pub, I don't even know if the person is sitting inside watching my every move, so taking a quick sigh I continue inside with my head held high trying to ooze confidence, and equally hiding the small chink in my armour. During our training we were taught to look for certain tell-tale signs using surveillance techniques on the lookout for any assassins or agents that are marking you as a target so casually looking around the bar area, there does not appear to be anything out of place or acting in any way I find worth more investigation. Walking to the bar, I order a drink of red wine and then sit near the main door, so I can study any people that pass by. On the empty table opposite to me another customer has left a local newspaper, so reaching over I take it and begin to look through the pages.

One of the waitresses walks over with a menu card, and asks, "Are you dining with us tonight sir?"

"Yes, I will thank you." She hands over the laminated menu card.

"I'll be back in a few minutes to take your order." I smile back.

Deciding what to eat from the menu the waitresses return's and takes my order. She brings cutlery along with some table sauces. I continue to pretend reading the newspaper as a few more people enter the bar area. Several people leave, but no one sparks any interest. Sitting waiting for the ordered food pretending to read the newspaper, my eyes are drawn to an article titled 'Australia Murders Government Cover Up.' Beginning to read the first column in the article it starts with the story of a murder victim who was found in a toilet cubicle of a roadside hotel in town of Mackay which is part of the Queensland state and situated along the Bruce Highway. As I continue to read the article, the story unfolds that during the investigation of the death, two government agents were sent from Sydney to follow up on a large drug deal.

The agents suggested that the drug dealers were in a turf war that resulted in one man being killed. Following the two agents leaving the site with most of the evidence, three police officers were then killed along with the two ambulance drivers who were taking the deceased body to the local mortuary. The bottom of the article shows a picture of the last Remaining Police officer Sergeant Haynes who is seen holding an evidence bag containing fingerprints smears on a film, and a spent bullet round found at the scene. His daughter Isabella Haynes was one of the forensic officers that attended the murder site. The article also mentions that she has now also been killed at the local police station.

Sergeant Haynes from the Mackay police department makes a statement of similar facts and praises the gallant efforts of the three officers that died during the events. The case still remains unsolved with no comments from the Australian government agency thought to be responsible for sending the two agents. My mind quickly remembers killing the assassin in pure cold blood just, because he didn't give me his name, and then the side of self-preservation kicks in knowing that McGough would instantly order my killing when it suits him. Looking around the bar again there are no visible indications that anyone is here and my sixth sense doesn't alert me to anything suspicious, but knowing that someone has followed me here does send a nervous shiver down my spine and thinking back to the story from Australia, I wonder if the two alleged agents were a clean-up team who were tracking not just the assassin, but me as well. Better him than me flashes through my mind. My thoughts are broken by the waitresses bringing my steak dinner with peppercorn sauce. Not the best I have tasted but it will suffice for tonight, as I take the first bite.

Gradually eating the food, I look around at the few couples and small families that are sitting around tables dining, and thoughts flash through my mind of being alone, and wanting more in life. My mind thinks back to when things changed so much, and the sacrifices that I have made with thoughts probably triggered off by the letter that was left. Being alone has never really bothered me, but loneliness is another emotion that unless you control it will lead to a world of hate and trouble, and thinking back now, I try to imagine if things could have been different, and what my life would be now along with who I might be sharing it with. Taking a deep sigh, I finish the meal and pushing the empty plate to one side, I try to do the same with these thoughts in my brain planning to unlock them another day.

The waitress walks over, and asks, "Would you like another drink or anything else?"

"No, I'm fine thanks just the bill please."

"Cash or card?" She asks.

"Cash please." I reply.

Drinking the last of the wine I place the newspaper back onto the other table as the waitresses brings over the bill.

"OK, that is £27.50."

Taking out one £20.00 and £10.00 note, I hand them over saying, "Keep the change."

"Oh, great thank you. Are you staying with us?" It's at that point she makes a mistake.

Quickly remembering that I noticed her cleaning one of the other rooms earlier, as I checked in, I know that someone has asked her to find out more and the lead I was searching for then reply,

"Well, I might be staying here."

"Your accent isn't from around this part of the country, and I've not seen you here before so I took a wild guess."

"Well, seeing that you saw me check in earlier, I thought you might have realised!" I reply.

She then realises that she had seen me and now feels very

uncomfortable with the situation, as she mumbles out a reply to hide her embarrassment, "Oh yes, I remember now sorry, I didn't recognise you."

She quickly walks away with the money, and reaching the till opens the drawer to deposit the cash. Watching her from a little distance she lifts a mobile phone from behind the counter then makes her way out towards the back of the pub past the kitchen area. Knowing that she must be contacting somebody, I stand, and quickly walk through the front entrance door into the darkness of the night then continue around to the left of the building towards the rear garden area. Reaching the corner of the building, the rear garden area borders onto the large wheat stubble field that can be seen earlier from my room. Looking forward the silhouette of a woman could be seen illuminated from the light passing through the glass Georgian style doors. Slowly creeping along the patio area almost brushing the wall, I can hear a female voice and by the accent it is the waitress. Finally stopping about fifty metres away in almost complete darkness, I hear the last of the conversation.

"He knows, and I'm not going back in there." She says in a raised voice then the ignited end of a cigarette can be seen as she takes a final draw. Throwing the stub end to the floor she stamps on it, and continues to speak.

"Look, I've told you where he is staying and done what you asked so, I need to get back to work, so he doesn't realise I'm missing." She switches off the mobile then opens the door to walk back into the pub.

Knowing that, it's no longer safe here my first thoughts are to pack my things and go, but where at nine forty-five p.m.? Whoever needed to know, I was here already suspected it, and besides I'll be gone early in the morning with the element of surprise now in my favour, and using this knowledge to my advantage. Making my way back towards the room using the rear entrance, I walk up the creaky staircase and along the narrow corridor, until I reach the door. Quickly checking the corridor for any sounds of footsteps or any other movements, I insert the key into the lock, and pushing the door open step inside then switch on the light. Lifting the bag from the floor and lowering onto the bed, I look through the few pieces of equipment taking out three motion sensors. Walking around the room one is attached to each window and the third onto the door. With all my bases covered, I lie on the bed fully clothed with a handgun underneath my pillow. Triangulating the signal from each sensor to my mobile, I set the device to vibration only a finally the alarm for a three thirty a.m. get up. A few hours rest is required, before the drive to Broadhurst's and McGough's wish of my death at the hands of Burns who will probably already know that, I will be sent to end the hostage situation.

My thoughts begin to replay the ideas for an escape plan, and presently with all my allies gone, being on my own allows me to be flexible, but not having any external support and help will make the escape practically impossible unless another opportunity presents itself. Lying in bed my brain registers the fear of walking into this deadly operation, but my confidence must remain high to avoid the only probable outcome of my death. I must feed on the previous knowledge and my experience, which has been gained from many other dangerous situations in order to survive. My only hope is a plan which needs to be worked to my advantage giving me the opportunity, and as the different scenarios play through my brain, I finally drop off to sleep.

BUZZ, BUZZ is heard as the mobile vibrates, so waking from my sleep, I quickly check around the room to make sure all the sensors are still active and seeing the small led green light on each device still illuminated, I know it's only the alarm sounding the three thirty a.m. call.

Gradually rising from the bed, I walk towards the bathroom, and switch on the main light illuminating the room. Using the toilet, I then undress and take a quick shower to wake myself before redressing and walking back into the bedroom, where I gather the motion sensors placing them into the bag. A brief thought passes through my mind that someone may be waiting for me outside, so reaching across to the pillow, I remove the handgun and tuck it into the trouser belt by my back and pulling on a jacket cover it. After gathering the last of my things, the bag is lifted, and I walk towards the door.

Opening the bedroom door, I quietly walk along the narrow corridor with the motion sensor lights clicking on and off, as I pass by. It feels like every footstep makes a conversation with every floorboard with each board having its own unique creak. Continuing down the noisy stairs, the room key is left on the reception counter, and I reach the outside door. Taking the car key from my jacket pocket, the remote is activated to unlock the doors. Opening the exit door of the pub, the dampness of the early morning dew touches my face, and as I begin to walk in the direction of the hire car the moisture in the air can be seen covering the car windows which are parked in front of the building. As the bag is placed on the front passenger seat, I walk around to the driver's side, and opening the door wait for a few seconds, to see if any car engines have been started. The eerie silence of the morning is only broken by an aircraft passing overhead.

Climbing onto the seat, the engine is started and headlights are illuminated, as I slowly pull away from the car park. As I continue past the village green and the narrow country road, I head for the direction of the A14. Glancing in the rear view mirror no headlights are seen behind or in front so whoever must be following me knows my next destination.

TWELVE

During the previous night, in a dimly lit public house, two men casually dressed in shirts and blue jeans sit at a table enjoying an early evening drink of beer. The door of the pub opens, and a well-built man wearing a dark blue suit and light grey hair walks inside. He quickly sees the two men and continues in their direction. The pub has three main areas, firstly, the bar section where four people are seen sitting on tall bar stools enjoying a drink. Then there is a restaurant area to the right with six tables, and to the left side of the bar past a large open fire is another dining area. The two men are sitting at table near to the fireplace. Three couples are seen eating inside the restaurant with a further four people sitting around a large round table in the other dining area. The walls and ceilings are an off-white colour with light brown oak beams exposed around the room. As the man walks along the large buff cream stone floor tiles, the latest easy listening chart music floats through the air.

Reaching the two men, he looks across at them, and gives the order, "He waits in the car for you both. I will look after your drinks, go now."

The men stand from their seats, and quickly walk towards the car park. The man wearing the blue suit sits at the table casually glancing around the pub for any reaction. Knowing that no one is taking any notice, he slowly reaches into his inside jacket pocket, then removes two small glass vessels which contain a clear liquid.

Removing the lids one at a time he gradually tips the contents of each vessel into the men's unattended drinks. Replacing the lids, he places the empty glass tubes onto the table top in-front of him.

Reaching to his right outside jacket pocket, he takes out a larger plastic container and lowers the two vessels inside closing the lid. Ensuring the lid is fully sealed, he returns the container to his outside jacket pocket. He can be seen peeling off a thin pair of latex gloves from his hands, and places them into his other outside pocket. The old man then continues to observe the clients in the pub making sure he wasn't noticed. Outside the two men reach the black Mercedes car, and tap on the rear passenger window.

The darkened window lowers slightly, and the command is given "Get inside."

The most senior of the two men walks around and opens the driver side rear door and climbs into the back of the vehicle. The subservient man opens the front passenger door and slides onto the dark leather seat.

"Leave us please." is heard inside the car and the driver's door opens. A man in dark grey suit exits the vehicle then starts slowly walking around the car park.

"So, what excuse do you two useless pricks have this time? How could you let him go?"

"Mr McGough, sir, I can only apologise for our actions."

"Your actions Wilkins have almost started an international incident with the Australian government. Who gave you the authority to kill those police officers?"

"Sir with respect, you instructed us to clean the area and remove all evidence."

"With respect Wilkins, you were told to be discreet and not to go in heavy handed. Killing half a small towns police force doesn't sound discreet and light handed to me" McGough snarls.

"Mr McGough, sir they were being very pushy, and we had to act fast. The forensic team had already gathered information about the asset."

"Yes, and your point is what?" McGough coughs.

"Sir, Nash had already moved onto Cairns, and the police were getting too nosey."

"You disobeyed a direct order, and that level of incompetence will not be tolerated. Is that clear."

"Sir we understand." Wilkins replies in a subdued tone.

"What of the target?"

"Sir, Nash boarded a plane back to the UK yesterday." Wilkins replies.

"I fucking know that level of information, do you idiots not realise who I am? I knew you were on a plane before you even walked to the departure gate!" McGough snarls.

"Sir what are your next orders?"

"Well, after the Australian adventure, I don't recommend a trip overseas, return back to the hotel, and await my next orders. I assume you know about Broadhurst's?"

"Mr McGough, who doesn't, do you think Nash will surface there?"

"Absolutely certain, he will be there next."

"How do you know this sir?" Wilkins asks.

"Because I have fuckin told him to be there, and because I am fucking smarter than you two idiots. You need to kill him."

The agent in the back looks a little shocked, but then a smile begins to form across his face, "Sir, I will not let you down again."

"You had better not, or I will ensure you both disappear never to be seen again!"

McGough looks to man in the front and says, "Preston, I have given you a chance to redeem yourself after the Wagstaff incident so you had better remember that and not let me down again."

Preston replies, "Yes sir."

"Once I know Nash is close to Broadhurst's, I will send a message to the pair of you along with the next orders. Now get out of here and wait at the hotel." McGough snaps.

"Yes sir." Both men open the doors of the car and climb out. The driver walks across, and then closes the doors, and waits standing next to the front of the car.

Wilkins and Preston walk back along the car park with their heads lowered slightly knowing that they have failed McGough. They enter the pub and continue towards the table with hardly a word said between them. The old man stands and smiles at then as they both quickly reach for their drinks taking a huge gulp of the liquid.

The older man can then be seen leaving the building heading towards the direction of the car, and as he reaches the Mercedes, the driver opens the door, climbs inside and starts the engine. The older man opens the passenger front door, and slides onto the black leather seat.

"Holmes, was it done?" McGough asks.

"Yes sir, I saw them both take a drink."

"Excellent, activate the trace elements for blood tracking. Let's see how utterly useless they are, but at least they can delay Nash, until he arrives." McGough stares at Holmes.

"Yes sir." Holmes takes out a mobile phone from a jacket pocket and with an integrated mobile app engages the trace elements that have been drunk by the two agents. The trace elements use the latest blood culture nanotechnology with pre-programmed molecules that when floating in the hosts blood stream emit a signal that can be tracked through GPS satellite software. The two agents finish their drinks and don't even realise what has been consumed.

"Where to sir?" Asks the driver.

"Continue towards Broadhurst's please, I think there is one last job to complete before I retire." All the men laugh, and they continue on their journey.

In the distance, the early morning darkness is illuminated by the blue and red police lights against the sky. Reaching ever closer to the Suxham Business Park, the road begins to be lined with all types of vehicles, and finally sections of security fencing. I pass the rows of vehicles which are parked at the side of the road in the grass verges and include police cars, minibuses, ambulances, fire engines, television camera vans, army trucks and unmarked cars. Several vehicles have slid into the deep roadside ditch to my left. In the reflections from the car headlights, people can be seen walking and running around everywhere with some wearing high vis jackets and others in body armour.

The road is completely gridlocked up front, and as I join the queue, people who are on the roadside stare at my car wondering who is inside. Suddenly, a camera flash illuminates the darkness and my eyes are instantly drawn to a group of people standing near a temporary stage which has dimly lit spotlights. Two people are seen standing centre stage in what appears to be Chief Constable and high-ranking Military Officer uniforms. I continue to weave my way towards the front of the queue in between the crowds of people, and suddenly, another camera flash goes off right next my car windscreen causing my eyes to sting slightly from the brightness.

As my eyes regain focus, I am confronted by four police officers standing in a makeshift line across the road holding torches highlighting the left junction for the Business Park. Behind them in the distance, the road looks more like a parking lot with more vehicles stranded everywhere. Finally, high level security fencing is noticed which prevents all access to the area, and as I quickly gaze along the fence line each metre feels like water has been poured onto my thoughts of escape after this job, and I sigh deeply. To the left is a small sign for the business park, and as I begin to turn the wheel of the car into the main entrance the road is blocked by two police Range Rovers parked with front bumpers just touching.

The highlights of the BMW shine against the whiteness of the vehicles and six armed police in full body armour stand behind the vehicles. Standing broadside to each car are six more officers in two groups of three, fully loaded with MP5's and body armour. Even in this dim light there is a seriousness across their faces confirming the difficulty of the situation.

One of the officers stands forward slightly, and beckons me to stop, and barks out an order, "Sir, switch off the headlights, open the driver's window and stop the engine, *now*."

Applying the brakes bringing the car to a gradual stop two meters away from the blockade, I turn off the headlights and open the driver's side window. As the window gradually lowers, the car is filled with the drumming noise and smell of diesel generators running some high-level temporary lighting stations and site offices. The vibrations from the generators can be felt through the seat of the car as the car engine stops running. The same officer then starts to walk over to the driver's open window, carrying the MP5 machine guns pointing downwards towards the road. All the officers have holstered pistols, handcuffs and CS gas canisters attached to their belts. Looking in the car mirrors five of the police officers have begun to circle the back of my car in a strategic formation as seen at checkpoints before covering both sides and the rear.

"What's your business here today sir?" The police officer asks sharply, leaning slightly towards the open window.

The redness in his eyes and two days of stubble confirms that he has been on duty for many hours and will not be the mood for any jokes. His voice and face show that he is under thirty years old, and he has probably only been on a hijack training course and never the real thing. I can hear one of the other officers start to report in that a blue BMW has been stopped at the main gate blockade through a muffled crackly radio communication.

"Dean Nash, here to see Commander Atkins on direct orders from McGough." I reply back quickly.

The same officer that was reporting my car, is now in the process of radioing through the licence plate details, so that a PNC check can be carried out. The police officer standing by my window leans back, and starts to lift the radio from his body armour jacket.

"Officer, do you know anything about hijacking incidents?" I sharply bark a question.

"What do you mean sir; I need to carry out proof of identity. Do you have a problem?" The officer snaps back.

The other police offices have now fully encircled the car after sensing some aggression with the conversation, and have begun to move closer to the car taking even more interest. The six officers on the other side of the blockade have now stopped talking to each other, and begun to stare in my direction as the atmosphere is beginning to become tense, and my pulse start to increase. Having been in this situation before, I am not afraid, but this time it feels very different, maybe, because it's my last. The police officer starts to lean back towards the car, as I snap out the answer to my own question.

"Yes Officer, I do have a problem. Do you know that all the police frequencies are probably being monitored, right now as we speak, by the hijackers. It is bad enough that your dumb ass colleague over there has already alerted the men inside to a suspect vehicle being stopped so instead of giving my name away, why can't you walk over to the main command centre, and ask in person. I will wait!"

The young officer beckons another officer on his left to come over, and asks, "Ben can you report to central control that a Dean Nash is here at the main gate to see Commander Atkins."

The second officer quickly runs over to the site cabin to the right side of the two Range Rovers and opens the office door slightly. There are no blinds on the windows with what appears to be around ten people inside, both police and army personnel in equal numbers with a heated discussion erupting from inside. Suddenly, one of the Army officers pushes the police officer away from the partly opened office door, and waving his left arm and hand he shouts out.

"Let him through right now, move them cars!"

The young police officer turns back looking at me and says, "You are free to move sir, sorry for any inconvenience." Sporting a cynical smile across his face.

"Officer, you had better wipe that smug grin off your face before I speak with the Chief Constable, or I will have you teaching road safety to primary school children for the next ten years." Replying with a similar smug smile.

The young officer stops and stares at me with shock all over his face. Pressing the ignition key back in the dashboard, the engine is restarted and switching back on my headlights, I wait at the blockade. The officer instantly stops smiling as two other offices run towards each of the Range Rovers and open the driver's side doors sliding onto the seat. Starting the engines almost at the same time the big cars begin to separate showing the clear road onto the business park.

Depressing the clutch with my left foot, and guiding the gear lever into first with my left hand, the car starts to shudder, and begins to move as the gears engage. The engine revs increase as the accelerator is pushed with my right foot and the car moves forward. The four remaining police officers are still standing around the back of my car, as I start to pass between the Range Rovers high front bumpers and the six other police officers now stare at me with some level of disgust.

Still having my window open, the ticking roar from the large V8 engines and smell of burnt petrol fills the inside of the BMW, and as the engine fan starts to whirl warmth air begins to circulate from the engine underneath the bonnet, which softly brushes against my face in the coolness of the early morning. I look at the car dashboard clock and notice the time of four fifty-five a.m. The Army officer has now made his way to the gap between the two police vehicles and is standing waiting. As my car bonnet starts to emerge from the opening of the blockade, I begin to depress the footbrake, and clutch bring to car to a stop.

"Sir, glad that you are here." He stamps his heels together giving a formal salute.

Saluting back informally, I notice his rank and reply with, "Which way Private?"

The soldier points towards another site office on the left side of a car park fifty metres forward. It appears to be a dark blue coloured site cabin dimly lit by outside lighting with a small yellow sign attached to the door that reads 'Strategic Site Operational Command Centre.' Having a quick smile to myself over the shitty typical formal sign thinking why they don't just use command centre.

"Sir Commander Atkins, and the others are waiting for you in the SSOCC sir."

"What's your name private, and what the fuck does that abbreviation mean?" I ask laughing.

"Sir my name is Private Ben Jackson, and the sign stands for Strategic Site." I stop him mid-sentence.

"Jackson don't worry I can see it." Still laughing, Jackson smiles back.

Starting to drive slowly towards command centre, I press the switch to close the door window as the two Range Rovers are driven back towards each other resealing the road, and blocking off one of my possible escape routes sealing my fate even further of entering certain death. My mind starts to drift slightly thinking about why I didn't just make a run for it again, and why my life is now at this stage of entering a probable no win situation. What will be the outcome for me from here? Reaching the command centre, the car is parked parallel to a black Mercedes, and as I activate the handbrake with two short 'clicks' my mind quickly remembers Wagstaff.

Switching off the lights and the ignition, the key is removed from the dashboard, and the interior light illuminates inside. Pushing the door open, I gradually begin to slide out from behind the wheel, and my senses are engulfed, and overpowered from all the noise, lights and smells being emitted from everywhere. In the background are the electric generator engines drumming away creating slight vibrations through my body, the smell of exhaust gases hangs heavily in the air along with reflections from the pulsating emergency lighting.

People's voices are suddenly overpowered by a police helicopter which is circling above. I see the image of the pilot and passengers illuminated by the cockpit display lights along with the red and green navigation tail lights, flickering against the dark sky. My thoughts suddenly flash back to Lloyd and the escape. Continuing to climb out of the BMW, I finally stand, turn and close the door behind myself, and start to make my way towards the command centre door. Reaching the door, I place my right hand on the door handle, and instantly, register the raised voices that can be heard from inside the building. Pushing the door inwards, I walk through the opening and into the main room. The office is quite bright with two sets of florescent tubes casting a yellowish white light across the area with a faint musty aroma hanging in the air.

I push the door closed quietly with a faint 'click' coming from the door lock engaging. My eyes are filled with the sight of a large flat table in the middle of the room with a set of architectural schematic drawings in the centre. Around the table are eight men and two women, all of whom are standing, talking and pointing at the plans. To the far-right side of the room is a frail old man around eighty years old who is resting in a large black office chair with a man in his fifties standing next to him. The people standing include two men and one woman in high ranking police uniforms, and four men in high ranking military dress. There are three men in smart dark suits and a lady in her late forties who is fussing around trying to keep busy.

At the far end of the room opposite the old man are four other men two in military dress and two in suits sitting at individual desks staring into laptop screens tapping away. On the wall of the office is a complete site plan of the business park showing all roads, buildings, and local land topography. The eight men standing are having quite a heated discussion. One man dressed in a Colonels military uniform is waving a piece of paper in his right hand trying to explain something, while the police officers try to ignore him. I stand in the doorway listening for a few seconds.

"Who is this man? What can he do that your military teams can't?" Asks the frail old man in his broken English voice.

"Well, Lord Broadhurst, it's complicated?" Replies one of the suits in a posh accent.

"Complicated in what way Jepson?" Asks Lord Broadhurst.

"This man is a specialist in these types of situations, and has a unique set of skills perfect for this type of job." Replies Jepson.

"Is it not possible just to pay these men and that will be it?" Asks Broadhurst.

"Lord Broadhurst that is not an option, England does not make deals with hijackers or terrorists on English soil." Replies another one of the men wearing a navy-blue suit.

"Well, why can't the SAS just do their thing like with the Iranian Embassy." Requests Broadhurst.

"Sir, The SAS are notified and, of course, on standby, but we do have a strange situation here." Replies the high-ranking military officer.

I look around the room and one man from his stance, voice and dress instantly gives away that this man is the new Director of Intelligence Commander Atkins. I remember another old thought of the first time we met.

"What situation is that? I seem to be getting a lot of parts but no full answers, maybe, a discussion with the Defence Secretary would be better." Snaps Broadhurst.

"Lord Broadhurst, I assure you that our selected candidate will be more than suitable for neutralising this situation." Atkins answers confidently.

No one has seen me standing in the door way, but I can tell that the situation is very tense, and the demands from the terrorist are clearly not going to be met.

"Good morning everyone, I hope, I am not the cause of all this confusion." I speak confidently but politely.

Everyone in the room suddenly stops speaking and turns around staring at me with what appears to be their eyes on stalks. The room is suddenly deadly silent with the only sound a drawing pin rolling off a desk and hitting the floor.

"Nash, thank god you are here finally!" Exclaims Atkins in a strong English accent.

Quickly scanning across the bewildered faces in the room, I can see from their reactions that they don't share a common acceptance, but some people appear to recognise me. I have already picked out several old acquaintances remembering when our paths had crossed in the past. Starting to walk towards the group of men around the table, the floor of the office 'creaks' and 'cracks' underneath the movement of my feet.

Atkins begins to lift his hand and raising my hand, we shake hands with a strong and confident grip, and it feels like greeting an old friend. Atkins smiles at me, and I can sense that a great weight has just been lifted from his shoulders.

"Would everyone clear the room for a few minutes, and grab some fresh air, I want to speak with Lord Broadhurst and Nash together, that also includes you Sandra." Atkins gesturing with his arms for everyone to move towards the door.

Lord Broadhurst slowly begins to stand from the black office chair and shuffles his feet with a level of frailty, as he walks in the direction of the windows to the side of the cabin. Atkins and I both watch him reach his destination and leaning on the window frame he takes a long hard sigh and has a slight cough as he stares into darkness of the approaching day. The man in his fifties who had been following closely behind then stands next to Broadhurst on his right-hand side with his back leaning on the wall close to the window staring at Atkins and myself.

Atkins then stares at me and starts to open his mouth saying,. "So, Dean do you feel this operation is possible?" Atkins stops to take a quick breath then continues to stare at me with dark brown sunken eyes.

I look across at him and can see that as with all the others people they have been awake for many hours and under extreme pressure then reply, "Well, I'm sure McGough has sent the file through and that you have studied the details."

"Nash, I need you to watch this broadcast that was sent through, we released an edited version out the news channels and press, but this version is un-cut."

Atkins turns and walks towards a laptop sitting on one of the rear desks. He beckons me to join him as he starts to operate the laptop, and open the DVD disk drive unit. He reaches inside his inner left jacket pocket with his right hand, and takes out a DVD case with a disc inside. He places the case on the desk and opens the box with his left hand and then takes out the disc with his right hand placing it onto the disc holder tray. He pushes the DVD tray into the laptop with an almost silent 'click' and the hard drive starts to whirr and buzz.

Reaching the desk, I can see the screen of the laptop start to change to a brightly lit room where the sobbing and crying of people can be heard in the background as the broadcast begins to run.

"To the Government of the United Kingdom and Lord Broadhurst, I Colonel Nick Burns confirm that my team, and I have taken over the Broadhurst weapons development facility and now hold five hundred and four staff hostage and hereby request the ransom of $100,000 per person for each employee of Broadhurst." Burns stands in front of the portable held camera demanding his money, then turns the camera and scans around to reveal the staff sitting in groups on the marble flooring shaking and sobbing.

"The monies demanded will be split evenly between my colleagues and the families of my fallen British Armed Forces comrades that have been killed in conflict by the weapons produced and sold by Broadhurst Industries over the last thirty years to our enemies. These include Gulf Wars, The Falklands, Bosnia and finally Afghanistan."

Burns then turns the camera, and walks into the main office area and the sales director's office and continue, "I have detailed reports and files showing where these weapons were sold along with all the official government documents from the Cabinet confirming that these transactions of arms sales were for training exercises only."

Burns then starts to move the camera over piles of Home Office and Ministry of Defence documents, "The last remaining documents are, of course, in the old archive files of Broadhurst Industries, and I have already started to extract this information."

Burns then turns the camera to a large digital clock on the wall, "The time as you can see is two nineteen p.m. on Wednesday fifteenth September 2010. You have until six p.m. Friday seventeenth September 2010, to arrange for the monies to be transferred to a Swiss Bank account, that I will give the information of in the next twenty-four hours."

Burns continues, "Of course, any form of rescue attempt will result in the death of all the hostages at Broadhurst Industries, and I will go public with this information delivering it to all the major news networks."

The Colonel warns, "I do, of course, fully understand that Her Majesties forces would like to set up camp on the front lawn, and they are more than welcome providing no one enters inside the fenced surrounding land around the factory."

Burns can then be seen smiling to the camera "It is also worth noting that any rescue attempt could force me to detonate the two hundred and fifty kilos of C4 explosive that I have distributed and armed around the site. Please keep your distance." Burns warns again.

The video stops and Atkins opens the DVD tray of the drive unit removing the disc and placing back into the case. He closes the case and places it back into his left jacket pocket. Atkins then starts to walks towards the large table in the centre of the room and starts to speak. I turn around and look towards the direction of Atkins then towards Lord Broadhurst.

"That's not the only problem Dean, Lord Broadhurst will you continue."

"Are you aware of what happens at this facility Dean?" Broadhurst asks still looking through the window.

"Well, yes sir, I previously worked here during the commissioning of the underground test chambers as a contractor." I reply.

"You have worked here before?" Broadhurst replies as he begins to turn around.

"Yes, the agency placed me here." Looking at Lord Broadhurst.

"That was over thirty years ago; my son Richard was just starting university." He gestures to his right.

"Nash, not only do we have a huge political problem here, but Lord Broadhurst's grandson William is one of the hostages. We are quite sure that Burns hasn't found him yet otherwise he would have made a direct request." Atkins stands leaning with both hands on the large table and continues to speak.

"We are running out of time fast Dean and the Home Office won't send in the SAS, due to the fact we believe looking at the video footage, some of the gunmen are in-fact ex SAS and the regiment naturally doesn't want any part." Atkins has concern in voice.

Lord Broadhurst then turns around and starts to walk over in my direction, with his son Richard following, "Look Mr Nash, I don't care about the factory, that can be rebuilt, but can you save my grandson and the other staff?"

Lord Broadhurst has tears in his eyes as he asks, "We can arrange for the money to be transferred now we have the bank account details, but our staff are just like family and my son means the world to me." Richard Broadhurst speaks with a posh crackly voice, fighting back the tears.

"Do you have family Dean?" Lord Broadhurst asks.

"I'm married to the agency sir and my only family is long gone." I reply honestly.

"Has Burns made any formal requests for evacuation off the site?" I ask trying to change the subject.

"Presently not." Atkins replies with another long sigh.

"Then that tells me he will either die with the staff or has another form of escape planned, and I would guess it could be aerial. I have seen Burns commanding before in Bosnia. He holds nothing back." I start to walk over to the large table.

"You know the Colonel?" Richard Broadhurst asks.

"Who are the other gunmen and how strong is the force?" I bounce around Richard's question.

Atkins replies, "Well, from the video footage we have confirmed eight gunmen around the hostages and office area to control the number of staff. If you include area patrols plus a few people in the security cabins he must have at least fifteen-eighteen men."

There is a knock on the door and a voice from outside asks, "Can we re-enter." A youngish voice shouts from outside.

Atkins replies "Yes, sorry forgot to invite you back in." Turning to wink at me.

The command centre door opens with Sandra walking in first and the other men following behind into the room. The air is filled with the smell of fresh coffee and tea from the cups they are holding in their hands. Steam rises from the cups creating a slight haze in the cool damp cabin environment. Sandra is carrying two cups of tea and walks over to Lord Broadhurst and his son handing them over. The two lower ranking military officers each have two cups of tea and hand them over first to Atkins and then myself. As the soldier passes me the paper tea cup, the warmth from the drink instantly sends a tingling sensation into the fingers of my right hand. I click off the plastic lid with my left hand and begin to lift the drink towards my mouth. I can feel the warmth of the rising steam touching my face, as I gradually take a small sip. The tea tastes stewed with no depth of flavour, but the drink is at least warming as the liquid passes down my throat.

"Burr it's pesky cold out there this morning." One of the grey suits proclaims.

"So what stage are we at?" Asks the Police Commissioner.

"I have just finished reviewing the video with Nash, and we are just starting to review the possible size of the hostile force inside." Commander Atkins replies.

I walk over to the table and start to look through the schematic drawings of the factory area, remembering as much detail as possible. There is also a pile of photographs of the gunmen that have been collected from the video footage. I place the tea cup on the table and pick up the pile beginning to thumb through the faces making note of any details that will help with identification. After a few minutes, placing the pictures back on the table I lift the tea cup and walk over towards the large map of the surrounding area and review any exit points along with entry area and limitations for any blast zones. The site map of the factory is broken down into several layers depending on the depth of chambers and foundations of the buildings. I notice something different from when I had previously worked here.

"What is this building here on the upper left side of the business park? This appears to be a new building?" I ask out loud.

"*Erm!* that's just a storage facility." Richard answers very quickly.

"Well, for a storage facility looking at the map scale it has walls almost two metres thick and a lower foundation of over fifteen metres.

What are you storing, gold bullion?" I ask with a sarcastic voice.

"That's not your concern." A voice from behind me instructs.

I turn around and look towards the direction of the voice and see a man in his late fifty's dressed in a dark grey suit and with light grey hair staring at me. I continue to turn around completely and start to walk over in the direction of the man who is almost two metres tall with slim build. His face has sharp chiselled details of chin and cheek bones along with a slight tan.

"It is of importance to me, and I will guarantee Burns will know exactly what is inside that facility. He could not only use it against me, but everyone in this whole area, so what's in the storage building?" I stand almost toe to toe with the man in the grey suit looking into his reddish-brown eyes.

"It's a chemical weapon test facility with water system purification." Atkins answers.

"So not only do you have a highly unstable military Colonel with evidence of illegal weapons sales, but you also have a demand for money and now chemical weapons at his fingertips." I turn and start to walk back towards the large table next to Atkins.

"The facility is in complete lockdown; it is operated remotely from the Home Office; there is no way that Burns will have the access codes to enter any of the doors." Replies the Air Chief Marshall.

"Who says he going to use the doors. You have heard Burns say he has a large quantity of C4 positioned around the site. One kilo of C4 can easily blast through a one metre thick concrete wall, if this is combined with a chain of C4 blocks and say a few claymore mines, a wall can quite easily be dropped." I answer back quickly.

"He doesn't have the quantity of explosives he would need a large van to bring them onto site and distribute them, he would have needed hours." Snaps out the man in the grey suit.

Just then another voice is heard, "Sir, it's finally confirmed from a farmers security camera that a large white Mercedes sprinter van passed his driveway on the A14 at twelve thirty-nine p.m. on Wednesday. The Farm is half a mile away from this business park and was not seen afterwards." The female solider looks back down at her laptop screen.

This piece of evidence suddenly sends the room into a spin with people grabbing mobile phone from their pockets. The man in the dark grey suit then walks over to the large table and clears away some pictures to expose the loudspeaker phone.

He presses the buttons on the control panel to get an outside line and a lady's voice is heard, "Yes, can I help you?"

"Ah good, Hastings here, can you connect me through to Home Secretary Allen immediately." He speaks with a Home Counties accent. The sound of the phone line can be heard ringing.

A familiar voice is now heard, "Yes, Hastings what is it now?"

"Home Secretary, it is confirmed the van on site has the C4 explosive and is a positive threat, repeat a positive threat."

"Well, how big is this threat? What is the expected blast zone? Has it been calculated yet Atkins?"

"Sir we do not have the final camera evidence yet for this allegation, but a large white van has been seen in the area prior to the facility being taken, therefore we will need to finalise all the risk factors and begin to prepare for the worst case."

Atkin pauses for a few seconds, then continues, "Initial indications confirm a blast zone close to one square mile which will be combined with fuel storage on site, but if the chemical weapons storage fails this would lead to major fatalities."

"Well, in figures man how many people?" Barks Allen.

"Sir, within the one-mile detonation zone, this would only account for less than two thousand casualties, but with the prevailing wind direction and chemical cloud exposure we would need to plan the complete evacuation of the Suffolk & Norfolk along with most parts of Cambridgeshire and Kent. The overall population exposure in the United Kingdom will be over two million people. There is also the risk, of course, to the Netherlands since it is still within the effective zone of the thorax chemical agent." Commander Atkins shares the bad news.

"Home Secretary, with the alleged C4 explosive and fuel storage onsite, there is over a seventy-five per cent chance that the majority of the thorax's deadly effects can be neutralised on explosion and this could be combined with a tomahawk cruise missile fired from a submarine off the Suffolk or Norfolk coastline." Admiral Jenkins replies staring across to Atkins.

"What vessels do we have in the area?" Allen askes.

"Well, HMS Ambush could be off coast in less than six hours, she has just finished a tour near to the Falklands and is already entering the North Atlantic Ocean." Jenkins continues.

"Firing a missile against ourselves is certainly a crazy idea, and I guess Burns will be expecting this not to happen. Am I right Atkins? On another note, how much devastation could we be looking at with this idea?" Allen gives a deep chesty cough.

"Well sir, if I may continue, we could send a phased thermal plasma fury type missile with a two hundred and fifty km range. The heat from the explosion combined with the fuel burn would vaporise the thorax chemical. The blast zone would still be within the one-mile detonation area and have minimal casualties." Replies the Air Chief Marshall.

"Christ, which idiot gave approval to build a chemical weapons factory to be built in this area?" Sighs the Home Secretary.

"OK look, I will, of course, inform the PM, but for now we had better start a low scale evacuation programme with anyone on the protection list living within a fifty-mile radius of the factory to be moved first." Requests Allen.

"Confirmed Home Secretary, I will co-ordinate with the relevant Police Constabularies with immediate effect the evacuation of the personnel from the protection list." Hastings confirms.

"Not you Hastings, leave the evacuation plans to Police Commissioner King I don't want another mess like last time. Now what is the status of this agent?" Allen continues.

"Sir, we have been carrying out a de-brief and formulating the action plan with Nash, when Hastings decided to make contact." Atkins turns and stares at Hastings.

"Of course, all approval is granted but the UK government stance remains that no negotiations with terrorists or hijackers will happen on UK soil. How quickly can Nash make an assessment and start?" The tired voice of Allen asks.

"Sir Nash here, I can be ready to commence Operation Deepdale in less than two hours." I reply.

The people in the cabin all turn and look at each other wondering how I have been able to find out the information concerning Operation Deepdale and then be in a position to execute the plans so quickly.

"Excellent Nash, continue as agreed Atkins, please give me a revised evaluation status update at six a.m. and put some more fat on the bones around this crazy idea of a missile launch. The PM and a few others in Whitehall will need some serious convincing to make that decision by seven a.m. Good morning, gentlemen." The phone rings off.

Another heated discussion now starts between the grey suit Hastings and Commander Atkins. All the other members of the team are present and throwing in questions based on fear and calculations.

"Do you really think that the PM will agree to a missile strike on UK Soil with UK weapons, you guys are living in the remains of a new cold war." Hastings laughs.

"It's unthinkable that the UK will fire missiles on itself!" Commissioner King replies.

"This is certainly not what I would have expected from Allen." Jenkins talking loudly with a strong West Country accent.

"Hastings, if the thorax gas escapes into the atmosphere then the south of England will be a quiet neighbourhood for about fifty years as the toxins are gradually released!" Atkins replies with some venom in his voice.

"Are you serious, the Home Office was informed that this is only a mild irritant with flu like symptoms and minor muscle damage?" Hastings snaps back at Richard Broadhurst.

"Gentlemen, please can we have some order of control!" Atkins raises his voice, then looks at Richard to continue, the latest generation of thorax agent is both respiratory and contact absorbent and any person inhaling the toxin or touching any surface where the substance has made contact will have fever and flu like symptoms first, but then the entire body is attacked by the thorax agent which completely breaks down the immune system and main organs with death to follow." Richard Broadhurst sighs.

"Well, how long from inhaling the substance until death?" Asks Admiral Jenkins.

Broadhurst explains, "We had an accident at the facility two years ago when three scientists where exposed to the thorax agent during a test exercise. In the isolation hospital zone four more scientists where affected even though they were fully protected in biohazard suits. The earliest case of death was five hours with the longest scientist surviving for twelve hours, even after the antidote had been administered! Broadhurst protocols were then actioned with all bodies, laboratory equipment and hospital zones all burnt at two thousand degrees Celsius for one hour to kill off the remaining thorax agent." Everyone in the room stands in complete disbelief.

"Why wasn't the Home Office notified of this incident?" Hastings snaps out.

"Whitehall, was notified that an accident had taken place with a fire in a laboratory and that seven scientists were killed." Richard Broadhurst replies back.

"I assume the thorax agent wasn't mentioned in this report?" Atkins asks.

"Of course, not, the accident was due to one of the scientists dropping a vessel of ten millilitres that broke on the floor." Broadhurst replies back.

"This critical piece of information was left out from the report. I knew there were more things happening here than Whitehall knew about. This must be reported!" growls Hastings. "Fighting between ourselves now will not help the five hundred staff being held hostage. These matters can be taken up once the problem at hand is sorted." Atkins stares around the room at all the people.

"We need an action plan drawn up for the concept of thermal plasma missiles, Admiral Jenkins can you work with Air Chief Marshall Downing on this idea with full status and projected timescales. If Burns knows the thorax chemical is on site, he will use it as another bargaining chip." Atkins looks across at Jenkins and Downing.

"Commissioner King, can you start the evacuation procedure for the protected list personnel as Home Secretary Allen has requested, the best option will be to fly them to Scotland from Marshall Airport telling them it's a training exercise." Atkins speaking in a calm and controlled manner.

"Nash, have you finalised your entry point and plan of attack routes?" Atkins asks staring hopefully at me.

"Plan of attack, I though Nash was just on reconnaissance?" Hastings answers.

"He is, but when the negotiations fail, he will be the first line of defence before any planned missile strike." Replies Atkins.

"A possible missile strike requires the approval of both the Home Office and the PM and from my information on the ground that's not been presented yet!" Hastings quickly responds, full of his own self-importance.

"Hastings, you and indeed the rest of us need to question why we have been sent here at all. If the thorax toxin escapes, we will all be certain casualties!" Jenkins speaks out quite openly.

"Gentlemen, this is a military operation that requires everyone to remain focused. Lord Broadhurst, I recommend that you and Richard make plans to leave ASAP!" Atkins continues.

"I can't leave this place, not now!" Richard speaks with raised voice.

"Richard, I fully understand, but there is nothing you can do." Atkins answers.

"No, my Father will leave, and I will stay, I can help if you need any more information on the site and besides, when this is finished, I must be here for my son." Richard now enforces his presence.

Hastings looks across at Broadhurst and from his body language, it is quite clear that he was not aware that Richard's son William is one of the hostages.

"Richard, is your son one of the hostages?" Hastings asks.

"Yes, he is, and we can give you immediate updates. You can be flown back here as soon as the hostages are freed, staying here is a major risk to your business and the security of this country." Atkins replies.

"Imagine if my son finds out that I decided to leave this place for the sake of my business, if my son isn't there for the future, there is no business, No I'm staying and Father can go. If anything happens to me or William, the exec board can continue the business." Richard continues his pleas.

"Richard, there is a big risk in you stopping here, but I fully understand if you need to be with your son. OK, but Lord Broadhurst must leave in case anything goes wrong." Atkins remains calm and collected.

Hastings then speaks, "With the government contracts for Broadhurst Industries, it would be better if both leave?"

"Hastings, the man's son is sitting in that room surrounded by terrorists. You may not have a caring bone in your grey stone body, but I fully understand Richard's request. I am in command here and Richard can stay giving any additional facility support." Atkins speaks with a raised voice enforcing his command.

Richard breathes a sigh of relief saying, "Thanks Director Atkins."

Standing looking all the people in the cabin, Lord Broadhurst and his son Richard start to make their way over towards me. In doing so the floor of the site cabin bends and flexes making a low creaking noise with every footstep. Lord Broadhurst reaches me and offers me his right hand. I see the gesture and reciprocate the action.

As our hands meet, he then places his left hand over the top cupping my hand completely giving a very strong and firm handshake.

"Please Dean, do what you can for my grandson and the staff. The whole country needs you now. The last thing we need is a missile being launched." Lord Broadhurst looks into my eyes with tears beginning to form.

Then Lord Broadhurst releases my hand and with his son they walk gracefully towards the door. I lower my hand and look across towards their direction and see Lord Broadhurst turning and looking at Richard. The two men have a firm handshake then embrace each other with a large hug.

I hear Lord Broadhurst say, "Good luck son, I love you and take care."

Richard replies, "I love you too Father."

Atkins look across to the two men and says, "Lord Broadhurst, we will try our very best for everyone. As soon as we know anything, we'll be in contact. Have a safe journey."

Lord Broadhurst releases his son, turns and opens the command centre door with his frail right hand. As he walks out of the cabin, Richard turns and with tear filled eyes walks in my direction. Standing a footstep away from me, Richard lifts his right hand, reciprocating the gesture again I can feel that Richard's whole body is shaking with nerves and adrenalin.

With a strong grip and a tear rolling down his cheek Richard looks straight into my eyes saying, "Nash, please save my son!"

I look back at Richard saying nothing, standing in the middle of the room, holding hands. My mind begins to fill with the thoughts of what Richard must be going through knowing his son may not survive, and that he could also be killed. Knowing that he has given the ultimate sacrifice for his son to stop in a place where they may never see each other again and about the sacrifice of Lord Broadhurst leaving his only son behind so that their business empire can continue as a lasting legacy. My thoughts are purely to stop alive, and how to ensure that McGough keeps his end of the deal. I release my grip on Broadhurst's hand and start to lower mine as a voice behind registers.

"Nash, have you been able to identify the most effective entry point on the site?" Atkins asks.

I turn and looking towards the men reply by saying, "Director Atkins, Air Chief Marshall Downing and Admiral Jenkins, I have professional respect and trust for all of you and your teams, but our friends from the Home Office and the Police, I do not!" Staring across at Hastings.

"The route I have selected will not be discussed in front of these people since they are potential sources of a leak to Burns, but what I will guarantee is that by five thirty a.m., I will give a status confirming my findings." I look towards Atkins.

"That's accusation is preposterous!" Shouts the Police Commissioner King.

"I have never heard so much rubbish in all my life!" Proclaims Hastings.

"I'm not going to spend the next two hours debating the facts, but will ask only two simple questions."

"Question One, when I reached this site earlier, the Police Officers on blockade duty used two-way radios to announce my presence? This action goes against all Official MOD and Home Office terrorist attack procedures."

"Question Two, how has Burns been able to source all the documents and entry codes for the facility? Only an internal leak could produce this information and since all MOD documents relating to weapons technology need Whitehall approval, this question kind of answers itself."

"What a load of bullshit, I have never heard anything like this before, with some jumped up agent telling me that my procedures are not being followed." Snarls King.

Hastings walks away slightly to the left of everyone else and calls across one of his other men and whispers in his right ear, "Wainwright, can you double check with Baines in the archive office when the Broadhurst documents were compromised and if there is a record of a signature in the archive log."

Atkins begins to walk over to me away so the other men can't hear and asks, "Dean, what can you do?"

"Sir, sometimes I can do the impossible, but with all these moving parts and if they find out William is a hostage, Burns is likely to hang him from a set of gallows on the front lawn, he will show no mercy!" I whisper back.

I continue, "Sir, all I ask is keep the police and the Whitehall idiots as far away from this operation and make sure that the missile isn't fired at all costs."

Atkins looks at me and holds out his right hand and responds with, "Dean, I hope you are everything we have been told, we don't have any other options."

Taking Atkins hand as a final handshake knowing he can't remember me I say, "Director, when have I ever let you down in the past, so failure isn't an option, besides it's been good to see you again."

Atkins has a look of shock all over his face, "You really don't remember do you?"

Releasing Atkins hand, I turn and walk towards the door of the command centre. Reaching the door, I begin to operate the handle and begin to open the door.

Atkins still in shock shouts, "Good Luck."

Turning around to smile at him, I nod my head and walk through the doorway back out into the darkness of the early morning and back into the drumming noise from the site generators. As I walk out from the building towards the back of the BMW hire car, the soldier ranked private from earlier at the blockade is standing holding two large black hard case bags.

Looking across at him I say, "Going on holiday Private?"

"Sir, no sir these are for you as requested." Jackson has no sense of humour.

Clicking the boot unlock button on the key fob, the lid pops open slightly and the interior lights illuminate the inside of the vehicle. As I reach the car to open the boot lid, a faint light can be seen leaking from around the seals which suddenly reminds me of a past memory, and as I gradually lift the boot lid, the image of a person lying inside the boot area fills my thoughts. The increasing glow which emerges from inside the boot clearly shows the dark green military kit bag which has been lying inside. My mind takes a few seconds, to refocus before I reach for the bag. Placing the carry strap onto my right shoulder, I pause for a few seconds trying to remember who the person was in the car trunk. Clearly the thoughts are not those from my previous exploits with Burns after the money robbery.

Closing the boot lid, the darkness then returns and my eyes take a few more seconds to re-focus, as I turn and ask Jackson, "Is there anywhere to change?"

"Yes sir, there is the main gatehouse over on the right." He points towards a small building.

I start to walk towards the gatehouse and Jackson asks, "Sir, what about the suitcases?"

"Bring them with you." I shout back looking over my left shoulder.

THIRTEEN

Private Jackson drags the two large bags across the tarmac road on their tiny wheels making a scraping sound as he quickly tries to catch me up. I reach the main gatehouse and quickly look over towards the car park and then in the direction I am planning to begin the operation. Lowering the lever with my right hand, the door is pushed open with my shoulder. The gatehouse is being used as a rest area for the police, and has ten officers inside with six men standing wearing full body armour and talking quietly while the other four men sit relaxing after removing their bulky jackets. Jackson finally catches up with me and walks into the twenty pairs of eyes now all staring at the two of us. My nostrils are instantly filled with an aroma that reminds me of a changing room with stale sweat and smelly feet, taking a small gasp, I look towards the ceiling and notice that some of the light bulbs have been removed from the holders to reduce the amount of illumination in the building. This helps the human eyes to focus faster between darkness and artificial light. The rest room smell is partly being masked by a coffee machine percolating away in the corner of the room. The only table in the room is filled with empty drinks cans, food packets and old coffee cups which have been thrown everywhere.

"Could everyone please leave the room, Direct orders from Director Atkins." Private Jackson continues to drag the suitcases into the middle of the room. Not looking at anyone.

"Who the fuck are you to tell us what to do Private?" One police sergeant blasts back.

"Officer, sorry but these are direct orders, and we need you to leave the room now!" Jackson repeats the request as he starts to lift one of the suitcases onto the table pushing the rubbish onto the floor.

A second officer walks over towards the Private asking, "What are you pair, the fucking comedy act?"

Jackson starts to lift the second case and another officer grabs his right arm forcing him to stop moving and lower the case back to the ground. I start to walk over in the direction of the second police officer only to notice, he is the same guy from earlier at the blockade. I can sense that the other officers are beginning to encircle me as the last remaining officer who was sitting is now standing in a defensive posture.

"Let go of Private Jacksons arm?" I snarl at the officer then continue.

"This is the second time you've pissed me off, there won't be a fucking third, everyone get the fuck outside NOW! Take your fucking rubbish with you it's a shit hole in here." I raise my voice stamping control on the area. Staring directly at the sergeant.

"Come on lads, its boy zone in here, pick up your mess." The sergeant, admitting defeat turns and walks out of the building slamming the door behind.

The remaining officers start to grab their guns, stab jackets, rubbish and other equipment and make their way towards the direction of the door, throwing rubbish in the large dustbin by the side of the exit door.

The last officer slams the door in defiance as Jackson finally lifts the second case onto the table. Taking the kit bag from my shoulder, I place it in between the two hard covered suitcases.

Turning to Private Jackson, I smile then say, "Thank you Ben, remember take no shit from anyone especially them idiots, thinking they are tough with a gun."

Smiling back, he replies, "Sir, thank you, but I was on top of the situation."

"Jackson, admitting defeat and asking for help isn't a failure, not asking for help and pretending it was under control is." He looks at me and smiles.

"Sir, are you really going inside to fight against Burns?" Jackson asks.

"I'm expendable Ben." I reply, as I start to open my kit bag.

"It's suicide though sir!" He has a look of shock on his face.

"We all gotta die sometimes Ben, why not today hey. Would you mind standing outside by the door while I change, I need to prepare." I shrug my shoulders and gesture with my hands.

Jackson turns and walks towards the exit door and as he reaches it, he turns and stamps his heels giving a formal salute.

I look across at him, turn and with a straight back, return the salute saying,. "At ease Private, it's been a long time since I've been formally saluted."

Jackson drops his salute and replies back, "Sir Good Luck." He leaves the building.

I turn back and start removing the contents from my kit bag and firstly, I pull out a neatly rolled pair of black tactical trousers. I unroll the pair of trousers and lay them on the table top. I reach inside the bag and then remove a matching black tactical shirt again neatly rolled. Next to be taken out of the kit bag is a pair of black lightweight military boots with a rolled up black tee shirt in one boot, and black belt, and camo face paint kit in the other. The final piece of clothing is a black assault vest. Removing my jumper, I start to undress and can instantly feel the coldness of the early morning air touching my naked arms as the jumper is folded neatly and placed by the green kit bag. I pull my blue polo shirt from my body and the cold instantly bites into my naked torso, so quickly grabbing the tee shirt, it is pulled back onto my skin along with the black tactical shirt.

Bending down and untying the laces from my casual shoes, they are removed with my right hand and unclipping my belt along with opening the buttons of my jeans. The hairs on my legs stand to attention as the warmth from the jeans disappears and the cold bites again. Reaching towards the table the jeans are placed next to the other casual clothes, and with my right hand I take the black tactical trousers and step into them giving back some warmth. After tucking the shirts inside the waistband, the trousers are fastened together, but the coldness from the floor is still biting at my feet so lifting the pair of black boots, they are placed on the floor. Sliding my feet into the boots, I stop for a second as my mind drifts towards the operation as the entry point and route start to flash through my brain.

Plotting the points and key landmarks inside the factory building from my past experience begin to unfold into a three-dimensional image as though it was only yesterday. I begin to remember the words of Lord Broadhurst and his son asking me to save everyone's lives and then the look on McGough's face when we were speaking. My thoughts are interrupted by a knock on the door.

"May I enter?" A voice is heard and instantly recognisable as Atkins.

"Yes, no problem Director." I turn towards the door.

The door begins to open as Atkins starts to walk into the room, "Dean, I remember now?" Atkins closes the door.

"Really, you're a long way from that young Private hey!" I look at Atkins.

"I don't understand, you have hardly changed?" Atkins stands in complete shock.

"Well, let's just say life has been good to me." I smile at him.

"I thought you had been killed in action!" Atkins still stands at the by the door.

"Lots of people thought or even hoped I was dead and after this operation my fate will definitely be sealed?" I continue to smile at him.

"You disappeared and now you are back!" Atkins just stares at me in disbelief trying to understand what is happening.

"Look Director, you haven't just come here to exchange old chit chat so what's the problem?" I ask calmly.

"Dean, after the tragic death of Wagstaff a few weeks ago, Whitehall doesn't seem to be making much effort in finding his killers, and it appears that because I was second in command this incident is placed squarely at my feet. I don't think I could live with the consequences if things go wrong here as well?" Atkins has stress in his voice as he looks at me.

"Atkins, the death of John Wagstaff was avoidable, but no one at Whitehall was prepared to stop it. Maybe, his use to the agency had come to an end so is it any wonder they don't want to get involved now. You know Burns, as well as me, and he will stop at nothing, until he gets what he wants. If he finds the Thorax chemicals then we are all in deep shit not just you!" I reply back firmly.

"Atkins, my advice for what it is worth is to stay focused and try to hold off those missiles for as long as you can. Whitehall will want the easiest solution to clean up this mess." I stare at Atkins.

I continue to speak, "Just watch that bastard Hastings, and make sure if things go bad, make sure he is last out of the door. You should know, you have seen him before?"

The director stands in-front of me with another look of shock on his face, and it is clear from his actions that Atkins had a huge amount of respect for John Wagstaff. I only hope he never finds out that I played a key part in his death. Lifting my left leg so that my foot is resting on the edge of the table, I start to lace up the left boot. Atkins turns away and starts to open the door still in a trance.

Turning back to me he says, "Dean, please do what you can for those people in the building, I would dread to think what things Burns could do with them."

"Sir, I have a score to settle with Burns, and I don't plan on losing today, there is too much hanging on the outcome." I reply still tying my boot laces.

Atkins finally turns and walks out of the room slowly closing the door behind himself. Lowering my left leg, I raise my right to continue with the boot lacing. With both feet now on the floor, the boots squelch and creak, as I move my body weight to each foot checking the support given from the supple leather. Wiggling my toes inside the boots, I make sure they are comfortable and nothing is rubbing against the cushion sole socks. Lifting the assault vest from the table, I thread my arms through the webbing and pull the vest around my abdomen securely fastening it with the plastic clip and zip. I move towards the kit bag and then fold all my civilian clothes into neat piles and so that I can place them inside the bag.

Walking across to the first black suit case, I turn the combination number lock to 1942 on both of the zip catches and flick open the small latch. Unzipping the upper flap of the first hard case, my nostrils are filled with the scent of fresh gun oil, as I notice the neatly packed guns held inside the protection foam. The guns shimmer in the light against the dark grey shaped foam that supports them along with the preloaded bullet magazines. Repeating the process for the other case, I unzip the lid which exposes various knives, detonators, grenades, motion sensors, a tool kit and a pair of night vision glasses. Taking my belt from the table, I start to thread it through the loops on my trousers including the gun holster for the right side and knife holster on the left.

The pair of small throwing knifes are lifted from the case and pushed behind the main belt buckle. Lifting out the Beretta handgun the rubber grip feels sticky against the palm of my right hand, as I click back the top slide with a quick movement of my left hand. Just from the noise and feeling through my fingers, the action is smooth and clean. With a click of the trigger, the top slide springs back into position, and I quickly examine the outside condition of the weapon using the dim light in the room. Clicking the safety catch onto safe, I reach with my left hand for a loaded pistol magazine from the suitcase, then push the clip into the base of the handle grip with a firm 'click' ensuring the spring mechanism is working smoothly.

Finally, the handgun with its increased weight is placed into the holster hanging on my belt with the safety strap clicked over the rear slide support position preventing the gun from falling out. Leaning forward, I reach into the suitcase for the MP5 sub machine gun and gradually lift the gun with my right hand. The coldness of the steel can be felt even through the anti-slip rubber grips.

As with the pistol the top slide is pulled back to check the action and then clicked forward to ensure the hammer spring operates smoothly. Taking the circular sound suppressor from the suitcase with my left hand, I engage it onto the threads at the end of the barrel and gradually rotate the lightweight tube. Finally pulling out the retractable stock, I lift the gun towards my right shoulder and look down the gun-sights checking the weight and feel of the gun. Pushing the stock back into the action and inserting a loaded magazine, the machine gun strap is passed over my left shoulder as the gun is hung across the back of my body.

Ten loaded magazines for the MP5 are then removed from the case and placed into the pockets evenly on each side of the assault vest distributing the weight. The six pistol magazines are also taken from the case and placed in more of the assault vest pockets. A large survival knife is the next weapon taken from the case using my right hand and softly clasping my left hand around the blade, I use my thumb to check the sharpness by rubbing it across the glimmering surface edge feeling the resistance and hearing the faint grating noise being generated.

The coldness can be felt passing into my thumb as the blade is checked millimetre by millimetre and after looking along the length of the blade for any dents or marks, the knife is pushed into the holster with the safety strap locked into position. The twelve motion sensors and ten grenades are taken from the case and placed into the rear pockets of my assault vest. Deciding to take only a couple of detonators since I may be able to find some of Burns pre-set devices, they are placed with the grenades. The toolkit is removed and placed into an empty pocket on my vest and the final item is taken from the case which is a pair of lightweight multi-purpose night vision glasses, these are inserted into the top pocket of my shirt ensuring they are protected.

Standing in the room the assault vest straps press heavy into the top of my shoulders from the weight of equipment and ammunition loaded inside the pockets. It is far less than I have carried in the past, but for this operation being light and agile is far more important than the burden of heavy backpacks.

The plan of the factory flashes through my mind again, as I begin to close the two suitcase lids and click shut the combination locks. Walking towards the door, I lift my kit bag and walk towards the door with the leather boots creaking slightly. Now standing at the door, I lift my right hand onto the handle and stop for a few seconds, to remember what has brought me to this place and now the certain truth that is waiting for me in the factory and no matter how much I try to blank it out death has finally up with caught me and may not be giving me another chance to escape.

Both fear and excitement now begin to race through my emotions, as I walk outside from the safety of the gatehouse into the darkness of the new day trying to make as much distance as possible before the morning light shows my progress. Starting to work my way through the rows of neatly parked cars away from the sound of the diesel generators, the only noise I can hear is the squeaking from my black leather magnum boots.

Approaching the rear security lodge, I wait next to a large tree which allows me to observe the surveillance camera's which are placed all over the site. I know by the manufacturer and information from the schematic plans that these cameras have dead-zones and once you know their operational field of view, the opportunity to melt into the darkness is easier. Quickly reaching the back of the rear entrance lodge, I peer through the glass door and see a man around twenty-five years old watching the large banks of security camera screens and from his actions, I sense that I haven't been spotted.

Taking a small detonator and charge from my utility pack, I place the device near the main electrical panel which can be operated from a remote-control signal. This would allow me to disable power feeds, and cause enough of a distraction at a crucial time. Slowly sinking back into the darkness away from the lodge, I turn and start to make my way to the far-right side of the facility near the main fuel deposit area, which I know from the screen is covered by a camera. This is another good place to set up more confusion with a remote-controlled explosive charge, but the risk of being spotted increases. Reaching the fuel storage area, there are two soldiers standing around one hundred metres in front of me near to a surface mounted service access hatch. Above the soldiers on the wall of the building is the surveillance camera. The duct access hatch is two metres square with all mains electric, gas and water supplies and the main access door is close to the outer factory wall and this is my entry point to the building. Taking these guards out now would cause more trouble and alert the terrorist team, who would then probably know my plans.

Better to wait and see if they move and sure enough after five minutes, one of the soldier's moves away walking parallel to the outer building wall leaving the other guy again with his back to me. This is my opportunity to set another explosive device and start my way to the duct if I can just negotiate the camera. I have been watching it gradually sweeping across from the left to the right in a one-eighty-degree arch of movement and know I have around four minutes each side of the sweep. Waiting for the camera sweep and the other soldier to move my heart rate is calm and collected.

The darkness of the night is beginning to change to dawns purple light, as I reach the area below the fuel tank, another explosive charge is set at the base to one of the rear support legs of the main fuel tank.

Only having limited time before the camera will sweep back over my position, the second soldier starts to walk in the same direction as the first man, this is my only chance, and I make a quick dash to the outer factory wall, where I can check out the service hatch in more detail.

A robin starts to sing in the nearby trees which breaks the darkness of the night, as the start of this new day begins to unfold. I take a look at the service hatch cover, and notice nothing from the outside, such as, a trip switches or vibration sensors, but there could be something underneath. I stare back across at the soldiers and from their stance, sense I only have a few more seconds before they turn around. I am now standing directly underneath the camera which will not pick up and of my movements. Bending down, I creep to the hatch and slowly start to lift the metal hatch cover plate, I recheck for any trip switches or sensors, but also know my time has run out so hearing nothing, I pull on the lid. The only resistance I can feel is coming from the rusty hinges which creak slightly with lack of lubricant.

I take one final look towards the direction of the soldiers and quickly start to climb down the steel ladder beginning to close the lid behind. Suddenly, I hear voices of the approaching soldiers and stop my movements on the ladder and through a small slit between the hatch and frame see the soldier's feet standing close by. Slowly continuing to close the lid, I can hear them talking above and know that I have not been seen.

Now in the service duct system, my eyes begin to adjust to the very poor artificial light inside the small tunnels being emitted from occasional florescent tube lighting. My nose is filled with the scent of stale musty air combined with heavy old hypod gearbox oil. My mind is in overdrive pulling together all the pictures of the tunnel system which runs like a rabbit warren maze underground. I need to remember the position of certain machines, where I can place explosive charges along with roof column supports that need exploding to cover any terrorist escape routes. Reaching into my shirt top pocket I place the night vision glasses on and a good level of light is now restored.

As I travel along the tunnel, my mind reaches back into my past, and I suddenly remember being taken along a dim light corridor to an interrogation chamber which was at the far side of this facility. Walking around the pipes and cables I occasional throw self-drilling motion sensors onto the ceiling that will pick up any people's footsteps and voices from the factory floor area. This is my last assignment, and I am taking no chances.

Meanwhile, upstairs Burns gets more frustrated with the slow pace of talks. Burns is disgusted that Lord Broadhurst has not transferred the money in to the account and snaps, storming into the main restaurant with a look of anger across his face. He stares around at the hostages deciding who to kill first, but also knows that he needs to wait for the right time. I continue along the tunnel and stop near a service hatch in the centre of the shop floor area. A faint dripping sound can be heard and on closer investigation blood can be seen dripping from the service hatch and clearly someone has been killed above.

Knowing that I have to place an explosive change in this area of the factory floor away from any cameras I need to climb the ladder. Trying to avoid the dripping blood, I remove the glasses then placing my hands on the blood drenched metal rails climb the ladder. Slowly reaching the service hatch panel, I check for any motion sensors, then begin to raise the lid. As I lift the panel, a person can be seen lying on the factory floor and lifting the panel further, there are a few more dead people who appear to have been sitting around a table having food. Pushing the panel sideways away from the body, I begin to emerge from the service duct checking all around for any terrorists but see and hear nothing. Now fully clear of the tunnel and ladder, the only noise that can be heard is the sound of machines still whirring and completing operations. I return the panel over the hole, but leave a small area uncovered, so that I can place my hands under the lip.

Taking an explosive charge from my assault vest and making sure no cameras are overlooking my position, I cross a small gangway and set the charge next to a large plastic injection moulding machine that is still producing parts. Placing the charge next to the main hydraulic pump, I turn to begin my journey back to the service duct. Suddenly, two voices are heard and two soldiers appear from nowhere. Now stuck between the machine and the service duct, I crouch close to the machine hoping they simply pass by but have already removed the knife from its holster. One solider looks across and sees the service duct panel not fully closed and stops.

With his back turned to me and before he can even radio in the concern, I jump forward with the knife pointing in his direction and stab the blade into the back of his neck straight through his windpipe and in a quick action grab the next soldier around the top of his neck and snap it with a quick sweeping action before the first soldier even drops to the floor. As they both hit the floor one of their guns strikes the hard floor sending out a metallic echo while a radio smashes against the concrete sending plastic fragments across the flat surface.

Leaning forward I check the pulse of the first man and knowing he is dead, pull the knife from his neck and wipe the blade on his jacket then slide it back into the holster. The second man was dead, as soon as, I twisted his neck so quickly, I begin to drag each man one at a time along the gangway next to the other dead men around the table in an attempt to hide them.

When both of the men are moved into position, I notice there is some blood and drag marks on the floor, but before I can return to the gangway to remove the evidence another soldier is heard, and knowing I only have a few seconds. I quickly hide next to one of the dead men, and pull one of them over me slightly. Slowly removing the knife from my holster, I watch the soldier stop and glance at the blood on the floor, then his head turns towards the direction of the drag marks and the group of bodies around the table. He turns and starts to walk in my direction. He is cradling a machine gun but hasn't reached for his radio at this time, but he is too far away from me at this time.

He stops and notices that some of the clothing is what the soldiers were wearing, and comes closer to investigate making his last mistake. As he reaches the dead soldiers, I am underneath the closest man and in a quick action grab hold of his left arm with my left hand, and with a quick sweeping action cut his throat and main jugular artery causing him to fall to the ground sending blood pulsating into the air.

Quickly moving from underneath the dead body, I grab him around the neck snapping it to make sure I don't meet him again and with hardly a sound I have killed three of Burns best men in a matter of minutes. Grabbing some cloth that was next to a machine, the blood marks are removed from the gangway, and I return back to the service duct as though nothing has happened. Continuing along the tunnel for a further four minutes and forty-five seconds, the pre calculated distance should bring me to the area of the building, where I need to lift the nearest service hatch closest to the restaurant which should be under the main office elevator maintenance shaft. If I carry on for another one hundred metres south, this will be the area where the van could be parked close to the staff restaurant building. As I continue along the corridor, the man in security requests all soldiers to check in. As they go through the list of call signs three are missing.

He asks again, "Team two, radio in immediately and confirm your position?" Silence is heard.

"Patrol party four, confirm your status?" Again silence.

He radio's forward to Burns, "Sir, there are three of the team not responding to calls?"

Burns replies, "Can you see them on the cameras?"

"Sir, no sir I have already checked."

Burns looks across to Reynolds and beckons him over then asks, "Reynolds, take Hobbs and complete a sweep of the shop floor."

"Sir, Yes sir."

"Be careful and report in anything that suspicious that requires additional investigation?" Reynolds nods his head in agreement.

"Heaton and Stubbs, report to the restaurant." Burns commands.

Burns sensing that several of his team may have already been killed starts to feel the noose beginning to tighten around his neck. Heaton and Stubbs report as ordered. Standing close by the restaurant entrance doors, Burns watches the two men appear, and they can see from the expression on his face that the Colonel isn't happy.

"Lewis, Brough and Swifty have not reported in, have you seen anything during your patrols?"

"No sir." They both reply with shock on their faces.

"I have sent Reynolds and Hobbs out to complete a recce but we may have a few rats in the cellar."

"Step up the patrols outside in case any unwelcome visitors start to breach the fence line and shoot on sight." Burns instructs.

"Yes sir, certainly." They both reply and quickly return to their perimeter patrols.

Burns radio crackles with some news, "Sir, we have found the three bodies, they were lying next to previously killed hostages."

"I knew it, return back here immediately." Burns with rage in his eyes storms into the restaurant wanting to seek revenge for the death of his team members then walks up and down the rows of hostages who gradually lower themselves closer to ground in an attempt to hide sensing that something is going to happen.

Burns stops next to a man dressed in a light grey suit and announces, "You look an important person at this company? What is your name and position?"

The man shaking with fear looks up to Burns and instantly regrets all of his previous actions, "My name is Gary Winters, and I am the vice president of finance."

"So, I guess you have a high salary and pretty wife hey?" Burns towers over him as Reynolds and Hobbs return.

"Please, I have only been here for a few weeks and have a wife and two young children."

"I don't give a fucking shit." Burns looks at Reynolds.

"Take him first."

"No please no I beg of you!" Winters cries and looks around the room for help, but people just look down to the floor praying that they will not be selected next.

Reynolds walks over as Winters begins to wet himself with the fear that his life is coming to an end. Reynolds places and hand under his armpit and starts to lift him from his siting position. As Winters stands shaking with fear, the large wet patch around his groin seems to be increasing and as tears begin to roll down his cheeks, he looks back at his latest conquest for help and support but she just looks away. Winters is dragged out of the restaurant screaming and crying and is taken into the office where the computer is running with the camera system attached.

Reynolds gives an instruction, "Kneel on the ground and place your arms behind your back."

Reynolds sensing that Winters won't move forces him to the ground and instructs him to kneel again. A piece of gaffer tape is removed from a roll and wrapped across his eyes. A second piece is then used to bind his wrists together.

"Britton, set up this man's death as a live feed broadcast, if these bastards will not listen to my demand's and kill three of my men, they can have their first live public execution." Burns instructs.

Britton who was sitting by the computer, connects the camera through the internet and starts a live broadcast.

In the main command centre one of the military personnel shouts out, "Sir, we are receiving a live broadcast feed from one of the Broadhurst offices computers?"

"OK, put it onto the main screen." Atkins points at the main communication wall. All the TV screens join together to show a man kneeling blindfolded with an unmasked gunman standing over him pointing a handgun at his head. Burns walks over and lifting the camera pushes it towards the victim.

"What is your name?" Burns snarls.

"My name is Greg Winters, please I have a wife and children." Winters is crying with tears streaming from behind the blindfold and fear racing through his voice as Burns drags the camera away.

He nods his head and a single gunshot is heard echoing through the room.

"You killed him not me, and you have one hour before I kill the next one." Burns gestures to Reynolds to drag the victim out of the way and drag him onto the main walkway of the office area.

Burns then takes the camera towards the restaurant and slowly moves the lens past the remaining hostages sitting on the floor shaking with fear and crying not knowing which one of them will be next.

In the command centre there is an eerie silence from everyone as the Police Commissioner looks towards Atkins saying, "Burns will not stop, until he is paid." King sighs.

"Or killed." Atkins replies hoping that Nash can get to him sooner.

"Do you really think Nash can finish this operation on his own? We need the SAS scrambled now, give me the Home Secretary." Hastings snaps.

"Hastings, we have one hour, and I have every confidence in Nash. If he hasn't reached them by then, we should send in the SAS, but at least give him a chance first."

"I don't care, I want to speak with the Home Secretary Allen, we haven't got any time to lose. Connect the conference phone to the HS."

A police officer dials the Home Secretaries number and says, "Connecting you now sir."

"Home Secretary, please its Hastings."

"Home Secretary, it appears that this agent Nash has failed and Burns has just killed a hostage live on Television, and we know this is not acceptable. Burns has threatened to kill another hostage in one hour unless we act now." Hasting pleads.

"So, we have another hour, this Nash is supposed to be the best so give him the hour, it will not change anything if a team go in now or within the hour." Home Secretary Allen replies.

"Sir, terrorism will not be tolerated on English soil so why are we not acting now."

"This is more than just terrorism, and you know that! Another hostage is acceptable risk at this time." Hastings complains, "Sir, I beg you to reconsider a person's life is worth more than this?"

"It's a calculated risk that both the PM and myself agree. Is McGough there?" Allen asks

Hastings replies, "He is dialled in to the conference call from his office."

A cough can be heard on the conference call as McGough clears his throat then speaks, "Atkins is right, I'm sure Nash can sort this thing out." Knowing full well, Nash has been sent to certain death.

McGough clears his throat again, "Home Secretary Allen, how are you keeping?"

"Fine thank you Edward, see to it that Nash is given his chance and if Hastings does this again you will have to take command, and I expect his resignation for insubordination. Is that clear McGough?"

"Yes sir, I fully understand Nash is to be given his opportunity first." McGough coughs and he can be heard moving around.

Hastings is whispering to the Police Commissioner who both stare back at the conference phone in disgust then Hastings turns and walks out of the command centre.

McGough rearranges his posture in his wheelchair, coughs and takes out his mobile from his old tweed jacket whilst still on his office telephone and continues to speak, "Gentlemen, have we finished for the moment on this call? I will be onsite in the next few hours."

The officers in the command centre all nod in agreement and the conference phone is disconnected. McGough lifts his mobile close to his eyes and starts to scroll through the numbers and stops at a certain name. Pressing the call button, he lifts the mobile to his ear as the noise of ringing is heard then a voice replies, "Yes sir."

"Patterson, I have a little job for you?" McGough replies then continues.

"Your cleaning services are required at Broadhurst industries, be there within the hour!"

"Yes sir, leaving now."

"I will meet you there shortly." McGough dials off.

FOURTEEN

Nearing the restaurant building, I lift the access cover plate slowly looking for any trip switches and realise that my calculations are correct, I'm underneath the service lift. The motion sensor grid which I have set up inside the tunnel start to bleep softly indicating that people are moving around on the factory floor which gives me the opportunity to check out the van which could have the explosives inside. I need to determine the extent of the threat along with any detonation devices that could be linked to the charges. I lower the service hatch plate and continue down the last part of the tunnel towards the area where the van is parked. I throw another sensor monitor at the tunnel wall and reach the final service hatch top panel.

Now finally after walking through the dimly lit confined tunnel which also included several dead-ends, I wait just inside listening for any voices or radio cross talk that could confirm if terrorists are the above. Hearing nothing, I slowly begin to lift the hatch door checking for any motion sensors, but nothing is seen or any type of resistance felt. Continuing to open the hatch, a set of vehicle tyres can be seen resting on the tarmacked surface and the darkness seen from underneath a parked vehicle is evident just two metres away. Scanning around I check for any cameras, people or any motion sensors, as I continue to slide the panel with just enough gap so I can climb out.

The sound of two voices can be heard, but judging by the distance I have enough time to slide under the vehicle. So, quickly crawling across the ground after carefully pushing the lid back slowly to avoid any noise, I reach the underside of the vehicle as the two pairs of boots can be seen walking past with a heavy stomping sound. The first job now is to deactivate the trigger system on the explosives and starting to look around the underside of the vehicle a small LED red light can be seen blinking next to the fuel tank. Taking a closer look, the timing of the light occurs every three seconds confirming it is active. The device is connected to a small block of C4 with a small wire pressed into the side. Simply removing the wire will not be sufficient and a closer look confirms that it has a magnetic switch so removal of the detonator is also difficult but not impossible. The amount of C4 is purely a secondary detonator for the main device probably inside the vehicle.

Knowing Burns there is probably a third or even fourth device, I remove the toolkit from my vest and concentrate on this first device. With my heart in my mouth, I gradually begin to unscrew the two pins that hold the explosive to the underside of the van using a small pair of pliers taken from my toolkit. After several minutes, and a forehead covered in sweat, I finally have the device in my left hand and slowly rotating the detonator see the magnetic switch and simple radio signal timer. Gradually removing the two small wires, I detach the device from the C4 explosive and place the block of material into a vest pocket. Knowing this device is now defective, I continue to look around the underside of the vehicle and find a second similar device attached to the main fuel line from the tank and as with the first device repeat the same operation.

I continue to look in every corner of the vehicle but don't find anything else. Next is to check the amount of explosive inside the van but I need to know if it is safe, so before moving any further, I check for any people and seeing that all is clear, slowly slide out from the underside of the vehicle. Standing up gradually between the van and factory wall there is just enough distance to move without being seen.

The van has a set of double rear doors along with a sliding door along the side behind the driver's door and finally the front passenger cockpit door. Continuing to scrape past the van side and wall, I reach the front passenger door and look through the window. A small cable can be seen on the driver's side door handle that passes through the handle on the rear sliding door which is certainly a trigger device for the main explosive charge. Looking into the rear of the van, a huge pile of C4 explosive material blocks are laid across the rear floor plan. At the lower edge of the rear doors there is another flashing red LED detonator. I must get inside to disarm all the charges so after checking all around the passenger door for any triggers, I take a deep sigh and place my hand onto the handle and slowly unlock the door checking every few millimetres of access for any possible motion sensors or trigger devices. Finally, after what feels like an eternity and a hand that is shaking with adrenalin, the door is open enough for me to enter the van.

A quick check under the seat confirm that no pressure sensor is present, but a check under the driver's side shows a weight sensor connected to the main detonator. Confidently removing the pressure sensor, I climb into the back of the van and begin an examination around the main trigger contact. All the other devices have been crudely assembled, but the last one shows signs of a professional finish which includes a mercury switch connected across the trigger system. This will be more difficult to remove since the mercury level must remain constant otherwise the electrical reaction will ignite the C4 explosive.

Looking around the device it is stuck into several blocks of the huge pile of explosive material, so lifting it without activating the mercury sensor will be very difficult. The red LED light keeps flashing as a warning, but also a welcoming invitation to switch it off so taking out a pair of pliers from the toolkit, I start to move through the wires that are connected to the mercury trigger and detonator. Red, blue, green, yellow and black wires are all evident and checking around the trigger, the red and blue wires appear to be the circuit maker for the mercury tube switch. Slowly, I begin to place the pliers around the blue wire as my hands shake even more, if I cut the wrong wire first, the circuit will be made, and it will be the final goodbye. Closing the pliers around the wire, I start to apply pressure and can begin the feel the resistance of the wire inside the plastic sleeving.

Making the final cut, I close my eyes hoping the decision is the right one and thankfully it was. I then cut the red wire and the main detonator is separate from the mercury switch, but if the mercury tube is moved, it would still blow up the material with the two rods attached to the blocks of explosive. Slowly beginning to pull the mercury tube from the explosive material my hands begin to shake again slightly. Minutes pass by, and suddenly voices can be heard outside returning in my direction.

It feels as though my heart has just stopped, as I kneel in the van over enough C4 material to flatten most of southern England and holding the mercury trigger device. As sweat pours from my forehead into my eyes making them sting, I want to wipe the liquid away, but watching the mercury level, it slowly begins to flow towards one side of the tube and with one final pull, I have it clear of the explosive material and safely in my hands. The voices now begin to depart, but I sense that a check through more of the C4 material is required just to be sure. Placing the mercury tube safely on the passenger front seat, I begin to move some of the blocks of C4 making sure there are no other hidden switches or devices. After several minutes of checking, nothing is found so lifting the mercury switch, I cautiously move in the direction of the passenger door and at that point notice the interior light had been activated and luckily the terrorists never saw it.

My hands stop shaking, as I finally reach the door and climbing out of the van, I drop to the ground firstly, to kiss it, and secondly, to place the deactivated the trigger system on the floor. I climb back into the van and take one final sweep around to make sure no more devices are left and sure enough there is another magnetic trigger device in the glove box. Burns certainty didn't want any mistakes and after removing it so I disconnect the wires and separate the C4. The last job is to lock the vehicle to make sure no one can get inside to the remaining explosive, and a quick check of the sun visor reveals the door keys that I catch in my hand. After climbing back out of the van, I lock the doors and place the key into my pocket.

Finally, after picking up the mercury switch, I slowly work my way back to the tunnel, and lower myself back through the hatch dropping the panel as though no one had been there. Working my way back along the tunnel towards the elevator shaft lower access area, I stop and look around the lower areas of the elevator shaft. The elevator car can be seen in the dimly lit shaft part way between the ground and first floor access doors. I notice the elevator guide rails along with the counterweight system. Finally, the hoist ropes can be seen hanging between the elevator car and rear side of the shaft. Knowing that this is my only access point, I stand slowly then begin to climb into the confined space using the metal framework structure to climb past the car side making my way towards the first-floor door access level.

As I climb, the raised aggressive voice of Burns can be heard shouting, clearly getting more impatient with the authorities not paying the ransom money. His tension over the situation hangs heavy in the air and can be felt even at this distance but not enough to hide part of the metal panel work creaking above me, as I climb. Suddenly, one of the soldiers hears an unfamiliar metallic noise and quickly releases the safety catch of his machine gun. Lifting the barrel, he starts to opens fire with the weapon sending bullets punching through the thin metal panel access doors of the shaft. Small rays of light then illuminate through the bullet holes as covering fire echoes through the elevator shaft.

Burns quickly runs out from the restaurant screaming, "Who the fuck is firing."

The soldier stops to reload the machine gun and lifts his hand submissively saying, "It was me sir." Taylor replies.

Burns walks over and with a loaded pistol kills him instantly firing a bullet to the side of his head, "No one shoots, until I give the command. Is that fuckin clear!" He storms back in to the restaurant not knowing how close I am.

Sensing both anger and nervousness in his voice, I see a different side of Burns usual calm and collected manner. Surely this must mean maybe, he is starting to lose control of this hostage situation. Now reaching the first-floor door access level, I manage to quietly move around the shaft standing on the top of the elevator car. Remaining at chest height to the access doors, I don't know if any of the terrorists will be on the other side just waiting.

Remaining at chest height in the shaft looking at the bottom section of the doors, my knife is taken from the holster, and the blade is gradually inserted into the gap between the doors, and very gently twisted allowing me to see if there is anyone outside. Seeing a second set of outer doors and a small balcony area, the elevator car suddenly begins to move upwards, and quickly grabbing my knife from the small gap, I lower myself onto the top of the lift. The car reaches the first-floor level and the doors open. Two different sets of footsteps can be heard entering the lift car with no other sounds made.

Knowing two possible terrorists are inside the lift, I quickly take my handgun from my holster which still has the silencer attached, and position myself quietly on the lift roof. Slowly looking through the small lift weldmesh access panel, I see two soldiers inside and one of them starts to move towards the call button panel.

With clear headshots at both men, I wait until the floor access doors close and take two quick shots dropping the men to the floor of the lift car. Before the lift starts to move, I reach for the top of the access framework with my right hand then lower myself onto the small step on the inside of the elevator shaft. Holding the knife with my left, I begin to prise open the metal doors once more. As a small gap starts to appear and feeding two finger tips through the space, the doors are gradually forced open against the springer counterbalance. The lift has completely lowered down the shaft and is slowing down to stop on the ground floor access point. I must be through the doors, and be hidden before the bodies are found. I continue to push the doors open and then wedge my knife between them so I slide through the gap. Now standing on the small granite finished balcony at the top of a staircase I turn slightly, and notice the spiralling black polished handrail leading downwards.

I glance over and wonder where the steps lead too, but I don't recollect seeing them on the plans. In front of me are a pair of light grey doors with large tubular handles. Trying to remember what is on the other side of the doors, I reach for a handle on the left side and after checking for any motion sensors, slowly start to pull it open.

I can hear one of the radio's crackle in the lift as a man's voice asks, "Heaton, Dale what is your status?" No reply is returned.
The voice asks again, "Repeat Heaton, Dale report your last position?" Hearing the instruction, I know my time is quickly running out and looking through the small gap between the doors, scan for any threats and my position in relation to the restaurant and the hostages. Seeing a line of storage cupboards, I slowly begin to exit from the balcony doorway and check my equipment knowing a gunfight is imminent.

I hear a radio crackle further down the office area and a voice says, "Colonel, Heaton and Dale have not reported in sir?"

A familiar voice responds, "OK Jones, keep me posted." Burns replies.

Knowing that there must be agents inside the facility, Burns now commands his team to take defensive positions, "Reynolds, Carla and Hobbs, continue to guard the hostages, Marcus, make you way here from the front desk. Evans, you and Stubbs begin a sweeping pattern moving forward with Britton supporting."

All the soldiers nod in agreement at their new orders and take positions.

I watch the three soldiers gradually move in my direction using office desks and cupboards as protection, and cover to break up the outline of their bodies. The two front men are similar build being short and stocky, but the third man seems a bit heavier and slower. I need to wait until they are in the right position just far enough from the others before I start the attack, then I must keep pushing all the way to Burns killing any obstacles in my way. Watching them slowly pass me with the two front men on opposite sides of the main office walkway, I wait for the third man to draw level, then with the safety catch clicked off fire three quick rounds from the MP5, and the man in front drops to the ground.

Before the two other soldiers can react, I have them in my sights and fire four short bursts hitting both of them one near the neck, and the other in the lower body and head. Now the ball starts rolling and gathering pace using whatever cover is seen in front, I work my way towards the restaurant area.

"Get the fucking bastard!" Burns commands as gunfire starts to echo through the office area.

Two more soldiers appear from the restaurant and begin taking shots across in my direction, suddenly from nowhere several bullets hit the cupboards to my left sending fragments of wood into the air and one bullet hits my left arm. Quickly turning around, a man can be seen working his way along the main walkway from the front area of the offices. Now pinned down in a crouched position, I am taking fire from both directions and need a plan quick. Removing two smoke grenades from my vest, I throw one towards my left and the other to the right. Two loud bangs are heard and the white smoke quickly starts to drift in my direction so allowing me to reposition.

I move behind the row of cupboards and backtrack towards the soldier who was behind me. I hear him stop and reload his machine gun and pinpoint his position through the white smoke. Quickly circling behind him and using the office cupboards and desks as cover,

I fire a volley of shots in his direction with the bullets ringing as they hit furniture and walls, but the last set of bullets fired have a different sound, and I can tell from the thud that I have hit him.

Quickly moving in his direction with the last of the smoke to cover my position, I find the soldier and fire two rounds into his head making sure he is dead. The two soldiers upfront continue to fire covering rounds in my direction in an attempt to hit me. Reloading the MP5, I work forward again at the sides of the office area towards the other soldiers who are still firing randomly. My actions are too aggressive for them and with precision shots keep them pinned down so they can't fire at me.

Suddenly, the ghost of my past exits the restaurant holding a male hostage walking in my direction and shouts out, "Is that you Nash?" He asks as I stop near a large cupboard to reload.

He continues, "I know it is you Dean, to take out those guys on the factory floor only a few people in the world could do that. Come show yourself." Burns shouts holding a pistol to a hostage's head.

"If you don't show yourself, I will kill this man." The man begins to wet himself almost crying.

Slowly I begin to stand and notice a dead hostage near the front of the restaurant and see it's my old manager from Harper and Harpers and with his death, thoughts of him receiving a punishment for the betrayal of his wife flash in my mind. Burns pushes the latest hostage to the ground and with him in a kneeling position, the gun is pushed to the back of his head and a single bullet round is fired. The body drops to the ground and a pool of blood quickly starts to form.

"I knew the agency would send their best and knew deep down they would send you, although, I thought you wanted to disappear?" Burns points the gun in my direction.

"A few things have changed since that basement Nick."

"Nash, I wanted you here with me, it would have been a great last job. Do you know how much money I will earn?" He starts to walk back slowly.

"I don't really care Nick, enough is enough."

Burns points at the remaining soldiers to move backwards then beckons me over asking, "Why don't you join us in the restaurant, there is someone you might like to meet?"

Slightly puzzled, I slowly begin to follow them, but knowing Burns assume it will probably be a trap, so holding the MP5 cocked and ready to fire at any time I keep moving forward. There is a third solider wearing a black ski mask standing holding an Uzi sub machine gun. I can tell from their shape they are considerably smaller than the other terrorists. A third person walks to the large doorway of the restaurant with Burns standing close by. The two other soldiers stand to each side of Burns with the red laser sights pointing in my direction. Burns raises his right hand and clicks his fingers and the smaller soldier removes the black mask revelling a very familiar face.

"Dean, how wonderful to see you." Carla appears.

"Well, I can't say I'm not surprised Sophie. I knew you were with Burns all along, and you certainly played a good innocent victim."

"Have you come to join us in the revolution." Sophie asks smiling, but shaking.

My thoughts race back to our past and from the first kiss on the dance floor at Nick's club along with the feelings of attraction between us. Even now her eyes lie, and I can see that Burns still has a strong grip over her. She needs to be released from this life and find a new freedom.

I sense the threat from the two soldiers and Burns and decide on the best actions.

I reply back, "Hmm let me think about that." I quickly fire two successive rounds at her with a head and chest shot killing her instantly. I feel no emotion to her any more and Burns needs to feel pain and be taken down.

"I guess you won't be joining me then!" Burns shouts as he starts to open fire in my direction, with Hobbs and Reynolds quickly following the Colonel.

I quickly dive to the left side and using a fallen solider as shield, manage to kill one of the terrorists with a clean head shot that was standing on Nick's far right. Burns and the last soldier retreat backwards towards the hostages.

Burns grabs the trigger system from a table and shouts, "Do you know what this is Dean?"

"Let me guess, a remote trigger device." I reply.

"Right, and if I don't get my money, we will all get blown to hell."

"Really is that so, I'm surprised, it's not your style Burns to wave around a trigger device you must be getting slow in your old age." I answer.

"Slow, I'll show you slow Nash, you failed me when you changed sides." Burns snarls.

"I've never changed sides, only now I think for myself."

As I notice, the last solider trying to move slowly in my direction. A quick set of shots is taken hitting him hard in the abdomen. and he drops to the ground.

"Enough of this warming up Nash, come on I'm not afraid of you," Burns shouts.

"You should be." as I start to move forward to face him. Burns laughing tries to depress the trigger system, but quickly realises the signal is not going anywhere, "You de-activated the trigger system. I fuckin knew it." He shouts.

Knowing he is out of options he will now try to kill me, and as I prepare, he throws the trigger device to the floor and quickly tries to fire his gun in my direction. In that instant, I have already begun to squeeze the trigger and with the faster hammer action fire several bullet rounds hitting him first, which drops him to the ground. I feel a bullet from his gun strike my right leg, as I roll to the ground. Standing back upwards, I start to limp towards Burns direction as the last injured soldier manages to fire off a round into my side that causes me to drop to the floor again. I drop the MP5 machine gun and quickly removing my handgun from the holster, fire two consecutive rounds into his head. Taking a deep breath, I start to stand again feeling the pain from the bullet wounds in my arm, leg and now the left side of my body. Blood now begins to soak into my clothes and a wetness touches my skin.

Burns can be seen partly rolled in a ball on the ground holding his side, as I start to limp over towards his direction. He begins to roll over onto his back and then turns his head to look at me. I can see already he has lost quite an amount of blood.

My shaking bloody hand points the handgun at him, and he starts to stand then begins to talk, "Well Dean, this isn't how I'm going to die, but you will suffer far worse."

Now standing opposite me, he spits out a mouthful of blood and throws away his guns. I can see that I have hit him in three different places near his left kidney, lower rib cage and mid abdomen. He takes a large hunting knife from his belt and beckons me over to fight. Knowing my gun magazine is empty, I lower the barrel and take out the empty magazine throwing it to the floor, then place the handgun onto a nearby table. Removing my knife from the holster, I notice some of the hostages beginning to move out of our way as they clearly sense Burns, and I have unfinished business.

"Have you figured it out yet Nash." He asks.

"I figured out that you wanted to kill me all those years ago and that you have always been jealous."

"Yes, and do you know why I wanted to kill you Dean?"

"Anything could come from your sick twisted mind Burns." I reply spitting out some blood which has formed in my mouth.

"It's because you were always given the best opportunities and, I was always given the shit jobs." Burns shouts.

"Maybe, I made the most of my opportunities, whereas you

expected them to be just handed over on a plate." I smile back at him making him stare at me.

Burns snarls and begins to rock slowly on the spot as we begin to size each other up. It is very different from those training days at the farmhouse, that felt like fun, but this fight will be to the death. Gradually staring each other up and down we are both looking for weakness points, and I know he can see my three wounds. I know he will make an attack and probably target one of the bullet wounds. Sensing him starting to move, he lunges forward clearly angry with my comments and tries to take a sweeping action towards my face with the knife blade, but I push him away and quickly make a deep cut into his left bicep arm muscle.

I punch him to the side of the neck very close to his jugular vein, and he lowers his head groaning as he stoops slightly. He turns around quickly and punches me into the wound on my leg which causes me to wince and step backwards. He tries to stab me in the leg with a low movement, but I lift my right knee, and make contact with his nose causing him to fall to the ground. I quickly kick him in the side of his body near the bullet wound around his kidney area a couple of times then stand back to wait for the next attack. He tenses his muscles on the floor, and then again lifts himself to a kneeling position beginning to stand again. Drips of blood start to fall from his body hitting the granite flooring. His face has a light grey look across it almost as though the life is draining out of him.

"You're still quick Nash, but not quick enough." He spits out more blood.

He lifts the knife again and then tries to stare into my eyes as he lunges forward again and this time catches me on the left leg thigh muscle. I move back and stab him into his left shoulder blade area causing him to turn and stumble slightly. I hit him in the back of the neck with the handle of my knife, and he drops to the floor again dropping the knife. He coughs and growls on the floor as he starts to stand again, but is clearly getting weaker.

"I loved you Dean, as a brother and as a good friend." Burns turns and looks at me from the floor with a look of both fear and disgust in his eyes.

Knowing an injured animal is always the most dangerous, I know Burns will try anything to gain the upper hand and win the fight so standing back slightly, I see him suddenly race forward hitting me square into the stomach, causing me to drop my knife as we both hit the floor. He now starts to punch and kick me in my bullets wounds in attempt to hurt me, but I manage to get several punches to his kidney section and then to his face.

He spits blood in my face, and then I manage to head butt him in the nose gathering enough energy to push him off me and to my right side. Quickly wrestling with him I punch him to the face and the kidney wound. He stops struggling knowing, I am a stronger adversary. I roll off him and start to stand once again staring at his every move. He lies on his back coughing and breathing heavily, and then gradually starts to look for the handguns he threw away. I notice his hand slowly reaching for one of the handguns.

Now standing near him, I remove a small pistol from my back pocket and fire a shot into his hand. He screams in pain and still tries to reach for the weapon with his opposite hand in the commotion, so I shoot him in the right shoulder, and he drops to the floor again coughing.

"You're too slow old man." I look at him.

"I'm not the old man." he replies before coughing out blood.

"So, what now Nash, hand me over to the authorities?" Burns asks.

"That will not be a good idea since they probably sent you in here anyway to tidy up some loose ends?"

"What then Nash, the final bullet?" Burns replies.

"Yes, when I am ready Burns."

"I want to know a few things first before I kill you."

"Know, what the fuck do you want to know Nash, why should I tell you anything?" Burns coughs.

"I would imagine you want the truth to be known and all this was for something." I reply.

"Yes, it was for something Nash, it was to show them bastards at that fuckin agency along with McGough who has manipulated our lives for so long that I have had enough."

"Why did you want to kill Wagstaff so much?"

"Wagstaff and McGough, they were working together and wanted to restart the cardinal programme. They needed you and me back together to select, train and command a new team for the kill squad."

"Wagstaff wasn't like that, McGough yes, but not Wagstaff." I shake my head.

Burns reaches into a pocket and takes out a mobile phone and slides it across the ground to me, "You know the unlock code, check the last few messages." He coughs and starts to move around clearly in discomfort.

I pick up the mobile, press the unlock code and start to look through the messages, there is one from McGough's mobile number giving instructions which read 'Last supper is a go.' There are also several more asking about my status and condition. I return back to the main menu and see messages from Sophie, Lloyd and finally several messages from an unknown number. These messages ask about the Pearson robbery payments, my recruitment back to the programme and communication to McGough. The messages have JW at the end.

"You see Wagstaff and McGough were both working together, and we were as always the pawns in the middle."

"What is Operation Last Supper?" I ask.

Burns coughs then tries to start laughing, "The old Cardinals wanted to retire McGough, so his instructions were to terminate them."

"Wait, Wait, McGough met me a couple of days after this message was sent. We had breakfast in Palm Cove, and he told me that you had taken over this facility."

"Palm Cove?" Burns asks.

"Cairns, Australia, he specifically mentioned that you had taken hostages, and I had to come here to kill you."

Coughing out more blood, burns now even more weaker replies, "Now it makes sense, he fronted this operation so that he could generate enough cash for the start-up programme. He wants to run the cardinal programme independently."

"He has played us both for idiots Dean." Burns smiles.

"This is all bollocks and doesn't make any sense." I look at Burns now more confused over whether to kill him or ask more questions.

"Dean, I only ever wanted the best for you and yes, I was jealous, but we have so much past, and I did want to get my revenge on you a few years ago. You remember that we were both in that same training facility and the tasks we had to complete, we were both left alone." He looks across to me with a tear rolling down his cheek.

"I was the outsider in that training programme and everyone else including you made my life hell, that's why I worked and trained harder than the rest of you. I had to in order to survive."

"Dean, please don't take things the wrong way."

My mind once so clear on this final operation, has now become clouded affecting my judgement and decisions over what to do next. Suddenly, the headset rings out in my ear, "NASH, repeat Nash what the fuck is happening in there." A voice from the central command asks.

I wait for a few seconds, deciding what to say then press the call button to reply, "All clear in here, send the team through rear entrance gates, there are claymore mines across front doors."

"It is about time what has taken you so long to reply Nash?" I regain my focus and look back at Burns.

"There have been a few developments, but the decision is now resolved."

"Decision? Resolved? What do you mean why are you talking in riddles?" Command asks.

"Nash out." I reply.

I lift the pistol barrel towards Burns then he starts to laugh saying, "You haven't got the fuckin bottle to kill me you little shit." Burns smiles and tries to laugh.

"Oh really, your crocodile tears don't wash with me Burns." I pull the trigger and an empty bullet case hits the ground. I look at the entry bullet wound in Burns forehead and know this chapter in my life is finally over. I fire two more rounds into his head to make sure he won't come back to haunt me and without another thought turn to my escape plans.

Holding my side with the increasing pain coming from the bullet wound, I only have a few minutes to escape before the rescue teams arrive, and ultimately face my death once McGough gets his hands on me. I switch off Burns mobile and tuck it into my jacket pocket, then lean down and lift up a woman's scarf that is on the floor. I rip it in half then tie one part around my leg as a tourniquet. The other half is pushed into my shirt in an attempt to slow the bleeding. I reach for my handgun which is still on the table top, where I left it and replace it into the holster.

"Are you OK?" A women's voice asks from behind.

Turning around I see a woman around forty-five years old who stands and has moved towards my direction, "Yes, I'm fine. Look get the people to their feet and wait for the rescue team to arrive don't use the front doors they have bombs connected across them."

"What about you? You need help and medical care for those wounds." As she looks at the blood drips hitting the floor.

I start to walk away, "Where are you going?" she asks.

Turning to look at her I reply, "I'm going home." With a smile across my face.

My main focus is now on my escape and how to disappear underneath McGough's agents and hitmen which I am sure are already gathered. Pictures of all the service ducts below ground flash through my thoughts and, as I plot the best escape routes, I suddenly remember where the small staircase on the lift balcony leads to and begin to walk there with haste. Reaching the staircase, I slowly start to walk down the steps, until I reach a dark grey door at the base of the staircase.

Opening the door, I continue into a dark tunnel with a small LED torch light as my only piece of comfort against the claustrophobic feeling inside. Reaching another dark grey metal door to the right-hand side of the tunnel, my brain instantly recognises the door and my thoughts are filled with past memories, as I remember images of what happened behind.

Reaching out my hand touches the coldness of the door handle and as my heart begins to beat faster which causes the hand to shake with adrenaline, as I try to push the handle downwards, but it is locked. Knowing I only have a very short time to escape pales into insignificance as my mind wants to open the door, so drawing the silenced pistol from my holster, a round is fired through the barrel lock breaking the internal action and sending a flash of light along the tunnel. Now that the lock mechanism is shattered, I try the handle again and this time the heavy door begins to move inwards. I gradually begin to walk inside shining the light across the room looking for any possible threats with only the sound of water dripping in the darkness. The light grey walls are still covered with flipcharts and formulas then to the far left is an organisation structure of professors and scientists.

I walk over to the chart and starting at the top take a mental image of each face and name with the eight people clearly already etched into my thoughts. A vivid image suddenly fills my mind, as I remember the operation and the orders from the cardinals. Quickly turning to the left is a separate chart titled exp group one. The chart shows pictures of Burns, Lloyd, Chris and Shaun with different colour coded bars of treatments but looking around I can't find myself.

Continuing to look around the room there is a large wooden desk and filing cabinet in the far-left corner. Quickly reaching the cabinet, I break open the drawers and start to flick through the files working through alphabetically, until I find one with my name. Taking out the file, all the contents have already been removed apart from a scrap of paper.

Suddenly, hearing footsteps splashing in the wet tunnel, I push the paper into my pocket, close the drawer and switch off the torch light then I continue back into the dark wet tunnel slowly closing the door behind. Torch searchlights can be seen flickering in the tunnel behind me, as I continue along the service duct remembering the route in almost complete darkness. Taking the last self-drill grenade from my vest, I change the setting to fire grenade and throw it against the service duct wall already knowing that the area is well safe of the fuel dump five hundred metres away. The grenade whirrs, as it attaches to the wall then beeps twice to indicate activation for motion sensor so moving away quickly, I continue towards the exit door of the tunnel and the escape hatch which leads to the outside world. The cold tunnel feels as though its suffocating me along with the darkness touching the skin on my face. Suddenly, a huge bang can be heard followed by voices screaming as the fire grenade activates. Then the sound of roaring can be heard getting closer as the flames from the explosion races down the confined tunnel.

I start to limp faster towards the small amount of day light in the distance, and begin to feel the warmth of the flames licking against my back. Knowing that I can't outrun the flames, I quickly drop to the floor of the wet tunnel and the heat plume passes overhead then extinguish along the tunnel. Luckily, for me there were no additional gases or combustible material in the tunnel that could have been ignited, but at least the area is now clear and hopefully the escape hatch will lead to my new life.

Standing back onto my feet, I continue along the smoky tunnel in the direction of the light with my footsteps splashing in water the only noise echoing through the darkness. My new life gets closer with every splash until suddenly from the other side of the escape hatch the noise of a radio break the silence. 'Fuck they have found me!' rushes through my thoughts as the gunshot wound on my side stabs with pain. My new life is so near yet so far, as I stand in the tunnel deciding what to do next.

My brain instantly starts to work on a plan b, and remembers a lower section and secondary escape route. Turning around, I quickly retrace my footsteps backwards and stop at a small grid in the tunnel side. Removing the metal cover, I gradually lower myself down the square ducting with dirty water running past me. Once, I am fully inside the duct, I reach forward and close the grid cover then slowly climb down the concrete duct wall trying my best to cling onto the wet cold surface sides with my elbows and knees. I continue to follow the square duct downwards as voices and footsteps running through water can be heard in the tunnel above.

My heart races so fast still waiting desperately to escape from this life and hoping that I don't get caught. I can hear from their conversations above they are running to try and help their fellow colleagues, but I know they would have just been killed from the fire grenade. Finally, after several minutes of climbing, I reach the lower grid cover and push the hatch cover open slowly. As I begin to lower myself through the hole, I sense that someone is already waiting for me, and emerge fully, the back of my neck is struck with the butt of a pistol. Feeling the pain racing through my body, I continue to slide out of the hatch and hit the floor of the tunnel landing in more cold-water tunnel and my escape plans start to evaporate into thin air.

"Nash what are you doing in all that water." I look across to see a man standing.

"I have a message to deliver from McGough?" He kicks me in the gunshot wound on my side.

Spitting out a mouthful of blood, I reply, "Oh I thought he would have the bollocks to tell me himself and not send a monkey."

The man leans down and pushes my face into the water,

"Now, McGough has given me the all clear to finish off the great Dean Nash."

Forcing my head up I reply coughing and sputtering, "Well, better get on with it you prick."

He stands away from me and drawing out a knife says,. "McGough is sick of your uncontrollability, and said that you can fight me for your life."

"Oh I can't wait." As I start to stand.

"McGough said you were once the best, but you look like a fackin mess now Nash."

"That's my disguise and your downfall. What is his Lordships message?"

"He said that you were once his best asset and that you were ruined by a woman's love. This love has turned you soft and unreliable. He has asked me to finish the contract." He laughs.

Slowly taking a small knife from my trouser belt, I gradually begin to lower the blade into my hand, "Let's hope for his sake you finish it otherwise McGough is next."

"That is not an option Nash, you will die in this tunnel today, what a waste but hey we all die sometime right."

"Your absolutely right!" I lunge forward towards him.

He swipes back cutting my right arm deep, but I manage to hit him straight in the neck pushing the small blade deep. Quickly stepping back he takes a second swing, but I counteract his move and grab his arm then twist his wrist, until he drops the blade. He takes a swing with his left fist hitting me in the face, and I drop the small blade. 'Crack' echoes through head as my nose feels as though it has been broken. Staggering backwards slightly dazed, we now begin hand to hand combat trying to hit pressure points, and weak spots on each other's bodies, but with my gunshot wound he is stronger than me. I need to turn the fight more in my favour so dropping to the ground, I lunge upwards and punch him hard into the groin area.

As he begins to fall, I quickly stand and kick him again in the same area. He sends out a scream of pain, as he continues to fall to the ground. The odds are now starting to move in my favour and quickly taking advantage of the situation. I kick him across the face breaking his nose and cracking his jaw. He sweeps his leg and hits me on the left knee knocking me off balance. As I start to fall, I land heavy onto his chest with my elbow hitting his lower rib area and then roll onto the floor quickly moving around and grabbing him around the neck with my right arm.

In the same movement I link my arms together and try to hold him in a pincer action applying pressure to his neck and windpipe whilst pushing my body next to his. He tries to kick and fight with me, as I start to strangle him applying more grip, but my injured arm is too weak to apply enough pressure. Releasing the grip, I stand then turn to watch him as he coughs lying on his back.

Holding his neck, he looks at me and asks, "Why did you let me go?"

"Do you know why you were sent to kill me?" I reply.

"McGough requested it." He answers, rolling over and starts to stand, resting on his legs and hands.

"What's your name?" I ask.

"Does it really matter." as he begins to move one of his hands into his jacket pocket.

"It matters to me. Stop going for that gun and give me your name."

He turns his head and now slowly begins to try and stand. "I've not asked you to move, *what is your name?*" I snarl at him holding a silenced handgun.

"It's Wilkins, my name is Wilkins."

"OK Wilkins, you were the one that has been tracking me from Australia correct?"

Coughing he replies, "Yes, how did you know?"

"I know McGough, and I knew he would send his best. Well, Wilkins you made two mistakes?"

"I think you made the mistake not killing me when you had the chance Nash."

"The first mistake is that you took this contract and the second mistake, you should have killed me when you had the chance."

He starts to reach for his concealed gun, so I fire a bullet round into each of his shoulders then into each of his knee caps. He drops to the floor and rolls over screaming in pain and must know that death is very close

"You know they just don't make assets the same way anymore and as for you McGough, because I know you are listening, you will be next." I announce.

"I underestimated you Nash, I thought this would be simple." Wilkins coughs and stares at me. I can see from the expression on his face and the look in his eyes that he is afraid.

"Lots of people think that, and I don't hold it against you Harris, but you picked the wrong side, and I don't have time to talk, so farewell." I fire two rounds into his chest then two in to his head.

As he takes his last breath his face changes slightly as his body releases his soul. His suffering is over but mine still has a long journey. The gun smoke clears and as the blood begins to seep from his head wound, I notice there is a small device in his ear and for sure McGough had been listening.

Leaning down, I take the device from Wilkin's ear and slowly lift it to mine as a familiar voice can be heard, "Wilkins, Wilkins, fuck he's killed him." McGough's voice has a level of tension.

"McGough, my old friend, how are you?" I ask as the voice goes silent.

"I know it's you McGough and I'm coming after you next." I throw the earpiece to the floor and then tread on it in a defiant action.

McGough knowing that I'm serious will for sure have a look of fear across his face as he realises his best man is down. I also know that he will now send every resource available at his fingertips to dispose of me. Continuing along the lower tunnel, my body aches with all the wounds and fight with Harris, but my heart is full of the thoughts of escape. I hope that this time the door at the end of the tunnel is clear and in the darkness my eyes pick out the image of the outer door. Finally reaching the door, a padlock through the catch stops my progress so removing my pistol again, I fire a single round into the mechanism breaking the lock apart which sends metal fragments flying into the air. Remembering from my past that this door is close to the main entrance, I know the police have a road blockade close by. Placing my hand on the cold metal handle, I push the lever system downwards, and as I start to push the door outwards light instantly floods through the ever-increasing gap causing my eyes to sting slightly.

After my eyes have adjusted to the brightness of the day, the door is slowly opened further, and I remove a small mirror from my vest. I extend the telescopic handle and push it through the small gap to check the threat level on the opposite side. My eyes can see police and military personnel standing around but no one is paying any real attention. I am sure that McGough will have sent a message forward to apprehend or kill following Wilkins's death. Looking to the left side of the tunnel exit there is a large pile of fallen timber and then a section of woodland and my thoughts race back to a past memory and similar escape. This time however the favour is more in my hand, but also knowing my window of escape is closing fast.

The mirror is retracted, and I replace it into my vest, as I slowly begin to push the door outwards just enough to squeeze past. Now fully outside, the door is closed and a heel of dirt kicked against the lower corner, as I stealthily make my way to the cover of the fallen timber. From this position and looking through the gaps between the logs, I assess the threat level of the police officers and military personnel then recheck the cover of the woodland and clearly there is enough time and distance to escape, but suddenly in the fork of a large tree there is a surveillance camera. The operation light can be seen flickering, as I stare closely to check the position of the lens and thankfully it is pointing in the opposite direction, but is beginning to gradually move in an arc towards my position. It is now or never and after checking the blockade again, I quickly crawl on my hands and knees in the direction of the woodland and a large oak tree that I can use as cover to escape.

Reaching the tree, I gradually stand, resting my back against the thick trunk and looking upwards into the canopy. My mind is filled with killing McGough and knowing deep down that he is probably onsite burns deep. I know that he will take any opportunity to kill me, and I know that he will never probably be so close again. Sensing that this may be the only time to execute him, the thoughts starts to take over my mind, however equally important is my escape today, killing him can wait for another day when he least expects it. Looking quickly back at the police road blockade, I heave a deep sigh then disappear deeper into the woodland. My past memories continue to haunt my every thought as the escape plans for a new life flash through my mind knowing that every government asset will be sent to hunt me to extinction on the instructions of McGough.

Knowing that Shaun was killed easily confirms that in order for me to live again McGough must be assassinated and my freedom will be the result of his death. Suddenly, there is a loud cracking sound and then something hits me on the back of the neck, turning slightly the figure of a person standing behind me can be seen.

Another loud crack is heard and a voice says, "You don't have eyes in the back of your head Nash, A man alone is easy prey." The voice sound familiar.

As I start to slip in and out of an unconscious state, I can feel two people starting to drag me by my legs along the forest floor and my training taught me to fight until the end, and I try to use my hands to grip at anything, to stop being pulled, but the blow to the back of my head has made me too weak to fight back. Hearing mumbled voices, then the sliding of a van door. I am dragged into the vehicle, then the feeling of a needle being pushed into my neck. Another familiar voice can be heard outside the van giving specific instructions, then the side door is slid closed. The van engine starts, and as I try to look around the vehicle, my eye lids start to feel heavy as the injection begins to take effect. The motion of the vehicle can be felt and finally after fighting for so long I pass out to the sound of laughter.